IT'S ALWAYS THREE O'CLOCK

"... In a real dark night of the soul it is always three o'clock in the morning. ..."
—F. Scott Fitzgerald

IT'S ALWAYS
THREE O'CLOCK

BABS H. DEAL

The University of Alabama Press

Tuscaloosa and London

The paper on which this book is printed meets the minimum requirements
of American National Standard for Information Science-Permanence of Paper
for Printed Library Materials, ANSI A39.48-1984

Library of Congress Cataloging-in-Publication Data

Deal, Babs H.
     It's always three o'clock / Babs H. Deal.
        p.   cm. — (The Library of Alabama classics)
     ISBN 0-8173-0494-0
     I. Title. II. Series.
  PS3554.E1218   1990
  813'.54—dc20   89–20626
                                                 CIP

British Library Cataloguing-in Publication Data available

FOR BORDEN

WITH WHOM THERE IS ALWAYS WORLD

ENOUGH AND TIME

With the exception of Captain Simms, who is based in essence on the character of my great-grandfather, Captain A. C. Card, the characters in this book are products of the author's imagination. Where historical characters are used they are given their real names.

Contents

For each age is a dream that is dying,
  Or one that is coming to birth.
                    —Arthur O'Shaughnessy

Preface

When The University of Alabama Press informed me it wanted to reprint *It's Always Three O'Clock* I was amazed to realize that twenty-eight years had passed since this book was published. I re-read the book. I wondered if in the temporal world of yuppies, stock market mergers, and electronic preachers it still had relevance. My conclusion was that, given the book's premise, it did.

When I began writing this book in 1959 we were on the brink of the sixties. Space, Woodstock, and Hey, Hey, LBJ were in our immediate future. JFK was my generation's hope. But the book isn't about that time. It is about my mother's generation: the flappers and sheiks of the twenties who had in their future 1929, breadlines, and FDR.

But, as the title implies, no matter into which generation or which segment of history we are born, we all have our heroes and villains, our gods and devils. As F. Scott Fitzgerald said, in a dark night of the soul, it truly is always three o'clock in the morning with all its attendant fears. Still, dawn comes; the name of the game is survival, and despair remains the ultimate sin.

Most of the reviewers in 1961 liked the book and agreed with its theses. One lady, however, took great umbrage. She said my heroine was "serene in the face of the ultimate weapon." Perhaps she misunderstood me and my heroine, who believed that if we insist on concentrating on ultimate weapons we aren't going to get very far with the day-to-day business of life. I'm not sure *serene* best describes my heroine. I see her today as resembling Rose Kennedy. She survives. Perhaps the book is about faith, which, however you define it, you either have or you don't.

Gorham Munson, in *Saturday Reveiw*, had this to say about *Three O'Clock*. "Mrs. Deal . . . wished to give the spirit of four distinct periods in American life: the twenties, the thirties, the forties, and the early sixties. One of her characters sees history as a train that went into a station 'where they played jazz and drank bootleg gin' [and] traveled on 'faster now, through the bread lines, the hunger, through fear,' into the time when her son was photographed on the flight deck of a carrier, and arrived finally at Cape Canaveral, where there were 'the single thrusting surges of light.'" I wonder if the train had traveled on through the seventies and eighties would the book's outcome have been any different. I think not.

When one lives as long as I have it becomes more and more apparent that life tends to be cyclical. It has been interesting to me to note that one of the basic symbols of *Three O'Clock* hinged on the hope of the space program—not for the launching of spy satellites or Star Wars weaponry but for the exploration of space, the new frontiers for the human mind. In 1960 many of us felt this way. Oddly enough, today these ideas are resurfacing, after a long hiatus, with the interest in *Voyager*.

A secondary symbol—if you like the term (I don't)—is the ocean. When I wrote the book I had glimpsed the ocean once, only briefly. But, like my heroine, I had always wanted to live near it. In later years I did so, for a long span of time, during which I raised my family and wrote most of my books. Later I was away from it for a long time yearning often, like Edna Millay, for "one salt taste of the sea once more." Today, cyclically, I have come back. This is, of course, only personal. But I still believe, as when I wrote the book, that the personal and the universal are intricately and inexorable mixed.

Recently my four-year-old granddaughter took me outside and pointed up at the stars. "Look, Granny," she said. "Aren't they *beautiful?* But sometimes there are clouds and you can't see them."

"Yes," I said. "But they're still there."

Her answer to this comment was her favorite one: "I know *that.*"

That is what *It's Always Three O'Clock* is all about. And after almost thirty years I still stand by it. I might write the book better today technically—and with more insight. But it is a book I will be happy for my granddaughter to read someday.

BABS H. DEAL
Gulf Shores, Alabama
October 1989

IT'S ALWAYS THREE O'CLOCK

Beachhead

She lived in a house on the beach in sight of the lights that went up over Cape Canaveral. There was only Eileen now, and the grandchildren, who came and went during the afternoons across the sand from their mother and father's house. At night there were the stars and the single thrusting surges of light that came often enough so that you were never wholly prepared for them and seldom enough so that you were always waiting for them—a fine smattering of suspense to give the nights a color.

She would sit on the steps behind the house and listen to the sea. Some nights someone would walk along the beach whistling in the dark—*When a lovely flame dies*—the sound sharp and clear against the subtle surge of surf. She slept on the sleeping porch where all night long the sea said *come back home.*

She worked at the hotel on the point during the day, keeping accounts, adding the meticulous rows of red and black, drinking Cokes. There were many people around the hotel, some of them old, waiting, others on vacation, bright in bathing suits and wide-brimmed hats of raveled straw. There were children too with sand buckets and tanned backs.

Her work was over at three o'clock in the afternoon. She would walk home down the wooden sidewalk that paralleled the beach, not having to shield her eyes from the sun any more, and she would take her sandals off and walk barefooted across the sand to her back door, her feet perfectly adapted to the roll and pitch that carries you in sand and over it.

The grandchildren swarmed over Eileen's strip of beach and over her screened back porch and her clean kitchen where the cakes sat on waxed paper in rows. They swam and sang and played games. They talked to Eileen.

3

Bambi was the oldest, eight now, brown-eyed, tanned golden, with hair like honey. She begged to spend the night. Eileen would tuck her into the extra bed on the sleeping porch and sit in the wicker chair and smoke cigarettes.

"Tell about when you were a girl, ma'am," Bambi always said. It made Eileen think of herself, of being eight and sitting on the wide front porch while the grownups rocked in outsize rockers and told the tales of accident and birth and death and idiocy—the long sad songs of night while she sat still and quiet in the little rocker in the corner, hoping no one would notice and send her to bed.

"Tell about flappers and sheiks," Bambi would say.

And Eileen would light another cigarette. "But it wasn't like that at all, Bambi love. I never even saw a pocket flask, and none of us had coonskin coats."

"Mother says you were a flapper."

"But it wasn't really that way at all. And there has been so much in between."

She would look at this child with the wise brown face to whom the lights above the Cape were part of night and home, and for a moment in the darkness know what it was that made that long-ago era bright and dear, remembering those who never let it go, holding the empty party favors in the after-midnight dark because the party was over and nobody wanted to go home.

"Well," she would say, "back home up in Alabama there was a little town, and people farmed around it and came into it to buy things. I lived on one of those farms."

So she would talk into the surf-sounded night until Bambi's eyelids were heavy and the last passing sound from the beach was gone. Then she would cover Bambi and sit on her steps and watch the sky, waiting without knowing it for the nights of the sudden searching light. Early enough she would go in to sleep. She slept soundly and when she dreamed the dreams were long and interesting and friendly. Sometimes they were filled with memories, but the sad memories no longer had the power to hurt and the happy memories mixed gently with the soughing water on her beach.

PART I

The Sheik of Araby

1. *April 1923*

The sky was gray with morning and soon you would be able to see the road that led from Maynard's Cove past the Holder farm until it joined the turnpike that led to town. Down the turnpike and past Five Points was Bellefonte, its white houses and gray shacks all gray alike with pre-dawn kindness, its square shuttered into stillness, the yellow frame station alone beside the stretch of silent rails. In a white house with a gabled roof an old man watched the sunrise; across town a young girl lay wakeful and anticipated her wedding day; in Maynard's Cove a man with a piece of steel in his head and ice in his heart waited for the sounds of battle to cease inside him; in the farmhouse on the cove road Eileen Holder opened her eyes. The world turned and the sun came up on Bellefonte. It was an April morning in the year 1923.

Eileen Holder always woke early in the morning. She could never remember a morning when she had not been awake before anyone else in the household, even her father who went to the fields at daylight, or her mother who had the biscuits in the stove before her father came into the kitchen. She would lie in bed, watching the grayness outside her window, trying to see by the intensity of color and texture whether the day would have sun or shadow, whether it would rain, closing her into a soft shell of comfort, or brighten, letting her out into the iridescent shell of the world. If it were already raining she would listen, hearing the warm drum on the roof that meant security; if it snowed she became alert with the small animal bright-eyed alertness of waiting. But always she was glad of weather. There were no bad days and good days to Eileen—not in the momentness of them. Bad and good days only came to her in retrospect.

This morning would be overcast. She could feel the trapped light of the sun even before that sun was fully up, and she lay still, remembering with her skin and bones and hands and eyes overcast days. It would be still, and the sun would threaten, but never quite come out until late afternoon, when it would shine low and suddenly. She turned over and sat up, leaving the warmth of bed gladly. I'll wear something gray, she thought, with a red ribbon, and I'll go up and see Vance before school time.

It was the day of the Sophomore play and she was spending the night in town with Veda Simms. If she didn't go this morning she wouldn't be able to see Vance until tomorrow. She tied the ribbon at her neck and went downstairs.

Her mother looked up from the stove when she came into the kitchen. "You're mighty dressed up for school, aren't you?" she said.

"I'm going up to Vance's before time," Eileen said, crossing to the safe to get the cracked tea glass that held the knives and forks and spoons. "It looks like a good dim day for Vance to be out in," she added.

"Ummm." Her mother grunted noncommittally, her hands busy in the biscuit dough. She kneaded the round resilient lump, thumping it in the dust of the floured biscuit board with a quiet plump sound. "What you going to wear to the party tonight?" she said.

Eileen smiled at her. "My green dress."

Mrs. Holder rolled the dough out with two quick thrusts of the green glass bottle and cut the biscuits neatly, cupping the tin baking-powder top into the dough with one hand, lifting the biscuits onto the skillet with the other. "You going with that nice Johnson boy?" she said.

"Yessum."

"They're nice folks for you to be with," Mrs. Holder said.

Eileen went to the bin behind the range for the chicken meal. She filled the round pan deftly, not looking at her mother. "Vance is nicer," she said softly.

Mrs. Holder shoved the skillet into the oven. "Ummm . . ." she said again.

Eileen went quietly out the back door into the yard. The chickens came toward her in a clutter of sound and movement. She threw the feed automatically, feeling it leave her fingers in an arc that brought her hand back to the pan again. Her eyes went across the fields toward the mountains, blue and hazy in the morning, dark with their lack of sun. She smiled, thinking of Vance. There wouldn't be any sun to hurt his eyes this morning.

Vance Maynard had been in the War. He had fought in the trenches in France and he had come home with a piece of shrapnel in his head. It was this that Mrs. Holder didn't like. Somehow that small piece of steel came between her and Vance Maynard as subtly and strongly as though she had seen it, lying hidden and malignant beneath the auburn hair. She could not wed her only daughter to that insidious piece of steel, and she knew of no way to stop that marriage. Eileen had loved Vance Maynard since she was a little girl, since the time before there had been a world war and bright marring pieces of steel. He used to ride by on his roan mare in the arrogance of fourteen years, and Eileen would run to the fence in her pink rompers, begging with five-year-old insistence to be taken up to ride. She had made him promise her then that he would wait for her, and when he had fought and come home Eileen had been waiting for him.

Outwardly there was no difference in Vance Maynard. He had always been a quiet boy, big, rawboned, moving slowly through the cove that sheltered the last of the Maynards who had been pioneers and who now numbered only two. But Mrs. Holder had known he was different, doomed, just as Mrs. Maynard knew. They were waiting. Eileen knew only that her love had come home.

The back door slammed and Eileen looked toward the sound. Morgan came down the steps and went past her toward the barn. She put the pan down and went after him. He was leaning on the fence behind the barn smoking a cigarette.

"Give me a cigarette, Morgan," Eileen said. "I know you've got some ready-rolls. I saw you with 'em last night. Come on now. Please."

Morgan shook his head. "You haven't got any business smoking," he said firmly.

He was taller than his sister, and darker. His hair was slicked down, parted carefully in the middle, and he wore a clean white shirt under his sweater. He was ready to go to town.

Morgan's world was Bellefonte. Bellefonte, which encompassed the drugstore and the poolroom and the wide white house of Veda Simms. It was a world of enchantment through which she moved like a small golden child, lighting the brick and pavement with her smiles. He was never sure whether Bellefonte had given him Veda, or Veda, Bellefonte. But it didn't matter. Both were the other world he yearned toward, the antithesis of the brown fields and bare comforts of home.

Eileen watched him, grinning. "You got a date with Veda tonight?" she said.

Morgan didn't answer her. He drew slowly on the cigarette.

"You have. She told me," Eileen said.

Morgan shrugged.

"She had her hair bobbed yesterday," Eileen said. She watched him, waiting for his reaction.

He didn't look at her. "What?" he said, attempting to sound casual.

Eileen laughed. "You should have come in to the dress rehearsal last night," she said. "She had it done yesterday afternoon."

"You know I didn't have any way in last night," Morgan said. "I don't have Ace Johnson to get me rides home if I stay after school either."

"Oh, shut up."

"What does your old beau Vance think about Ace Johnson?" Morgan said. He put his cigarette under his heel and carefully ground it into the ground.

"What do you care if she bobbed her hair?" Eileen said. "It's real pretty."

"I *don't* care," Morgan said. He buttoned his sweater across his white shirt and went toward the barn. "You better not miss Mr. Wright," he said over his shoulder. They rode into town with Mr. Wright, the mailman, when he went in to pick up the daily mail.

"I don't aim to," she said.

Eileen hurried through breakfast and through the dishes. Then she was on the road, hurrying toward the mountains and the dark opening that would lead her into the cove. At the entrance to the cove road she stopped and put her books and the small black hat-box behind a roadside bush, then she walked more slowly into the cove road, stopping to look up at the bushes and trees that grew around her, rising up and on toward mountain. It was quiet here, as it always was. Sometimes she heard a bird or the rustling of a small animal somewhere in the roadside bushes, but that was all.

She was happy, she was going to see Vance. And she would be happy today at school, and at the party before the play. The various threads of her life waited on each other and if today she went with the warp, tomorrow it could be the woof, with no disturbance to her. She loved Vance, but she liked the people of her own age she went to school with, and she was pleased and flattered that Ace Johnson always sought her out—even though she found him only a nice boy. That was all anyone was to her—ever had been—except Vance. She wasn't like Morgan, who longed always and every minute to get into town and see Veda. She could be happy with the others in the brightness of town and automobiles and Mayhill parties, but her real life was with Vance in the solitude of the hidden house in his private world.

She turned the small curve on the rutted road and the house

was in her sight. Nothing disturbed the quiet of the morning sun on the rough-hewn walls. She had loved this house since she was a little girl. She always paused for a moment here at the turn in the road to look at it, holding inside her the secret, half-ashamed joy that she knew was pride—pride in the hope of ownership. That house, so long loved, was going to belong to her. She walked on toward it softly, watching the way the doorway lay in the shadow of the gable, the heavy oak door, with its plain iron latch, opening into the polished hall with its sad wonderful deer heads, mounted to grow right out of the wood.

She knocked and Mrs. Maynard's voice came to her as it always did. "Come on in, honey." She stepped inside.

She stood for a moment until her eyes became adjusted to the gloom of the inside, then she turned, stepping down the two steps, worn into a shallow trench in the center with the passing feet of years, and she was in the living room. Mrs. Maynard was sitting in her wheel chair in the corner. From the kitchen came the sounds of Ida, the hired girl, banging the milk pans. Mrs. Maynard smiled.

"He's out with those snakes," she said. "Sit down and let me look at you for a minute."

Eileen sat down on one of the handmade benches, resting her chin in her hand and sniffing the odor of the house. It smelled of something old and delicious and forgotten. Her mother said it was only the smell of wood and smoke and mangy animal hides and preserves, but she couldn't believe that. It smelled too strongly to be only ordinary things. Eileen knew the smell of ordinary things; that was home: biscuits and jam and feed and clean linen and earth. She knew too the sophisticated smell of town. Mayhill's smelled of furniture polish and flowers and chocolate and spice. But the Maynard house smelled of time.

"I hope you're feeling well, ma'am," she said to Mrs. Maynard.

The old lady smiled. "I don't ever feel well, Eileen," she said. "But there's good days. This is one of them."

"Can I get anything for you?" Eileen said.

Mrs. Maynard shook her head. "You might open a window over in the dining room," she said. "Ida'll never get around to it and it seems right stuffy in here this morning."

Eileen got up quickly, glad of a reason to look at the house. She went up the steps and across the hall and down two more steps into the dining room. It was darker here for the shutters closed out the morning light. She crossed to the window and raised it, reaching out and throwing the shutters open. The hazy light fell across the broad floorboards and a breeze stirred into the room tinkling suddenly the prism that hung over the round oak dining table. She looked up at it, then down at her arms, speckled by the prismed light. She ran her finger tips over the oak table for a second, then went back across the hall.

"Go on out to him, child," Mrs. Maynard said. "He's at those cages. Reach me my book over there and go on."

Eileen brought the book, a dark, double-bound library book. She put it gently into Mrs. Maynard's hand and went down the hall and onto the back porch.

Vance was standing beside the wooden and wire cages that backed into a rocky ledge on the edge of the back yard. Eileen stood on the porch for a moment, looking at him. She loved him so much that sometimes, coming on the sight of him suddenly like this, she felt surprise that flesh and blood and bone could be so much more than just what it was. She watched him raise his arms above his head to stretch, then lean over and look into one of the cages. She went down the steps and stood beside him.

He didn't turn toward her, but he spoke softly. "Look at that one, Eileen," he said. "Have you ever seen a marking like that before? It's like jewels that have been buried for so long they've forgotten what they're for."

She looked through the meshed wire. The snake stirred restlessly at her presence, sliding toward the corner of the cage. The snakes didn't frighten her; they never had. They were something

Vance liked and wanted to keep and although she could not imagine why anyone would want to keep snakes, it was all right with her. He had snakes of every kind to be found in the county. Some of them he had removed the poison sacs from, others he hadn't. She wasn't sure which were which, so she was wary with all of them, but not afraid.

"Do you want to climb up and sit on the slope a little while?" she said.

"All right." He turned and looked at her, his eyes somber as they always were when he wasn't communing with some of his snakes or animals, or looking at one of his guns. He whistled, a clear warbling note, loud in the morning.

"What was that?" she said.

"Mockingbird . . . his real note. You don't hear it very often. Come on."

He took a long stride toward the flat ledge behind the cages and clambered up, giving her his hand. She came up onto the rock beside him and they went on up the mountain, climbing over the rocks that were embedded in the lower slope. When they came to the pine line he stopped, sitting down on a clump of slippery needles. "Why do you tag along with me, Eileen?" he said.

She sat down too, looking down toward the house in the cove, watching how quietly it seemed to sit there on its spot of owned ground with no one around it to move and mar the landscape. "I always have," she said.

"Yes." He stretched out on the pine needles with his arms under his head. "It's going to be a nice sort of day. There won't be any sun, you know," he said softly. "It's mighty strange to me to think of a good day being a day without any sun. I don't reckon I'll ever get used to that." He rubbed a hand across his eyes.

Eileen sat beside him, watching his face, glancing occasionally toward the opening in the trees where the road was visible and where the Ford mail truck would pass.

"I wish you'd come to our play tonight," she said. "Marty May-hill would like you to come to the party at his house too."

He shook his head. "That crowd's too young for me, Eileen."

She looked down at her feet, feeling the hurt of his words. "That's not a nice thing to say," she said.

"Aw, honey, you know I don't make a habit of saying nice things," Vance said. "That's one reason me and you can get along. You don't expect it."

She wouldn't look at him and he got up and came over to her. He put his hand under her chin and lifted her face toward him. "You have fun, baby," he said gently. "All you want. I know it gets dull out here sometimes. You can't spend all your time running around through the woods with an old man. But ... I don't know. All that's too noisy for me. Huh?"

She shook her head, smiling. "Sometimes it seems like I'll never be eighteen," she said. "You'd think it would just come along, wouldn't you? But it never does."

He laughed suddenly, his head thrown back. "Is eighteen the magic one?" he said.

She felt herself blushing. "Daddy says you can get married when you're eighteen," she said defiantly. "He says then you're a woman of your own. He's always said that."

"Well, I'm still waiting for you, ain't I?" Vance said.

"Are you? Are you really? Or do you still just say that to kid me?"

He looked down at her, wondering suddenly whether he *was* still saying it just to kid her. She comforted something in him, he knew that. But he wondered if he had a right to take all that beauty for comfort. So he laughed again. "You don't see nobody else beating your time, do you?" he said.

"Oh, there's Mr. Wright, stopping for the Wheeler kids." She stood away from him, already starting down the slope. "I'll see you tomorrow," she said.

"Have fun, baby."

She threw a kiss at him and was gone, half-sliding down the rock face, then racing down the cove road toward the mail truck, pulled up now across the road.

He stood for a long time after the truck had pulled away, thinking of the way the bright figure had run out of the cove, leaving it strangely empty in the morning.

Veda Simms never woke up until her grandfather had pounded loudly on her door with his cane. Breakfast was always served at exactly seven o'clock in the Simms house, but Veda had never been able to wake without being wakened. Captain Simms always woke her. He would begin by tapping gently on the white panels of her door, then a little louder, until at last he would pound mightily with his cane, and she'd stretch and yawn, and say, "All right, Grandfather."

He would say, "I'm staying right here, miss, till you're on the floor." Then she would laugh and get out of bed and make it up very quickly so she couldn't get back in it.

This morning she didn't mind getting up at all. This was the day of the Sophomore play, and the day of the dinner party at Mayhill's with Morgan. There was what she called her good-streak feeling clear through her. She stepped lightly on the cool floors to the french doors that opened onto her tiny balcony and looked out at the morning. "Oh, don't rain," she said, pulling her mouth down at the corners. Then she laughed. "Oh, I don't care whether you do or not," she said.

"What's that, Veda?" Captain Simms' voice asked gruffly.

"Nothing, Grandfather. Go on to breakfast. Tell Mama I'll be right down."

"You up now?"

"Yes *sir*."

She could hear his cane tapping gaily down the hall toward the stairs. She was fifteen. And life for her hadn't begun and was half over. She had met Morgan Holder, she loved him, she was going to marry him. She had decided that a year ago when she first met him and there was nothing to change her mind or her decision. It was the one thing she wanted or that held interest for her. She liked pretty clothes, she liked parties, but she had no desire to design clothes or to become a belle. By nature she was wife and mother, and at fifteen she knew it. What being a wife and mother involved she didn't know, but she knew her destiny.

She went to her chifforobe and took out her silk teddies and stockings and her new pongee blouse. She put on the underwear and went to stand in front of her vanity mirror, watching the fall of her new bob across her cheeks. She giggled. She could still feel the sharp pointed snip of the barber's scissors on her neck and the fluffy dust of powder from the brush. And she could hear her daddy too when she came home. He hadn't liked it at all. She tilted her head again to feel the soft brush across her cheek. Grandfather had liked it though—the old sheik. He always liked everything new.

She put on her raw silk suit. Then she went to the door and locked it. She came back to the dresser and opened her hair receiver, the pyrolan box that went with her matched dresser set. She dipped her fingers into it and brought out the small round box from the bottom. She opened the compact and put her nose to the rosy cake inside, sniffing the ashy rose odor. Then she took the puff and delicately touched her cheeks. She put the compact down and rubbed her face hard with the palms of both hands. Satisfied, she put the compact back in the hair receiver and unlocked the door just as her mother's voice came up the stairs.

"Veda Simms! Are you coming to breakfast with the family this morning?" she said.

The dining room was large and light, filled with Mrs. Simms' potted plants and the heavy oak furniture of the dining room suite. The table seemed to stretch very bare and long now that there was only Mozel and R. V., their youngest daughter Veda, and the Captain. Bill and Elizabeth Ann Simms were away at college now and Veda missed them terribly, even though her mother said they had never done anything but fuss when they were all at home. It was nice, though, having a room all to herself. When Elizabeth Ann had gone off to school Mozel had moved her absent daughter's things into one of the empty bedrooms and told Veda she could have their old room for herself, and for Christmas her daddy had let her pick her own new suite of furniture from the catalogue. She had a bed with four tiny posts and a triple-mirrored vanity dresser and a cedar-lined chifforobe. Besides, she could shut and lock her door and burn incense in her own Buddha burner, and sit as long as she wanted in front of the mirror without being laughed at. But she got lonesome sometimes anyway. If it wasn't for Catharine Graves who lived just down the road she thought she'd bust sometimes for somebody to talk to—especially about Morgan Holder.

Her parents thought she was old enough to have her own room and furniture now, but not quite old enough for beaus. She could have a party date, but she wasn't supposed to go anywhere in a car. She was the youngest person in her class at school. She sat down at the table and took her napkin from its silver ring. Grandfather winked at her. "How's the first lady of the stage this morning?" he said.

Her mother was watching her closely. "Have you got anything on your face, Veda?" she said.

Veda shook her head, feeling her face grow hot under the rouge.

"Young folks are just high-colored," Captain said.

Mozel shook her head at him. "You spoil Veda," she said. "That fan, for instance."

Captain laughed and drank from his large coffee mug. "She'll be the prettiest thing in that play tonight," he said.

Grandfather Simms had been an old man when he came to live with his son and his family, but he didn't act like an old man, nor talk like one. He looked like one, tall and white-haired and mustached, imbued with dignity. But he wasn't really old—not even as old as Veda's mother and father.

Grandfather Simms had fought in the Civil War. And he had fought on the wrong side. He had been a Captain of Light Infantry for the Union. "That's what I happened to believe," he said. And that was all. In Bellefonte Captain Simms was accorded the same respect as the veterans of the Confederate Army. He was called Captain, more in affection than in deference to title, and he was accompanied on his morning walk through Bellefonte by Captain Hudson, formerly of General Coffey's Division of the Confederate Troops.

Captain Simms loved life. It was that simple. He liked to get up in the morning and go to his room at night. And he wanted to live a century because he wanted to know what was going to happen next.

He read the encyclopedia for amusement. He had purchased a set when he came to live with his son, because, he said, they wouldn't want him around all the time and that would keep him busy in his room. He stayed on the second floor with his books and his Morris chair, and his neat blue captain's hat that hung on the gable of his wall.

Each month he received a pension from the United States Government. Each month he went happily to town to buy presents for everyone in the family. Not useless presents, but what he called *real presents*—things that the person wanted, but would just never get around to buying for himself. He had bought R. V. Simms a gilt shaving mug with his name on it, and he had bought Mozel Simms—who couldn't help loving him in spite of the annoyance his presence sometimes caused her—the first McCormick victrola record in Bellefonte.

Now that Veda was going to be in the Sophomore play she had needed a fan, and Grandfather had gotten her an ostrich feather one. He had had to send off to Memphis for it and he had gone to meet the train to get it before Veda got to the post office. It had come wrapped in brown paper and underneath that in a gay striped box. Captain had stripped the paper off and come home, swinging the striped box in one hand, tapping his cane smartly along the road with the other.

"Damned if he don't look like Diamond Jim Brady," R. V. had said when he handed the box to Veda with a flourish.

She had screamed and hugged him until he almost lost his balance, and Mozel Simms had said, "That's certainly an odd present for a grandfather to make." And R. V. had said, "What about

John McCormack for his daughter-in-law?" Mozel hadn't said anything else.

"It's a beautiful fan, Grandfather," Veda said, beginning to eat her steak and eggs.

"Well, I want you to use it," Captain said, brushing crumbs from his mustache with a light elegant movement of his hand. "Nothing's any good at all if it isn't used."

"Oh, I'm gonna use it," Veda said. "But the first time has to be tonight."

Mozel put down her fork. "I wish you wouldn't be so mysterious about this play," she said. "What are you going to *do* with that fan anyway, Veda?"

"It's part of my costume," Veda said. "I told you. I'm a vamp."

Captain Simms chuckled. "Vamp," he said. "That's a fine-sounding word. Who is that woman? Theda Bara?"

"That's her," Veda said.

"Picture shows!" Mozel said. "Sometimes I think that's all any of you think of."

"Well, I sure enjoy 'em," Captain Simms said. "Lord, if anybody had told me back when I was riding my horse up to the sawmill before the War, that they'd have moving pictures, I'd never have believed it. Now I'd believe anything that came along. Why just take the electric light . . ."

"Don't get started, Father," R. V. said.

Captain shrugged. "You talk, Veda," he said. "I like to hear the words you young folks use nowdays."

"Grandfather," Veda said. "Your war's not The War any more. There was another one."

"Yes, I know that. But my war's still The War to me. That other one don't deserve the name anyway. Sitting in ditches and jumping out to be cut up by machine guns . . . machine guns, now; that's another one . . ."

"Father," R. V. said.

Veda finished her breakfast and asked to be excused.

"Veda," her mother said as she started out the door, "is it just

Catharine and Eileen that are spending the night with you to-night?"

"Yes ma'am."

"All right. You can go to the grocery after school and get some things for your midnight feast as you call it."

"Thank you, Mama."

"You won't be here for supper?"

"No, Mama. We're having the party at Mayhill's."

"Well, go on. You'll be late for school."

"All right. 'Bye Daddy, Grandfather. 'Bye Mother."

She took her books from the space between the posts in the living room and went out onto the shaded porch and down the steps and the concrete walk to the chert road that led toward town and toward Catharine's house. She started running, her feet plumping softly into the dust of the road, her silver bob switching against her cheeks.

Mozel sat watching the door long after she had gone through it. "I'm not sure I approve of this play," she said finally.

"Oh pshaw!" Captain said. "They're having a good time, Mozel. Let 'em alone."

"That's what I'm doing, isn't it?" She sniffed.

Captain chuckled. "You sure are a put-upon woman, Mozel," he said. "I do declare you are."

R. V. suppressed a smile.

Mozel sniffed again. "It's this Sara Butler, *Mr.* Kenneth Downs thing," she said. "I must say they're an odd choice of sponsors."

"He seems a right nice young fellow to me," R. V. said. "He was down at the barn the other day with some other young fellows, and I thought he was real nice."

"Pushy," Mozel said firmly. "Fast." She stood up from the table and delivered her last remark with the sound of doom. "Christine Butler will never allow him to marry her daughter," she said, and went regally out the door.

Mozel Simms was quite right. Christine Butler had no intention of allowing her daughter to marry Kenneth Downs. If she could

have helped it she would not have allowed her to collaborate with
him on the Sophomore play. But she had found no way of preventing this without casting doubt on the character of her daughter.

Sara Butler was twenty-two years old, but to her mother she was
still a child, to be guided in the right paths toward the altar with
one of the members of a pioneer Maynard County family. No
power on earth could reconcile Christine Butler to a Yankee
schoolteacher. And that was what Kenneth Downs was. He came
from "someplace" in Ohio, an unfortunate event for Mr. Downs,
whether as leader of the Sophomore class or as suitor for the hand
of Miss Sara Butler. That he was the best history teacher ever seen
in Maynard County, and the most popular teacher of any subject,
was not in his favor. Quite the contrary, in fact. There was still
an inherent suspicion attached to intelligence in Maynard County,
and an even greater one to the powers used to influence young
people.

Bellefonte, Alabama, in 1923 had not caught up with the rest
of the world. The children might ride in automobiles and bob
their hair, they might watch flaming youth on the screen of the
movie theater, but their parents did not think of them as flaming
youth. They thought of them as The Kids; they thought they were
rebellious and too loud and impertinent—as parents always have
done—but they didn't think they were very different from the children of the previous decade. Not, at least, until after the events of
the night of the Sophomore play, the night that opened Pandora's
Box on the postwar generation, and changed forever the lives of
the participants.

Sara Butler had gone away to college at Shorta and come back
to Bellefonte as a music teacher. She was a conventionally pretty
girl, with a prim white face and a small bowed mouth. She liked
her job as teacher and she relished the hours in the small music
room at the high school, tapping the time to Couperin exercises
with her small, neatly shod foot, glancing importantly at her small
necklace watch when the thirty-minute lesson was coming to an

end. She had beaus. They called on her in the living room with the tasseled pillows and fringed lamps, and brought her boxes of Whitman's candy. She liked the attention and she liked the boxes of chocolates, but that was all the young men meant to her . . . until Kenneth Downs.

Kenneth Downs was dapper and scholarly at the same time. He carried an aura of great places of learning to the north, tempered with a gallantry that she had hitherto attributed only to southern gentlemen. Moreover, he thought Sara Butler an exotic flower of the south, and he treated her as though she were.

Mrs. Butler had made it quite plain the first night Kenneth Downs had come to call on Sara that he was not welcome. She had been very nice to him, and she and Mr. Butler had left the front room early to allow them to be alone. But the very set of her head had been disapproving, and she had not changed her mind.

Still she had allowed Kenneth to come to the house until the episode of "Omar the Tentmaker." After that he was firmly turned away at the door with the message that Sara was out or in her room unable to see him.

It had happened in February. Sara Butler had a Chevrolet coupé that had been her father's present to her when she graduated from college and came home to teach in the high school as a dutiful daughter should. It was her habit to take the car and drive up to Chattanooga once every three months or so to do her shopping and to see a picture show. She always took some female colleague with her, and these schoolteacher jaunts were looked upon with mild amusement and pleasure by the older members of the faculty. But when in February Miss Butler and Miss Cartwright, the calisthenics teacher, had gone to Chattanooga to see "Omar the Tentmaker," they had met Kenneth Downs in front of the Rialto Theater.

Now Miss Cartwright could not have known that *The Rubaiyat of Omar Khayyam* had any special meaning for Miss Butler. She had certainly not seen the leather-bound copy which Sara Butler kept in her locked bureau drawer, nor the inscription on the flyleaf

—To my chosen companion in the Wilderness, Your Ken. No, Miss Cartwright could not know this. Neither did she know that there was anything prearranged in the meeting with Mr. Kenneth Downs in front of the Rialto Theater. But she knew when Sara Butler shamelessly held hands with Kenneth Downs through two showings of "Omar the Tentmaker." And in forty-eight hours so did everybody in Bellefonte. If Kenneth Downs had ever stood an outside chance with Sara Butler, that chance ceased to exist after that episode.

Sara Butler did not want to make a break with her family. Girls of her class and age did not make that break hastily in 1923—not in Bellefonte, Alabama—and she did not. But she continued to see Kenneth when she was quite sure her mother was not likely to find out about it.

The Sophomore play had been an inspiration on Kenneth Downs' part. He was the sponsor for the Sophomore class, and he thoroughly enjoyed the job. They were a bright bunch of kids, fun to teach, fun to be with. And now they were the answer to his own personal problem. The Sophomores had never had a play; this had always been the prerogative of the Juniors and Seniors. It had been Mr. Downs' contention, duly brought up in faculty meeting, that the Sophomores deserved a chance to show what they could do with dramatics, that it would be good training for the future, that it would give them experience needed in the Junior and Senior plays. He was most persuasive, and the faculty enthusiastically backed him up. He then suggested that the play be in the nature of a revue—singing and dancing. He would, of course, need the assistance of the music teacher in putting on this revue, but he would be glad to take over all the other duties connected with the play.

There was no way to object to this without voicing the gossip concerning him and Sara Butler, and the high school faculty had no intention of antagonizing the Butlers—Mr. Butler owned a flourishing hardware store and was on the school board. The motion was passed.

The Butlers couldn't say anything against the venture without admitting the truth of the gossip about their daughter. So Kenneth Downs and Sara Butler had two weeks in which to rehearse the students of the Sophomore class, and two weeks was all the time needed for Sara Butler to decide that she wanted to spend the rest of her life with Kenneth Downs, whether in Bellefonte or the wilds of Ohio.

Now, on the morning of April the 20th, she was waiting to be married. Her new blue dress hung in the closet, and she had not slept the night before. Outwardly her morning was no different from all the other mornings of her days as music teacher at Maynard County High School. She dressed, she ate her breakfast, she went out to her small car and drove the four blocks to school. After chapel she would begin on the lessons for the day, after school she would check the stage and auditorium, she would go home and dress, she would help Kenneth Downs put on the best play Maynard County High School had ever seen. Then she would be married—to her darling Ken. She parked in the graveled space behind the school and got out of the car.

Veda Simms ran down the road until she came to Catharine Graves' house. It was a big white house with flowers growing around the margins of the yard. She went up the walk and knocked on the door.

Mrs. Graves let her in. "She's not ready," she said. "She's never ready. And, I'll vow, you always look as good as she does. It takes her two hours to dress and I can't see where she's put it."

Veda laughed. "You know she always looks better than the rest of us," she said.

Mrs. Graves shook her head. "Tell her you're here and come have a cup of coffee with me," she said. "She won't be ready before that first bell rings."

Veda went down the hall and out onto the back porch. She knew Catharine would be in the bathroom. As in most of the older, larger houses in Bellefonte the bathroom was built onto the end of the back porch. There was still an idea in the minds of most people that the bathroom was not quite clean and the fact that the porcelain fixtures were scrubbed daily with Old Dutch and Bon Ami did nothing to lessen this feeling. In the winter going to the bathroom still partook of the old-time feeling of going out back, and the daily bath was preceded by a chilling walk down the open porch.

Catharine had been in the bathroom for a long time. She had taken a leisurely soaking bath, using too much of the hot water in the tank. She knew that she would get a lecture about it when she got in from school, but she didn't care. She had powdered herself liberally and gotten into her pressed teddies. Catharine Graves ironed all her own clothes. She knew that if the wash-woman did her clothes they would come back starched too stiff and not ironed right around the buttons. The Graveses didn't have an old family servant to do the wash. It was picked up and done at one of the shacks across the railroad, and brought back home. They hadn't lived in Bellefonte long, they had moved in from Martin Town six years ago. And six years was not a long time in Bellefonte. Mr. Graves had been an itinerant preacher but he had given up his calling when they moved to town. He had purchased an interest in a rural sawmill some years ago and that had grown steadily until now it took most of his time—what time he didn't spend on the front porch of the sprawling white house he'd bought from old Mr. McCloud.

Veda knocked on the door and opened it when Catharine yelled, "Come in."

"Lord, it's steamy in here," she said. "What are you doing?"

Catharine put down the eye-brow tweezers she was using and grinned at Veda. "Well, hot damn, gal, it's the big day," she said.

Veda perched on the edge of the bathtub. "I can hardly wait till tonight," she said. "A party at Marty's and the play on top of that. It's too much."

"Um-hmmm." Catharine rubbed Pompeian cream into her flaw-less complexion and wiped it off with a piece of toilet paper. Veda watched while she discreetly powdered her face and skillfully applied rouge, most of which she wiped off.

"Let me try just a little of your lipstick," she said.

Catharine handed it over and Veda bent over her compact, putting just a dot of lipstick on her mouth and smearing it in with the tip of her little finger.

"I bet I forget every word of my song tonight," she said.

"Nope. It'll be me who forgets in that sketch I do with Graham. I won't be able to talk," Cat said, stepping into her crepe de chine dress.

There had been a lively debate between Miss Butler and Mr. Downs about this sketch. It was a standard domestic-dilemma sketch, but it ended with a stage kiss. Miss Butler had been doubtful but Mr. Downs had laughed at her and he, of course, had won. Sara Butler didn't want to appear provincial, even if it did fit her southern belle role exceedingly well. The kiss stayed in the script.

Catharine put on two strings of beads, looked at the effect carefully in the mirror and took them off again. "Is Morgan coming to Marty's tonight?" she said.

Veda nodded, blushing. "Eilcen's going to date Ace Johnson," she said.

"I wonder what *that* means," Cat said. "I thought she had a beau out there in the country somewhere."

"She does," Veda said. "Vance Maynard. He's *old*, but real . . . you know . . . attractive."

"Sexy, you mean," Cat said.

"I remember once when Daddy had some business with his daddy—oh years ago seems like—and Vance was in the army then. We went out there in that old buggy we had and Vance was home on furlough. I remember he looked ten feet tall to me in those puttees."

Catharine was putting all her make-up carefully into a cloth bag. "Well, I'll settle for your cousin Graham," she said. "And I reckon Miss Veda'll settle for the Sheik, Morgan Holder, eh, Pickles?"

"I reckon you're right," Veda said. "You better hurry, Cat. We're late now."

"Oh, what if we do miss chapel," she began, then laughed. "Damn if you're not right," she said. "I *don't* want to miss chapel. I won't get to see Graham until fourth period after that." She opened the door and they stepped onto the porch.

"Your mother wanted us to have coffee," Veda said.

"No time, Pickles. No time at all," Cat said. They went into the hall, and she picked her books up from the table. " 'Bye Mama," she called toward the kitchen. "We're late."

Mrs. Graves' voice came to them as they went out the door. "Never a bite of breakfast," she said automatically.

The alley beside the Graves' house cut through to the high school and they went down it between banks of honeysuckle, green now, but not blooming yet. They crossed the road and the bridge over the creek that ran through the school grounds. "There goes the damn bell," Cat said. She began to run, her high heels sinking into the grass of the campus.

Maynard County High School stood on a hill two blocks from the town square. It was a dark red brick building, high and oblong with identical rows of tall small-paned windows on each floor. The front entry was built out from the rest of the building and it contained the high-arched double door with two narrow windows above it. These windows looked out from the alcove in the center of the upstairs hall, and they were a favorite place at recess and lunch hour. There were two smaller windows on either side of the alcove, looking north and south, so that anyone standing in the alcove could look three ways across the campus. The auditorium was in a single-storied wing at the rear of the main building and its high windows were overhung by white cement arches. The building had two side doors, north and south—these too were favorite places at recess and lunch.

Miss Constance Jones had been with the school since the days when it had been the Baptist Institute for Higher Learning and she still retained the flavor of the Institute in her teaching. She taught English literature. Most particularly she taught Alfred Lord Tennyson. *Elaine the fair, Elaine the lovable, Elaine the lily maid of Astolat.* There was no trace of Elaine in the bobbed hair and slyly painted faces that looked back at her from the square wood-and-iron desks. And what had *Ring out wild bells* to do with the noise made by the klaxons of the automobiles driven by the slick-haired young men, who practiced dilating their nostrils in sheik-like passion and wore on the back of their heads small round hats which they never removed in the presence of ladies? *I saw the Holy Grail and heard a cry—"O Galahad and O Galahad, follow me!"* The thing that most disturbed her was that she knew she still taught the elite of the county, the members of the best families, or the oldest families, or the most ambitious families, and she could not reconcile these children with them—with their mothers, who still prided themselves on their roses and their fig preserves and their nectar, and their fathers, who still plowed straight furrows and made honest mule trades and kept sober account books in their well-run stores. *Yet I would the rising race were half as eager for the light.* She taught them, with the same words she had used for twenty years, but she was no longer sure that they heard her, or understood her, or cared. She watched them, gathering their books so eagerly at the first sound of the bell to go into the recessed hall and stand together, always looking for the moment of meeting, always dressed for the opposite sex. *In the spring a young man's fancy lightly turns to thoughts of love.* Lightly? Miss Jones wasn't so sure. When even Veda Simms came to school in a silk dress and high-heeled shoes, and held hands with Morgan Holder in the halls, the eternal verities no longer applied. Miss Constance Jones *But I was born to other things* had never heard of Rupert Brooke.

After the events of April 20, Miss Jones always thought of herself as possessing Cassandra-like powers—she had seen it coming, but had been in no position to state her opinion. She had been against the Sophomore Revue (as Mr. Downs called it) from the beginning but the other faculty members were all for it and who was *she* to say different? She was against the students' being allowed to bring their automobiles to school, too, but the teachers themselves wanted to drive cars and they could hardly deny the privilege to students who were members of the town's most influential families—not when they themselves did so. Still the thought of Marty Mayhill's roadster, an outlandish car called a Jordan Playboy with spoked wheels and nickel-plating, made Miss Jones cringe. She was standing just inside the auditorium door this morning, watching the students file in to chapel. She knew that today, as on every Friday, after everyone was settled and waiting for the announcements, she would hear that outlandish car come up the hill, disturbing everyone in the room, and that Martin Mayhill would come down the aisle, flouting authority while every head turned to watch him.

She nodded stiffly to Sara Butler and watched her go to her place with the Freshman class. It was a shame about her. She looked sharply toward Mr. Downs, who was waiting for the Sophomores to settle into the front rows which they had pre-empted over the Senior protests. But he had not glanced toward Sara Butler. They cover it up well, she thought smugly, but where there's smoke . . . "Settle down here, boys," she said to a scuffling pair of freshmen in the doorway.

Eileen and Morgan Holder were late getting into the auditorium. Mr. Wright had been late and they'd had to hurry to their lockers to get their books for first period class. Eileen stopped to speak to Miss Jones as they came in the door. "She always looks like she could murder us on chapel days," she whispered to Morgan as they went down the aisle. "She's right nice in class, but lord, outside!"

"Old maid," Morgan said curtly. He searched the front rows, looking for Veda. He couldn't see her at first because he wasn't looking for the bobbed hair but he spotted her finally and went

down to the empty seat beside her. Catharine Graves and Graham
McCloud were sitting on the other side of her. Eileen went to
sit in front of them in the first row.

"Hi, Morgan, Eileen," Veda said. She smiled and took Morgan's
hand when he reached for hers.

The room was gradually quieting down and Mr. Johns, the prin-
cipal, had gone to take his place on the stage. He was a tall skinny
man whose suit fitted him as though he had been greased and
slipped into it. The pants legs rode a good two inches from his
ankles. He cleared his throat and the last whispers and flutterings
faded.

"Good morning," he said in his precise nasal voice. "It is Friday
again."

Cat Graves snickered.

Mr. Johns looked around the room. "Let's not be mis-*chiev*-ious,"
he said.

"Oh, God," Graham said. "Mis*chie*vious!"

Mr. Johns cleared his throat and began again. "It is a good
fine day," he said.

The sound of a motorcar came through the narrow windows.
It was in second gear, pulling up the high school hill. Everyone turned toward the windows. "I see that Mr. Martin Mayhill
is tardy again this morning," Mr. Johns said. They laughed.
Mr. Johns put his hands on his hips. "We will just wait," he said
in a resigned voice.

Two car doors slammed simultaneously, then there was silence
for the space of two minutes. The door at the back of the auditorium opened and everyone turned to watch Marty Mayhill and
Ace Johnson come down the aisle. Marty wore a bright red cable-
knit sweater and white duck pants, he had a small round red felt
hat on the back of his head. Ace Johnson came behind him, carrying a ukulele in his left hand. They marched solemnly down the
aisle and sat down in the front row, one on each side of Eileen
Holder.

Mr. Johns looked down at them. "Miss Holder," he said, "don't you think you could do something about getting these gentlemen to school on time?"

The audience laughed. "Mr. Mayhill," Mr. Johns went on, "if you are going to take it upon yourself to give Mr. Johnson a ride to school every morning, couldn't you do him the courtesy of getting him here before second bell?"

"I'll try, sir," Marty said. "But Miss Holder would probably have more influence on him."

Mr. Johns looked pained. "We have many announcements this morning," he said. "You two boys report to my office after chapel. First I would like to say that tickets are on sale in the office for the Sophomore . . . er . . . Revue. It will be presented at eight P.M. tonight. Anyone desiring tickets for your family and friends may see me or Miss Butler or Mr. Downs. Tickets will be on sale at the door, but it will be much handier to have them already purchased. Second: There is to be no more smoking in the Gentlemen's Room. Third: Those still delinquent in tuition fees will not be permitted to take final examinations . . ."

They had stopped listening to him, engaged in their own thoughts and plans or feeling merely the presence closest to them on the hard folding chairs of the auditorium. Mr. Johns was not known for the brevity of his remarks.

It was a long day—for everyone. Sara Butler felt as though it dragged purposely to thwart her. She hated the sound of the piano by the time she gave her last lesson in the afternoon. It was a long day for Kenneth Downs too. He had dreamed of taking the captive maiden away from her castle for a long time now, and with the hour fast approaching for his act of heroism, time seemed to have stopped suddenly. He felt, as the day wore on, that all of life had evolved into a room of blank round faces into which he unavailingly tossed the ramifications of the Bill of Rights.

For the Sophomore class it was time to be gotten through before the afternoon and night, before the supper party at Marty's and the play. It was always a good time at a Mayhill party but the revue made this special. They did not know yet that this would be a day they would remember out of time as the day the world changed, so they went through it as through any other school day. And when the last bell rang at three o'clock they went to town to the drugstore because that was what they always did.

It was two blocks to Cartwright's Drugstore from the high school and Veda and Cat and Eileen walked it, with Marty and Morgan and Graham driving slowly alongside them in Marty's Playboy. Ace walked beside Eileen, still carrying his ukulele. They cut across the lawn of the Baptist church and went past the new Ford agency. They came slowly, laughing and talking, into the afternoon square.

The courthouse was in the middle, square and brick with a silver tower, and around the courthouse were trees, stretching to the concrete fence with the round-balled gate posts. Next came the wide stretch of pavement, the place of wagons and cars and horses and people; then the street, curving around the square, a black laid pattern of progress; and between the street and the sidewalk, trees again. There were fewer of these, the forgotten ones only, at the corners toward the ends of the square. But behind the town they reached into the sky—they weren't gone yet. The houses lived between them and not too far away they possessed the land again.

They came into the square from the southeast side, past the trees and the newspaper office, the first solid brick building. It sat back from the sidewalk as though it too, like the trees, did not belong to the business of the square. On the strip of lawn that stretched in front of it was the original hand press, glinting dully in the afternoon sun, straight and strange in the grass, placed there in memory or dedication, as useless as the empty guns on the courthouse lawn but holding forever the memory of the word.

Past the newspaper office the square really began. There were the buildings that housed the grocery stores, spilling their smells onto the awninged sidewalks, the furniture company, the hardware store, the post office, dark and waiting now for the afternoon train. Along the other three sides of the square were more grocery stores, another furniture store, the barber shop, and on the west

Cartwright's, dark and cool and smelling of vanilla. They cut across the square and waited on the other side for Marty to park his car.

Virgil Cartwright waited on them at the round marble-topped tables with the spindly wire chairs, bringing Coca-Cola and Eskimo Pies and root beer.

"Look at him," Cat said to Graham. "Listening to every word we say. He's just like an old woman. I can't stand him."

"Ah, he just hasn't got anything to do since his precious Dudley went off to school," Graham said.

"Well, I don't know how Dudley would give anybody anything to do anyway," Marty said. "What a blockhead."

"Oh, I guess he's all right, really," Cat said. "Just dull. Dull. Dull. Dull." She sipped her Coke.

Cat would never have admitted it but Virgil Cartwright made her uncomfortable. She always felt as though he disapproved of her in some way and she couldn't think how or why. It had been a long hard fight for Cat to be the sort of person she was now and she thought she had succeeded admirably well. But if she couldn't fool old Virgil Cartwright it made the whole thing doubtful. She looked at Graham. Well, she had him, anyway, and that had been the whole purpose, that was what really mattered. She smiled brightly at him.

She remembered vividly the first time she had ever seen Graham. They had come into town for her father to talk to old Mr. McCloud about buying the house. They had come in the wagon, and she had been embarrassed and ashamed—of the wagon, and her mother and father, and of herself in a dress made out of flour sacking dyed bright green. Old Mr. McCloud's wife had died that year and he had decided to sell his house and move in with his son. It was to his son's house that they went first. They came into Bellefonte from the east, through the square and on to the half-empty country on the western side of town. That was where Byron McCloud lived, in a tall brick house with columns in front and green shutters on the windows. She had wanted to stay in the wagon but they made her get out and come into the yard.

Graham had been sitting in a wooden swing in the front yard and her father had motioned for her to stop and stay there with him. She sat down, pulling her skirts around her skinny legs.

"Hello," he said.

And she said, "Hello."

"I'm Graham McCloud. Are you the folks who're going to buy Grandpa's house?"

She nodded, not looking at him.

"It's a real nice house," he said. "I like it a heck of a lot better than this one. I bet you'll like it."

She looked up at him then, watching his brown eyes and the way his hair grew up and away from his face. "We've never lived in town," she said.

He winked at her. She was confused and felt herself blushing. She couldn't think of anything else to say to him and after a few minutes he got up and went away around the house. She sat very still in the swing, feeling unhappy, and then her father came and they went to look at the new house.

It was a long time before Catharine talked to Graham McCloud again. They were in the same class at the City School and she saw him every day but the memory of his abrupt departure around the red brick house stayed with her and she was always too embarrassed to speak to him. She had been best friends with Veda Simms for months before she knew that Veda was Graham McCloud's first cousin.

When she did speak to him again it was on her own terms and from the steady ground she'd built for herself in Bellefonte. The first date Catharine Graves had in Bellefonte was with Marty Mayhill. He took her to a B.Y.P.U. social at the Baptist church and afterward they had gone to his house for hot chocolate. By that time Catharine was fourteen years old. She knew how to dress, how to fix her hair, and how to make up her face without her mother knowing about it. She knew how Veda Simms held a fork and that you said, "I'm so pleased," rather than, "I'm so proud." Her clothes were in meticulous taste and she could play neat little Chopin etudes on the piano.

For Graham McCloud, Catharine Graves became the logical choice. He knew nothing of her striving to be that choice and would not have cared one way or the other if he had. She was the logical choice because she was pretty, vivacious, and popular.

Life was simple for Graham McCloud. He was the only son in a family for which the son was the symbol of futurity and his future was as well-defined as his past. He would go to college and become a lawyer as his father and grandfather had before him. After that it was up to him—the local courts, the legislature, the statehouse. The ways were open. In the meantime he dated the gayest girl in town.

Cat looked away from Graham and smiled at Ace Johnson, who was picking out "The Sheik of Araby" on his uke. Eileen was singing with him, laughing over his shoulder as he made the chords.

"Eileen, you do look good today," Graham said. "It must be clean living."

Eileen laughed. "It's Ace's music," she said. "Inspiring."

Cat looked sharply at Graham. She had an ambivalent feeling toward Eileen Holder and she was half-conscious of her reasons for it. She liked Eileen but somehow she always felt aggressive toward her. She knew, without really admitting it, that she resented Eileen's immediate acceptance in the circle she had worked so long and so hard to belong to. Eileen and Morgan were from the country and it didn't seem to make any difference to anybody. Not even, she had to admit, to Catharine Graves.

"We've got to go to the grocery store before train time," Veda said. She'd been sitting quietly beside Morgan, not joining in the conversation.

"Grocery store?" Marty said. "Don't you reckon Buz'll feed us enough tonight?"

Buz was Marty's mother. They all called her that, although it embarrassed Veda. She could never feel that it was right to call anybody's *mother*, Buz. Not even Mrs. Mayhill, who looked as young as Marty's sister Sue, who had her hair bobbed and smoked cigarettes in a jade holder.

"Of course she will," she said to Marty. "She always has enough for an army. But this is for the Midnight Feast."

"Ah," Ace said. "The girls are having a spend-the-night. We'll serenade you long about twelve."

"You'd just better not do any such thing," Veda said. "Daddy'd think you were the K.K.K. and run lock all the doors, and Mama'd know just exactly what you were and go lock all the windows."

Eileen laughed. "I bet your Grandfather'd like it though. He's the nicest *grown* person I ever met."

"He is," Veda said. "You can *talk* to him."

"I bet if he was a few years younger he'd be the biggest sheik in town," Cat said.

"He's already talking about wanting a car," Veda said. "And you can imagine what Mama and Daddy think of *that!* They're convinced automobiles are the devil's own invention. I don't know what they'd do if Grandfather *bought* one. They couldn't stop him. He has money in the bank besides that pension. I guess they'd try to hide it as though he *drank* or something." She stood up. "We're going to the grocery store. Anybody want to come?"

The boys shook their heads. "See you at the train," Marty said.

The girls went out of the drugstore and the boys sat watching them. Their silhouettes darkened the doorway for a moment, etched sharply against the late slanting afternoon sun. Then there was only the sound of their laughter, bright on the cooling air.

"You got a date with Eileen tonight, Ace?" Marty said.

"Hey yes," Ace said. "Who you got in mind, Marty?"

Marty shrugged. He had dated every girl of datable age in Belle-fonte, and some who weren't of datable age. It was rumored he had dated older girls too, some of the Ward-Belmont crowd, but nobody knew for certain. Sometimes when they were all together he didn't date anybody, preferring to watch the others in the slightly paternal fashion he assumed at such times. "I've sorta had my eye on that little Marshall girl this week," he said.

"Ruby?" Ace said. "Lord, Marty, she's no more than fourteen years old."

"Chronologically, maybe," Marty said. "Actually, she's years older than your Eileen or Morgan's Veda. I'm not so sure about Cat."

"Damn, boy," Graham said. "Whose gal you think you're talking about?"

Marty shrugged and reached into his sweater pocket for a pack of cigarettes. "Have a Fatima, boys," he said. "I didn't mean anything, Graham. We all know these gals *talk* a good petting party, and that's about it." He lit his cigarette. "That's why I've got my eye on the Marshall kid."

"Think so, huh?" Graham said.

He nodded.

"You ought to date somebody in the class tonight, though," Morgan said. "After all, I'm only here because of Veda myself. Maybe a girl wouldn't want to be an outsider that way."

"Don't kid yourself," Marty said. "A freshman would love a sophomore party."

"Especially if she got to come to it in Marty's Playboy," Graham said.

Marty leaned back, propping his feet on an empty chair. "I wonder if I could grow a mustache," he said.

Hudson's Grocery was a dark cavernous store with oiled floorboards that creaked with the weight of your feet. It always smelled of coal oil. There were long wooden counters on each side and, in the back, the meat market where the sides of beef and the newly slaughtered hogs were chopped on round heavy wooden tables. The floor here was covered with sawdust and a bladed ceiling fan moved slowly.

The girls wandered between the counters, looking into the round glass jars, peering over toward the shelves and bins behind the counters.

Mr. Hudson came toward the front of the store, wiping his hands on his apron. "Hello, Veda," he said. "You girls getting taken care of?"

"Yessir. We're just shopping around right now."

He laughed. "Well, take your time. Your Dad just called from down't the mule barn. Said for you to get what you want and put it on the bill. How's your mother?"

"Fine, thank you."

"I heard from Charles the other day from the university. He says he sees Bill right often. Even though they don't belong to the same fraternity."

"Yessir." Veda smiled politely.

"Well. I reckon you girls know what you want. I'll go on back to my meat." He started away, then turned back. "You children putting on the play tonight, aren't you?"

"Yessir."

"Well, I reckon me and Mrs. Hudson will just have to come to that," he said. He turned to Catharine. "I hear your daddy's been thinking about going into some Florida real estate," he said. "You know about that?"

Cat shook her head. "Mr. Hudson," she said, "to me Florida might as well be Timbuktu."

He laughed again. "Well, you tell him to come round talk to me about it some. I've been thinking that way myself."

"All right."

"How's the spring planting coming?" he said to Eileen.

"Fine."

"Um-hmm. Well . . ." He stood for a moment, his hands folded across his apron. "I reckon you'll want some Coca-Cola," he said.

Veda nodded in relief and he went to the back of the store where he kept the cases of soft drinks.

"Lord, he can talk," Cat said. "I thought he'd never shut up."

"He's just trying to be nice, I reckon," Eileen said.

"You mean he just wants to be sure we all keep buying groceries from L. J. Hudson," Cat said.

"Well, let's get started," Veda said. "Everybody pick out something you want, and then we'll add what goes with it." She picked up a handful of Peters chocolate bars and laid them on the counter. "Let's hurry before he gets back to wait on us."

They bought Tak-homa biscuits, and deviled ham, and sardines in mustard sauce, and Planter's peanuts and hoop cheese, and three boxes of Dromedary dates. Veda went to the back and selected three big pickles from the glass-topped pickle barrel, and added a sack of buckeye chocolates.

When they came out of the store the air had cooled but there was still plenty of light. "You think we've got time to go to the train?" Cat said.

"We told the boys we would," Veda said. "Besides we might have mail."

The 4:17 came down out of Tennessee into Bellefonte, bringing inside its slick black steam-wet sides the pencil and pen marks of communication, the packages and bundles of surprise, before curving up to Memphis and Tennessee again. It was usually late but it was always waited for; the afternoon train brought not only the communications of the outside world but furnished the excuse for communication among those who waited for it. The young people of Bellefonte would walk through the dusty afternoon streets or ride in Model-T Fords or the occasional open roadster to gather on the gravel-edged platform by the yellow frame station and wait for the mail. Afterwards they went on back through the bluing evening to the post office to stand together in the dark box-lined room and watch anxiously the glass-fronted squares for the appearance of the envelope or slip that would darken the front of the box and that might mean—anything.

The station flanked the town. Between it and the square with its two-storied brick buildings interspersed by high-gabled wooden

ones, there were the trees, a wide swath of forgotten woodland
still alive between the rails and the town, cut through by the dirt
road but tall enough to be remembered as forest, thick enough to
shelter or panic.

The girls went up the road together, walking between the trees
that were fully leafed out now, but pale still in the afternoon
sunlight, assimilating rather than reflecting the wested sun. They
heard the sound of a motor coming up fast behind them and they
went to the edge of the road. Marty roared past them, the spoked
wheels throwing dust over their shoes. Veda looked down at her
white pumps covered with a brown patina of dust. She laughed.
"No use to dress atall," she said.

"No use to dress," Eileen and Cat said behind her. They walked
on, laughing, toward the station.

Marty's car was parked at the end of the line of automobiles.
He sat under the wheel with one leg thrown over the door of the
car. Graham McCloud and Morgan Holder sat squeezed together
beside him and Ace Johnson, his ukulele firmly clutched in his
hand, sat on top of the other car door, his legs dangling over the
side.

"Look at those fools," Cat said.

There was a stir among those who stood closest to the rails,
communicating to the others; there was a shifting and regrouping,
a sharp tingle of excitement in the air. "It's in the block," somebody said. Then they could hear it—the long whistle for Holly
Springs Crossing, pricking the back of the neck with its sound,
then the thunder riding in under the whistle, the clicking against
the steel, and, finally, the sigh of steam.

Cat stopped just short of the platform, the paper sack she was
carrying clutched against her. "I love a damned train," she said.
"I plain ole love 'em."

The mailbag was thrown off, dropping with a heavy clump onto
the platform where it was picked up immediately and hoisted into
a Ford that waited at the end of the line of cars. Eileen and Veda

came up beside Cat, watching the mailbag transference, waiting for the jerk and hiss that would signal departure, the wave of the conductor's hand from the steps.

"I forgot my hatbox," Eileen said suddenly.

"What?" Cat said.

"I left my hatbox in my locker," Eileen said, her eyes clouding. "Now I'll have to walk all the way back to the school before I can dress."

"Marty'll take you," Cat said. "In fact, I bet he'd love to take you."

Eileen shook her head. "You all go on to the post office," she said. "I'll meet you at Veda's."

The train began to move slowly out of the station and they turned to watch it, looking down the length of rail until the small red light disappeared into the west. Ace walked up behind them. "Going to the P.O.?" he said.

"Eileen's got to go back to school and get her hatbox," Veda said.

"I'll take her," Ace said quickly. "I haven't lost anything at the post office anyway. You all go on to town."

He put his hand under Eileen's elbow. "See you later," he said, starting away with her.

"Where you going, Ace boy?" Marty yelled across the platform. "Want some company?"

"*We* do," Cat said. "Let's go see if the mail's up." She reached over and took the paper sack out of Eileen's arms. "We'll carry the feast," she said. "Just get back in time to dress, and *don't* run into old man Johns."

Eileen laughed. "We'll hurry," she said. She turned and went down the road, Ace hurrying to keep up with her.

Ace Johnson had liked Eileen since the first time he had seen her getting out of the battered old mail truck in front of the high school. He liked her light hair and her slightly snub nose and the way she smiled. He liked the clothes she wore and the way she moved and talked. But he was afraid, with an instinct that he had to trust whether he wanted to or not, that Eileen Holder belonged to somebody else.

She had not said so. She went on their parties and she talked to him in the corridors of school, she sat with him in chapel, and rode with him in Marty's car. But he had never touched her except for a hand under her elbow once or twice. He felt that not knowing was better than knowing. And so he deceived himself and her. He was Ace, always around, always friendly, ready to play the uke and tell a joke. That was all.

Until Eileen, Ace had been lonely in Bellefonte. He had come there to live with his aunts in the neat brown house next door to the Mayhills' when he was twelve years old—too old to forget his mother and father and the house they had lived in, the way they had been together before the accident. They had been good to him here—Marty especially. He had come over the first week, running across the empty lot that separated the houses, swinging a tennis racket in his hand and asking Ace to come over and play a set. He had been part of Marty's gang from the beginning, but he never ceased to be lonely. Somehow Eileen Holder had changed that. So he hadn't questioned her. He hadn't asked for more. She was his friend.

They walked together through the square and toward the school, talking slowly in the coming dusk.

"Reckon we'll get to listen to Marty's radio tonight?" Eileen said.

"Always big doings on the radio at Marty's," Ace said. "Always big doings of some kind anyway. What I'm worried about is my part in this darned play."

Eileen smiled at him. "You'll do fine," she said. "You can play that uke better than anybody I know."

Ace shook his head and reached up to brush his hair off his forehead with his long-fingered hand. "You don't have to worry," he said. "Just being the prompter. I don't see why you wouldn't be in something, though."

"I can't *do* anything," she said. "I don't play the piano very well, or sing or dance. So—I hold the book."

"None of the rest of us *do* anything either," Ace said.

They came up to the school and went around to the side door. "What if it's locked?" Eileen said.

"It won't be. It'll be open for tonight if nothing else."

"That's right."

Ace turned the knob and the door opened inward. They stepped into the dimness of the downstairs hall. It was quiet, with the unbelievable stillness which can belong only to a place that you have always associated with noise, and they stepped cautiously as though afraid of disturbing the silence. Halfway down the empty hall he took her hand. She didn't move away from him, and they went on toward the wooden lockers at the other end of the hall, holding to each other mutely in the dark musty stillness. A stab of sunlight crossed the hall in the center, coming in under the front door. Ace stopped and looked at Eileen through the dust motes in the sunlight but she walked on and he followed her.

At the lockers she stopped and worked the combination, taking her hatbox, a small round black leather bag, from its depths. He took it from her and she shut the locker door and snapped the lock, turning around so suddenly that she bumped against him. He felt her standing against him with such an instant impact that he dropped the hatbox, and had half bent over to pick it up when he saw Eileen's face. She was looking at him, her eyes wide in the half-dark. He reached for her instead of the hatbox and pulled her into his arms. She came against him naturally and he kissed her, feeling the softness of her mouth tremble for a moment against his before she suddenly pushed him away.

"I'm sorry, Ace," she said. "I shouldn't have let you think ... think anything."

She was confused and she stammered a little, her voice unnaturally loud in the echoing corridor. "We'd better go on to Veda's now," she said.

He looked at her, trying to meet her eyes, but she looked away.

She had for a moment liked him so much that she had forgotten Vance and the entire world of her future; and she knew it. She examined this and was not afraid of it, but because it was the first time she had ever been kissed she was afraid of cherishing the moment, so she laughed, too suddenly, and said, "Let's go, Ace. Big doings tonight. We can't be late."

He followed her back down the empty hall, trying to get the hatbox away from her because she had firmly picked it up herself and wouldn't hand it over at all.

He walked silently beside her to Veda's, which was only two blocks away, and left her at the gate, hurrying home, cutting across lots and through back yards, swinging the ukulele against the weeds at the ditch edges, whistling uncertainly under his breath in the coming night.

Eileen went up the cement walk between the spreading water oaks and onto the wide front porch. Mrs. Simms was sitting in a rocker on the end of the porch, rocking placidly across the floor-boards, the rockers making a series of rhythmic creaks.

"Hello, Eileen," Mozel said. "Who was that with you? Alvin Johnson's boy?"

"Yes ma'am."

"He's turned out right handsome," Mrs. Simms went on. "Never thought he would . . . too skinny. But he makes a right nice appearance. Sit down, Eileen. How's your mother?"

"Fine, thank you. She said to tell you hello." Eileen sat down in the swing and put her hatbox at her feet.

"What do *you* do in this play?"

"I'm just the prompter," Eileen said.

Mozel grunted. "Well, I'll be glad when it's over . . . so much commotion about it." She looked up the street. "There's Veda and Catharine," she said.

They came up the street together, swinging the paper sacks. Catharine had her dress on a hanger over her shoulder and a box with her other clothes under her arm. "Eileen's already here," she said as they came up the walk. "She didn't give ole Ace half a chance."

"I told you," Veda said. "Vance Maynard."

"Got the mail, Veda?" Mrs. Simms said.

"Yes'm. It's all for Daddy."

"He's out back. You all better get ready if you're going over to the Mayhill's any time tonight."

"Come on, Eileen," Veda said. They went through the three-parted glass door and into the reception hall. To the left was the living room, dark and smelling of furniture polish. In the reception hall there was a big table with a silver tray for calling cards and a set of reed furniture. Around the walls were ferneries filled with soft green feathery plants. There was a pleasant smell of steak and biscuit in the air.

"You all go on upstairs," Veda said. "I'll take the mail to Daddy." She went down the long back hall, lit with a single dangling bulb, and into the kitchen. Aunt Betty, a tall thin Negro who wore floor-length skirts and aprons, was standing in front of the stove stirring gravy with a long-handled spoon. She looked at Veda and nodded toward the back door in silent communication. Veda went out onto the porch. She stood for a moment, looking through the screen across the back yard. She could see the shadow of the well outside the door, covered now that they no longer used it, and the great hump the wisteria arbor made against the dark blue sky. She could smell her father's pipe smoke and knew he was sitting in the arbor. She went through the screen door, slamming it behind her. "Daddy," she called softly, "I brought the mail."

"Well, bring it in, child," he said. She walked on into the arbor, seeing his shape against the light from the other end. He was sitting on the iron bench, leaning back, watching the faint wind-motion of the vines around him. She walked nearer and saw that he was in his shirt sleeves, his galluses standing out blackly against the white shirt. She handed him the mail. "Sit down?" he said.

"No sir. We've got to hurry to get to Marty's."

In the darkness she heard him chuckle. "You kids sure have fun at Martin Mayhill's place," he said. "Can't imagine him adding to it any. Guess it's Mrs. Mayhill that puts on the parties."

"Yessir."

"I thought so. Who all's going?"

"Cat and Graham and Eileen and Morgan—Ace Johnson—you know."

"How you going to get there?" he said.

"Walk, Daddy."

"All right. We'll all be sitting on the amen row tonight, baby. Put on a good show."

"Yessir."

"No automobiles now, Veda."

"Yes, Daddy." She turned and ran out of the arbor. The night was lighter here and she skipped lightly around the well and went in the back door.

Captain Simms was standing in the hall, leaning on his cane. "Hello, Miss Pickles," he said. "Where's your vamp outfit?"

"Oh Grandfather. We put our costumes on at school. We're going to supper at Mayhill's first."

"Who you sparking tonight?"

Veda blushed. "*You* know."

"Mr. Morgan Holder, I presume. What's that they call him? Sheik?"

"Yes."

"Well, just don't let him take you off to the desert on a prancing steed now."

Veda giggled. "I don't reckon Mama and Daddy would care," she said. "As long as it wasn't in an automobile."

Captain laughed. "Just you wait till I buy *us* an automobile," he said. "We'll show 'em."

"You going to be at the play?" Veda said.

"Wouldn't miss this for anything I know of," he said. "Get on now."

She started up the enclosed stairway, then stopped and called over her shoulder. "Grandfather," she said, "I love you."

"Don't you go off without that fan now," he said.

Ace Johnson cut across the empty lot that separated the Johnson property from the Mayhills'. He was dressed in his good suit and he still carried his ukulele in one hand, swinging it lightly against his pant leg. The field was clean and flat and mowed because it belonged to the Mayhills, and it was planted with cedars on both sides. On the other side of the far row of cedars was the Mayhill house. It was three-storied, built of white overlapping boards and mellow brick. And it was full of surprises. There were bay windows, jutting out suddenly from the side or from a third story, there were gables and turrets and scrolls, all gleaming with fresh paint—it was painted regularly every second summer. Spiraea grew in clumps around its white-railed porch, snowball bushes sheltered the side entrances, and below the bay windows honeysuckle fought with roses over high straight trellises. The brick walks were lined with perennial borders and the grass was smooth and green, merging into moss at the base of the maples and oaks of the front yard, growing between the roots of the willows in back. The outbuildings were painted as trimly and whitely as the main house: the smoke house with its salty, throat-catching odor of pork, the tool shed, the well house, the pergola with its own tiny cupola, and the playhouse with its own porch and scrollwork.

But the one object which made the grounds of the Mayhill house different and delightful to Marty Mayhill's friends was the red clay tennis court, lying deserted now behind the willows of the back yard. It was the only tennis court in Bellefonte. In fact, it was the only tennis court in the county and it was always filled in the summer; and always, winter and summer, enchanted. You could sit in the window seat of the third-story playroom and look out of the multipaned triple windows across the back yard toward it, watching the figures in white flitting to and from the fragile net, prolonging the moment of going down and joining them, watching from a distance before taking part in the enchantment, hearing dimly the voices calling, the faint muffled sounds of play.

Ace cut through the cedars at the point where the court began and stopped for a moment, looking at the canvas-covered plot. In another week or so it would be rolled and marked, the iron benches would be given the yearly coat of paint and set out around the margins. He walked around the court and up through the trees to the back yard, grinning at the thought of playing tennis again. Ace was the best tennis player in the gang next to Marty.

He rounded the well house and stopped, hearing Marty and Morgan's voices from the driveway. They were sitting on the running board of the car, smoking.

"Hi," Ace said. "Are you gentlemen planning your get-away?"

"Hi, Ace," Marty said, extending his cigarette case. "Sit down and have a cigarette. We're waiting for the ladies to arrive."

"Why don't we go get them?" Ace said.

"No, no, sir," Marty said. "They are to come together and alone as befits ladies—except for my date. I'm going after her."

"Ruby Marshall?"

"That's right."

"Where's Graham?" Ace said.

"Probably delayed by his old man," Marty said. "They're always expecting him to do this or that with the family. Those McClouds are a strong bunch for family."

Morgan looked around the driveway. "How far you reckon Graham goes with Cat?" he said.

"Not far," Marty said. "Take it from me."

"Meaning Marty Mayhill never went very far?" Morgan said. He took out a comb and carefully combed his hair.

"Maybe."

"Play the uke, Ace," Morgan said . . . "something hot."

Ace strummed on the uke, stretching his legs out in front of him. Graham came around the corner of the house. He was wearing white flannels and a new blazer. "Well, goddam, boys," he said. "I thought I'd never make it. Just as I tie my tie and start out the door who should just happen to drop in but old Aunt Caroline Simms that nobody's seen since winter set in last year, and she had to know this and know that and 'Aren't you turning into a handsome boy, Graham?' and 'Why do you boys part your hair in the middle?' and 'What's this about Miss Butler and that Downs man putting on this play?' till I thought I'd go out of my damn mind."

"I reckon everybody in town has something to say about poor old Downs and his woman," Ace said.

"Well God knows if she *is* anything to him," Graham said.

"And Morgan here," Marty said. "Morgan says it's all true."

"How come?"

"Oh, I told you—what I heard," Morgan said.

"Not that old talk about 'Omar the Tentmaker,' I hope," Graham said, sitting down on the gravel and pulling his knees up. "Why the hell shouldn't anybody go to a damned picture show anyway?"

"Oh, not that," Marty said. "He heard them talking during rehearsals one night when he was waiting for the fair Veda."

"What were they saying?" Graham said.

"Oh, nothing much," Morgan said. "But it wasn't just talk between two play sponsors."

"Well I for one am damned glad to hear it," Marty said. "So evil. Wouldn't the high school faculty love to get hold of that?" He stood up. "Well, boys, time for me to go give Miss Ruby Marshall a thrill. You all go on up to the playroom and get the crystal set going for the gals."

They went up the back steps and past the white-coated boy standing in the back door. "Ham," Marty said, "did you change that spark plug?"

"Yes *sir*." Ham grinned. "It's right much of a pleasure to work on that automobile, Mr. Marty."

"Why don't you take it down and gas it up while we're having supper?" Marty said.

"Yes *sir!*" Ham slipped away toward the pantry, moving with alacrity.

They went up the back stairs and into the third-floor playroom. "I'll see you," Marty said, retying his tie. "Try to tune in Chicago while I'm gone."

The playroom was the gathering place for Marty's gang, which included most of the sophomore class of the high school, at least all the important ones—the bright, or the handsome, or the interesting. Marty had the first crystal set in town and it had become a tradition to gather in the playroom to take turns with the earphones, listening over the crackling and popping of incomprehensible interference to the voices of the North—that impossible world which they all thought of as the Outside Place. It was as though the world they lived in were a cocoon of sky and mountain and water and somewhere above it, away from it, outside of it —always outside—there existed the cities and plains of North or West. The earphones brought it all into the cocoon—the music and talk and laughter of the Outside.

Marty Mayhill had the first roadster in town, he had a jade and ivory mah-jongg set, but the radio, like the tennis court, was, for a long time at least, unique. It was magic, or the next best thing.

Graham went over to the set and picked up the earphones. "I wish the women would get here," he said.

Downstairs Buz Mayhill stood looking down at the buffet she'd had set in the dining room. She checked the napkins and silver and the stack of hot plates under the warming cloth, she went into the kitchen to look at the gelatin salad she'd made herself. Satisfied, she went into the living room and took a cigarette from a china box. She lit it slowly, watching the flame ignite the paper and tobacco with a sensuous pleasure. She was very glad she had been permitted to live in a time when women were beginning to be allowed to live. She was also very glad that Martin had made so much money, that her world was made of the miracle that changed a dirt field of cotton and a dirty noisy gin into this white house and green gardens. And she was glad she had Marty and all Marty's friends to make the white house noisy itself with a different sort of sound.

Her daughter had been a disappointment to Buz. From the time she was born she had waited for Sue to be a companion to her. She had dressed her in handmade dresses and fed her delicate foods, and curled her hair around her fingers. But Sue was dull. There just wasn't anything else to say for her. She liked to talk to her father about the gin, or read books of biography, or change her bedroom around. But Marty . . . Buz smiled. Marty was just the sort of boy she'd wanted. He was charming, indolent, handsome. He was intelligent too, more intelligent than Sue with all her dull biographies. Even Martin Senior had to admit that. Buz picked up the book she was reading—*Jurgen*, covered with a plain brown paper cover—and settled back to wait. When the doorbell jangled she went to let them in herself.

They went up the wide front stairway and along the carpeted hall, Veda, Eileen and Cat, smoothing their skirts and touching their hair as they walked, raising a foot behind them to inspect a shoe-heel, their beads swinging forward to brush their cheeks.

"Don't you just love this house?" Veda said.

"I love the yard," Eileen said. "It always smells wonderful in this yard."

"That's Mrs. M's flowers," Cat said. "She has them planted for every season of the year."

"It smells good inside too," Veda said.

"That's money," Cat said. She went through the doorway into Buz's white bedroom and they followed her, stopping to peer into the white-framed mirror, to repair the unseen ravages of a ten-minute walk.

The boys were waiting in the playroom. Morgan took Veda to the window seat and sat beside her, holding her hand carefully. He watched her face covertly, seeing the small smile that came and went as she watched the crowd around the radio across the room. Graham had the earphones on and Cat was leaning against him trying to hear too.

"It's Chicago, boy," Graham yelled excitedly. "Hot damn, it's really ole Chicago, booming in plain as day."

"Let me hear." Cat grabbed the earphones from him, putting them over her short black hair. "What's that they're playing?" she said.

"It's Eileen's turn," Ace said. "She hasn't gotten a chance yet. How about it, Cat?"

Cat handed the earphones over and Eileen placed them on her head. Her eyes lit suddenly, the blue glittering with excitement.

"Lord, Eileen, you're pretty," Ace said.

Eileen blushed. She took the earphones off and handed them back to Ace. He stood for a moment, the phones dangling from his hand. "Veda?" he said, not turning to look toward the window seat. "You want to hear Chicago?"

"She's not interested in Chicago," Graham said. "She's dreaming about a tent on the burning sands."

"Say, Sheik," Ace said, "are you gonna abduct our Veda?"

Morgan grinned. "I like it right here," he said.

Then the gong, that Buz Mayhill had ordered all the way from California, called them to dinner in the house below. Marty and Ruby had arrived. He stood against the wall, watching her with amusement as she flitted around the living room like a tropical bird in a red dress.

In the dining room Martin Senior sat stolidly at the table eating his supper. He wasn't interested in the children and he devoutly wished Buz wouldn't serve things off a buffet. He liked to sit down to a well-cooked, well-served meal, and the devil with style. This was all bad enough, but what was worse he was going to have to go to this play thing they were putting on. Buz insisted. He sighed heavily and helped himself to more potatoes. He wished Sue was home from Ward-Belmont. She appreciated a peaceful meal too.

Buz had agreed to take all of them to the school in her Oldsmobile and she began trying to get them together as soon as they finished eating. "Sara Butler will never forgive me if I don't get you there in time for this," she said, pushing Marty toward the door. "Are you and Ruby coming with us or in your car?"

Marty grinned at her. "I just think we'll come along with the rest of you," he said. "I'll let one of the others have my car. They don't get to ride much."

"Do I detect an ulterior motive, darling?" Buz said lightly.

"Naturally." Marty laughed and winked at her. "If I drag Miss Ruby along with the crowd to the play she'll be all the happier to ride home all alone in the joy buggy with Marty."

"Oh, Marty," Buz said. "You're impossible."

"You love it, madam."

She shrugged, moving away from him to get her wrap. Marty stood in the middle of the floor, the car keys dangling from his finger. "Silence, children," he said loudly. "Highest bidder gets to transport his date to dear old M.C.H.S. in Marty's Playboy." He glanced at Ruby, who was pouting sullenly. "Don't worry, child," he said into her ear. "We have all night after the play."

"Well, what are we gonna do?" Morgan said. "Flip a coin?"

"Oh, let Morgan have it," Graham said. "He and Veda never get to joy ride."

Veda shook her head. "I better not," she said. "You know how Mama and Daddy . . ."

"I sure do," Graham said. "That's why I think you ought to go."

"No. I'm sorry, Morgan." She smiled at him. "But if they found out I might not get out at night at all any more."

"We go with Mrs. Mayhill," Morgan said. "You and Ace match for it."

"All right," Graham said. He took a nickel from his pocket and pitched it into the air.

"Heads," Ace said.

"Sorry, old man, you lose," Graham said. He reached for the keys, but Cat reached across his shoulder and grabbed them from Marty's finger. "Ta ta, everybody," she said, running toward the door. "See you back stage."

"Hey, wait a minute," Graham yelled, running after her. "I'm driving."

"I've got the keys," Cat said, going out the door.

She ran lightly ahead of him across the porch and into the moonlight of the drive. He slowed down, not trying to catch her any more, watching her figure moving shadowily in the moonlight. She stopped and stood looking down at the car. Graham came up behind her and put his arms around her.

She turned toward him, her moon-washed face glowing softly. "Just look at that damned thing, Graham," she said. "That's the prettiest damned car I ever saw."

"Um-hmmm," Graham said. "Let's get in it."

"Just look at those spokes." Cat leaned over and ran a hand lovingly around the yellow spokes of the wheels. "Wouldn't you know Marty would have a car like this?" she said. "A car nobody in Maynard County ever heard of." She laughed, excitement making her voice unsteady. "I've been wanting to drive this thing ever since he got it. Let's get in her and *go*." She put one foot on the running board and vaulted easily over the door into the driver's seat.

Graham got in beside her and put his arm around her shoulder. "Aw, Cat," he said. He leaned over and kissed her cheek.

She moved away from him, leaning over to advance the spark and throttle. "Graham, honey," she said, "you've got to get out and crank."

"Oh, hell," he said. "I thought *you* were going to drive." He vaulted over the door and went to the front of the car. He ran back around and got into the seat beside her as she backed out of the drive with a spurt of gravel, tapping the horn to the others, who were getting into Buz's car now.

"I'm gonna drive all the way to Holly Springs," she said, feeling the wind take her hair and lift it. "Listen. It doesn't rattle at all."

"We're supposed to be going to put on a play," Graham said mildly. He took a cigarette from his pocket and lit it elaborately.

"In a minute, in a minute. Just let me drive it a little first."

"We've got to get dressed," Graham said.

She shook her head. "Oh, Graham, I never get to drive. Daddy has a fit every time anybody touches that damned Ford. We aren't on till last thing anyway. Please Graham. Don't be proper. Don't be *old*."

Graham slumped down in the seat. "All right, baby," he said. "Drive."

They went up the chert road, moonlight making it almost as bright as the headlights. It was getting close to eight o'clock and they didn't pass another car but once on a straight stretch, a wagon, going home slow and late from some social, the children curled in the bed sleeping, the mother sitting up straight in a splint-bottomed chair. Her eyes followed them as Cat put her foot hard on the gas to go around.

Graham watched Cat's face in the moonlight, the angled jaw, the lips pressed together now as she watched the road. He reached over and touched her gently. "Park, baby," he said. "We're nearly to Holly Springs." He could hear her laughter above the sound of the motor. She braked abruptly, backed across the road, turned around, and stopped.

"In the middle of the road?" he said.

"There's nothing coming for miles."

He leaned over and touched her chin with his fingers. She moved over and kissed him lightly on the lips. He put his arms around her and kissed her, but she pulled away. "Got to go put on a play," she said.

"They're already mad by now," he said, kissing her ear.

"No reason for them to get madder."

They drove back up the road, passing the wagon again, seeing the slow stare turn toward them as they swept by. She drove fast and expertly to the school and around to the stage door, braking with a spurt of gravel.

Marty was standing on the steps watching them. "I see you got her all back in one piece," he said, looking at the car.

"We sure did," Graham said sullenly.

They got out of the car and went in the stage door.

Sara Butler stood coolly in the middle of a crowd of chattering people. She was highlighted by the stage behind her and they stopped in the doorway, looking at her, surprised a little by her magnificence. She wore a blue dress in two shades, powder and copenhagen. The skirt was straight with a long sash ending in square cut cording, the jacket had wide sleeves and hung loosely over the hips, belted at the waist with another belt that fell to the same tasseled effect on the other side. Her hat was a round twist of copenhagen ribbons, shading her eyes and held in place by one large pearl hatpin in front. She wore patent-leather shoes with dainty pearl buttons, and the sheerest hose Catharine had ever seen.

"What's she doing all got up like that?" Graham said.

"I don't know," Cat said. "See how Mr. K. Downs looks."

"Where have you two been?" Sara said, coming toward them, the tassels on her skirt swishing against the silk.

"Sorry," Graham said. "We had car trouble."

"Cars are so convenient," Sara said. "Horses never had trouble with their insides. They just always ambled on toward home."

Graham laughed. "We'll get dressed," he said.

"You'd better hurry. The curtain's ready to go up now." She looked around distractedly. "Where is Ken—Mr. Downs?" she said.

"Right here, Miss Butler," he said, coming out from behind a back drop, dapper in white flannels and navy coat.

"Ah, ha," Cat said.

"What was that?" Miss Butler said.

"I said I'll hurry," Cat said quickly. She pressed Graham's hand, went behind the stage and across to the partition where the girls were dressing. She stuck her head in and whooped. "Here's the lost one come home," she said.

"Cat! We thought you were gone for good and all," Veda said. She was already in her vamp costume, standing uncomfortably in the tight black skirt. "Can you help me fix this thing?" she said, tugging at the bandeau that sat lopsidedly on her forehead.

Cat took it and pinned it to her hair in the back with swift quick movements. "You look wonderful, honey," she said. "Where'd you get the cigarette holder?"

"Buz. Isn't it something? I feel like Mata Hari."

Cat slipped out of her skirt in one quick movement and reached for her costume. "Notice anything peculiar around here?" she said.

"Peculiar?" Eileen said. She was helping two girls with their tulip costumes. "How, peculiar?"

"Well, Butler being all diked out with hat and all," Cat said, slapping grease paint on her face.

"Probably going to another movie after the play, ha, ha," Veda said.

"I bet it's more than that," Cat said.

"You don't mean—eloping or something?"

Cat grinned. "Maybe. They're sure dressed up enough for it."

"That'd give Mrs. Butler a fit," Veda said.

"That's the truth. They say she won't let him in the front door. My Lord. They're *old* too. Sara Butler graduated from college ages ago. I hope to God my family don't try to boss me around that long."

"It's just cause it's him," Veda said. "They'd like her to marry anybody else."

"Shhh," Eileen said warningly.

Sara Butler came into the room. She was moving in a daze tonight and she knew it, so she over-compensated by trying to be everywhere and do everything at once. She had rearranged the set several times, she had personally supervised the costuming, she had tested the lights and the curtain, and the stage door. She had even checked the water bucket in case of fire. "You look fine now, Veda," she said. "You too, Cat. Come out front and take a look through the curtain. We've really got a full house."

They followed her onto the stage and took turns peeping

through a hole in the dusty wine curtain. The auditorium was almost full and people were still coming in a steady stream.

"Everybody in the damned county must be here," Cat said. "There's my mother and daddy—and there's yours, Veda, and the Captain."

"Where?"

"Right in front," Cat said. "Catch your grandfather missing anything."

"Let me see," Veda said. The Captain was sitting in a front-row seat, his cane dandily held between his legs. "I don't see Morgan," she said. "Eileen, can you see your family?"

Eileen looked through the curtain. "Right in front of that post in the middle there," she said. "Lord, Mama's got on a hat."

Veda looked and saw Morgan, his white shirt gleaming in the darkness of the semi-lighted room. "I'm so excited I think I'll bust," she said.

Marty stepped up behind her and picked her up, waltzing her grandly around the stage. "Come with me to my tent, oh lovely," he said. "I'll dilate my nostrils for you endlessly."

"Marty, stop it," she said, struggling weakly. "You'll ruin my costume."

"Vamps have to expect that sort of thing," he said, putting her down.

It was a good play, and the audience was pleased. They had expected something modern and different and they were gratified to find that the most daring thing in the revue was only Veda Simms, looking as though she were got up in her mother's old clothes to play lady.

From her place in the wings Eileen watched the stage, listening to the rise and fall of applause, the brightness of voices pitched out toward the auditorium, the scuffle of feet across the rough boards of the stage. When Miss Butler came up behind her just before time for Graham and Cat to go on with their skit and handed her a square violet envelope, she took it automatically. She nodded when Sara said, "Will you give this to my mother when she comes backstage after the performance?", and slipped it into her prompt book.

Sara saw Catherine and Graham onto the stage for the last number, she told Eileen to see that everybody got on for the last song as soon as the curtain came down on their skit, then she turned and went out the stage door and got into her Chevrolet coupé beside Kenneth Downs.

"It's an awful thing to do to those kids," she said suddenly. "I don't think I can . . ."

Kenneth reached across her and slammed the door firmly. "Can you think of a better way?" he said.

She shook her head.

"Then let's get on to Tennessee," he said. "We need a good start."

On stage Catharine and Graham went through their skit, the audience laughed in the appropriate places, and Marty stood in the stage door watching the tail light disappear down the hill. He laughed and came back to where Eileen stood. "They've gone, by God," he whispered.

She jumped and looked around at him. "Who's gone?"

"Butler and Downs," he said. "They've flown the coop."

Eileen looked down at the letter in her book, addressed in the precise copy-book handwriting of Sara Butler. "Marty," she said, "what will I do?"

He picked the note up, holding it carefully between his thumb and forefinger. "Let me deliver it," he said. "I wouldn't miss this for anything in the world."

"What's going on?" Ace Johnson said. "It's nearly time for the finale and I can't find either of our dear sponsors anywhere."

"It seems," Marty said importantly, "that we'll have to put on our own finale. Our sponsors are on the way to the state line right now."

"Hot damn!" Ace said, doing a dance step across the narrow space in the wings. "There'll be a hot time in the ole town to-night."

On stage Cat and Graham went on with their act while the rest of the cast gathered around Marty and absorbed the news as quietly as possible. "Look at ole Graham and Cat," Marty said, looking onto the stage. "Going right on with it all." He laughed.

The skit ended and Graham put his arms around Cat and they went into their stage clinch. Eileen jabbed the boy who handled the curtain and he pulled on the ropes, the heavy curtain swishing together to the sound of applause. Onstage Cat and Graham still sat on the sofa, kissing each other under the bright lights of the stage.

Marty looked over Eileen's shoulder. "Glory to God," he said. "This is gonna be a night to remember. Let's really give 'em something to talk about." He pushed the curtain boy aside and opened the curtain with a strong yank on the ropes.

The applause stopped. Bellefonte Alabama sat in stunned silence and watched Graham McCloud kiss Catharine Graves.

Buz Mayhill laughed. The sound was sudden and silvery in the silence of the auditorium. Cat and Graham jumped and looked into the footlights. Then they sat still, their arms around each other, blinking toward the shadowy figures in front of them.

Mr. Graves moved. He fought his way across the people sitting between him and the aisle and moved down it and up the little flight of steps onto the stage. He grabbed Cat's arm and marched her back down the steps with him and toward her mother who still sat in silence, watching her daughter uncertainly. "You're coming home. Right now," he said loudly. Buz Mayhill laughed again.

In the pandemonium that followed it was some time before anyone missed Sara Butler and Kenneth Downs. Catharine had been marched up the aisle and out the auditorium. The rest of the parents were all backstage, endeavoring to take their children home with them, towing them behind them like cubs, shouting at them, instructing them to get the paint off their faces.

By the stage door Captain Simms and Buz Mayhill stood in a space of quiet, watching the scene.

"Jerusalem!" Captain Simms said feelingly. "It looks like the

camps used to on the night before battle." He chuckled. "Young
folks don't ever change atall, Mrs. Mayhill. This is just like the
time my sister Flora got caught kissing the boy that was supposed
to be tending the horses at a play party."

Buz laughed too, but she sobered suddenly. "This isn't going to
make it very easy on any of the kids concerned though," she said.

"No, I reckon not," Captain Simms said. "Parents don't ever
change either."

There was a sudden lull in the commotion and into it Mrs.
Butler stepped grandly, the note Marty had handed her clutched
dramatically to her bosom. "She's gone," she said. "Gone!"

"This is too much," Buz said. "I simply can't stand anything
else." She doubled over, laughing. "Sara Butler has run off with her
Yankee schoolteacher. I feel it in my bones."

"I think I'd better go home," Captain said, tapping his cane.
"Mozel is going to be all the hysterical woman I want to see to-
night." He bowed gallantly to Buz and marched over to where
Mozel was standing over Veda Simms, her mouth in a grim line.
R. V. stood just behind her, his hand on her shoulder placatingly.

"She hasn't done anything, Mozel," he said soothingly. "Not
anything at all."

"How do we know what she's done during all this rehearsal?"
Mozel said. "Rehearsal indeed! With Sara Butler and that man
lally-gagging around here themselves. That poor woman!" She
looked toward Mrs. Butler sadly.

"She'll be reconciled by the time the first grandchild comes,"
Captain said. "Come on, Miss Veda. Let's all go home." He put
his hand under Veda's elbow, then looked around the crowd.
"Where's that little Holder girl?" he said. "She's spending the
night with you, isn't she?"

"I trust her mother's taking her home too," Mozel said. "I don't
think there's going to be any spending the night or feasting or
whatever tonight."

Morgan had come up onto the stage and was talking to Eileen
in the wings. "You going to come on home or what?" he said.

"I better," she said. "Mrs. Simms is awful mad. And if I were you I'd get on back down before she sees you. All they need is to find out Veda was seeing you after rehearsal all last week."

Morgan nodded. He took one look at Veda, standing sadly rumpled in her finery. Her tight skirt had split and trailed down behind her raggedly. Her bandeau rested rakishly over her left ear. He turned and went back across the stage. "We'll wait for you out front," he said to Eileen before going back down the steps into the auditorium.

Eileen moved toward Mrs. Simms, embarrassment making her awkward. "I think I better go on home tonight," she said hesitantly.

Mozel nodded curtly and Eileen turned away, going out the stage door toward her family, the forgotten prompt book still in her hand.

"Come on Veda," Captain said again. "We all need some sleep." They went out the stage door and up the road, Veda's torn silk skirt trailing behind her.

In the McCloud car Mr. McCloud was calmly but firmly telling Graham that it was two more years before he could go to college and that there would be four years of that and three more of law school—and that money was always tight.

Ace Johnson was walking home between Miss Mattie and Miss Trudy Johnson. He held his ukulele in his hand and occasionally he cursed under his breath. They talked across him, the words irritatingly slow and doom-laden on the night air. "Alvin would never forgive us," Miss Mattie said. And "This is what comes of raising other folks' children," said Miss Trudy.

"That sort of thing wasn't going on all the time during rehearsals, was it, Eileen?" Mrs. Holder asked on the way home, and when Eileen said no, that had been the end of it in the Holder household. Mr. Holder was dubious, but his wife calmed him. "Eileen don't lie," she said firmly. Mrs. Holder was not afraid of petting parties. She was afraid of a small sharp shining piece of steel. She said nothing else, she was waiting.

Marty Mayhill didn't take Ruby Marshall home. Mrs. Marshall took her, thanking Marty politely, but firmly, before she whisked the small figure in the red dress out the stage door.

Martin Senior was already sitting in the Oldsmobile. He had had enough for one night. Buz and Marty stood on in the emptying wings. Buz was trying to calm Mrs. Butler now. "Sara is twenty-two years old, Christine," she said, her voice soothing. "I'm sure Kenneth Downs comes from very nice people. It will work out. Believe me."

Christine Butler sniffed. She did not want to be consoled. She turned away, and Buz shrugged. "Let's go home, love," she said to Marty. "We've done enough damage for one night."

"You want a spin in my car?" Marty said.

"Sure," Buz said. "Why waste it? I'll tell your father to go on."

They drove home through the silent streets, Marty gunning the motor in a last burst of defiance in the darkness.

In the Graves home the parlor lights were still on. Mr. Graves was praying. Cat and her mother sat stiffly on the edge of the sofa while he knelt in front of the wing-back chair. He had not forgotten the words and rhythms of his old calling as preacher and his voice droned into the quiet room, quavering at the highest pitch of each pleading sentence. Mr. Graves always pleaded with God. He pleaded for Him to look down and see the things that were put upon His poor servant, W. W. Graves. Tonight his burden was his daughter, and he was at the top of his form. He had reached the sentence of the "serpent's tooth" before he noticed that his wife and daughter still sat upright on the sofa. "On your knees," he said grimly, his voice not losing a beat as he continued with his supplications.

Mrs. Graves went down on the floor dutifully. Cat continued to sit on the sofa.

"I said kneel in the sight of God," Mr. Graves said.

Catharine knelt down. "God," she said silently behind her clenched teeth, "God, look down and see what a pompous, ignorant, ranting old fool W. W. Graves is." She rubbed at her knees that were already itching from the rough carpet. She closed her eyes, and sighed.

Then April was over in Bellefonte and May came heavily and dully. The young girls stayed at home on the spring evenings and learned to crochet, sitting in the big rockers on the front porches. After dark Marty Mayhill drove his roadster through the streets, blowing his horn at the houses where the captive maidens rocked, and went home early because there was nobody to have any fun with.

"It's ridiculous," Buz said to him one Saturday night when he came into the living room at eight o'clock and asked her if she wanted to go get a Coke with him. "They can't keep them shut up forever."

"They won't," Marty said. "But they'll do it long enough to change them."

Buz looked at him soberly. "Don't sound so wise, darling," she said. "It gives me a chill."

He shrugged. "I feel wise. Tonight," he said. "It's all this being alone."

"Why don't I call some of their mothers?" Buz said. "I could have a dinner party."

"Not you, sweetheart," Marty said. "Remember, you laughed."

Buz smiled wryly. "Well, darling boy, you opened that curtain."

"I know." Marty kicked at the rug. "I wish to God I hadn't. Hell, I didn't know this was still the dark ages in Bellefonte."

"It is. And to some extent it always will be," Buz said. "That's one of the curses of knowing all your townsmen." She stood up. "Come on," she said. "Let's go get that Coke."

"It sounds silly as hell to me," Vance Maynard said to Eileen. They were sitting on a rock behind the house, watching the sun go down on another Saturday afternoon. "I don't see how one little kiss and a couple of high-school teachers eloping could make all the mamas in Bellefonte decide their children were up to something."

Eileen smiled. "I don't guess it's just that," she said. "They've been reading all this stuff about flaming youth, and seeing movies, and talking in whispers about the awful things that happen up North. Now they think it's come to Bellefonte, that's all."

Vance stood up, his hands in his hip pockets. "Well, I see more of you now, anyway," he said.

Eileen stood up too. "Are you glad?" she said.

He smiled down at her. "Don't be fishing for compliments, little one," he said.

She came close to him suddenly. "Are you glad?" she said again. "Yes."

"I think I want to kiss you now," she said.

He looked down at her, wanting to put it off again, turn her from sixteen to six, ride her piggy-back across the back meadow. "I reckon it's time," he said. He leaned over and put his lips over hers.

Eileen came into the kitchen slowly, walking quietly, hoping to get to her room before her mother saw her. But it was no use. Mrs. Holder was sitting in the rocker by the window. She looked at Eileen calmly and sadly for a long moment. Then she got up and took the frying pan from the back of the stove and slapped it onto the front eye. "All right," she said gruffly. "Go on to your room for a while. I'll get supper."

"Mama," Eileen said.

Mrs. Holder looked at her. Eileen's face was soft and her eyes shone in the dim light from the banked fire of the range. "You gonna marry him?" Mrs. Holder said.

"I've always been going to marry him," Eileen said.

"But not yet?"

"No'm, not yet."

Mrs. Holder sighed, whether with worry or relief she wasn't sure. "Well, it's good stock," she said finally.

"Oh, Mama." Eileen laughed a small laugh. "I love him."

"Are you telling me something, miss?" her mother said. "Now, get on to your room. I've got enough trouble with Morgan mooning around like a lost soul because they've got Veda Simms shut up in that house, without you carrying on too. You just go have a rest before supper. You're not going to get out of washing dishes afterwards," she called after her as Eileen went silently out the door.

On June 23 Mr. and Mrs. Kenneth Downs came back to Bellefonte. And on June 24 Kenneth Downs went to work in Mr. Butler's hardware store. They had been in Ohio, where Sara had cried day and night to come home. Kenneth Downs, who had had more than enough of Bellefonte, Alabama, had held out against her for two months. But on the morning she had blushingly told him they were going to have a baby he had told her to go on and pack. He knew when he was beaten.

On June 25, Sara Butler Downs, accompanied by her mother and armed with a case of calling cards, made the rounds of the mothers of the girls of the sophomore class and did her penance while drinking nectar and lemonade in the musty drawn-shaded parlors of the white houses. She apologized prettily and assured them that nothing untoward had occurred at rehearsals before the play. But it was much longer before the girls involved were allowed to finish their penance.

Gradually, as summer turned into fall, the parents relented for church socials, and when Buz Mayhill gave her annual Christmas Eve party they were all allowed to go. Mainly because Buz took the neat precaution of asking Mozel Simms to help chaperone. She was rather pleased with herself for this stroke, though unfortunately it dampened the party.

During the winter the Simmses and the Graveses, after careful talk and consultation, decided it would be proper for Morgan and Graham to call on Veda and Cat—if they would sit in the living room or kitchen and not stay too late. Automobiles were forbidden. And Marty Mayhill was dating a girl from Morgan City who went to a finishing school in Virginia.

Winter brought with it a problem for Eileen and Vance. In winter there was no place to go. Summer had been warm and beautiful. There were the woods, infinite and varied, full of hollows and groves of thick-leaved bushes—quiet and hidden—and sunlit through the greenness. Summer was a time for love, laying-by time, a time to rest in the lushness of tree-filled afternoons. To Eileen summer forever after had Vance's face, brown and smiling, between earth and sky, leaning over her in silence and in light. For Vance, summer blotted out forever the trenches and the blast-streaked skies of France.

Then the trees turned, the grass was dry, and after three o'clock in the afternoon it was too cold in the woods and the night came on too soon. The cotton had to be picked, and the days closed in. They sat together at night in the parlor—at Eileen's house or at his—and for them it was not a time to be together at last as it was for Cat Graves and Graham McCloud and Morgan Holder and Veda Simms. For them it was a cozy warm prison where the family talked interminably, and the piano must be played by Eileen, and the nuts cracked and picked, and the apples eaten, and the fire chunked, and the doors kept closed.

They sat in the living room with Mrs. Maynard one Saturday night, watching the fire on the floorboards, holding hands. Vance straightened up suddenly, reaching over and putting one hand on Eileen's face. "We will have to get married," he said. "That's all."

"I have to finish school," Eileen said.

"Finish then," Vance said. "I don't care. But we will get married. Now. I'm not going to sit by the fire and hold your hand any more. I want you under my damned patchwork quilt."

"Vance," Mrs. Maynard said. "It's late. You'd better be thinking about taking Eileen home."

He looked at Eileen, laughing. "You see?" he said.

They were married in the parlor of Eileen's house, and she wore her mother's wedding dress with its faintly yellowed veil. Veda was her bridesmaid and Cat ladled the punch into the small crystal mugs that were gotten down from the back cupboard. Bellefonte mothers thought it was scandalous because her mother *let* her marry that young, and they cast worried eyes at their daughters' Saturday night dates.

They went to Chattanooga for their honeymoon. And he bought her a star sapphire in a jewelry store on Broad Street where a little man in a high white collar took them into a dark little room with a table spread with velvet to look at the stones.

They were uneasy with each other in the big white bed in the plain hotel room, so he brought her home the next day and carried her up the old enclosed stairway to the hand-turned spool bed with its patchwork quilt.

On Monday morning she went to school, going down to the end of the cove road to catch the mail truck. Miss Constance Jones looked up startled when she came into English class, the girls were envious, the boys thought how pretty she looked, and Ace Johnson flunked his algebra test that afternoon.

They had six months together before Vance began having the headaches.

2. *August 1925*

The T-model came over the bridge on the east side of Bellefonte. It was going fast, rattling loudly over the chert road, its side curtains flapping wildly in the late afternoon breeze. Morgan clutched the wheel firmly, looking straight at the road in front of him. Beside him Veda sat quietly. She was wearing her best dress, blue silk with polka dots, and her beige straw cloche with the blue flowers. She held her hands tightly clasped in her lap, the new ring with the orange blossoms carefully out of sight under her bag. She was frightened. There hadn't been time to be frightened before: not that morning while she was sneaking her clothes out of the house to leave at Cat's, nor that afternoon when she and Morgan had wheedled Captain Simms out of the car, nor even, she thought, during the ride to Tennessee or the brief ceremony performed by the fat justice of the peace in the musty parlor. But she was frightened now. She wished Cat had come with her. But Cat hadn't come. At the last minute she and Graham had backed out, and Veda couldn't really blame them. It wasn't going to be pleasant facing her mother and father; and they would have blamed Graham. Because Graham was family and should have taken care of her. She looked toward Morgan and he reached out and put his hand over her clenched fists.

"We're nearly there, baby," he said. "Come on. Don't be scared."

She shook her head. "I just can't go home," she said softly.

"We don't have to," he said. "I told you. We're going to Eileen's."

"Eileen's got troubles enough of her own," Veda said.

"This isn't trouble, Mrs. Holder," Morgan said lightly, pulling her against his shoulder. "This is our wedding night. It's supposed to be happy. Aren't you happy?"

She smiled. "Yes. But I'm scared anyway."

"Aw honey."

"I know." She sighed, resting her head against his shoulder. "I just don't know what Daddy will do."

"Nothing after tonight. You know that. He won't try to get it annulled after tonight."

She relaxed against him, watching dusk coming onto the road. The sky purpled and the trees stood out green against it. They could feel the heat coming into the car, heavy and thick with approaching night.

"Here's the pike," Morgan said. He turned onto the road and slowed for the railroad crossing, then he stamped the gear pedal and pulled up and over the graveled grading. It was night when they passed the Holder farm.

"We could stop here," Morgan said, "but I reckon you'd rather be with Eileen."

She nodded and he drove on up the road to the cove. "I hope to hell Vance is feeling all right tonight," he said as they stopped in front of the house. "He must be. I don't see a light in the bedroom."

He got out of the car and opened the door for Veda. "Come on, Mrs. Holder," he said. "It ought to be about supper time." He pushed open the heavy door and they went into the dark hallway. "I wish to God they'd get some kind of lights out here," he said irritably, feeling his way along the wall. "Hey, Eileen, you got company," he called.

"In the kitchen."

They followed the sound of her voice, stepping down into the living room and going through the tiny passage into the wide kitchen that stretched halfway across the back of the house. Eileen was frying something at the stove. Vance sat straddling a kitchen chair, drumming his knuckles rhythmically on the seat in front of him. "Well, look who's here," he said.

Eileen turned. She looked at Veda's hat and dress and Morgan's suit and tie. Then she shoved the skillet to the back of the stove. "Uh-oh," she said.

Veda smiled.

"That's right," Morgan said. "Meet Mrs. Holder."

Vance stood up. "Well, well," he said laughing. "I wondered when you two were going to get up the nerve to take the jump."

Eileen reached over and took a cigarette from the pack in Vance's shirt pocket. She took a kitchen match and scraped it slowly across the stove and lit the cigarette, watching Veda and Morgan, half amused, half angry. "How far behind you is R. V.?" she said.

Veda laughed then, relaxing visibly. She reached up and took off her hat. "They don't know it yet," she said. "We took Grandfather's car and a picnic lunch to go over and see Tallulah Falls."

"Oh, brother!" Vance said. He stretched, his arms almost touching the darkened ceiling. "Well, I reckon you could use some supper," he said. "Where'd you go? Fayetteville?"

Veda nodded. "Have you got any coffee, Eileen?" she said.

Eileen took a cup from the cupboard and poured from the big pot on the back of the stove. She still watched Veda closely. "Sit down, for God sakes," she said finally. "You make me nervous standing around like that."

They sat at the table and Eileen went back to the stove again. "I better put on some more meat," she said.

Vance started out of the room. "I'm going up and see to Van," he said.

"He's asleep," Eileen said.

"Just look in a minute." He went out.

Eileen looked at Morgan. "Well, you've fixed it, haven't you?" she said.

"Now don't start, Eileen," Morgan said. He unbuttoned his coat and leaned back in the chair. "Where's my cup of coffee?"

"Morgan," Eileen went on, "you haven't got a damned bit of sense. You never did. Don't you know what Mozel and R. V. are going to think about this?" She handed him the pot. "Pour your own coffee."

"Well don't be blaming Morgan," Veda said. "We've wanted to get married ever since school was out this year. I don't want to go off to any girls' school. My Lord, Eileen, you've been married two years. What's the matter with you?"

Eileen shrugged. She lifted an eye on the stove and threw her cigarette stub onto the coals. "O.K.," she said. "I won't say anything else. Just one thing. Are you planning on staying here tonight?"

"Well hell yes," Morgan said. "You don't think we're going in to Simms' tonight, do you?"

"All right," Eileen said. "If I don't say you can, Vance probably will. But I'm not going to have anything else to do with it. I might as well let you stay, 'cause if I don't you'll just go on up to Mama's." She laughed then. "O.K., all settled. Now I guess we'll have to celebrate. Vance!" she called.

"What is it?" he said from the living room.

Eileen smiled. "Come on back now, and just go on out to the back and bring in a jug of that corn. I reckon we might as well have a toast."

It was midnight when the persistent rapping on her door got Eileen out of bed. She came up out of sleep suddenly, quickly, from long practice. She looked at Vance, sleeping quietly beside her, and across the room at the baby. Then she threw on her robe and went to the door. Morgan was standing in the hall, his face worried, his hair tousled, Vance's pajamas hanging loosely on him.

"What is it?" Eileen said sharply and softly. "Don't wake Vance or the baby. It's seldom enough Vance gets a normal peaceful night's sleep." She stepped into the hall and closed the door quietly behind her.

"You better go see about Veda," Morgan said worriedly. Embarrassment crossed his face briefly. "I . . . I can't do nothing with her. She's half hysterical or something."

"For God sakes, Morgan," Eileen said. "What did you do to her? Scare her half to death?"

Morgan looked away from her. "Honest, Eileen, nothing. Just . . . just made love to her. That's all. What the hell . . ."

Eileen stared at him. "Go on downstairs," she said. "Chunk up the fire and put on the coffee. I'll be down in a minute." She pulled her robe around her and went down the hall to the door of the guest room. She stood outside for a minute, listening to the muffled sobs from inside the room. Then she sighed and pushed open the door.

Veda was curled up in the corner of the big bed, her face red and swollen and her blond hair standing up in wisps all over her head. She looked at Eileen and put her face into the pillow.

Eileen looked around the room for a cigarette. She saw the pack on the floor by the bed and picked it up and shook two out and lit them. She touched Veda on the shoulder. "Here," she said briskly. "Have a cigarette."

Veda shook her head, still crying quietly.

"Come on," Eileen said firmly. Veda looked up and Eileen thrust the cigarette between her lips. Veda caught her breath, drew uncertainly on the cigarette and began to cough.

Eileen went over to a chair by the window and sat down. She waited until Veda experimented with the cigarette for a few moments before she spoke. "O.K.," she said finally. "What is it? Did Morgan pounce on you?"

Veda began to cry again. "Oh God," she said uncertainly. "Oh, God. Why didn't somebody just tell me?"

"Tell you what?" Eileen said. She yawned briefly. I'm so damned tired, she thought. Always so damned tired.

"Anything!" Veda moaned. "I'm so ashamed..." She gulped. "And I hurt."

Eileen stared at her, startled wide awake now. "Tell you?" she said. "Tell you? You mean you didn't know?"

"I didn't know anything," Veda said. "I thought... I thought ... You kissed and held each other... and..."

"Oh Lord," Eileen said. "I might have known. Mozel probably wouldn't dare let you know little boys aren't made of snips and snails and puppy dog tails." She got up and came over to Veda. "Do you love Morgan?" she said.

"Of course I love Morgan." Veda sat up straight on the bed and stopped crying. "I just was so scared and surprised... and I hurt so." She began to cry again.

"You better let me see," Eileen said practically.

"No!"

"All right," Eileen said. "I'm going down now and bring you some water to wash with and some milk and a couple of aspirin tablets. How's that?"

Veda nodded.

"Do you want to go home?"

Veda shook her head.

"You sure? If you do, I'll take you in myself. It's probably not too late anyway. Do you want to go home? For tonight or from now on? Tell me now."

Veda sat still, shaking her head. "I'm so ashamed," she said.

"Oh, hush. Everything will be all right. It gets all right. Understand?"

"I don't know," Veda said.

"My God," Eileen said. "I'll be back in a minute." She went out the door and down to the kitchen.

Morgan sat hunched over his coffee at the kitchen table. He looked up at Eileen, a puzzled expression on his face. She shrugged and went to fill the tea kettle with water from the bucket. "Well?" Morgan said.

"Pig," she said shortly.

"Damn it, Eileen. I was as gentle as anything. I . . ." He stopped, embarrassed. "She acted like I wanted to kill her or something."

"She probably thought you did," Eileen said sharply. "She didn't know what was going on."

"Didn't know what was going on?"

"That's right, lover boy. That's right, ole sheik of the desert. Didn't know what was going on. Now shut up and drink your coffee."

She fixed a tray with warm milk and crackers and coffee and poured a panful of warm water. "You're lucky," she said over her shoulder as she started out the door. "She wants to stay with you anyway. I'm going up and fix her up. And when you go back up there you better leave her alone."

"My God," Morgan said. "Of course I'll leave her alone. You think I'm crazy or something?"

"Yes," Eileen said. "I do think you're crazy. How you planning on supporting her anyway?"

"The farm . . ."

"You aren't any farmer, Morgan. You never were. You better think about it."

She went on out the door and back up the enclosed staircase, balancing the tray in one hand and the pan in the other. She kicked at the door with her toe, and Veda came to open it.

"Get washed up," Eileen said. "I'll be right back. Think you could eat some crackers and milk?"

Veda stood hunched over, holding the bedspread around her with one hand. With the other she brushed ineffectually at her hair. "I guess I am sort of hungry," she said.

Eileen grinned. "Hurry up. Your coffee'll get cold," she said.

In the Simms house they sat in the living room. Captain Simms leaned on his cane. Occasionally he tapped it impatiently on the floor. Tonight he was the scapegoat. R. V. sat in a straight chair, the back tilted against the wall. Mozel paced the floor.

"R. V.," she said for the twentieth time, "why do you just

sit there? Aren't you going after her? Can't you stop it? Why do you sit there? And you!" She turned on Captain. "Gave them that automobile to go in. I knew it. I knew it when you bought it. Cars lead to no good. Damned old fool. Can't drive it yourself so I'm feeding that nigger boy that's been out in that kitchen all night with his mouth hanging open because he's got no use with his play toy gone." She turned back to R. V. "Do something," she said.

R. V. shifted back in the chair. "Too late to do anything, Mozel," he said placidly. "If they have eloped they've already eloped. It's too late."

"It's not late bedtime yet," Mozel said firmly.

"It's past early bedtime," R. V. said. He reached in his pocket and brought out a crumpled sack of Bull Durham. Mozel frowned. He rolled the cigarette quickly and neatly, licked the paper and put it into his mouth. Then he lit it with a kitchen match, scraping the match across the bottom of the chair seat. "She's made her bed," he said.

Mozel stamped her foot on the floor. "Well if none of the menfolks in this family are going to do anything, I *am*," she said. "They're bound to be somewhere and Catharine Graves probably knows where. I'm going down there and talk to her."

"Mozel," Captain said, "why get her all worried? She didn't have anything to do with it."

"Of course she did," Mozel said. "Veda can't breathe without Catharine Graves to help her. Of course she did. I'm just going to go down there and have a word with her." She went out of the room and came back with her tapestry bag. "Are you going with me?" she said to R. V.

"I reckon I have to," he said.

"Jerusalem!" Captain said softly.

Cat Graves and Graham McCloud were sitting in the porch swing at the Graves' house. They were wearing wet bathing suits and occasionally Cat scratched herself inelegantly. "This wet wool is hell," she said. "But if I go in to change they won't let me back out." She grinned at Graham, tossing her hair off her forehead. "What you bet they'd hear the first squeak of that damned door?"

"You ought to oil it," Graham said. He stretched out in the swing, looking down at his legs. "That's a pretty damned good swimming place old Marty found out there," he said. "Cold as blazes, but private."

"Um-hmmm." Cat turned toward him. "How about a little lovin' before this little sheba goes in for the night?" she said.

Graham put his arms around her and pulled her to him. He kissed her on the mouth, running his hands down her body. He broke away suddenly. "Hell, you're wet!" he said.

Cat laughed softly. "I told you. This suit is stinging the daylights out of me. I think I've got sand in it somewhere too."

"Let me see. I'll fix it."

"No thanks." She moved slightly away from him. "Well," she said slowly. "Reckon Veda and Morgan have made it by now?"

"Oh sure. It's late. They're all tucked in out at Eileen and Vance's by now. My, my. Sheik and Veda. I wondered for a while if they were ever really gonna make it."

Cat shrugged. "They wouldn't have if they hadn't run off. Mrs. Simms was all set for Veda to go up to Sullins with Elizabeth Ann. Lord knows why. Veda don't need any finishing school. She's the damnedest lady I ever saw just naturally."

"Yeah. What's Morgan planning on doing anyway? They ain't gonna want to stay out there on that farm. He's no better than a hit and run farmer at best."

Cat sighed. "I guess they figure R. V.'ll fix him up."

"I don't know," Graham said. "What's Morgan know about mule trading? I can't see it."

"Oh, they'll find something," Cat said. "Everybody's working. Why I heard Daddy say just the other night he could hardly find help even with the good wages they're offering out at the mill."

"Well thank God I'm off to the University come fall," Graham said.

Cat frowned. "You all set up to go, aren't you?" she said.

"Hell yes. Aren't you?"

"I don't know whether I'm going or not."

"What's that all about? I thought you'd already talked your old man into all those new clothes."

Cat nodded slowly. "I'm not much good in school," she said.

"Hell, honey, you don't have to be. You were just made for promming and partying. You'll manage to pass well enough to stay for all that, huh?"

"I don't know. I was thinking. Daddy said something about going to school being about the price of a car. I don't know but what I'd rather have the car."

Graham sat up straight in the swing. "Well to hell with that, Cat," he said. "You come on to school. Then you can probably talk him into the car later anyhow. Everybody knows he's rolling since he and ole man Hudson made that killing with real estate. How come 'em to sell?"

Cat giggled. "Mama and Mrs. Hudson just got scared and made 'em. Mama said no piece of land was worth what that stuff down there was going for, she didn't care if it was on all the water in the world. She said there were always mosquitoes." Cat laughed and pushed the swing with her foot. "I sorta wish they'd saved enough to build a house on though."

"Nothing down there any prettier than right here," Graham said.

"I reckon not."

He reached for her again and they sat still in the swing, holding each other, forgetting the wet bathing suits. Cat cuddled against him. "Graham," she said softly, "kiss my ear. I plain love it when you do that."

They didn't hear R. V. and Mozel until they had turned into the walk leading to the house. Cat pulled away quickly when she heard the determined steps on the concrete and pulled ineffectually at the legs of her bathing suit. R. V. and Mozel came on up onto the porch.

"Catharine," Mozel said, her voice loud in the stillness, "do you know where Veda is?" After one quick look at the bathing suits she looked carefully over the top of Cat's head.

"Yes ma'am," Cat said softly.

"Graham," R. V. said, "maybe this would be better discussed between us. It's man's business."

"No it's not," Mozel said sharply. "Cat says she knows where she is. You and Graham can just hush up."

Graham, who had not said anything, looked from one to the other of them uncertainly. "Aunt Mozel," he said, "Cat didn't have anything to do with it. Veda just told her. That's all."

Mozel waved a hand at him impatiently. "Has she gone off with Morgan Holder, Catharine?"

"They're getting married, Mrs. Simms," Cat said hastily. She stood self-consciously, one foot poised as though to run.

"Well I should hope so," Mozel said meaningfully. "At this hour of the night."

Graham laughed. "Which way do you want it, Aunt Mozel?" he said. He put his hand firmly under Cat's elbow.

"Don't talk back to me, Graham McCloud," Mozel said. "I want my daughter home like a decent girl should be. Now you two tell me where she is."

"They went to Fayetteville," Cat said. "They were supposed to get married this afternoon. I guess they're at home at his house or somewhere now."

"You see," R. V. said. "It's too late to do anything about it, Mozel. You might as well accept it. You've got a new son-in-law. And I, for one, reckon she could have done worse. The Holders are fine folks."

"And what does he do?" Mozel said. "What does Mr. Morgan Holder do? Does he help his father run that farm like he ought to? No sir, he does not. Everybody knows he spends half his time hanging around downtown here. And that Eileen, marrying that half-sick Vance Maynard and leaving her mother with all that work to do. Neither of them amount to much, I say . . ."

"Mozel," R. V. said quietly. "It's late."

A window shade snapped up above them. "Catharine, what's going on down there?" Mrs. Graves said sleepily. "Can't anybody ever sleep around here? You're gonna wake up half the neighborhood."

"Flora," Mozel said. "It's me. Mozel Simms. Veda has run off with that Morgan Holder. And I'm trying to find out what Catharine knows about it."

Flora Graves sighed heavily. "I'll be down to let you in," she said. She devoutly hoped they wouldn't wake Walter. She opened the door and, after one quick look, sent Cat upstairs to put something on. The rest of them crowded back into the kitchen where she put the coffeepot on the stove and tried to make them sit down.

R. V. looked at Graham in the light from the harsh overhead bulb. "For God sakes, boy," he said, "haven't you got any clothes to put on?"

Graham moved uncertainly. "Yes sir," he said. "They're in the car."

Mozel glared at him and he went quickly out the door. She sat down heavily in a kitchen chair. "My little girl," she said, beginning to cry.

"Mozel," Flora said sharply. "Drink this coffee. Veda's all right. She was gonna marry that boy no matter what you folks said or did, and everybody knew it. It's just come a little sooner than you thought, that's all."

"She's a baby," Mozel said. "She's seventeen years old, Flora. She doesn't know anything about men."

Flora shrugged. "Women are born knowing about men, Mozel. Don't tell me different."

Mozel continued to cry. "We ought to go get her," she said.

R. V. shook his head. "You know better than that," he said

sharply. "She is Morgan Holder's wife. What we got to do now is find something for Morgan Holder to do."

Mozel stopped crying and looked at him. "So that's what you propose?" she said. "I reckon you intend supporting them?"

"I didn't say that. I intend to help him find what he wants to do. That's all. And until I do I intend to bring 'em home where they belong."

Flora shook her head. "You reckon that's a good idea, R. V.?" she said.

"It's what I aim to do," he said.

Graham came back into the room, his white ducks and striped shirt clinging damply over his bathing suit. "I reckon I'll get on home," he said.

Mrs. Graves glanced at him. "Yes," she said. "I don't think Miss Cat'll be back down."

"Did you have anything to do with this, Graham?" Mozel said.

He raised his hand. "Word of honor, Aunt Mozel. They just told us."

She sniffed. "You better get home. It's an outrageous hour," she said. She glanced sternly at Flora.

Flora shrugged. "Goodnight, Graham," she said.

"Yessum. Goodnight." He waved his hand and went out the door. In a few moments they heard the sound of his car starting up, and a final backfire as it turned the corner.

Flora poured herself a cup of coffee and sat down by Mozel. "Walter might give Morgan a job," she said.

"Well," R. V. said. "I hadn't thought of that."

"Sawmilling," Mozel said scornfully. "What kind of job is that?"

"We've done all right by it," Flora said shortly. She got up. "It's late."

"It is, Mozel," R. V. said quickly. "Let's go home."

"Yes. I reckon so." She stood up heavily. "I reckon I'll get on back. That A. C. Simms will be waiting to hear every word of it.

Lent them his car," she said to Flora. "Can you beat it? Actually let them have that car. I knew when he bought it . . ."

"Come on now," R. V. said. He pushed her gently toward the hall.

They walked back up the early-morning silence of the street, silently together in the darkness. R. V. spoke as they turned into their front gate. "It's not what I ever wanted for her either," he said.

Mozel sighed and patted his hand.

The living room lights still burned brightly out into the dark. They went slowly up the steps and through the doorway into the silent house.

Morgan sat stiffly beside Veda on the living room sofa. Across the room Mozel sat stolidly in a basket chair, R. V. standing beside her. Captain sat beside Veda, occasionally patting her hand. Veda still wore the blue silk dress but it was wrinkled and soiled now. She held her hat in her lap.

"Mr. Graves is going to give you a job in his sawmill," R. V. said. "It'll pay all right—not any whole lot—but all right. You'll stay here for the time being, of course. Veda's got her room all fixed up. You can just stay right here for a while."

"But Mr. Simms," Morgan said. "I thought we'd . . ."

"Stay at your house? Too far in to work. Better all round if you stay here."

"Yes sir. But I thought . . . I thought we'd get a place of our own."

"What for?" R. V. said. "We got more room than we know what to do with here. We rattle around. I haven't got any renter houses empty now either. Can't help you that way. Besides Veda here can't cook. She can't clean. You'd do better to stay right here, son. For now, anyway."

Captain Simms cleared his throat. "R. V.," he said, "maybe the boy's got something. It's nice for young folks to get out on their own, away from both the families, so to speak. What about

that house down below the back pasture? Isn't the lease about
up on that one?"

R. V. frowned. "That house isn't fit for Veda," he said. "One
bedroom, kitchen built on, cold in winter. No sir. I think they'd
better stay right here."

"Mr. Simms," Morgan said again, "I appreciate all this. But
we would like to . . ."

"Morgan," R. V. said. "Don't you reckon it would be better
for Veda to keep right on having the things she's used to till
you can afford to get 'em for her? Don't you think that?"

Morgan didn't answer him. There wasn't really anything for
him to say.

Mozel hadn't spoken. She watched R. V. stolidly and when he
finished she spoke. "If you're going to do all this for Veda and
Morgan," she said quietly, "you better be thinking about what
you're going to do for your son Bill, when he gets home."

"Bill?" R. V. said. "I'm sending him to school, ain't I? What
else am I supposed to do for him?"

"Well now," Mozel said. "Elizabeth Ann is already planning
on teaching music, but Bill, he's not so sure what he wants to
do." She paused, waiting until they all looked at her. "I hear
Virgil Cartwright is trying to find a buyer for the drugstore," she
said. "It ain't common knowledge yet, but he's fixing to buy the
Coca-Cola plant."

They all stared at her.

R. V. spoke angrily. "I don't have the money to buy any drugstore," he said firmly. "I don't know how this got into the conversation anyway. What would Bill want with a drugstore? He
hasn't studied any pharmacy that I know of."

"Just hush your poor-mouthing, R. V. Simms," Mozel said.
"It can be a sundry store. He can sell to the young folks and
carry some patent medicines and things like that."

"What makes you think he wants a sundry store?" R. V. said.

Morgan and Veda looked at each other. They were forgotten
in the sudden shift of the conversation. Captain winked at them.

"He needs a place of business," Mozel said. "Your trading and swapping and buying and selling isn't going to last forever. Bill hasn't got any talent for it anyway. He needs something to do."

"Mama," Veda said.

"Hush, Miss Veda," Mozel said. "You've had your say for this week. I'm now going to tend to business for the rest of the family."

Veda stood up. She looked at Morgan uncertainly. "I reckon we ought to get on upstairs," she said.

Morgan stood beside her. "Veda," he said, "I don't like . . ."

"Hush about it for now," she said softly. "We'll work it out somehow."

They went out of the room and Captain followed them. On the stair landing he stopped. "Come on down to my room," he said solemnly. "I've got a half-pint rye that that black rascal, Nip, got for me, and a bag of rock candy. We'll just have us a little toddy."

They followed him down the dark hallway, holding hands mutely, listening to the sound of his tapping cane.

Graves' sawmill was on the east side of town. Once it had been a small one-man rig. Today it was fast becoming a lumber company. There were two cutting sheds and an enclosed yard where the lumber was stacked in square piles for drying. There was an office too, actually only a lean-to room leading off the smaller planing shed, but it was an office. There was a chair, and a desk with a telephone, squeezed into the space behind the round-bellied stove and the rows of nail kegs and paint cans that lined and almost filled the room. Walter W. Graves was expanding. He was, even now, reading literature about dry kilns.

Morgan stood uncertainly outside the office door. There were several men that he recognized under the planing shed and he nodded toward them stiffly. He didn't want to go in and talk to Mr. Graves about a job. He didn't want to go to work in a saw-mill. But just now he saw nothing else to do. There was Veda, she was his; and there were her father and her mother, who still thought she was theirs. Between them he knew he had to work. He was honest enough with himself to know that he wasn't going to do anything with his father's farm. He hated to farm. He stepped onto the wooden step outside the office door and stopped again. He wondered what he did want to do. He couldn't, right offhand, think of anything. Work on cars, maybe. He sort of liked that. But all the garage jobs he knew of were filled and people waiting to get on. He pulled open the door. Wood wasn't so bad a thing. It smelled good and clean and new and the feel of it in your hands was good. Maybe he'd learn to put things together with wood after a while. The thought comforted him and he went on into the office.

It was quieter here. Outside the thin whine of the saw and the higher smaller whine of the plane came distantly through the one window. He reached into a keg for a handful of nails to keep his hands busy while he talked. "Hello, Mr. Graves?" he said.

Walter Graves leaned back in his swivel chair. "Round here, son," he said. "Just come around them nails and past that paint and turn right again."

Morgan came around and stood beside the desk.

"Well sir," Walter Graves said, "I can sure use me another hand right now. Fact is, there's so many places I can use you I don't know where to put you on. Finished high school, did you?"

"Yessir." Morgan fumbled the nails in his fist.

"Well." Walter nodded. "How was your math?"

Morgan's face brightened. "My best subject," he said, pleased suddenly to be able to say it.

"Well sir. Yes," Walter said again. He shifted in the chair and pushed back his felt hat and scratched his head, all in one motion of his left hand. "Reckon you could learn to use that plane?"

"I could sure try," Morgan said. He felt better and he reached behind him and dropped the nails he had been clutching into a keg.

"That's good enough for me," Walter said. "Can't pay much

to start. Oh, say, dollar and a quarter a day till we see where we stand, hmmm?"

"All right," Morgan said. He had no definite idea of how much he would be worth.

Walter heaved himself out of the chair. "Come on outside then," he said. "Chris Martin's running the planing rig. He'll break you in."

Morgan followed on the creaking wood floor, around the kegs and cans and outside again. He stepped onto the sawdust-covered ground confidently and followed Mr. Graves over to a tall thin man in overalls.

"Here's your help, Chris," Mr. Graves said. "Morgan Holder —from up Tupelo way. He just married R. V. Simms' little girl. I want you to give him a hand now and show him the ropes."

Chris Martin leaned back and spat tobacco juice into the pile of sawdust behind him. He looked at Morgan carefully, first his hair, slicked and parted, then his clothes. Lastly and most importantly he looked at his hands. He studied them for a moment, then he nodded slightly and grinned at Morgan. "I reckon the first thing we better do is git you a pair of overhalls," he said.

Ace Johnson sat in front of the linotype machine in the semi-darkness of the newspaper office. Behind him the presses thumped and roared regularly, but he didn't hear them. The only time he ever heard the sound of the presses any more was at the end of the day when he stepped into the street and became aware of them by their absence.

He was setting the small paragraph that announced the marriage of Veda Simms to Morgan Holder. The letters bounced along the bar and dropped into place and there it was in small metal slugs, set and ready to go, irrevocable and caught forever. For somebody, somewhere, always keeps newspapers. The world is filled with yellowed and crackling memories of births and marriages and deaths. Yesterday's newspapers may be dead but their announcements reverberate forever.

HOLDER-SIMMS

Mr. and Mrs. R. V. Simms an-
nounce the marriage of their
daughter, Veda, to Mr. Morgin
Holder, on August 10, 1925.

Ace shook his head. He got up and went around to the cluttered
desk where Mr. Marshall, the editor, sat checking galleys. "Is this
all we're gonna run on Veda Simms getting married?" he said.

Mr. Marshall looked around and took off his glasses. "That's
all Mrs. Simms called in," he said.

"I feel like we ought to put a little more," Ace said uncertainly.

Mr. Marshall thought a moment. "Well, if you want to run up
a little something we could run it in editorial I guess. They
wouldn't mind that. Guess Veda'd like to have it to keep. Run up
a little something, Ace." He put his glasses back on and turned
away.

Ace went back to his chair. He thought for a few moments,
pushing his hair impatiently out of his eyes. Then he composed
three short paragraphs and ran them off quickly without thinking,
as he always did. They were not much longer all together than
the original one.

HOLDER-SIMMS

Morgan Holder and Miss Veda
Simms stole a march on their
friends and family by driving to
Fayetteville, Tenn., last Saturday
and getting married.

The bride is the popular daughter of Mr. and Mrs. R. V. Simms of
this place and the groom is a son of
Mr. and Mrs. M. L. Holder of
Tupelo. The bride was a member
of the graduating class of the
M.C.H.S. last yeat, and the groom
graduated from that place in 1924.

The young couple have many
friends who will wish for them a
long and hippy life.

When he had finished it Ace was not sure it was any better than the announcement paragraph. He shrugged. What could you say when there was no dress or cake to describe? He went on to the rest of the social news: Mr. and Mrs. Martin Mayhill, Sr., had returned from a vacation in Florida, Mr. and Mrs. L. J. Hudson had as their guests . . . the letters clicked automatically into place.

Ace had been working for the paper for more than two years now. He had begun by delivering handbills after school in the afternoon during his junior year at M.C.H.S. Now he was head typesetter, and the only person in the office Mr. Marshall could depend on any more. Old Jake Burke was getting too old and too short-sighted, and he drank too much. His son just wasn't much use in a newspaper office. And Mr. Marshall himself didn't seem to have the interest in the paper he used to. Sometimes Ace felt as if he ran the whole damned paper himself. He did write most of it, and set all of it. He wondered if the day might not come when he would have to deliver it too.

He got up, wiping his hands on a grimy handkerchief, and went to stare out the small front window across the green strip of lawn. The sun was going down and the last rays shone brightly against the hand press in the grass. He looked at his T-model, parked against the curb. I should have left her in the shade, he thought, seeing the shine of sun across the leather seats.

"She set up, Ace?" Mr. Marshall said behind him.

"Ready."

"Whyn't you go on home then?" Mr. Marshall said. "We'll roll 'er tonight. You look tired."

Ace squinted around at him. "I'm fine," he said. His eyes hurt, but he was used to that.

"Go on home," Mr. Marshall said again. "Have a party, get drunk, get a girl. You stay in this damned office too much anyway."

Ace grinned. "I warn you. I'm gonna take you up on it," he said.

"I mean it. Git on."

"Thanks, sir. Somehow I don't feel too good today."

"I thought so. Come in late in the morning. She'll be out by then. We can worry about the next one later."

Ace went to the back and washed his hands at the tiny sink. He scrubbed ineffectually at his grimy nails for a moment, then shrugged and dried his hands. He took his battered straw hat and went out the door.

The sun had slipped down behind the courthouse and the trees on the lawn cast shadows out into the street. It hadn't cooled off much yet and Ace got into the car gingerly, feeling the hotness of the seat through his pants legs. He stretched his legs out and pushed his hat back and just sat for a moment, savoring the light and the stillness. Ace seldom got depressed, he was by nature cheerful; but today he felt sad. He knew the feeling was connected with writing the announcement of Veda and Morgan's marriage, but he couldn't figure out why that depressed him. Everybody had been expecting it for years now. He got back out of the car and cranked her, running around to set the spark and then back to the crank. The motor caught and he jumped in and pushed the pedals, backing into the street and cruising gently to the corner. He braked there and stopped, careful to keep the motor going. He didn't know where he wanted to go—not home. Aunt Mattie and Aunt Trudy didn't expect him tonight, they wouldn't have supper. He went on around the square and parked at Cartwrights'. He went in and ordered a Coke and two hamburgers. Then he went to the magazine rack and got a couple of magazines to look at. He didn't read them. He never felt like reading print after work, but he looked at all the pictures and he carefully noted all the layouts of every page. His hamburgers came and he ate quickly, gulping the Coke in two long swallows.

Virgil Cartwright leaned over the counter, watching him. There was no one else in the drugstore. It was suppertime in Bellefonte.

"You seen Dudley around today?" Virgil said.

"Dudley?" Ace looked up, startled. "No. I don't reckon so. I haven't been out of the office today."

"Thought you might have seen him," Virgil said. "He's supposed to come in here and go over some papers with me tonight." He wiped at the counter with a damp rag. "Him and me and Mr. R. V. Simms," he added.

Ace looked at him blankly. "Yes sir," he said.

Virgil sighed. He felt full of importance about the drugstore deal and his Coca-Cola plant deal, but nobody ever wanted to talk to him any more. "You want anything else?" he said.

Ace shook his head. He got up and went out onto the street. Night was coming, and some coolness now with the sun gone. He got back into his car and drove around the block. Finally he went on up the square to the southwest corner and drove out to Graham McCloud's house. It was good dark now and the lights from the house rayed out into the new driveway. He pulled into it and got out of the car.

Cat stood in front of the mirror in her bedroom looking at her new dress. It was bright green. Her green hose, rolled just below her knees, had little gold clocks on them that danced when she walked. She had a new pair of long green earrings too, but she didn't put them on yet. She put them in her purse and went down to wait for Graham.

He brought Ace Johnson with him. She saw them getting out of Ace's car in front of the house, and she sighed. They'd be drinking. They always drank when they got together, white corn whiskey out of an old syrup bottle with a corncob stuck in the top, the corn whiskey made by one of her father's men out behind the sawmill. Cat didn't have anything in particular against whiskey. She had to be for it in a general way because her father was against it. But she didn't really like to drink it. It burned and she thought it tasted like musty old corncribs where the rats had been. She didn't like Graham to drink it because he didn't look at her when he was drinking. In fact he just didn't pay much attention to her at all.

They came up the walk, laughing loudly, and Cat got up out

of the porch swing. "You all better get right back in that car," she said. "Before Daddy comes out here." She stepped between them, taking an arm of each, and they went down the walk together, her high heels clicking sharply on the sidewalk.

They got into the T-model, giggling suddenly at nothing. "Let's go up and shivaree Veda and Morgan," Ace said.

"No thanks," Cat said. "I'm not welcome around there just now."

"Well, let's go get Marty then and call them to come over there." Ace lifted the bottle and looked at the level. "We've got plenty for a nice congratulations party."

"You mean André Lacoste, old boy?" Graham said, laughing.

"The very same," Ace said.

"Isn't that just the cat's?" Cat said. "Marty going French like that? He's crazy."

"He's that all right," Ace said, swinging the car around the corner and onto the highway. "But never dull, my dear. Never dull." He felt better now with a good belt of corn in him, almost gay. He put his arm outside the car and banged loudly on the door. "Here we come, André," he yelled. "Toute suite."

He pulled into the driveway beside the white-trellised Mayhill house and stopped the car. The tree frogs sang shrilly in the darkness, their eerie chorus rising rhythmically and dropping to silence in sudden quiet union. "He's here," Graham said. "There's the Caddy."

He opened the door and helped Cat off the running board. "Roses," she said, standing still in the gravel. "Roses, roses. This place smells of roses all summer long."

They went up the side steps and pulled the door bell, watching through the frosted pane until Ham's shadow loomed against it and it opened inward. "They's down at the courts," Ham said.

Buz and Marty Mayhill sat beside each other on one of the white iron benches beside the tennis court. That summer they had talked Martin Senior into lighting the court for night playing, and they were always here in the late afternoon and early dark. The

Mayhills ate late if there were guests, early, for Martin's sake, if there were not, so the time of first dark was always free.

Buz had on a white tennis dress. She sat smoking quietly in the shadows, her slim legs crossed neatly, one tennis shoe resting lightly on the grassy margin of the court. She and Martin had just returned from their annual two weeks in Florida and she was glad to be home. She didn't like Florida any more. Once they had stayed in a small town on the west coast where only local people swam and fished and went on with their daily lives. Now they went to a place on the east coast where there was a new hotel. It was a good hotel and Buz appreciated the luxury of it, but the old vacation feel of Florida was gone for her. It was like being on one of Martin's business trips to go there now. It was bright, crowded and noisy; she was always glad to come home. I'm getting old, she thought. I miss my roses.

It was during the annual Florida trip that Marty had gone into his French phase. Marty had been through many phases in the last two years, but this one seemed almost virulent in its exactnesses. He had traded the Playboy and acquired a long black Cadillac, elegant, chromed, sleek. He wore a black beret, tilted rakishly over one eye, and an ascot. He smoked cigarettes with a faint perfume in a long black holder. And with a thoroughness which bothered Buz more than she admitted, he had paid fifteen dollars and legally had his name changed to André Lacoste.

"Well, Mamá," he said now, accenting the last syllable. "The darkness falls. Would you care to indulge in that horrid British habit known as a sundowner?"

Buz stretched and stood up. "I could use a drink," she said. "If there was anything fit to drink. That last gin your daddy got was abominable. I've gotten to the point where I'd just about as soon drink white lightning."

"The wine of the provinces," Marty said.

"Oh stop it," Buz said irritably.

"Stop what, Mamá?"

Buz picked up her racket and walked onto the court. She started angrily lobbing balls across the net.

Marty-André stretched indolently on the bench, watching her movements on the lighted court. "I declare, dearest," he said. "You look just like Gloria Swanson in this light."

"Sure," Buz said. She knocked the last ball into the net and lifted her head. "Somebody's in the drive," she said. She picked up the balls and put them into the can.

"They'll come on back," Marty said. "Probably Ace..."

They stood, waiting until the footsteps came across the back yard and toward the court.

"Hi André," Ace said, poking his head and arm through the bushes and waving the bottle in front of him. "We've come to rescue you from the dull world. Let's get Morgan and Veda and celebrate."

"How très chic," Marty said.

Cat and Graham came through the trees and Marty stood up, bowing grandly toward Cat. "Mamselle."

Cat giggled. She tossed her hair off her forehead and grinned at Buz. "He never slips up, does he?" she said. "Why do you suppose he never slips up?" She had sampled the whiskey on the way over and she felt a little lightheaded.

Ace was handing the bottle around.

Buz watched them, frowning. "Let's go to the house and have a decent drink," she said suddenly. She picked up the rackets and a white sweater from the bench and ducked through the bushes surrounding the court. They followed her, stumbling over each other in their haste to hold the branches back for her and Cat.

"How's that Caddy operate?" Graham said.

"It's a joy," Marty said. "I've got a cut-out on the muffler, and the roar! Magnifique!"

"I'll say, magnifique," Ace said. "It sounds like it's coming through our house every time you take her out."

They went up to the playroom and Buz sent for ice and gin. She wandered around the room restlessly, watching the others.

"Well, all off to college soon," she said finally, sitting down on the window seat. "It's a shame Veda and the Holder kids won't be going with you."

"That reminds me. We meant to get hold of Veda and Morgan tonight," Graham said. "Why don't I run over and get them?"

"Do, child," Marty said.

Graham took the keys from Ace and went out.

Cat sat watching the doorway for a moment. "I don't think I'm going to school either," she said finally. She took a pack of violet-scented cigarettes from her bag and lit one elaborately, waving the match out with a theatrical gesture.

Buz smiled at her. "Of course you're going," she said. "Think of all the parties."

"I'm no good at studying though."

"Oh nonsense. It isn't all that hard." Buz went over to the Edison and glanced through the stack of thick black records. "I wish I'd been able to go," she said. "You'll like it. Wait and see."

Cat took her earrings out of her purse and twisted them on. "I don't know," she said doubtfully.

Ham came in with the tray and Marty mixed drinks. Buz put a record on and sat down beside the phonograph. "They were sure playing this in Florida," she said.

" 'Sleepytime Gal,' " Marty said. "Veda's theme song."

Cat laughed. She took the drink Marty handed her and tilted it up. "This is sure better than that stuff you've got, Ace boy," she said. She went over and looked through the records. "Got any good Charlestons, Buz?"

"Sure. Second stack there."

"Say," Ace said. "Did you hear about Ruby Marshall breaking her ankle learning the Charleston?"

Cat leaned over the Edison, laughing. "That makes me feel real swell," she said. "Real swell-elegant. Come on Marty, dance with me."

Marty took her hand. Buz sat drinking steadily, watching them dance. "You look more like Charlie Chaplin than whoever it is you're trying to look like," she said suddenly.

They all looked at her, startled. There was an undercurrent in her voice that none of them could place. Cat sat down abruptly on a cushion. Ace went over and picked up a record.

Marty stood alone in the middle of the room, smiling slightly at her. "Ma petite," he said mockingly. "Ma petite mamá."

Ace looked from one to the other for a moment. "I think I'm tight," he said suddenly. He picked up a cushion and balanced it on his head. "Listen all good people and you shall hear my tale," he began in a quavering tenor. Cat stood up. She came beside him and they sang through as many verses as they could remember of "The Death of Floyd Collins." The tension eased gradually and Marty mixed another round of drinks.

Buz stood up and went to the door. "I'm going down to wait for the others," she said. "I told Ham to stay in the pantry in case you want anything." She went out the door, her small dark head held haughtily.

Marty stood looking after her for a moment. Then he poured straight gin into a glass and tossed it down. "A little more than kin, a little less than kind," he said. Then he laughed loudly and went to dance with Cat again.

"No, I'm not going," Morgan said. He lay stretched out across the bed in Veda's room. His voice was stubborn. He had come home from the sawmill tired in every bone of his body, more tired than after a hard day in the fields. It must be I'm using a different set of muscles, he thought, coming up the concrete walk to the strange house. It didn't even bother him that the house was strange. He could think only of lying down across a bed—any bed.

Veda hovered over him, solicitous. She brought him a Coke and two aspirin tablets and rubbed his head. When it was time to go down to supper he felt fine again. He ate heartily, enjoying the good meal and the nice tablecloth and Captain Simms' remarks. He was uneasy with Mrs. Simms, but the Captain didn't let him stay that way long.

After supper they sat in the big rockers on the front porch and he and R. V. had a cigarette. The tree frogs sang in the hot night and the creak of the rockers soothed him. He was happy to think of going up to bed with Veda and they went in early.

She followed him up the dark stairway, stopping at the turn to kiss him. They went into their room and Veda threw the doors of her little balcony open wide. It was hot here upstairs but the heat wasn't oppressive. The fact was, nothing was too uncomfortable for Morgan tonight, because he was proud of himself. He had worked hard today and he had earned a nod of commendation from his foreman. He was earning money to support his wife and now he was at home with her. He felt fine.

He had just stretched out across the bed and taken his shoes off when Mozel called up the stairs. "Graham's down here," she said.

"I'll go." Veda jumped up from her boudoir chair and ran out of the room. Morgan lay still, hearing the summer night outside his room, filled with all the insects of August.

"They're having a party for us at Marty's," Veda said, running back into the room.

Morgan groaned. "Not for me," he said. "I got to get up at daylight in the morning. I'm still tired, too. Tell Graham not tonight, honey."

Veda stared at him. "Why, Morgan," she said, and there was a faint pout in her voice. "They're having it for *us*."

"I'm not going," Morgan repeated. "I got to work in the morning. I can't spend half the night drinking gin and listening to records and Buz Mayhill."

"Buz Mayhill?" Veda said. "What are you talking about?"

"I don't know," Morgan said. "I just don't want to fool with all that tonight. Cat doing the Charleston, and Graham and Ace drunk, and Marty being a damned Frenchman." He got up and walked to the balcony doors. "*And*," he finished, looking out into the darkness, "Buz Mayhill acting like she was one of the crowd."

"Why, Morgan Holder," Veda said. "You're out of your mind. I never saw you mind any partying before we got married. Are we gonna be dead because we got married? I don't see why we have to be dead. I don't know why you've got to talk like that about Mrs. Mayhill either," she added angrily. "It doesn't sound nice."

Morgan sighed. "Now, honey," he said. "Don't start crying. You know damned well I can't stand that. But I have to work now. That's all. We can't keep up with that bunch if I have to work."

"Ace Johnson works," Veda said stubbornly.

"Yeah. And he likes to drink a damned sight more than I do too."

"Oh Morgan, let's not fight." Veda went to the dresser and ran a comb through her hair. "We won't stay long. But we *have* to go. It's for us."

"Yeah. Sure." Morgan put his shoes on. "Do you know where my ties are?"

Veda smiled. "I hung 'em right in my chifforobe," she said. "There was a little bar there just for 'em. And it's been there all the time and I never knew it." She came across the room and put her arms around him. "Oh, Morgan. I love you," she said.

"We're coming back in just a little bit now," he said warningly.

"Well you know I want to," she said.

Eileen came out of the house and got into the Chevrolet with the self-starter that Vance had insisted she get when he started having the headaches. She looked back toward the house, reluctant to leave, afraid not to go for Doctor Matthews. She saw Ida's tall shadow against the shade in Vance's room and she pushed the starter and drove out of the yard.

She had sent for Ida to come and live in the little house in the back yard when Vance first started being sick. Her mother had wanted her to come down home with Vance and the baby, but she wouldn't do it. This was her home and she was going to stay here. It had been her home from the moment she moved into it and Mrs. Maynard, in the year before she died, had relinquished it to her. Mrs. Maynard had wheeled herself around the house, negotiating the levels on the little strips of oak Vance had made for that purpose, showing Eileen the linens and the jars of preserves and jelly and chowchow. She had showed her the quilts, packed in a long cedar chest in the back hall, and the crocheted bedspreads, yellowed with non-use and folded carefully in tissue paper.

"You'll want to get those out and use them," she said. "They're all of a size for the big beds except the one. That's for the trundle in the bedroom. I reckon you'll be needing that one too."

They had needed it. The baby had come the second year, before Eileen had been able to finish high school. But Mr. Johns had been awfully nice about it. He had let her study at home and take the tests and get her diploma anyway. Mrs. Maynard didn't live to see the baby. She didn't live to see Vance begin to die, either.

Eileen drove carefully along the side of the road. She didn't like to drive. She felt vulnerable in the machine, vulnerable to whatever lay outside in the dark and to the machine itself, which responded to her hands and feet only because it had to. She felt better when she got onto the turnpike; there were more lights along the roadside and fewer ruts in the road. She could have stopped and gotten her father to go in for her, but she never had, and she wouldn't this time, she told herself, no matter how bad it was. It was her job and because she hated doing it so she had to all the more. She didn't let herself think of Vance, drawn tightly against pain in the poster bed, fighting the pain inside himself. She thought instead of Doctor Matthews and his little black bag with the hypodermic to stop the pain. "You are going to have to learn to do this," he had said the last time. "I can't," she told him. "You will," he said.

She came to the railroad grading and stopped, hoping that the car wouldn't stall. It had once before and she'd had to get a man from a house down the road to come help her get started again.

Now she kept her foot lightly on the gas pedal, looking up the track fearfully. Then she rattled over it and turned onto the highway and knew that the worst was over.

Dr. Matthews was sitting in his shirt sleeves listening to the radio. He got up immediately when Eileen came in and put his coat on. "I wish to God you had a telephone in that place," he said. "I'm going up to Maynard's," he told his wife when she came into the room.

"Let me fix you some coffee, Eileen," she said.

Eileen shook her head. "We ought to hurry," she said, watching the doctor anxiously.

"We're going," he said. He went outside and cranked up his T-model.

Eileen waited until he started off up the highway, then she followed him, watching the red light bobbing in front of her with an intensity that blanked her mind against anything else.

When she went into the house Dr. Matthews was already upstairs. She sat down in the living room, volitionless now that her errand was done. She wanted coffee but she was too tired to put it on. After a few minutes she called for Ida.

Ida came down the stairs and went to the kitchen and came back with the coffee. "Done had it heated," she said. "He's all right now. Sleeping like a baby already. Van's sleeping too. You better sleep while you can."

"When the doctor leaves," she said. She sipped the coffee, flinching when it burned her tongue, swallowing anyway, enjoying the hotness.

Doctor Matthews came down the stairs and into the room. He put his bag on the sofa beside Eileen and went on into the kitchen. She could hear him pouring coffee for himself and asking Ida for an orange. He came back into the room and sat down beside her. He sipped at his coffee, watching her face. "When did this one start?" he said.

"Just before I came for you," she said tiredly.

"So quick?"

"So quick."

"All right." He put down his empty cup and reached into his bag. He took out a hypodermic and balanced it on his palm. "Go get me some water," he said.

She looked at him numbly, seeing the instrument of glass and steel lying on his hand. It looked alien to her in spite of the times she had seen it used. This is not true, she thought. She got up and went to the kitchen and brought the water back. He picked up the orange and held it in the other hand. "I am going to teach you how to do this," he said. "An orange most nearly resembles the feel of human flesh."

She watched him, seeing the way his strong wrist held up the syringe and let a little fluid escape, seeing the needle prick the orange, the plunger go in, and the quick release. She took the orange and the instrument from him and went through the same series of motions mechanically.

He watched her and nodded. "You've got to get out quicker and smoother," he said. "Try it again."

She practised doggedly on the orange until he nodded. Then he went to the kitchen door and called Ida. "You find me a small pan, just big enough to boil this in." He held up the syringe.

Ida nodded and went away to rummage in the cupboards.

Doctor Matthews came back to Eileen. She sat quietly, holding the orange with the scarred pricked surface in her hand. She looked up at him.

"A month at the most," he said.

"No."

"Yes. I've told you before, Eileen."

"Why can't you just go in and cut it out?"

"I've told you before, Eileen. It's inaccessible. They took out what they could before he came home. Eileen, please believe this. You have to believe it. Now. Vance is going to die."

"I believe it."

"No you don't. You never have."

She looked at him bitterly. "All right. I never have." **Suddenly** she leaned forward and put her face in her hands. "I can't," she said.

"Probably less than a month, Eileen," he said again. "The pain is going to get worse and it is going to last longer. The steel is pressing on his brain, Eileen. Eventually it will rupture a blood vessel. That is the way it is." He spoke harshly because he wanted to reach her. He had been trying to reach her for a long time but she wouldn't listen. Sometimes he was not sure she actually heard the things he told her.

He had come out here when old Mrs. Maynard died. Eileen had been busy then, working to keep Vance from being upset, working to take care of the house full of mourners, but with it all serene in her pregnancy. He had gone up to her in the kitchen where she was putting damp cloths over the food that had been brought. He had thought how young she looked and how well pregnancy agreed with her. "How are you feeling?" he said.

She smiled. "Wonderful. There's nothing to this having a baby after all, is there? Except I'm getting too fat. I bet I get to where I can't tie my shoes."

"This is awfully far out for you to be," he said.

"Mama's right up the road," she said. "And we've got the car now."

"How is Vance?"

She frowned at him, straightening the already straight cloths.

"He's all right," she said. "He knew his mother didn't have long to live."

"That's not what I meant," he said. "How are the headaches?"

"Not too bad. Not too often, you know. Just when he's outside too much, or works too hard. That powder you gave him always lets him sleep and it goes away."

He stared at her, not sure how much she was admitting to herself. "It's going to get worse," he said. He felt he had to prepare her because even now, he thought, Vance had been lucky. It couldn't be too long.

She shook her head. "He seems better to me," she said.

Vance had come into the room then, and the doctor had stopped. He knew that Vance had told her himself. He knew Vance knew the truth of his mortality. But she wasn't going to know it yet. He thought that perhaps it was a protective device until the baby was safely birthed. So he had let it alone for then.

He knew now that she had never accepted it, not even when she had said she had, and he was afraid for her. "Eileen," he said, "you must plan what you are going to do when Vance dies."

She put the orange down on the table in front of her, slowly and carefully. Then she looked at him, her eyes wary. She didn't say anything.

"You won't be able to keep this place up by yourself," he said.

He saw her eyes change then and he thought, Now. Now I've hit the right spot. Now she knows it. He sighed. It would be bad for her tonight. But it was better than what would happen later if she didn't believe it now.

"No," she whispered. "No. I'm not going to leave this place. Never, never, never. Do you hear me? You just go on and cut people open and take things out and leave mine here to suffer. Go on. We'll stand it somehow!" Her voice rose hysterically. Then she jumped up and ran out of the room and up the stairs.

The doctor sat watching after her for a moment. Then he went to Ida and left some sleeping pills for Eileen and showed Ida how to sterilize the syringe. "She's going to have a bad night to-night," he said. "Take care of her. Vance'll be all right till the next time. I left the envelopes with the proper amount written on them in his room."

He put on his hat and went out and cranked the T-model and went back to town.

Eileen ran up the dark stairway. At the door of Vance's room she stopped, leaning her head against the wood of the door. Then she turned the knob and opened it. There was a lamp burning on the dresser with a newspaper propped in front of it to shade the glare. It gave the room an eerie, murky light, strained through the black newsprint and rough, faintly yellow paper. She pulled a straight chair close to the bed and sat down. Vance lay quietly, his eyes closed, breathing regularly and peacefully. She looked at his mouth, the corners turned slightly down in sleep in just the same way Van's did. Then she began to cry. She cried quietly at first, the tears falling freely in spite of the hard ache in her chest, but after a few moments she knew she wasn't going to be quiet any more. She got up and went down the hall to the guest room where she slept with the baby when Vance was sick. No, not here, she thought, seeing the baby sleeping too. She went back down the stairs and out of the house and got into the car parked in the front yard. There, in the discomfort of the alien and cold machine, she put her head on her arms and cried aloud for the first time since she was a little girl.

Two weeks later, on a Sunday morning, Mr. Holder was coming home to breakfast from a walk up on the back forty. The back forty was a trial to the Holders. It was a mile away from any of their other land, up past the cove and through a woodland. But it was the best land they owned and they couldn't afford to let it go. It was a nuisance to work and a nuisance to harvest and they never had a moment's peace about it because they were afraid something would happen to the crop. It was planted in cotton this year and on Sunday morning Morgan Senior went up to take a look at the neatly laid-by rows. It was a good morning, clear and still cool, although there was no breeze and the sun felt hot between his shoulders.

When he passed the cove road he decided to walk up and see about Eileen before he went on home. He shook his head, looking at the laid-by fields around the house. All that crop and nobody to harvest it. He thought of the sort of folks they'd have to hire to do the job and it made him feel bad. Seemed like the hands that put it in the ground ought to take it up. He harbored no illusions about Vance. He knew he wouldn't harvest this year.

Just as he reached the doorway he heard the sound of a rifle, sudden and sharp in the Sunday stillness. It was close, too. He raised his head, puzzled, and the rifle cracked again. He opened the door. The house was oppressive. There was no smell of breakfast, no sound. He walked quickly through the house to the kitchen and, as he did so, heard the rifle again. Ida was sitting on a straight chair in the kitchen. She had her apron over her head and Mr. Holder knew immediately from the age-old gesture that Vance was gone. He was wary suddenly, but not really alarmed. He knew Eileen too well. "Where is she?" he said.

Ida jumped and pointed toward the back. "Lord God, Mr. Holder, I'm glad you've come," she said. "He's gone, and I can't do nothing with her. She went to sleep settin' there by him about daylight, or some before I reckon, and he just didn't wake up this time. And Lord!"

He went past her hurriedly and out the back door. From the steps he could see Eileen. She had her back to him and for a moment he couldn't understand what she was doing. Then the gun exploded again, the sound pushing into his ears with sudden pressure, and he ran down the steps toward her.

She was standing in front of the wire and wood cages, shooting into them. The snakes writhed and hissed and coiled into the corners, slithering up the sides of the cage, dropping raging onto each other and biting at themselves. She had hit some of them and the blood from the mangled bodies spattered the cages, goading the other snakes to further frenzies. She looked calm and steady and completely expressionless as she raised the gun to her shoulder and fired into the cage again.

"Eileen," he said loudly. "It's Daddy. Eileen. Stop it. Eileen."

She didn't even look around but he knew she'd heard, from the tenseness of her back. He reached over her shoulder when she paused to reload and took the gun out of her hands.

She turned around without a glance toward the cages or a word to him and went up the back steps and into the kitchen where she sat down in the chair Ida had vacated. "I reckon you can go ahead and notify folks now," she said.

Through the open door the sound of the snakes was sibilant and strange in the morning.

One day it was autumn. The trees were still green and there were still roses, but it was autumn. In the way smoke drifted, in the way the evening came, in the way light lay when the sun was going down, there was a feel of old time. The light suggested light that lay on Rome before it left the arches for the west. It was hotter than before and very dry. A patina of dust lay on the still-green leaves.

Marty Mayhill went to Chattanooga to get fitted for new suits for college and to buy a set of matched luggage the color of his new overcoat. Graham McCloud brought the old suitcases his father had used down from the attic and restrung his tennis rackets.

The first crisp apples appeared in the grocery stores.

Mr. Graves bought Catharine her car. It was an Oldsmobile sports roadster, not so elegant as she would have liked, but elegant enough. She had decided definitely against going to college and she spent the days, while the others prepared for school, in re-doing her room. Her wall was repapered in plain buff and she covered one side of it with pictures of Valentino. She bought a Japanese screen and yellow and red pillows and an oriental rug. After that she was bored with it. She drove the car, fast and for long distances, wearing a jaunty polka-dot hat with a scarf to match. It was told that she had torn through the town of Sinclair, Tennessee, known as a tourist speed trap, and when the patrolman had stopped her and told her it was a five dollar fine for speeding she had handed him a ten dollar bill and said, "Keep the change. I'll be back through here late this afternoon."

Eileen's father had hired the help to gather her crops, but he couldn't get her to come home. Through the last of summer she stayed on in the house with the baby and Ida. She aired the quilts and winter spreads. She canned. When the leaves began to turn she took the baby and spent long afternoons with him in the woods, shuffling through the browning pine needles, holding him on one hip. During the day she was not as lonely as she had feared, because she kept very busy, but at night she was afraid of the coming fall. She didn't sleep well, the wind seemed to wake her, even the west wind that had once soothed her. When she was awake in the night it *was* lonely, more lonely and more terrible than she ever had imagined it could be. Lying awake in the dark spaces of autumn morning she knew that she had made no plan for anything. She was volitionless at night and she knew that she was actually volitionless in the daylight, in spite of all the things she found to do with her hands. Sometimes she cried until, spent and with burning eyes, she could sleep. Other times she sat stonily by the window, staring into the blackness, afraid to stay there, afraid to go to bed.

Then one morning she woke cold and shivering and had to get up to get the quilts from the quilt box. She went down the dark stairs and opened the heavy box and took them out, smelling the musty cloth in the darkness. She covered the baby and took a quilt to Ida. Then she came back to her own bed. She spread out the quilt and snuggled into the warmth of the bedclothes. Then for the first time since Vance had died she enjoyed something sensuously, immediately and personally; the feel of comfort when the year turns cold. She lay in bed remembering fall, the smell of smoke and dry leaves, the feel and smell of new school books with slick white pages full of newness, the first day of the sweater with its stinging harsh warmth on bare arms and, most of all, anticipation. For to Eileen fall *was* anticipation, the newness of a bare beginning after the drag-end of too-lush days. She touched the anticipation gently with her grief and it was still there. I am going to get over this, she thought. And then—Tomorrow I must buy some clothes for Van. There was no lessening of loneliness but the wind was not frightening any more. Before morning she slept, her legs no longer drawn up against her but stretched comfortably and warmly under the many-colored quilt.

Buz Mayhill worked her chrysanthemums. She knelt in the dirt bed, digging with a trowel around the burgeoning plants, loosening the too-hard-packed earth. In a week or so now they would open, yellow, orange, and red feathers, round and soft and bright. She leaned back on her heels and wiped her hands on her white knickers. The sky was immensely blue. She felt lonely so she got up and lit a cigarette and went to the house to take a bath. She knew by now that her loneliness of autumn didn't mean anything. It was a physical feeling, like the feeling of excitement with snow, or comfort with steady rain.

In the hall she met Marty. The beret was gone and the ascot and the bright French phrase—overnight, when the weather turned.

"Well," she said. "Only a few more days now."

"I don't want to go," he said.

"Nonsense."

"No. No, I don't. It'll all probably be completely different from what I think."

She smiled. "Of course it will. That's why you'll like it so much."

He shook his head, looking at her. "Oh, Buz," he said suddenly, the words harsh in the dim cool hallway where everything was so completely in its place. "Oh, Buz!"

He reached one arm toward her but she stepped around him quickly and onto the first step of the stairs. "I'll buy you a silver pocket flask," she said. "Wouldn't you like that, Marty? I bet nobody in Bellefonte ever had a silver pocket flask."

She went on up the stairs quickly, leaving him looking after her up the carpeted steps, the odor of dirt and sun and leaves behind her in the clean white hall.

Captain Simms liked to sit in the arbor in the afternoons. The grapes were ripening and the smell was dark and sweet under the vines. He would sit at the end of the arbor where the sun shone in, looking out onto the dusty road where the sun seemed brighter from his hollow cave of tendrils and leaves.

Veda sat with him sometimes. She was learning to cook from Aunt Betty and after a batch of sticky rolls or a leaden cake she'd come out the back door and shake off failure in the sunlight, stretching and running in the back yard where she hoped nobody could see her. For grown women with working husbands did not stretch and run across the grass. She'd drop down beside the Captain and he'd talk to her about the falls he'd seen up in the mountains, and the fall of the War that still seemed to him the brightest bluest fall there had ever been.

"They aren't so bright any more—the falls," he said. "But there's something about them I like better. When they're too bright they're hard too. And here there's a smoky thing in the air that makes them soft. Even those slick-leaved trees of Mozel's are soft like. They don't turn pretty, but when the leaves come down they come down silky—and they lay quiet. They're not a bad kind of tree. Now Mrs. Graves' leaves up the street are a sight prettier. They turn all at once and you come on them one morning red and yellow—like that. Sudden. But when they fall they crackle and turn dusty. Both kinds are nice in their different kind of way."

In the field behind the high school they practised football. Ace would go over after work to watch them. There was a ledge on the back of the auditorium and he'd sit there with the other watchers, smoking, talking about the new football team. Everyone talked about the new football team. It was a time for it.

Some afternoons Cat Graves would drive over and sit watching them, or she would stand leaning on the door of her car, her high heels delicately held off the ground, the skirt that matched her sweater swirling in the small wind.

On the weekends they danced at Miss Alta's Barn. Miss Alta Compton was a widow and the Barn was her hobby. It was a little building, sitting just off the football field and down the hill behind Miss Alta's house. Once it had been used to store things;

now it had a hardwood floor, and electric lights hung from the exposed rafters. On Saturday nights Miss Alta had an orchestra brought from Hunter City and charged a quarter a couple to dance till twelve.

On the last weekend before they left for college Marty and Graham took over the dance. They brought in tubs of punch, concocted from gin and white lightning and fruit juice; they dug out Buz's old New Year's Eve favors; and they paid the band to stay on all night.

It was a good party. Even Dudley Cartwright, who had come alone and dignified in his neat serge suit, got drunk and tried to kiss Cat Graves on the edge of the dance floor; Ace Johnson knocked down an out-of-town boy who said the local girls weren't as pretty as the ones in south Alabama; and Marty sang "That Old Gang of Mine" to his own accompaniment of brushes and drums.

It was a hot night, and in their room under the rafters Veda and Morgan lay together in the gladness of solitude. In Maynard's Cove Eileen and Ida worked crossword puzzles while the last of the summer's gnats circled the kerosene lamp. And in her white bedroom, with the door locked and the blinds drawn, Buz Mayhill got quietly and solitarily and thoroughly drunk.

3. October 1927

CAT: Graham's coming home this weekend. And he's gonna want to know when again. It seems like that's all he ever wants to know any more. I don't know, maybe I ought to just go on and do it, but Daddy convinced me with all that talk or something. I just don't want to. Maybe I'm scared. I'd feel like Peaches with Daddy Browning or something. And then—and maybe this is really it after all—I don't think Graham would marry me if I did. What really worries me is that nothing is as much fun as it used to be any more. Seems like it's gotten spoiled with me and Graham somehow, because when he's home there's just one thing he thinks about and how are you going to have any fun dancing or drinking or petting, or anything else, when all the time that's the only thing he thinks about. Marty's not like that. He dates everybody and I don't think they do it at all. I just know they don't. Well, maybe Ruby Marshall, but not anybody else. And Ace and Eileen. I bet they don't. Or maybe they do, Eileen having been married and all, but I don't think so. Anyway it's the only thing *Graham* thinks about. I don't see why he don't just marry me if he wants *that* so damned bad. Daddy'd help us; Morgan and Veda are making out pretty well. Graham says I ought to want it his way, all that talk I do about romantic deserts and stuff, but that's different. And anyway Rudolph Valentino's dead. I don't see why that had to be that way. Just dead. All of a sudden like that. No reason. What if Graham were to die? Then I'd wish forever and forever that I had done it. But what if I did and then he didn't love me any more? That'd be like dying, only maybe worse. What if he married somebody else? Then there wouldn't be anything to look forward to . . . ever again. Sometimes now I wish I'd gone on to school with the rest of them. I could have gotten by somehow. And I wouldn't be just here waiting, waiting for Graham to come home and start that talking about it all over again. He says I cheat because I get more out of petting than he does, and I guess he's right. I like it all right. It just about makes up for all the fussing and fighting, how I feel when he loves me —like the last time before he went off to school and we were out in the back of the house in Mama's dahlias and he lay down by me and held me against him and I could feel him so. All the air smelled like those peppery damned flowers, and dirt, and sunshine, and I felt like I was gonna die. He says it'll be like that a hundred times better, but I don't know. I reckon I'm scared.

GRAHAM: Well, I'll try one more time. Damn, that woman's like a brick wall. She wants to get married, I guess. That's what they all want. Get married, like it'd change the universe. And where would I be? Dad would probably cut off the money—no more school. I can see me slaving away like ole Morgan, sawing up pieces of wood, or messing around in printer's ink like Ace. Hell, I ain't cut out for a trade. Besides, I just don't want to marry anybody. If I did, it'd be Cat, but I don't want to marry anybody. But Jesus Christ! How long am I gonna be able to stand it? All that kissing and feeling and wanting and going home with an ache every night. And it's her I want, not some little nothing just to get 'em off for me. Damn women anyway! Why are they all so one way? That Gloria the other weekend at school. As ready as you please and enjoyed it one hell of a sight more than I did, tossing and moaning and all that stuff, and then crying and saying, "You got to marry me." Marry me, my ass. Where do they all think they get off, anyway? What do they all want with diapers and babies and little fences and radio sets and kitchen tables? Jesus Christ. Look at that Veda. Half-sick all the time since she lost that baby. Is that what they all want? Ole Marty's got the right idea—love 'em and leave 'em. But how does he get away with it? I guess it's all that money. Damned if that don't help anything. Well. After the football game tonight I'll try again. It's still warm enough to be outside and I don't know, maybe just once more. She sure the hell wants it. I know that.

VEDA: I feel better today. Maybe it's because Mama's flowers are blooming so pretty and the sky's so blue. You can't feel too bad on a day like this. Grandfather says I have to buck up. That's Grandfather, all right. I bet he never was sick. He doesn't seem like it. And I guess he's right. If you like everything the way he does you don't have time to be sick. Mama hangs over me too much. She thinks I'm going to turn out delicate and she and all the old ladies in Bellefonte can bring me calf's-foot jelly and nectar and junk. Morgan thinks it too—that hurts. Men don't like you to be sick. They want you to laugh and look pretty and not ever have anything hurt or be wrong. One day he said country girls didn't get sick over losing a baby. But I can't help it if I'm not a country girl. If that's what he wanted he could have married one and stayed out there and plowed up fields forever. Maybe the sawmill's not much, but he likes that wood. He can't say he doesn't. All those little chests and book ends and things he's made for me. I know what he really wants is to move out of here. I don't blame him. Mama makes me tired too. But where are we gonna move on what he makes, and then we'd miss Grandfather . . . both of us. Sits in the sun so much now, just watching. He probably knows every way there is for the fall to come. He'll be in, in a little while, to listen to the radio. That's when they have that program with all the records. "Hard Hearted Hannah." Isn't that a song for an old man like that to like? It *is* a pretty radio. I don't know how Morgan ever saved enough money to buy it for me. I'm gonna dress and go downstairs, and I'll eat supper tonight. That's what I'll do. And maybe Morgan'll drive me out to see Eileen. No, it's ball game night. Maybe I'd feel like going to that. I wonder if I'd feel like sitting on those bleachers? I reckon

I ought to. Look at that old man out there, sitting pretty in the sun.

MORGAN: Told me today I was going to get a promotion—going to get more money too. I don't know, this is probably as good a place as any. Since I'm learning to read those blue prints it's all more fun. It's wonderful how you can look at those white lines and see the beams and feel the flooring. There's no getting around it, it's pretty nice. And maybe . . . maybe after a little I can get a transfer. Maybe we can get the hell out of that house and living somebody else's life and go away. Then Veda'll be like she always was. And we can have another baby—and buy a car of our own. I wish she'd go to the ball game with me tonight. I wish I could take her and show her off like I used to. We could dance at Miss Alta's later. Veda still does the best Charleston in town. She's got the prettiest legs too. It's nice to have a wife with the prettiest legs in town. Maybe if I got Eileen and Ace to come by we could all go together. I bet Eileen's gonna marry Ace, and a good thing too. Somebody ought to help her with that kid. I'll go out and get Eileen to come by. That's what I'll do. Right after work. That kid of Eileen's sure is a boy for you. He sure is a sight.

BUZ: What is it about this room when I wake up in the mornings? White—and cold—and damp somehow, like a winding sheet would be . . . if people in our culture knew about winding sheets. Of course I know perfectly well that this is ridiculous. I have only to get up and open the curtains and look out and it will be a fall day with the sun shining and all my flowers blooming in the sun. Only those few steps across the room and there will be no more darkness. What was it that I dreamed last night? Only parts of it left now, like wisps and strays and corners. Something about Marty. I was afraid. I remember that all right. I was afraid. It was so silly too. He had on a Little Lord Fauntleroy suit, like the one my mother gave him when he was ten. Little Lord Fauntleroy. But Marty never had yellow curls. There's nothing like *that* about my Marty. And that wasn't it anyway. That wasn't what frightened me so. It was that bad kind of fright too, like the time when I was a little girl and I looked up at the sky and thought God's face was behind it. I ran all the way home and bawled like a baby. And that's when my father told me that God wasn't a giant man. Oh, yes, I remember that. And then one day there wasn't any God at all. And maybe that's why I'm afraid now. Because if there is nothing behind all that sky, how lost we are, how sad we are. And how insignificant. He has such strong hands, Marty does, really very good hands. I wonder if he sleeps with that little Marshall girl? I bet he does. There's something ruthless in him. I've always felt it. Even when he is laughing and talking, even when he was being a complete dunce with that André Lacoste thing. He isn't happy either. And that frightens me too, of course. Because I have transmitted fear to my son and he will know what the fear is. Because he is stronger than I, and more ruthless, and he never minds facing anything. I do. I've been afraid all my life. I don't like to think too much about what I feel. It isn't natural somehow, it's like seeing that giant face behind the sky. And if you ever once did see it, what then? What then, with all our insignificance? I am going to get up. This is nonsense. Marty's coming home tonight. I have to go down and plan the meals and see that his room's been opened and aired, and check the gin, and cut some flowers for the dining room. And I have to plan what I want to wear to the football game tonight. What is that song? "Dear one, please don't be angry, for I was only teasing you?" That's it. That's what I was so afraid of. How perfectly ridiculous. Why on earth should Marty be angry with me?

MARTY: In just a couple of hours I'll be there. And I'll stop in the drive and just sit there for a minute and look at the flowers and the grass and the trees. Then I'll walk across the porch and into the hall. And it will be cool and quiet and peaceful, like diving or hiding. I'll set my suitcase down loud and she'll come out of the room on the right. She'll have on something white and she'll still be tan from the summer, only not so tan as when I left in August. There'll be bracelets on her arm that'll jingle a little when she puts her hand out toward me. Then she'll take it back, quick, like that, because she always does. And I'll say, Hello, Buz, and she'll say, Hello, Marty. Glad to be home? And I'll go and pick her up anyway. Though she'll pull away from me and laugh a little and say, Oh, Marty. Put me down. But I'll hold her a little, just till she struggles. Then I'll put her down, quickly, and she'll frown. We'll have the drink then, a good strong one in a frosted glass that takes the finger prints from her hand on its foggy sides. We'll drink that one pretty fast. Then I'll mix another one. And after that we'll talk. *She'll* talk, and light cigarettes and get up and wander around that room. And finally she'll put her hand on my head and leave it there for a little, cool and inert. And then he'll come in. He'll say, How're things at school, Marty?, and I'll say, Fine sir. He'll say, That's good. They ought to be. You're spending enough money. And he'll say, Where's my paper? to her, and she'll go quick and get it for him. He'll sit down across from me and I'll say, I'd better go clean up. All through dinner he'll talk to me and I'll talk to him, and out of the corner of my eye I'll see her, with the candles making her face soft and her hands crumbling bread that she never eats. Then I'll take her to the ball game. She'll wear a little hat and her hair'll stick out around the edges of it; she'll laugh a lot and when she sits on the bleachers she'll say, This is no place for an old woman, and I'll say, You're right, my dear, of course. You're absolutely right. And when it's late and dark and everybody sleeps I'll lie in my own room in my own bed and know she's lying sleepless too.

ACE: I guess we'll go to the preacher's house and get married. She can't have any church wedding, but I want a preacher to do the job. I don't want any running off with Eileen. I want her to wear that blue dress with all that fringed stuff on it and I don't want any of the rest of them there... just us. I sure don't want Aunt Trudy and Aunt Mattie. Not the gang either. They can come later and bring their bust-head whiskey if they want. But when I marry Eileen I don't want nobody else there. We'll go to that ball game tonight and then tomorrow we can act like we're going to that singing business at the high school, and just go on over to the parsonage. I'm gonna call Brother Jones this afternoon. I really didn't ever believe in this. I never thought Eileen'd belong to me. Not even after I went out there that time and I knew she saw me again—really saw me, after all the time of being polite and letting me sit with her and play with the kid. Not even then, nor after, when I kissed her, not even when she said she loved me too. I never really thought she'd belong to me.

EILEEN: Mama always said you had to live through just one day at a time. I guess I did that—somehow. I love Ace. I love him so terribly that I know it's right. I guess what makes me feel a little guilty is that he excites me more than Vance ever did. I don't understand that. I loved Vance so. I loved him in a way I'll never have for anybody else again. I loved him just thinking about him almost as much as when he was there. I never seemed to not be loving him deep inside somewhere. It's never been like that with Ace. When I think about him sometimes I don't love him at all exactly. But every time I see him I get weak and wild and crazy . . . like I'd never had any sex before . . . he can just put his hand on my breast and I nearly die. I don't see how it happened like that all of a sudden. He'd been sitting there talking to me for months and then he got up that night and went to get a drink of water and when he came back I could see the shine of it across his mouth, and I thought *I want him.* I want him awfully right now. I guess I scared him to death because I just got up and went across the room and kissed him. But he was as ready for me as I was for him. That was for sure. God. I can't stand sitting here thinking about it. I don't think I'll be able to stand it till tomorrow night. Mama'll keep Van and we can go somewhere all by ourselves and get in a bed together and love each other all night long. Oh Ace. Ace. Ace. I love you so.

The lights from the high school auditorium rayed out into the early night. They shone across the cars parked around the hill and down the hill to the creek with the little stone bridge where Marty Mayhill sat, tossing rocks down into the small stream, listening intently to the splash and ripple in the darkness. He had been sitting there for an hour perhaps, since late twilight, before the lights had gone on and the people had begun arriving in their cars, before the sounds of feet scuffling gravel and voices lifted in excitement. He was dressed carefully and neatly and his nails had been manicured. He sat very straight and stiff on the bridge and occasionally he smiled to himself in the dark.

He had been looking forward to this weekend for a month now, and of course nothing had gone as he had wanted it to or expected it to. Because things overplanned and over-thought-on never turn out right. It was, he felt, one of those perverse laws of life that made ever counting on anything impossible. A friend of his at school had once told him that he would not be in the least surprised to go home and have his mother meet him at the door with a knife ready to cut his throat. He had laughed at him at the time but he wondered now if perhaps there wasn't something in what he had said. There is nothing predictable except unpredictability. Why shouldn't your own family turn on you? The world is rife with turnings and turnings out. Out into the darkness and the gates shut and shielded behind you, lighting the night with the flame of their barring swords.

He tossed another pebble, listening intently in the darkness for the splash. He'd known when he pulled into the driveway yesterday afternoon that things weren't going to go right. It had been late afternoon but instead of looking cool the shrubs and flowers had seemed dusty and hot and there was a haze in the air. He parked and walked across the porch and before he reached the front door he could hear them—all the clutter and cackle of sound that meant a party—glasses sounding their crystal snaps on table tops, voices raised beyond the pitch necessary for conversation, heels clacking across the spaces between the rugs. He went on in. The air was blue with smoke and the house felt close. He tried to get by the door and up the stairs, but she caught him. She came toward him, pulling Dudley Cartwright with her by the sleeve, her other hand holding a glass. "Marty! Darling!" she said. "I'm having a party for you. Isn't Graham with you? Cat's in here. I'll go call him right now. Everybody wants to get in the mood for the game tonight."

"Hello, Marty," Dudley said constrainedly.

Marty nodded, his eyes going back to Buz. "You all started a little early, didn't you?" he said.

She frowned, her eyebrows pulling together crookedly, and let go of Dudley, who immediately bowed and went back into the living room. "What's the matter, baby?" she said worriedly. "It's just your friends here. Ace and Eileen are getting married soon and it's sort of a get-together for them too." She set the glass carefully on the banister post. "I knew you were going to be mad at me," she said flatly.

"I'm not mad," Marty said. "I'm tired. That's all. I want to go up and change."

"All right, Marty. I'll call Graham." She went to the phone and he went on up the stairs, bathed and dressed, and went back down and joined them.

It was a party indistinguishable from all the other parties they had had in the last five years—too much to drink, too much cigarette smoke, too much noise in an overheated room. They had all gone on to the ball game together later. Nobody remembered who scored, but Bellefonte won and they had gone back to celebrate at the house again. Veda had been sick on the dining room rug and Morgan had taken her home, and Cat had had a terrific row with Graham in the pantry. Marty had walked in on them while looking for extra glasses. He left the house by the back door and wandered down to the tennis court. He stepped through the bushes surrounding the court and almost stumbled over Ace, who was stretched out on the ground with his head in Eileen's lap.

"Hell, Marty," Ace said, laughing. "Look where you're stepping."

"You two don't look tight," he said, feeling a momentary relief, longing to talk to somebody.

"Just with each other," Eileen said.

He sat down on the grass beside them. He could hear Eileen's breathing in the darkness, soft and happy, and it made him sad.

"When's the big day?" he said.

"Tomorrow, but don't tell anybody. We don't want anybody there," Ace said quickly. "No wedding . . . just us, getting married."

"The best way," Marty said listlessly.

Ace struck a match and their faces flashed whitely in the darkness, Eileen's happy, Ace's intent. Marty stood up. "I'm in the way," he said abruptly. "This is no damned place for the host anyway."

"It's no place for the guests either," Eileen said, laughing. "Sit down. You're too sober for that crowd in there."

He had let himself be persuaded and he stayed, talking to them about where they would live and what they would do. He felt that he was intruding on them and that he had no right to, but he couldn't leave. He wanted suddenly to be close to somebody, anybody, and he stayed for an hour before he stood up abruptly and left. "I do wish you the best of everything, always," he said, turning momentarily, and he could hear the murmur of their thanks in the darkness as he walked away from them.

He stood at the well house for a while, watching the lights from the house, hearing the crunch of tires on gravel as guests departed and others came in. Later he heard Buz calling him, her voice questioning and quiet and sad. She was standing in the back door with the light behind her. He watched her, but he didn't answer her, and after a while she went back in. He sat on the back steps until the last of the sounds from the house died down and until Ace and Eileen went past him around to the front of the house. After the lights were all off he went up the back stairs and went to bed.

He threw a last rock into the stream but, though he listened, there was no echoing splash. He leaned over the bridge and peered down into the darkness but he couldn't see anything. It must have fallen onto the bank, he said, and stood up and started up the hill toward the school.

There was a male chorus singing tonight. It was directed by Sara and Kenneth Downs. Marty smiled as he went toward the auditorium, thinking momentarily of Sara, in her blue finery, running away with Kenneth Downs in a Chevrolet coupé. She was the mother of three children now and she had begun to be plump—a short, plump matron who wore black dresses and had let her hair grow to be put up in a bun. She still taught music to reluctant little girls with pigtails and on Saturday evenings she and Kenneth conducted the glee club. Tonight they were presenting a program and a good deal of the depression that accompanied Marty Mayhill into the high school was caused by the simple fact that there was no place better than this for him to go on a Saturday night. He had thought of calling Ruby Marshall but at the last moment he had put the phone down without giving the number, hearing the operator's mechanical voice dully sounding until he replaced the receiver . . . Number please? Number please? Number please?

He had stayed in his room all day, half-dozing with the blinds drawn, waking to smoke a cigarette, going back to sleep again. He had done this often at the University. Many mornings there he did not get up at all but slept through the sun's coming and going, getting up at twilight into a strange and useless world where he was the strangest and most useless thing abroad, walking the streets behind the campus, looking at lighted windows in a sort of wonder at the abundance behind them, ending up perhaps in the bus station where he would sit on a bench and watch the faces coming and going, in and out in the darkness, to and from God knew where or for what purpose. People who rode buses always seemed tired, they carried bags and bundles and shapeless bulging sacks, they dragged whining children behind them, they checked and rechecked their pocketbooks. He would watch them all, trying to fathom purpose behind the faces which were so carefully blank with transit. Sometimes there would be an expectant one, a waiting, hopeful face. There were never too many of these. Once he had gotten on a bus and ridden in to Newcastle but at the end of the sixty-mile journey there had been only a larger terminal, with more faces. He had turned in his round-trip stub and come back.

He spent hours in the old quadrangle behind the new campus. It was a strange place at night, dark and deserted, the three-storied buildings casting black shadows from the one small street lamp at the corner. He would sit on the steps of one of the buildings, looking into the shadows, remembering the stories of how the Yankee cavalry had burned the old university, until his eyes would gradually change the time to suit the place. Then he would wait, breathlessly almost, for the skulking figure that would turn the corner of a building and set the torch.

He dated a great number of girls. They were all alike in some undefined way: small girls, graceful girls, girls that laughed a lot. They weren't very real to him. One—older than the others and with a quiet way of looking at him—he brought to the quadrangle once. But she was frightened when he tried to talk to her about the shift in time he felt here sometimes, and he never dated her again.

He drank with Graham McCloud. They would sit all night in the window of the fraternity house, drinking and looking down onto the empty campus. Early in the morning they would watch the first signs of life come into the streets—the janitors, the dining-room workers, the first professors. Graham talked about Catharine Graves, Graham talked about politics. Marty would listen. Politics were as remote to him as the thought of marrying a girl from Bellefonte and settling down to run a cotton gin. By the beginning of his junior year he knew that there was really nothing at all he wanted to do.

When he came home this weekend he had planned to stay. There had been in his mind a picture of himself going back to school alone to get his clothes and books, being an outsider at last in the place where he had always felt an outsider. He would miss the quadrangle, and the trees, but there are trees and dark places everywhere.

After yesterday afternoon he knew that it had all been a ridiculous dream. Nothing is what we expect or what we plan. There was no place for him at home either. He couldn't spend the rest of his life in a party. He couldn't be a gigolo for his own mother. It was as simple as that.

He went on up the hill to the auditorium and through the door and down the hall and inside with the people and the lights. The concert was already more than half over. He sat in the back row so Buz would not see him, looking out across the tilted heads of Bellefonte, watching the black and white pattern of men across the stage, listening to the sentimental inane songs for male voices, laughing somewhere deep inside himself at the folly of all mankind.

They sang "In the Evening by the Moonlight," and "The Mocking Bird," and "The Quilting Party" . . . all silver songs. That was the way Marty thought of them, silver, like the moonlight on that quadrangle or bright across the road to Holly Springs. "A Spanish Cavalier." When he had been a little boy he had thought the cavalier stood in his retreat like a statue in a niche, wearing the armor of the soldiers in his history book who had explored Florida. Somehow the niche had been imposed on him—the fortunes of war—but they had allowed him to keep his guitar. They sang the Italian songs, "Marianina," "Santa Lucia," "O Sole Mio," and he wondered why the Anglo-Saxon personality liked the songs it had no emotional contact with. Italian boating songs —like jazz—imposed on reluctant minds that never felt the incipient passion in anything.

They saved Mother for last. He had known they would. It was the great rouser. It was just the type of closing medley Sara Butler Downs would like. He was surprised that they didn't have a little old lady in an armless rocker for background. They began with "I Want a Girl Just Like the Girl That Married Dear Old Dad." They went on to "M Is for the Million Things She Gave Me," and knocked them cold with "Tie Me to Your Apron Strings Again." It was during this one that he started to laugh and found that he was crying. It enraged him so that he stood up and went out of the auditorium, slamming the door behind him with all his strength. He walked past the place where he had parked his car and had to go back for it. When he got in and tried to start the motor he was trembling so hard he couldn't do the muscle-automatic task. He put his head on his arms and sat there, cursing bitterly in the darkness. He straightened up finally and started the car, driving into town and through the deserted streets, looking for somebody, anybody. He thought that if he saw one person anywhere that he could speak to about the absurdity of human existence in 1927 he would be all right.

He made up the imaginary conversation in his head as he drove. "What a joke on all of us old Freud has played. Sara Butler can still have her Mother program, but it won't be long—it won't be long before it'll be snickered off the stage. Tie me to your apron strings again. Oh, Brother! *Rise up, my love, my fair one, and come away. For, lo the winter is past, the rain is over and gone. . . the time of the singing of birds is come, and the voice of Freud is heard in our land."*

He didn't see anyone at all on the square. He drove on home. The house was dark except for the lights over the garage and the side entrance, and the small glow from the lamps left on in the halls. The servants had been given the night off because of the concert. He put the car carefully in the garage and got out and walked around it, looking at the tires. Then he took a rag from the shelf and polished it. There was no sound from the neighborhood. He might have been alone in the world. He tried to think of that—an imaginable future with only Marty Mayhill left on a wide and empty planet—but the image wouldn't stay with him. He finished the car and went into the house. It was very quiet here. The few lamps that had been left on cast lonely little pools of light onto the carpets. He walked to the stairs, going carefully around the circles of light, and went up to his father's room. The gun was in the drawer of the bedside table. He didn't know whether it was loaded or not. He didn't know enough about guns to know. He hefted it gingerly in his palm. It was an ugly damned thing. Then he went back down the stairs and into his father's study.

There were no lights on here so he switched on the desk lamp over the desk and sat down in his father's chair. There was a sick, sweetish smell in the room and he couldn't place it. He worried about it but he wouldn't get up to see. After a moment he placed it. It was the bowl of sliced O. Henry his mother put on his father's table for a midnight snack. He got up and picked it up awkwardly with his left hand—he was still holding the gun in his right—and took it into the kitchen and threw it into the garbage can. The refrigerator cut on with a faint hum and he jumped, looking around. I guess I have to hurry, he thought.

There was something he wanted but he couldn't think clearly enough to know what it was. He went up the stairs hurriedly and into Buz's room. He began to go through her dresser drawers hastily, pulling out wisps of underwear, beaded bags, earrings, and throwing them in heaps on the floor. Whatever it was he was searching for, he couldn't find it, so he went back down stairs and into the study and sat down in the chair. He didn't think about it at all. He just put the gun to his head and pulled the trigger. It was harder to pull than he had thought. He had to concentrate on it, so when it gave he didn't have time to really think, No.

Buz Mayhill was bored with the concert. She suffered it, sitting beside Martin Senior, fidgeting on the hard wooden seat, glancing back over the auditorium to see if Marty had come in. She didn't see him. She hadn't seen him all day. She wondered if he was unhappy about some girl. It didn't seem likely. She had never known him to be unhappy about a girl. At intermission she saw Cat and Graham in the hallway and they smoked a cigarette together. "Seen Marty?" Buz said.

Cat shook her head. "I bet he went with Eileen and Ace," she said.

"Uh-uh." Graham shook his head. "They didn't want anybody.

In fact, we're not supposed to know they're getting married tonight. Remember?"

Cat shrugged. She was very thin this year and she fancied the shadows under her eyes were becoming, so she emphasized them with cosmetics. It gave her a slightly sinister look of which she was very proud.

"I guess he has a date," Buz said. She went back into the auditorium to Martin, who remained in his chair, looking at the closed curtain as though it contained a message of consuming importance.

When they came out of the concert they were exhilarated. They stood in groups on the gravel parking space, talking to each other, making bets on whether the drugstore was still open, enjoying being dressed up and made up and out of the house. Nobody wanted to go home.

The night was warm but clear, and the automobiles stood in random ranks waiting to transport them—anywhere but home. The crowd was a long time breaking up. Martin Senior was in the car but Buz made him wait. She was looking for Marty and, failing to find him, for someone to talk to. She finally spotted Graham and Cat again and asked them to come home with her. She didn't want to be alone and she knew that Martin would go to bed the minute they got in the house. He would go to his study, have his milk and chocolates, glance at the market page of the newspaper again, and go to bed. He always did. He would tonight.

Buz was never ready to go to bed. She put it off even when there was no one in the house. She would read or rearrange the flowers. She would take a bath. Sometimes she would sit on the porch, smoking cigarettes and looking out at the dark empty streets of Bellefonte. Tonight she didn't want to do any of these things. She asked Graham and Cat to come to the house.

They came with her because Cat was eager to go any place where she didn't have to be alone with Graham. Each weekend that he was at home had become a crisis weekend and the role she was playing was beginning to wear on her. She knew that something had to happen, and soon, but whether she would win and it would be a wedding or Graham would win and it would be something entirely different she didn't know. She told Buz she'd love to come over for a drink and Graham, cursing under his breath, went along.

Buz drove the Buick sedan with the same dash that Marty displayed in his roadsters. She turned corners on two wheels and tapped the horn briskly at each car they passed. Martin sat stoically beside her; he was sleepy. In the back seat Graham tried to put his hand on Cat's thigh and she pushed him away.

"He's home," Buz said suddenly as they turned the last corner. Her voice was so intensely relieved that they all stared at her—even Martin. Looking out the window, Cat could see the open garage doors and, as they turned into the drive, the shine of metal from Marty's car. There was a light in the study, raying out onto the driveway, lighting up the yellowing rose vines and the last wilting fall roses, making the thick clustered bushes bulk dark and heavy around the house. Buz braked the car so suddenly that they were jolted forward in their seats and she jumped out in the same instant of turning off the key. The others followed her. At the front door she paused, tapping her foot impatiently as she waited for them to catch up. Her face looked tense and drawn and Cat had a sudden sharp sense of wrongness. She put her hand on Graham's arm.

He looked down at her and put his hand over hers. "What you reckon Ace and Eileen are up to right now?" he whispered.

She shook her head impatiently. Buz opened the door and they went in. The light from the study shone into the hallway and the small lamps that had been left on cast their circles. Buz flipped on the overhead light and they blinked at each other in the sudden illumination. She went to the stairs and called up. "Marty?" And louder, "Marty?"

"Maybe he's asleep," Cat said.

"Marty? At this hour?" Buz laughed. She took a step toward the living room, glanced in and walked on across to the study. Cat saw her silver dress sweep into the doorway, stop, rush through. Then she heard the scream. It was as though the scream came from nowhere and everywhere. It was so completely horrible in its suddenness and certainty that none of them could do anything. They stood there in the bright clean hallway, not even looking at each other. Then as the scream went on and on in the midst of their silence Cat felt the perspiration start on her body, drenching her in a sudden cold sweat. She turned and started for the front door, running. Graham stopped her as she was fumbling with the screen door and the movement propelled Martin across the room and into the study.

Graham took hold of Cat's arm roughly. "Come on," he said. "It could be..." He stopped and pushed her in front of him to the study.

Buz was on the floor, the silver dress crumpled around her. She held Marty in her arms and she was still screaming. Martin was trying, with no success, to get her up.

When Graham and Cat came in the door she turned toward them and they could see the reddened front of the silver dress and her bare shoulders. They could see Marty, too.

Graham came on into the room. He pushed Martin away and slapped Buz across the face. She stopped screaming, and the silence was worse than the screaming had been. She sat on the floor, looking at Graham like a child while he moved Marty and laid him on the rug and took off his coat and put it over him. Cat was still standing in the doorway. "Come here and take care of Buz," Graham said sharply and Cat moved into the room. She came over, walking carefully across the rug, trying not to look at the spot on the wall in front of her and unable to look at anything else. When she reached Buz she stopped and put her hand out to her and Buz got up and went with her out of the room and up the stairs.

"We better telephone," Graham said to Martin. "Do you want me to?" When he got no answer he turned and saw that Martin was standing perfectly still in the middle of the room, tears running down his face. He hadn't heard him at all. Graham called Doctor Matthews. He was not sure whether to call the police or the coroner or not, so he left that for the doctor. When Dr. Matthews arrived Graham left him in the study with Martin, and with Marty, and went up the stairs. Buz was sitting in the middle of her bedroom floor. There was a heap of underwear and scarves and purses around her and she held a scarf in her hands. Cat sat on a foot-stool beside her, looking at her helplessly. Graham shook his head. "I thought I told you to look after her," he said

"Graham, dammit, Graham. We came up here and all that stuff was all over the floor and she . . . she just sat down in it. I didn't know what to do."

Graham picked Buz up and put her on the bed. She tried to smile at him and then she began to cry. He watched her for a moment. "She's all right now," he said. "Get that damned dress off her."

Cat went to the bed and Graham picked up what looked like a gown and negligee and handed them to her. He stood for a moment looking down at the litter on the floor. Then he nodded and leaned over and slowly and carefully picked up the garments and ornaments and bags and put them back in the dresser drawers.

Cat was watching him silently. "They don't mean anything," he said. "They don't have any significance at all."

He finished the job and went on back down the stairs to talk to the doctor and coroner.

The sun came into the room through the new organdy curtains, slanting brightly across the floor and the foot of the bed. Eileen raised herself on her elbow and looked at Ace. He lay on his back, completely relaxed. She put her hand out and pushed his hair off his forehead. He murmured and turned away from her and she smiled, settling back under the bedclothes against his back.

It had been a most satisfactory wedding in the stuffy little parlor of the parsonage with Brother Jones in his black suit and his wife nervously waiting for him to finish and get her to the glee club concert. Eileen giggled and Ace turned over and looked at her. He put his hand on her cheek and smiled. "What's so damned funny?" he said sleepily.

She shook her head, moving closer to him. "Mrs. Jones," she said softly, looking at his eyes. "Mrs. Jones in her finery so all-fired anxious to get to that concert."

"We didn't delay them much," Ace said. He put his arms around her. "What I can't get over is that damned spray of arti-ficial goldenrod in the fireplace. That was a lovely thing."

"Beautiful," Eileen said. "Almost as lovely as the lace doilies." She kissed his chin. "Almost as lovely as you in a suit and tie . . . almost as lovely as you like this."

He kissed her slowly, feeling drowsy and still half-asleep in the early light of morning. Her body felt alive and soft and warm against him. "I reckon it's really true," he said.

"It's true all right," Eileen said. "It's about the truest thing that ever happened to me. I love you."

"You right sure?"

"This sure."

"I reckon that's sure enough."

It was a small room they lay in but it was a private room be-cause it was a house in itself. It had been the Johnsons' laundry house and Ace had painted and papered it and installed a small bathroom. It was in the Johnsons' back yard but it was their house, and to Eileen it was as much home as the whole of the cove had been. She had felt the apology in Ace when he brought her here and she had tried to combat it. If it had been only a bedroom in the bigger house, the place belonging to Mattie and Trudy, she might have rebelled, but this was hers and a present from Ace. It was all she wanted. She kissed him, longing to erase all the doubts from his mind. She had been his only love and he was her second and there was no changing that. There was only the hope it would cease to matter to him. Holding him, she thought it might.

The door opened and sunlight splashed suddenly into the room.

Eileen felt the shock coiling inside her. Her body stiffened and she pulled the bedspread over her. Mattie Johnson stood in the middle of the room, looking carefully at a spot on the wall several inches over the rumpled bed.

Ace sat up. "What the hell do you want?" he said.

Mattie drew herself up portentously. She was a stout woman with elaborately waved gray hair. She wore lavender and green and two dinner rings on her left hand. She didn't approve of Ace marrying a widow and she had said so, many times and in many ways. Miss Trudy didn't approve either, but she was never as vocal as Miss Mattie.

"Marty Mayhill shot himself last night," Mattie said, the words falling into the quiet room with physical impact.

Ace stared at her uncomprehendingly. "Who?" he said.

"Your fine friend, Mr. Martin Mayhill, Jr.," Miss Mattie said. She still did not look at them. "In the study over there. Blew his brains out. They came in from that concert and found him in there. Mr. Martin and Graham McCloud and that Graves girl— don't know what they were doing there—and his mother, of course."

"Are you sure?" Ace said.

Eileen looked from Mattie to Ace. Then she pushed herself up against the headboard, holding the bedspread carefully around her shoulders. "We'll have to dress," she said.

Mattie continued to look at the wall. "I wouldn't come in here with a story like that if I wasn't sure, would I?" she said.

"We have to get dressed," Eileen said again.

Mattie looked at her then. She looked straight at her, at her tousled hair and the rumpled bed. Her lip curled slightly and she turned and went to the door. "Breakfast is at seven-thirty here," she said. She went out of the room, closing the door carefully behind her.

Eileen got out of bed, indignation and shock warring in her. Ace stood up and pulled on his pants and buckled his belt. He looked at her helplessly. "Did you hear what she said?" he said.

"I heard her." Eileen came to him. She put her arms around him and drew him down to sit by her on the bed. "Don't look like that, darling," she said softly. "Please don't look like that."

"Marty," Ace said. "That just don't seem possible somehow. Why would Marty do that, Eileen? Why would *Marty* do a thing like that?"

"I don't know," Eileen said. "But he wasn't happy. He's never been happy, Ace."

Ace turned to look at her. "Why do you say that?" he said. "I thought Marty was happier than any of us. He had more to live *for* than any of us." He stopped and tried to smile at her. "Except me, of course," he said.

Eileen shook her head. "Everybody will think that," she said. "Everybody will say 'he had everything to live for.' But that's because most people think that if you're being loud you're being happy."

Ace leaned his forehead against her shoulder. "You're too deep for me, baby," he said. "I can't see it like that." He stood up suddenly. "God! All last night he was lying over there . . . maybe if we'd just looked out the window we'd have seen something wrong and could have gone over . . ."

"No, Ace." Eileen stood up too. "Don't start thinking like that."

"I wish I had a drink," Ace said. He felt frightened with the inevitability of life and with the suddenness of its possible ending.

"You don't need any drink at seven o'clock in the morning," Eileen said. "You need a cup of coffee. I'm going into that house and make you one." She started putting on her clothes. "I don't care whose kitchen it's in, either. I'm gonna make you a pot of coffee. A whole pot." She put her arms around him and kissed him hard on the mouth. "And then," she added firmly, "we're going back to bed, darling. I'm going to love you very very much before you have to go over there." She watched his expression carefully and added judiciously, "That's what Marty would like us to do."

She opened the door and went out and across the narrow space to the Johnson kitchen.

Veda cried. She cried for a long time with Morgan standing helplessly by her, not wanting to leave for work until she felt better. "I wish to hell Graham hadn't called so early," he said. "He knows you don't feel good."

"Go on to work, Morgan," Veda said. "I'm all right. I just feel so miserable about Marty."

Morgan shook his head. "It was one hell of a thing to do, all right," he said.

Grandfather Simms knocked on the door. Morgan let him in and he leaned over and whispered in Morgan's ear. "Get on to work, boy. I'll take care of Miss Pickles. I don't know what the nation that boy meant myself, but I guess he had his reasons. Get on now."

Morgan looked helplessly at Veda on the bed and went out and downstairs and to work.

"Miss Pickles," Captain said gruffly. "Get up from there now."

Veda sat up on the bed and tried to smooth down the wisps of hair around her face.

"Let's get downstairs and have some coffee and sit in that arbor for a spell," Captain said. Then he turned his back and waited until she combed her hair and straightened her skirt and came to the door with him.

They went downstairs together and Captain stopped in the kitchen and called Aunt Betty. "Where's that mug of mine?" he said, and when she brought it he gave it to Veda. "You're the one needs a big cup of coffee right now," he said. "Fill 'er up and bring 'er on out."

He sat down on his iron bench in the arbor and made Veda sit beside him. "Now," he said after he had watched her drink her first sip of coffee. "This is a real sad business about that Mayhill boy. I've known him since the day he was born and I've known his folks a sight longer. I've lived a long time, Pickles. Long enough that for me life is a gift every morning. And when I say life I mean everything from that first cup of coffee to the sound of the last mockingbird at night. So it makes me sad to see the ending of a life so young. But it happened. I've lived long enough to know that when things happen it don't do to say 'why,' and it don't do to say 'if,' and it don't do to say 'no.' Have your grief and cry about it, but accept it at face value. No 'why,' no 'if,' no 'no.' Understand?"

Veda nodded, watching his face. "Yessir," she said.

"I couldn't quite get hold of the words to talk like this to you when you lost your baby," he said slowly. "But I can now, and it's a thing to remember. It's not just for now."

She nodded again.

"All right," he said. "I just wanted to say that for the other time and for now too." He smiled at her. "Just like I think that crying of yours has been. For now and for the other time and for the uncertainty of the future. One more thing, Pickles. Just one, and this old man will hush and leave you in peace. It's worth it, Veda. Never forget that, no matter what happens, it's worth it all to be born and live and breathe on this earth."

He stood up then and blew his nose loudly. "I'm going out in that sunshine now," he said. "And take a little walk down to the pasture."

"I won't think of it. I won't think of it. I will not think of it," Cat told herself over and over as she lay on her white iron bed, staring across the room at the pictures of Rudolph Valentino on the wall. Then the scene would develop in her mind as though it were etched somewhere on the back of her brain and would suddenly print itself on the front of it in black and white and red. That was the way she saw it, black and white and red. The study and the wall and Marty and Buz on the floor and from the hallway the scent of the last roses, faint and sweet and thick. There was a line from a poem they had studied in senior lit. that ran through her mind too, over and over across the scene: *I shall never again be friends with roses, I shall never again be friends with roses. I shall never again be friends, I shall never, roses, friends.*

She slept once and woke suddenly, drenched with sweat and crying. The dream had been about Rudolph Valentino. He had been standing on the street in front of the drugstore and he'd turned to Graham McCloud and said, "Betcha it won't be long now, Graham boy," in Marty's voice. For some reason which she couldn't understand the words had been fraught with sinister intent.

She got up and began taking down the pictures of Valentino. She took each one from its place carefully and stacked them in a neat pile on the floor. She felt better, then, but she still couldn't sleep and after a while she went down to the kitchen and sat with her mother, watching the clean efficient motions with which Flora Graves prepared potato salad to take to Mayhills'.

Marty Mayhill's funeral was the largest ever held in Bellefonte. This was not only because he was a Mayhill, but because he was young. The young were the ones who created attention by their deaths. That he had died by his own hand had no significance. In Bellefonte, death was death.

They held the funeral at home and there were so many flowers that they lay on the front porch in the boxes they had come in, the cards neatly placed on top of each wreath and spray by Sue Mayhill's capable hands. She had come from the camp, where she taught the daughters of the rich to weave baskets and paint pottery during the idle summer months, and she took over the business of the funeral. Martin Senior sat alone in his bedroom, Buz lay in the white bed in hers, while Sue received the flowers and calls and offerings of food at the front and back doors, cool and efficient and dry-eyed. She dressed her mother for the funeral and afterwards put her into the back of the family car for the trip to the cemetery. She tied her father's tie and helped him in beside her. She stood at the grave and dropped the dirt on the casket. Then she went home and packed her suitcase.

"You're not going back?" her father said, watching her preparations in surprise.

"Yes."

"Please stay. Your mother and I need you."

She shook her head. "I've never felt at home here. I wouldn't now just because Marty's gone. You should take Mother to Europe or somewhere for a while. I'd only be in the way."

Martin shook his head. "You're all we have," he said slowly.

Sue snapped the catches on her suitcase and set it on the floor for Ham to take downstairs. "You shouldn't be in this house right now," she said. She brushed past him, then turned and came back and kissed him on the cheek. "Believe me, Daddy," she said. "It would only make her feel worse to have me here. Take her away somewhere. I'll go in and tell her goodbye."

She went to the door of the dimly lit bedroom and looked at Buz, lying still in the bed. "I'm going back to camp, Mother," she said.

Buz looked at her. "All right," she said. "You know best."

Sue came across the room and kissed her mother on the cheek. Then she went past her father, who was still standing in the doorway, and down the stairs and out of the house. "That's that," she said, looking back at the flowers and shrubs, already showing neglect from the absence of Buz's hand. She got in her coupé and drove out of the drive and onto the highway and out of Bellefonte.

"You have to marry me now," Cat said.

Graham was ready to go back to school and they were sitting in his car, telling each other goodbye for the tenth time. "I'm afraid," she said. "Something will happen if we don't now. Please."

He stared at her, watching the lines in her face as though he had never seen her before. Something in him wanted to say yes and be done with it—marry her and have her the way she wanted it. He loved her, didn't he? He thought that he did. "Not again, Cat," he said. "Please don't start it all over again."

She leaned against him and kissed him, her mouth open before it touched his. "Please, darling," she said.

"Oh hell." Graham threw his cigarette out the window and put his arms around her. "All right. Thanksgiving weekend."

She didn't want a big wedding. She wanted to be married at home. She bought the material for her dress. She wanted it white, but not long; dressy, but not impossible to wear again. She wanted Veda and Eileen to attend her and she wanted to serve punch and cake.

Graham came home the first weekend in November and they rented an apartment. It was in an old house that belonged to a cousin of Mrs. Graves and it had a living room and a bedroom and built-into-the-closets kitchen and bath. It was in very bad shape and Cat went to work on it.

Mr. McCloud was unhappy. "Are you going to quit school, boy?" he said to Graham.

"Yes," Graham said sullenly. "I'm going to sell insurance for Mr. Browne down at the First National."

"What the hell about law school?"

Graham shook his head. "I'm gonna quit. I can't go to law school and support a family. That's all there is to it. Maybe I can get into politics later anyway." He avoided looking at his father.

"Well I think you're an imbecile," Mr. McCloud said calmly, lighting a cigar. "We're not going to help you, you know."

"I know it."

"Why the hell can't that girl wait a couple of years? Maybe if she'd just wait until you're in law school we'd help you out. Don't you think she . . .?"

"She ain't gonna wait any more," Graham said. "Not after Marty and all . . ."

"What the hell's that got to do with it?"

"I don't know. It scared her, seems like. She can't get out of her mind something might happen to one of us, I guess." Graham sighed. He wasn't sure himself what was the matter with Cat. But he knew with a certainty that if he didn't marry her now he would never get her. It was a slow sure thing in himself that told him so. Now or never. Just like that. "We'll get by somehow," he said sullenly.

Mr. McCloud looked at him. "You don't have to marry that girl, do you?" he said suddenly.

Graham burst out laughing. "Cat?" he said. "Cat? Hell no, Dad. Holy hell, no." He laughed again mirthlessly. "She's a virgin all right," he said. "I wouldn't worry my head about *that*."

"Stand still, Catharine," Mattie Johnson said around the pins in her mouth. "How am I going to get your hem straight when you fidget around like that?" With the exception of Eileen's, Mattie Johnson had made every wedding dress that had been made in Bellefonte for the last fifteen years.

Eileen sat in a rocker in the littered sewing room, watching the fitting. "It's beautiful, Cat," she said. "You're going to look just wonderful."

Mattie gave a short disgusted grunt. "Not going to look any way," she said, getting up from her knees. "If she don't keep still long enough for me to pin this thing up. Short dress, indeed!" She ran a hand down a seam and stood back to look at it. "It's a pretty dress, Miss, but it's not any wedding dress. Look at those knees! Why don't you let me make this up for Sunday and do a nice long one for that wedding?"

Cat shook her head and Mattie shrugged. "Your wedding," she said shortly.

"I better go help Aunt Trudy with supper," Eileen said.

"She hasn't needed any help with it till yet that I know of," Mattie said. "Might as well stay here."

Eileen shrugged. "I'll set the table," she said, and under her breath as she went out the door, "Any idiot can manage to do that."

"'Bye Eileen," Cat said. "Come over to the apartment and help me paint."

"Sure," Eileen said. "I'll bring Van and let him help. You might get some real decorative effects that way."

Cat laughed. "I bet."

Eileen went through the living room and into the kitchen where

Miss Trudy was stirring soup on the black range. "What can I do?" she said.

"Nothing to do," Miss Trudy said. "Go on and talk to your friend."

Van was sitting on a high wooden stool beside the table, watching Miss Trudy. "Aunt Trudy makes good soup," he said solemnly.

"She sure does, Buster," Eileen said. "You gonna eat a big bowlful for supper?"

"Uh-huh." Van nodded vigorously. "Then take a bath, go to sleep."

"That's right." Eileen lifted him down and held him for a moment.

"When's Daddy coming home?" he said.

"In a little."

"He's all right here," Miss Trudy said. "Leave him alone, Eileen. He's fine."

"Sure," Eileen said. She put him back on the stool and went out on the back porch and across to her house. She took a book from the mantel and sat down to read till Ace came home.

Cat was painting the walls of her apartment blue. She had on an old smock, paint-streaked already. Eileen was helping her. She wielded the brush rapidly and efficiently, never having to go back over an area.

"You slay me, kid," Cat said. "Where did you learn to paint?"

"You learn a little bit of everything on a farm," Eileen said. "Van—stay over there."

Van looked at her and sat back down in the corner to play with the spool cars Eileen had brought with them.

"What makes him so good?" Cat said.

"Probably scared not to be, with all the authority he has to live with."

"Bad, huh?" Cat said. She put down her brush and lit a cigarette.

Eileen shrugged. "Can't be helped," she said. "They're so used to waiting on Ace hand and foot they don't think anybody else has a right to do anything."

"It would drive me nuts," Cat said. "That's the reason I wanted this place. I can see me trying to get along with that bunch of Mc-Clouds, or Graham trying to get along with Mother and Walter W., for that matter."

"Won't be long now," Eileen said. "Move. I'm ready for the second wall." She moved around and started painting again.

"I know," Cat said. She went to the window and stood looking out at the blankness of a sun-filled November afternoon. "I love September and October so," she said. "I don't see why November is so sad. Even when the sun shines—more so when the sun shines. Look at it out there now."

"Doesn't bother you this year, does it?" Eileen said.

"No. I reckon I'll always feel sort of grateful to November now. For heaven's sake. Stop that and have a cigarette. You'll have the whole place painted at this rate and then how'll I spend my time till next weekend?"

Eileen laughed. She put the brush down on a piece of newspaper and began cleaning it with paint thinner.

"Leave it," Cat said. "Let's go down to the drugstore and have a Coke."

"All right." Eileen continued to clean the brush, then put it neatly in a jar of thinner and started on Cat's.

Cat shook her head. "Be efficient, dammit," she said, lighting another cigarette.

"I guess I really don't have enough to do," Eileen said apologetically. She picked Van and his spools up from the floor and scrubbed at his face with the end of her slip.

The door banged open and Graham McCloud came into the room. Cat stared at him, her face surprised and wary at once. "Why, baby," she said. "What are you doing home this weekend? The wedding's next week, you know?" She smiled tentatively.

Eileen took one look at Graham's face and shifted Van up on her hip and went outside. She sat down in the swing in the front yard of the old two-storied house and stared at the peeling paint on the side of the gutters. She had not needed the slight waving gesture of Graham's hand to leave. She knew by his face that he wanted to be alone with Cat and she also knew that she'd better stick around for a minute. She lit a cigarette and gave Van his spools.

Graham stood still in the middle of the bare room and looked at Cat. He tried not to see the paint-smeared smock, nor the look in her eyes. She moved toward him and he opened his mouth, knowing he had to speak quick and get the hell out. There wasn't any other way.

"I can't go through with it," he said, embarrassment and shame making his voice harsh. "I thought I could, but I can't. That's all. I'm sorry I let it go this far. I'm really sorry, Cat."

She didn't say anything.

"Cat?" he said.

"What did you say?" she said slowly, watching his mouth.

"I can't," he said. "I can't marry you . . . law school . . ."

"All right," she said. There was no expression on her face at all.

"Do you understand, honey? I'm sorry. I'd give anything if this hadn't happened. But two years . . . in two more years . . ." His voice trailed off.

"Sure," she said. "In two more years. All right. I'll see you around."

I'm not going to cry, she thought. I'm not ever going to cry about this as long as I live.

He moved toward her but she brushed past him and went out the door. She went around the side of the house to where Eileen sat in the swing. "Let's go down to the drugstore," she said.

"Where's Graham?" Eileen got up and picked up the baby.

"Come on now," Cat said impatiently. "I want a Coke."

Two weeks later she came by the brown house and picked up her wedding dress. She paid Mattie Johnson for it and tucked the box under her arm and went home and bathed and got into it. She had a date with Dudley Cartwright. Four weeks later she

married him in her parents' living room. They went to Bermuda
for their honeymoon, something no one in Bellefonte had ever
done before. When they came back Dudley built her a house on
a hill on the right side of town and she kept very busy furnishing
it. She bought quite a lot of new clothes.

The library was in the city hall. You walked up a long dirty
flight of wooden steps and turned a corner and went inside. It
smelled of paste and old bindings and floor polish and they really
didn't have many books at all, but to Eileen they seemed inex-
haustible—at first. She had never read before; there had been no
books to read in her home and at school there had been too much
else to interest her. Then she had married and there was enough
to do in the cove to keep the thought of books from touching her.
Now she read every day. There was no work to do. She polished
the little house until it shone, she played with her child, she saw
her friends, but there was still a long empty space of time before
Ace came home at night. She was used to the busy days of farm
life, to the cooking of big meals, the baking of bread, the tending
of the kitchen garden, the cleaning of lamps, and the separating
of milk. Even with Ida to help her the cove work was never done.
And now, in the stillness of long afternoons, she would think of
the family who were farming her land and tending her house and
there was something like envy in the thoughts. She had known
when she married Ace that she would have to make an adjustment
to town living. There was never any question of Ace's learning
to be a farmer. He had his own work and his own life in town.
She accepted it when she accepted him, knowing there would be
the times when she longed for the country again, knowing too
she could never let him know it. So she read, she read everything.
Coming to it late she had never distinguished between fiction and
biography, history and myth. She liked it all. She began at random
in the library, reading the titles that appealed to her. Then she
read the other books by the authors she had liked the first time.
Then, overwhelmed by the wealth of words, she began with the

A's and worked through to the Z's. She read *Ben Hur*, she read *Arrowsmith*, she read *St. Elmo*, and *The Keeper of the Bees*. She read through a shelf of James Oliver Curwood and another of Gene Stratton Porter. She read *So Big* and *Chickie*, and *At the Earth's Core*, she read *The White Rose of Memphis*, and the *Travels of Marco Polo*.

Then she thought of Veda's house and the glass-fronted bookcases in the reception hall. She worked her way through the complete set of Stoddard's Lectures, a leather-bound set of Sir Walter Scott and another of Charles Dickens. Veda lent her her children's books and she enjoyed *Black Beauty* and *The Wind in the Willows* and *Alice in Wonderland* as much as *Lorna Doone* and *What Happened to Mary*.

On winter days with the fire burning in her little coal grate and her one-roomed house shining and quiet around her, she was very happy. Because she was happy Ace was happy too.

The Mayhills closed the house and went to Europe. One afternoon in late February Cat Cartwright drove up to the front of it in her new sports roadster. She stopped the car and got out and went through the hedge and up onto the porch. It was very cold and the wind cut through her short fur jacket. She sat down on the banisters and stared into the blank windows. She thought that if she could only will it hard enough the lights would go on and the music would start and she could get up and go in. She sat there until she was very cold. Then she got up and looked across the empty field toward the Johnson's. She could see smoke rising from Eileen's chimney and she thought of going over and sitting with her in the cozy warmth. She went on down the steps and got back in her car. She had trouble starting it but she succeeded, finally, and drove on past Eileen's. She thought of going to Veda's, she'd heard that she was pregnant again. But she didn't go there either. She drove on up town and parked on the square and went into the hat shop and bought a pair of red gloves. She didn't have anything to wear them with and she knew the purchase would necessitate the buying of a complete costume. The thought pleased her and she hummed to herself as she got back in the car and drove to the Coca-Cola plant to pick up Dudley.

Captain Simms sat in his room looking carefully at a piece of cellophane. He held it up and looked at the fire through it, then he placed it around his finger and looked at his finger through it, then he crumpled it carefully and noticed the noise it made. He smiled, gratified. He had liked the idea of cellophane since they had first begun talking about it several years ago. Now it was here, on cigarettes and bread and candy, and the thought of it made him feel good, as all new things did. He had a fine picture in his mind of life starting somewhere in a lush jungle and continuing in a beautiful straight line toward now and on toward a miraculous future which could contain anything, but which would be beautiful and terrible and which would go on.

He was very thankful for the past year. It had been full of many things, the biggest being that young idiot crossing the Atlantic Ocean in an airplane. It made him happy just to think of it. He wished he had been born a little later so that he too might have ridden in airplanes, not just once or twice at a carnival as though it were some sort of new-fangled and more dangerous ride, but as an everyday thing just to get around. He felt sure that day was going to come. Probably by the time the new baby Veda was carrying was grown up that would be the way he would travel.

He got up and went to look out his window at the bare yard. It was a fine winter, cold and bleak and beautiful. He wished he could live a hundred more years. He thought they might get to the moon by then. He felt that was on the line too. A going out. He liked to think of that. If one young fool wanted to fly a little machine across all that ocean a bigger young fool would get the idea of flying a bigger machine across that bigger ocean. *Fish out of water* . . . He chuckled. Captain Simms could not believe in the theory of evolution—he had been raised a hard-shell Baptist, and he had to take the other side in the Scopes case—but in his heart he believed in evolution. He believed in the evolution of life.

He could chuckle at his own musing no matter what he gave lip service to.

He thought of Veda and Morgan and he hoped for them suddenly. He hoped for the child Veda carried. He thought about Eileen Holder and he remembered that she was pregnant too. She had been as excited about Lindbergh as he had. He remembered her last spring, driving into town like a maniac in her car because her radio wasn't working and she wanted to hear whether he made it. Veda had laughed at her. But he hadn't. He wanted Lindbergh to make it too. It seemed to him a lot healthier to be excited about than, say, the death of that Italian fellow some time back. They'd all pulled long faces and wept and mourned about that face on a screen dying. He'd liked Eileen's being glad about Lindbergh and his machine. He'd liked it when she married again too. She was as pretty a little thing as he'd ever seen and she looked like she ought to have a dozen children. All those children to fly in the flying machines. He grunted. He wanted his coffee and the stairs weren't quite as easy to negotiate as they had been. He went down to the kitchen grumbling at his legs because they weren't going to last another hundred years. "I wonder why that fellow wants to sit on flagpoles?" he said half aloud. "It'd take a body more than a hundred more years to figger out the human mind."

Beachhead

Wednesday afternoon was Eileen's half-day off from her job at the hotel and she had taken Bambi into town to see a Walt Disney movie. It was a hot still day and the town was shuttered into silence by the closed stores and banks and offices. They came out of the theater into the harsh sunlight and walked down the sidewalk together, sniffing the smells of hot tar and dust. "Mama's sick," Bambi said.

"What?" Eileen looked at her sharply.

"She's sick. She stayed in bed today and cried."

"Has she been sick before?" Eileen said. She knew of no illness of her daughter's, no reason for sickness, had heard nothing of sickness from Veda herself, or from the children, and for a moment she felt afraid. Then she smiled. She must be pregnant again, she thought.

Bambi watched her. "Not sick to throw up," she said.

"Do you always read my mind?" Eileen said.

"Sometimes." Bambi smiled.

"Well, we'll take her something from the drugstore," Eileen said. "What do you think she'd like to have?"

"Candy," Bambi said.

"Who? Your mother or you?"

"Both of us."

They went into the drugstore and Eileen bought a pound of peanut brittle and a box of suckers. "That'll take care of everybody," she said. They got into the car and drove out to the beach. The tide was out and the wet sand lay grayly smoothed along the edge of surf. Umbrellas dotted the upper beach and automobiles drove along the hard-packed sand above the surf line. "That's such a stupid business," Eileen said, annoyed as always by the state law that permitted automobiles on a public beach where children should be able to run in safety.

"We always stay away from the cars," Bambi said.

"You better."

She parked behind her house and looked toward Veda's. Cliff's car was there and he and the younger children were stringing fishing lines on the back steps. Bambi broke away from Eileen and ran toward them. "Daddy's home," she yelled shrilly, her feet throwing up sand behind her as she ran.

Eileen followed her. Cliff looked up when she came up to him. "What's the matter with Veda?" she said.

He shook his head, looking at the children, and she sat down on a piece of driftwood.

"She's all right," he said, seeing her anxious expression. "Nerves."

"I know about that," Bambi said. "That's when you holler and get mad about nothing."

"Who's talking to you, bright eyes?" Cliff said.

"Veda's never had any nerves in her life," Eileen said. "My children aren't nervous."

"Just a manner of speaking," Cliff said. "Everybody's nervous these days, Eileen."

"I'm not."

Cliff grinned. "I know you're not, madam. But you have a built-in stabilizer. Everybody isn't so lucky."

Eileen lit a cigarette. "All of you think too much about your own minds," she said. "It isn't good for you. If there's one thing I've learned from living it's not to worry too damned much about what goes on in your own head."

Cliff stood up. "All of you go in and get your suits on and we'll take a dip before supper," he said. They scrambled up the steps: Bambi and Lyn and Tommy and Cliffy, brown and lithe and loud. The screen door banged behind them.

"O.K.," Eileen said. "What is it?"

"What I'm doing," Cliff said.

"Making rockets go up? My God, I think it's wonderful. I

thought Veda did too. She certainly raved enough about it to begin with. My, the times I've had to listen to what a bright young man you are, Cliff Taylor."

"Yeah. It's the payload that worries her."

"What?"

"Missiles, sweetie."

"Oh. That. Chicken Licken again."

"Sorry. You are a beautiful, young and intelligent mother-in-law, but there are times when I don't follow you at all."

"Chicken Licken. Surely you remember that. 'The sky is falling. Let us go and tell the king.' "

"This time, though, it looks like it might fall."

"Cliff, it always has."

"Well, that's the story anyway. She's been sort of funny about it all summer. I haven't said anything 'cause I didn't want to worry you. I don't think my doing anything else would help, either. She's got the real bug about it."

Eileen sighed. "To each era its own devils," she said.

"I don't know," Cliff said. "She's got a lot of company with this one. It's like the old story of pushing a button and ending the world. You start worrying about how many trigger-happy people there are."

"I know. But you can't let it stop you."

"From what?"

"Living. What else? I'm going in and talk to her."

"Don't tell her I told you. She has some sort of idea you don't realize how bad things are and she doesn't want to be the one to tell you."

Eileen laughed. "Your own children never really know you, do they?" she said. "Veda ought to know enough about me by now to know I can't live right down the beach from a bunch of hot-rod scientists and not know what they're up to. Besides, we went through this once, back when Hiroshima happened."

"She remembers that but she thinks you look at it naïvely."

"Ah, the young," Eileen said. "I wish to God I remembered

what naïveté was like." She grinned at Cliff and went into the house.

Veda was in the kitchen. She was wearing shorts and her hair was pulled back from her face with a ribbon. She looked pale and tired.

"What you having for supper?" Eileen said.

"Hi, Mama. Shrimp again, I reckon. It's the only thing they'll all eat without a mumble."

"I brought you a present." She handed over the two boxes of candy. "You want the kids to have this now or after supper?"

"Better put it up, I guess." Veda took the suckers and put them on top of the kitchen cabinet. She opened the peanut brittle and broke off a piece. Then she smiled at Eileen. "Just a bite before supper . . ."

"Uh-huh." Eileen sat down on a stool. "You feel bad?"

"No. Well, yes. Sort of."

"Not pregnant again?"

"No!"

"Well, you don't have to sound so vehement about it. I thought you wanted a dozen."

"I think four's enough."

"So do I. You're the one that used to want a dozen."

Veda began peeling onions. "Who snitched?" she said.

"Bambi," Eileen said. "She said you were sick."

"Well I'm not. I just felt bad this afternoon. It's so damned hot."

"You want me to fix supper?"

"No. I'm fine. I want you to stay and eat with us though."

"All right."

"No fuss? That's not like you, Mama. Where's your independence?"

"I happen to want to spend the evening with my daughter and family. That's all."

"Don't kid me. You think I'm sick. Honestly, it's just the heat."

"It is hot," Eileen said. "I had a letter from Betty Al this morning."

"She say anything about getting married?"

"No. Give her time."

"Lord, Mama, she's twenty-six."

"She's happy. Don't worry about her. If she wants to go to school for the rest of her life that's her business."

Veda shrugged. "Maybe she's right at that," she said.

"Well, I could use a few more grandchildren," Eileen said. "I only have ten. A round dozen would be nice."

"Set the table, will you?" Veda said.

They ate on the porch because the kids were still in their bathing suits. After the younger ones were put to bed they sat on at the table, drinking coffee.

"When you going to send us up another night-light, Cliff?" Eileen said.

He looked at her. "You know I can't talk about that."

"I know. I was just thinking . . ."

"Thinking what, Mama?" Veda said impatiently. "You're always starting something and breaking off when we start to listen."

"About old Captain Simms," Eileen said. "How he'd love to have seen these rockets."

"Why?" Veda said. She was interested in spite of herself, although she'd told herself all during supper that sooner or later her mother was going to try something to make her feel better and she was determined not to listen. Her mother was always so calm and logical and certain about things that it made disagreeing with her impossible. The best recourse was to not listen; but tonight, as always, all her life, she knew that she would listen because—dammit—she wanted to hear what Eileen had to say.

"Oh, because he was always so interested in anything new," Eileen said. "He used to say he wanted to live a hundred more years just to see what they'd think of next."

"Well I bet he could have done without some of the things they've thought of this go-round," Veda said.

"I don't know," Eileen said. "He was interested in the bad things as much as the good things. I guess he was just interested, period."

"You know, I remember him," Veda said.

"I don't reckon anybody that ever saw him doesn't," Eileen said.

"I remember him because of something he said to me at a birthday party once . . . a party for Martha Ann." She got up and went into the kitchen to reheat the coffee.

Cliff made a face at Eileen. "Devious," he whispered.

Eileen ignored him. "Did I ever tell you about the time he bought himself a car?" she said.

"Ma'am, you've told that a hundred times that I know of," Veda called.

"I don't remember it," Cliff said. "Tell it."

"Yes," Bambi said. "Tell it, Ma'am." She had been sitting quietly in the corner of the couch, trying not to be noticed and put to bed.

"What are you doing there, little one?" Cliff said. "Isn't it past bedtime?"

She shook her head. "Let me hear Ma'am tell a story—just one— then I'll go."

Veda poured coffee and handed around the peanut brittle. "Yes, you too," she said, passing the box to Bambi. "Thirty more minutes. Then bed."

Bambi nodded.

Eileen lit a cigarette and sipped her coffee. Through the screen the sound of the ocean came, soft and regular in the dark. The coffee tasted very good and she felt warm and cozy, except for the nagging worry about Veda.

"Well," she said. "His son and daughter-in-law were against cars from the word go. They wouldn't let your Aunt Veda within a mile of one. They thought the only way a girl could get in trouble was to ride in a car, and if she did ride in a car she was automatically in trouble. Captain Simms had some money of his own and he wanted a car. He wanted one because they were new and different and would go fast. So he bought him one. He just drew some money out of the bank and went down to the Ford place and bought one off the floor and had the salesman drive it out to the house. Then

he took out the money and paid him for it. He had him park it on
the edge of the back pasture behind the house.

"Mozel and R. V. came running. They saw Captain drive up in
that car and they knew what he'd done. They tried to talk him into
letting the salesman take it back, but he just sat there with his
hands folded over his cane and grinned at them. Then he turned
to the salesman and said, 'I can't drive this contraption yet, so I
reckon you'll have to walk back to town, son, but first you just
show me how to get 'er to start.' "

"How old was he then, Mama?" Veda said.

"Lord, at least eighty. But you'd never have known it.

"Well, the salesman showed him how to crank it and set the
spark and all— It was a lot harder to start a car in those days,
Bambi. Your Aunt Veda was hanging over the back fence watching
all this but scared to come down because she knew how mad her
mother and daddy were. Well, the salesman let Captain Simms
try starting the car and then he said he'd show him how to drive
her and Captain said, 'No, son, you get on back to work. I'll learn
to drive her myself.'

"The boy got down and walked back to town and Captain
Simms just sat there in the car looking at R. V. and Mozel. Then
he said, 'I reckon you old folks had better get out of the way. I'm
fixing to drive this contraption across that pasture.'

"Well, they stepped back—there wasn't much else they could
do—and he climbed down and cranked the car and got in and
started across the pasture. Veda said he was doing fine, but he forgot about the branch. It cut through the pasture in three places,
winding in and out, and Captain hit 'em all. He went bumpity-
bump across the first branch ditch, and hell for leather to the next
one and across that too. His cane fell out of the car and his hat
fell off and he was yelling, 'Jerusalem' at the top of his lungs.

"Mozel and R. V. ran after him. Veda climbed over the fence
and ran after him too. Then the cow stood up and he had to turn
the wheel to miss her. Veda always said that damned cow just
stood there looking astonished. She said all her life she'd thought
cows were the most placid-looking creatures in the world, but that

cow looked astonished as all get-out. She didn't move, she just stood stolid and waited for that tin lizzie to run her down on the hoof. Captain missed her but he had to turn into the third branch crossing to do it and he wasn't going fast enough to bump on over it like he had the other two. The car stood straight up on its nose in the branch, the motor grinding away, and Captain standing practically on his head. They all came running to get him out but by the time they got there he had already climbed out. He stalked past them without even looking at them, retrieved his hat from the middle of the pasture and his cane from the far side, and started for the barn.

" 'Father!' R. V. shouted. 'Where the hell do you think you're going now?'

" 'I'm gonna hitch up your buggy,' Captain said with dignity, 'and drive over to niggertown and get me a chauffeur. I'm too old to learn to drive it, I reckon, but I ain't too old to set back and ride.' "

They were all laughing when Eileen finished the story. "You're making that up," Cliff said. "I don't believe half of it."

"It's the absolute truth," Eileen said. "He was a fabulous old man. I wouldn't have missed knowing him for anything on earth."

"Did he get him a chauffeur?" Bambi said.

"He sure did. A gangly Negro boy named Nip that was as proud of that car as if he owned it. He'd sit up there driving like he had on livery, with Captain Simms in the back seat poking him every once in a while with his cane to tell him to speed it up a little. They used to drive all over the county. They drove all the way to Druid City once for Captain Simms to see his brother—took them a whole damned hog when they went, cut up and hanging from the sides of that car like it was a butcher shop."

"Did Aunt Veda ever get to ride in it?" Bambi said.

"Well, she ran off and got married in it," Eileen said. "But that's another story. Now you go to bed." She picked Bambi up and took her into the house. When she came back Veda was sitting next to Cliff on the couch. "Why don't you spend the night?" she said.

"Think I'm too lazy to walk fifty yards up the beach?"

"No. Thought you might want to tell us some more tales," Veda said.

"Don't be sassy."

"I'll walk over with you," Cliff said.

"Oh, nonsense." Eileen picked up her cigarettes. "You can lend me some matches though. I'm out."

Veda got them for her. "Want the flashlight?"

"Heavens no. The moon's bright as day."

"Haven't you ever been afraid of anything?" Veda said.

"Are you kidding? I'm human, am I not?" She went down the steps and started across the beach. "Veda," she called.

"Yessum."

"You chirk up."

"Oh, Mama."

"You heard me."

She went on across the sand to her house. She didn't feel like going to bed so she put her coffee pot on and found an old cinnamon bun in the cabinet. She took her coffee and bun to the porch and sat down to eat. Down the beach she could see the lights going out at Veda and Cliff's. "Poor Baby," she said. "I wish I knew what to tell her. We have nothing to fear but fear itself. It's a fine phrase, but how do you tell the frightened what it means?"

PART II

My Blue Heaven

1. *1931 Van*

In the year 1931 the winter was long. Looked back on, it seemed to be a year of winter, a time of gray and black and white with low-hanging clouds and cutting winds. The fires burned low and fitfully and cars passed slowly in the hardened roads bearing the marks of mud and time.

At night the lights from the picture show splashed a circle of light onto the darkened square and the light in the newspaper office burned late as the paper was put to bed in the morning quiet. The house lights were turned off early behind drawn shades and Bellefonte slept uneasily.

In the cove house strangers swept Eileen's wide-boarded floors and stored what provisions there were in the too-large pantries. The Mayhill house stood black and silent on an unkempt lawn; and across the hedge Van Maynard lived with his mother and stepfather and his brother and sister, in a one-room house with a grate fire and colored pictures on the wall.

They had oatmeal for breakfast even on Saturday mornings now and Van didn't like oatmeal. Something about it made him feel horrible inside, made him want to scream and beat his fists on the table. It hurt his chest. When he was much older he found out the word for the way oatmeal made him feel . . . frustrated. Now he only knew that they had it a lot. That was because his Aunt Trudy sold the eggs.

They ate at the kitchen table in Aunt Trudy and Aunt Mattie's big house. It was covered with blue oilcloth and the dishes were blue too with the story about the Chinese princess on them. Sometimes he'd take the oatmeal and push it around and make islands and mountains and rivers and lakes but Aunt Mattie would catch him and he'd have to stop. He had to sit in a chair now because Veda got the stool and Martin the high chair. He had to go to school too and he didn't like that either.

Inside the school it was dark and smelled of chalk and dirty people and something they put on the floor. His room was sunny though. There were charts and pictures and blackboards. There was Miss Benson too. She wore black dresses and a comb in her hair and she was all right. Reading was all right too.

What he didn't like was drawing and numbers. What he didn't like most was lunch time. Mama always fixed him sandwiches in a brown paper sack. There'd be peanut butter and jelly and cheese. Sometimes there'd be ham, but not much. Some of them had biscuits and ham. He would have liked to trade with them for some of that, but he didn't like to ask. They ate at the desks and you could still smell the chalk and what they put on the floor and the people and what they had for their lunch. There was something else too; it was soup. They made it downstairs in the lunchroom and sold it for a nickel. He didn't get it because he had lunch but some of them did. The boy across the aisle did. He wore overalls that were ragged at the bottoms and his hair wasn't cut. The soup smelled real strong and not very good and he could look over and see that it had pieces of tomatoes all shredded up in it. Then he wouldn't want his lunch. Even the oatmeal at breakfast was better. It smelled all right anyway.

When he got home from school Aunt Trudy and Aunt Mattie would give him something, milk or sometimes a Coca-Cola and crackers. Then he'd have to play with Veda. Mama was going to have another baby. He knew that because she was fat in front. Last year the cow had gotten fat and had a calf and they had all been excited because that made more milk and they didn't have to sell it like the eggs. He hoped the baby would be a big brother to play with. Veda was always falling down and crying and Martin was too little to play at all.

Sometimes Aunt Veda that Veda was named for would be there when he got home from school. She was real thin and pale and wore lots of lavender and pink, colors that made him head-achey. She made him feel sad too. She was pretty but she sighed a lot. She had a little girl like Veda and he'd have to play with both of them. Her name was Martha Ann and she was his cousin. Some-times Aunt Veda brought them cheese tid-bits. Sometimes she'd cry and Mama would cluck her tongue at her. Then they would talk and talk. Grown people always talked and talked.

Aunt Veda'd say, —Daddy just don't do any good with the mules any more. And Mama'd say, —Nobody's doing much good with anything. —Morgan wants us to move and I don't see how we can, Aunt Veda'd say. And Mama'd say, —I gave up on *that* busi-ness a long time ago.

Van knew what that business was. Mama wanted them to have a house somewhere, a big house like Aunt Trudy and Aunt Mattie, but Daddy said they were doing pretty good to have something rent-free.

Daddy made the paper and Daddy was fine. He was tall and he squinted up his eyes when he talked and he was always kissing Mama. He brought them suckers with Amos and Andy faces, and sometimes he'd take them all in the car to Doc's to eat ham-burgers. That made Aunt Trudy and Aunt Mattie mad though, so they didn't do it very much. The best thing about Daddy was he didn't fuss. He'd get mad and spank sometimes but he didn't worry and fuss like everybody else.

Aunt Cat was another grown person who didn't fuss. She was the most wonderful grown person he knew. She always looked beautiful and smelled good. She wore pretty clothes and long earrings that dangled around her face when she leaned over to talk to him. When she came everybody was happy. She always brought presents, candy and flowers, and perfume for Mama. She'd come in with a big bunch of flowers in her hand and say,

—Find me something to put these in. Then she'd take out a big sack of candy and say, —I bought this stuff and then didn't want it at all . . . and give it to him and Veda.

Aunt Cat didn't have any little boys and girls. She was married to Mr. Cartwright who worked at the Coca-Cola plant and that never did seem right to him. Mr. Cartwright was like an old man and Aunt Cat wasn't an old lady. But Mama said Yes, that was right. Aunt Cat was Mrs. Cartwright.

One time he had made Aunt Cat feel bad. Everybody had been talking about Graham McCloud coming home to practice law. Daddy had put a piece about it in the paper and the next night Uncle Graham came. He was big and had a loud voice. He stood with his elbow on the mantel and talked about the things grown people talked about. He talked about Democrats and Publicans and Governor Roosevelt and Former Governor Smith; and about court cases and venyous. That sounded like it ought to mean something, but it didn't that he could see. Then he talked about the Depression. Everybody talked about that some. It had something to do with no eggs for breakfast and sewing up stockings.

Then Aunt Cat came. She was coming in the door laughing and talking and with a sack of Hershey bars; then she just stopped and stood there and she laughed the way grown people did sometimes when it wasn't really funny at all. Uncle Graham said, —Well, hello Cat and she said, —Hi Graham, and went over and sat down on the footstool Nannie Holder had made out of tin cans. And she didn't give them the candy. She just sat there holding onto it. Then Uncle Graham didn't talk about venyous and four closings any more but about funny things because everybody laughed and talked. But Aunt Cat never did give him the candy. Then he said, —Why isn't Aunt Cat married to Uncle Graham? They match. That's when he made Aunt Cat feel bad. He knew because everybody quit laughing and talking and Daddy made him get to bed. He didn't mean anything bad. He wanted to say that because Mama had just explained to him about things matching and he knew Aunt Cat didn't match Mr. Cartwright.

When he got up the next morning there were the candy bars on the dresser where Aunt Cat had left them and that made him feel terribly bad and he gave them all to Veda and wouldn't eat any. Then Mama tried to tell him about how Aunt Cat was going to marry Uncle Graham once, but didn't and married Mr. Cartwright instead, and he thought that was pretty funny of Aunt Cat.

*   *   *   *   *   *   *

> Our young friend, Attorney Mc-
> Cloud, seems to be making good
> headway with his practice here.
> Lawyers are one set of men who
> usually give the young newcomer
> "a break" and especially in Belle-
> fonte. I told McCloud that Ham-
> bone says "De lawyer I likes is de
> one whut kin fuss de most for
> twenty-five dollahs!" Big fees are
> on the list of Vanishing Americani-
> zations now and you'd be surprised
> how much Blackstone a hundred
> smackers will buy you when in
> trouble.
>
> —From the *Maynard County Mast*

*   *   *   *   *   *   *

His Aunt Mattie had money in her house all the time. That was because she sewed for people and she made people give her the money before they got the dress. He knew that because Martha Ann told him. She said her mother had a dress made and Aunt Mattie was mean about it. Aunt Mattie had a round tin box with the money in it on the shelf by the lamp that had all the things stuck on it. It was a fine lamp. It had a dog on a silver chain and shells and colored glass and even a tiny Coke bottle. He would stand on a chair and look at it. That's how he saw the money. He told Mama and she said he must never never never touch Aunt Mattie's things, and he hadn't. He'd just looked.

Sometimes Aunt Mattie would take money out of the tin box and give it to him to go downtown and get thread for her at Hertz

Bargain House. He liked to go there. It was a brick store with a red front and big black letters on it, H B H, with little letters in between. He asked Mama what the little letters said. She laughed and said Hurry Back Honey was what it said. It was dark inside and smelled like material. There were bolts and bolts of it.

He liked Mrs. Hertz. She was a big lady with a mole on her chin. She would thump the bolts out on the counter and turn them, plump plump plump, and there would be a pile of cloth that she'd take and measure quick on a yardstick nailed to the counter. Then she'd wrap it in a pink paper with Hurry Back Honey on it and ring up the money on the cash register. Then she'd put her hands on her hips and say, —What can I do for you today, Mr. Johnson? to him. Lots of people called him that, but his name was Maynard. He knew that was important because he was the last Maynard there was. Mama said he ought to keep the name, but that when he got older if he wanted to be Johnson like Veda and Martin he could.

After he went to school he could read the things it said on all the little cards all over the store. They said: Outing 10¢, and Special! Sweaters! 49¢, and Pillow Slips Nice Quality 5¢ No one else ever did this!, and No. 2 Lamp Chimneys 5¢, and Khaki Cloth all colors Look it up in Mail Order Books. He knew that 5¢ was a nickel and would buy a candy bar or an ice-cream cone or a hamburger. After that he wasn't sure of money.

On Saturdays he got to go to Mr. Hudson's grocery store with Aunt Trudy. The grocery store was dark inside too. It smelled of all kinds of good things. Aunt Trudy would go to the back where Mr. Hudson was doing things with big pieces of cow and pig and Mr. Hudson'd take out a new folded paper bag and write figures on it. Then Aunt Trudy'd give Mr. Hudson the eggs and poke at the meat. Van would look at the jars of candy while Mr. Hudson got sugar out of a big barrel and put it in a sack with a string around the neck, and coal oil out of a big can into their little one, and coffee out of a big machine. They he'd say, —Here's your free potatoes, and push a little string sack across the counter. Then he'd reach into a round glass jar and get a big yellow cookie and give it to him and they'd go home.

All the way home Aunt Trudy would say, —Thirty cents a pound for coffee! Hmmp! Hmmp! He could just see a little sign like in Hertz Bargain House saying Coffee 30¢ Hmmp! Hmmp! —How do you spell Hmmp? he asked Aunt Trudy. And she said, —Don't be sassy, boy.

He always saved The House for Saturday afternoon. The House belonged to him and he never took Veda there . . . she was too little anyway. He never played at The House during the week either. He saved that for the one day when he could play in the afternoon by himself.

He'd put a piece of cornbread in his pocket, in case the dinner wore off, and collect what he wanted to take with him. Sometimes it was marbles, sometimes his car with the real rubber wheels that Santa Claus brought last year. He would put that in his other pocket. Then he'd look all around and go behind the hedge. There was a big hedge all along the side of their house. It was a good place to play. You could pretend it was a tunnel or a cave or a train; but on Saturdays he went right on through to the other side.

On the other side was a whole lot full of weeds. They were fun to play in too. They could be a jungle or a forest. They played Tarzan in them in the summer. Now they were dry and brown, and whispered. They scratched too when you tried to crawl through them. They'd scrape on the back of his hands where he was cold and hurt like everything. Then he pretended he was a prisoner who had to escape through spears. After the weeds there were a bunch of trees and then a lot of bushes, and then . . . The House. If he came in the back way there was the desert. It was a flat red place where nothing grew much but straggly grass and around it were lots of bushes. In the summer they had flowers, now they were dry too.

Past the desert and the little houses and the well was The House. He had never been inside it. It was locked and besides he knew you weren't supposed to go inside other people's houses. He thought that Mama knew he played over here, but she wouldn't like it if he ever went in. He never had. He looked in the windows though. He would climb on the trellises and look inside where the curtains were pulled back. He could see into the kitchen. It was big and full of white iceboxes and stoves and things. He could see into the front hall too where there was a big stairs that went up a long way. He could see part of a room where there were white sheets over everything. It made him feel funny to see the house so quiet. It was such a big house and so empty. He had always lived in such a little house with so many people. Still, it wasn't the sort of house he'd want to live in. It was the sort of house you looked into on Saturday afternoons and went away from.

The lady came the day of the autogyro. That is how he always thought of her ... with the autogyro, as though it had left her on the spot, going away into the sky with its shining whirling blades.

Daddy knew about the autogyro the day before it came because the man let the paper know. It was that way about a lot of things. The man's name was Captain Tracey and he had flown across the ocean to Rome, Italy, in it. The day he came they got to go downtown to the square to see him put on a show. They sat on the square in Daddy's car and looked up and waited and waited and waited and then he came. He had never seen a real plane before. He had seen the Zeppelin that flew over one time and that looked like a big silver pig in the sky, he'd seen the pictures of the airplanes in books and papers and once at the picture show. But this was the first real thing that flew that he ever saw close.

It came into the sky over the City Hall, low and big and beautiful, with the thing on top going round and round in the sun and the Captain sitting in it like he was outside. He flew it right over the courthouse and made it stand still in the air. Then he came straight down to the ground in it and they all got to go up and look at it and get the Captain's autograph.

Captain Tracey was a big man with a mustache and a helmet
on his head. He talked to Daddy like they knew each other and
leaned over and shook his hand. Then Uncle Graham came up
and he and Captain Tracey started all that talking about Democrats and Publicans. Then they talked about the autogyro instead
of cars to get to Hunter City because they couldn't get the highway put in.

Grown people all talked about that too. They wanted a new
highway to Hunter City ... all except Aunt Mattie and Aunt
Trudy. They didn't because they said it would take half their yard.
He couldn't see how a highway could take anybody's yard, but
that's what they said.

Just as the Captain was going to get back in his plane and go
up again here came old Captain Simms just a-tapping along with
his cane and laughing fit to bust. He and the airplane Captain
started talking about the plane. They looked at the propeller and
the blades on top and the instrument panel. The air Captain got
so excited he got right out of the plane again and talked and
waved his arms and pointed and bent over and showed things
underneath the plane. Then he let Captain Simms climb in it and
look at the things inside.

Then he said, —Why are they both Captain? and Mama said,
—Lord the questions you think of, like she always did. But after
they got home she tried to explain it to him about the different
wars.

*　　*　　*　　*　　*　　*　　*

BOND ISSUE MEETS
2–TO–1 DEFEAT

Gov. Miller Now Advocates 3½¢
Additional Gas Tax to
"Pay-As-We-Go"

The proposed $25,000,000 road
bond issue for Alabama was defeated in Alabama Tuesday by
about two-to-one or even greater

majority, only a few counties going for the bond issue.

Maynard County voted favoring the bond issue by a small majority. Bellefonte handed up a three-to-one vote favoring the bonds.

Governor Miller opposed the issue, and stated publicly today after its defeat that he would advocate the legislature passing laws to levy an additional 3½ cents per gallon tax on gas to create a "pay as you go" plan for road building in Alabama.

Maynard County was interested in the bond issue in the belief we would be able to get at least a part of the Lee Highway built through the county, but now it would appear we are in for a long wait to couple to that long wait we have already experienced.

—From the *Maynard County Mast*

*   *   *   *   *   *   *

He was so excited that day he could hardly eat his dinner and Aunt Trudy kept saying, —Have some more beans, Van. I don't cook all day for you to mess around with your food. Daddy winked and said, —You thinking about flying one of those things, boy? He nodded and tried to eat up all the beans because it made Aunt Trudy mad to throw anything out. —I saw that old fool Captain Simms down there trying himself in that thing, Aunt Mattie said. —You'd think he would stay home sometimes at his age. —I reckon he's got as much curiosity as the rest of us, Mama said. Then Aunt Mattie left the table and everybody looked mad, so he ate up the beans real quick and left too.

He hadn't meant to go to The House that afternoon. It was cold and he was still excited about the Captain's autogyro. He wanted to go out back and play flying on the chicken coops, but if Mama and Aunt Mattie were going to be mad and funny he thought he'd go.

He knew as soon as he crawled through the bushes into the back yard that something was different. It felt different. Then he saw the car. It was a long black car with a silver lady on the front of the hood. He looked at it for a while, thinking that it was really his day to see things. Then he went around to the front and saw that the door was open.

It surprised him so much that he just stood there. There were rugs hanging over the banisters on the porch and then Aunt Callie Perkins that worked for them sometimes on canning days came out the door with a white thing tied around her head and said, —What you doin' there, Van? You best go on home now. —I'm not hurting anything, he said. —You go on, boy, she said and shook her mop out over the banisters.

—What is it, Callie? a lady's voice said. Then she came out the door. She wasn't like any lady that he'd ever seen before. Something about her was like Aunt Cat, but she was an older lady, and he couldn't imagine Aunt Cat ever being an older lady. This lady was thin and wore a pretty dress and a hat with a little bird on it and earrings that dangled down like Aunt Cat's. She was smoking a cigarette in a long thing like Mae West at the picture show and when she saw him she came down the steps and leaned over, like Aunt Cat did, and said, —Well, hello. Who're you? She smelled good like Aunt Cat too.

—My name's Van Maynard, he said. She frowned a little and stood back like grown people did and looked at his face and said, —Is your mother named Eileen? That was Mama's name, so he nodded and she looked sad a minute and said, —How old are you? How's your mother? all together. He said, —Six and she's fine. She's going to have a new baby because she's fat in front.

Then the lady put her head back and laughed and Callie said, —Boy, that ain't no way to talk. But the lady said, —That's fine.

He liked her, so he said, —I live right over there and I play here Saturday. Is it your house?

—Yes. But I don't live in it much any more.

—It's an awfully big house, he said.

—Yes. She looked off at nothing the way they did. Then she said, —I don't want to sell it.

—I saw a man in an autogyro today, he said.

The lady looked back at him and smiled again. —You certainly look like your mother around the eyes, she said. He said, —Yessum, because everybody said that to him.

The lady took one cigarette out of the holder and put another one in and lit it. Then she sat down on the steps. —Would your mother let you go down and have an ice cream with me? she said.

—I don't know, he said. —Everybody's funny about buying good things to eat.

When he said that the lady jumped up and stamped her foot and said, —Oh damn this thing. Damn this money thing. I will buy you a banana split. She went into the house and came back with a pocketbook. She started rummaging through it and taking out things for powder and letters and papers and handkerchiefs. They she took out a little leather purse and looked in it and said, —Yes. A banana split.

Then Callie came back out on the porch and said, —Mr. Martin say you to stay here till he get back from down't the gin.

The lady looked real mad at that and said, —Oh, yes. I might get into trouble at the ice-cream parlor. And Callie said, —He say. The lady said, —Oh what the hell. I'm sorry, Van Maynard. But if I want to keep my house I have to do what Mr. Mayhill wants, just like you have to do things for your Mama and Daddy, huh? He nodded because she looked like she wanted him to. Then she reached into the purse and took out a quarter ... a whole big shining quarter ... and put it in his hand. —You go buy the banana split, she said. —That is what that quarter is for. That is the only thing it's for. You tell your Mama and she'll understand. A quarter only for banana splits. Then she turned around and went into the house and shut the door.

—You go on home now, Van, Aunt Callie said. He said, —All right, and went home.

The really funny thing about it was that Mama cried when he told her about it and when Daddy came she talked to him and he took him to the drugstore and he had the banana split. It was the first one he ever had. It had three kinds of ice cream and pineapple and whipped cream and a cherry on top. After he ate it he got a dime back. It was his good-luck dime and he kept it a long long time.

He didn't see the lady any more. They closed the house back up and went away. One night he heard Mama and Daddy talking about her after he was supposed to be asleep. Mama said, —It's a shame. They say she's never sober any more. Daddy said, —Well, that's a lot of money to lose. Mama said, —Money doesn't have anything to do with it, Ace. And Daddy said, —It has to do with everything now.

*   *   *   *   *   *   *

We were glad to see our old friends, Mr. and Mrs. Martin Mayhill back in town last Saturday. Mr. Martin was here to transact business with Mr. Roy Summers down at the gin. He says he still has faith in the economy of this country of ours and he's holding on to his Bellefonte holdings. Mr. and Mrs. Mayhill have spent the last several years in Europe and Martin says we don't know what we've got to be thankful for till we've seen how some of those other folks live. The Mayhills have left for a visit to the West Coast, but we hope to have them back here soon in the old house on what we hope will be the new Lee Highway.

—From the *Maynard County Mast*

*   *   *   *   *   *   *

The new baby came. It was red and had a fuzzy head like all of them. It was a brother like Martin; they called him Holder. Mama was in bed with a blue thing on over her gown and a ribbon around her hair. Aunt Veda came and brought some of those knitted things. Martha Ann came with her and she looked at the baby and said he was awful little and went to play with his lead soldiers. Aunt Veda gave Mama a silver dollar from Captain Simms. He had sent them all one. His was put up in the cedar chest with his old baby shoes and sometimes Mama would let him take it out and look at it. Aunt Veda brought Coca-Colas. They all had one and she took a B.C. with hers. He liked to watch the way she held up the little paper and tapped it and threw the powder on her tongue. —I want a B.C., he said. Aunt Veda laughed and said, —You don't have headaches, do you? And he said, —No I don't. Martha Ann came over and said that *she* did real important like so he pushed her and Mama sat up in bed and said, —Stop that now this minute, Van. So he went out back by himself and let all the women look at the new baby.

It was better when Aunt Cat came. She brought a box of candy and flowers and a silk cover for the baby. She sang him a song. Sometimes Aunt Cat would do that. She'd sit in the rocker and sing songs for them about Yes We Have No Bananas and Alice Blue Gown. She sang about Barney Google with the goo-goo-googly eyes, this time, and Mama said, —Do you remember the words to every song that ever was? Aunt Cat said, —All *those* songs anyway. Mama shook her head and said, —Oh Cat!

Aunt Cat said, —Well looks like it's going to be me soon. And Mama said, —What are you talking about? And Aunt Cat said, —Yep. Finally. I'm p.g. Mama said, —Thank heavens. It's just what you need. Aunt Cat said, —Oh yeah? And Mama said, —Yeah. Definitely. Aunt Cat said, —I don't know. And Mama said, —I do. You'll see. Aunt Cat said, —I sure will. I hope it's a girl.

Then Aunt Cat looked at him and said, —Why don't you go out and play, Van? He said, —I don't know what it means if it's like that anyway. Then Aunt Cat hugged him and said, —You're such a fine boy. Maybe I want a boy after all. He said, —Are you going to be fat in front? Aunt Cat said, —Don't know what we're talking about, my foot! Get on out and play.

* * * * * * *

It's a good thing Dr. Matthews has a new young assistant—we mean Dr. H. Clifton—to help him out with the bumper crop of new residents we're getting in Bellefonte these days. Our right-hand, Mr. Alvin Johnson, is a proud papa agin himself. This new one is called Holder after Mrs. Johnson's folks, and we can see Grandad and Grandma are out buying new walking canes to celebrate the addition to the family. This makes four for the Johnsons and a mighty proud and happy father they have too. He wasn't wroth a darn around here for two whole days.

—From the *Maynard County Mast*

* * * * * * *

One night he heard Mama crying. He listened though he knew he was supposed to be asleep and she was saying to Daddy, —It's going to be Christmas, Ace. What are we going to do? Daddy said, —We'll make out, honey. And Mama said, —Why do you always have to be so damned cheerful? It's the way they do you that's killing me. It's *your* money, little as it is, that's keeping them in their house with the nice parlor nobody can go into and their four bedrooms and their filled linen and china closets. You know it is. They couldn't make it with that sewing money. But they have to put on a show of buying all the groceries with it and let on that me and my children are living on Mattie's damned sewing machine. Oh, I hate it. I hate it. Why do we have to pretend it's their way? Why? Daddy said, —They're old, honey. And

Mama said, —Yeah, sure, and blew her nose loud. —I feel like taking what little I get off that cotton and giving it to them, she said. —You know that has to be put up for doctors and medicine and "in case," Daddy said. Mama said, —I could sell the farm. And Daddy said, —And who'd buy it? Then Mama laughed and said, —O.K. You win. We'll get by.

He didn't go to sleep for a long time after that. He lay still under the covers so he wouldn't wake Veda and Martin and the baby and watched the fire on the ceiling. After a while he knew what it was. It was money. That was what all the grown people kept talking about and fussing about and doing their mouths funny about. Money.

He knew about a nickel and what that would buy and about a quarter, and the dime left from the banana split, but they were talking about money altogether like in Aunt Mattie's tin box and that Daddy got on Saturday. There wasn't enough of it. That's what the lady at The House meant when she stamped her foot and said, —Damn this money thing, and what Aunt Veda meant when she said, —Daddy isn't doing any good with the mules, and what Aunt Trudy meant when she said, —Coffee, 30 cents a pound, Hmmp! He thought about all the different money he had ever seen and where he'd seen it and how people got it, and he knew then what they would have to do.

He felt very important when he got up the next morning and after he was dressed for school and brought in the eggs and had his oatmeal he told Mama he had to talk to her. She said he'd be late for school and she had to bathe the baby, but he said it was important, so she put the water on to heat and sat down in a chair, and said, —O.K. Shoot.

—I know what you have to do to get the money, he said.

Mama's eyes went all funny and she put her arm around him and said, —What money, baby?

—The money nobody has, he said.

—What makes you say that? Mama said.

And he said, —That's what's wrong, isn't it? That's why everybody fusses all the time?

Then Mama looked like she was going to cry and she said, —Is that the way it seems to you, honey? Is that the way everything seems to you?

He said, —Listen, Mama. I know what you can do. I know because I've seen people do it. I saw Aunt Mattie once, and Mr. Simms, and I've seen Aunt Cat do it, too.

—Do what, baby? Mama said.

—You write a check, he said happily. —You get a book with them in it at the bank and you write a check and they give you money for it.

Then Mama started to cry, and she cried and cried, and finally Aunt Trudy came in and made him go on to school.

*   *   *   *   *   *   *

> Laying all jokes aside, the depression is getting lighter despite all the depressors can do. Bellefonte has had some real fine business the last two weeks and it looks like old times at times. Now is a good time to spend money for necessities such as newspaper subscriptions . . .
>
> —From the *Maynard County Mast*

*   *   *   *   *   *   *

2. *1932–34 Martha Ann*

In the late afternoon before they turned on the lights the fire made the room a cave. She would lie close to the fire and color and all the colors were different and strange.

Mama was always sick. She stayed in bed almost every day. When Daddy came in he would turn on the lamp with the pictures of camels marching around the edge and Mama would sit up and talk. Mama listened to the radio. There was the Hit Parade on Saturday nights. When Daddy came they heard the news. The radio was big and stood on four legs. It had a picture of the sun on it . . . not the sun with a face that she liked to draw, just an ordinary sun coming up or going down, she didn't know which. When she was little she thought there were little people in the radio. The best little people were Asher and Little Jimmy. Once Mama let her send off a cereal top and she had a big picture of Asher and Little Jimmy and Little Brother Buddy. Little Jimmy had bangs like hers which was funny for a boy. He wore a polka-dot shirt and he played the guitar and sang. One time everybody listened to the radio . . . Mama and Daddy and Grandmama and Granddaddy and Grandfather Simms too. They came in Mama's room and sat around in chairs. It was about a little baby being taken down a ladder and everybody said the man ought to be electrocuted but they didn't tell her how they electrocuted people.

Another time they all listened was when He won the election. Cousin Graham came and slapped his hands together and yelled and drank out of a bottle. Grandfather came in and leaned on his cane and said, —Jerusalem!

Grandfather drank out of a tall cup and wiped crumbs with a napkin off his white mustache. Sometimes he took her with him for a walk. He sang about the frog went a-courting and old man at the plow and coffee growing on white oak trees.

They went, more than any place, to Aunt Eileen's. Aunt Eileen had a lot of babies and she and Veda played with Van's lead soldiers. To get to Aunt Eileen's you had to cross where they were making the new highway. It was a big pool of black tar. You had to walk across planks. If you got it on your feet it didn't come off. She knew because once she'd stepped right in to see. Aunt Eileen was nice. She laughed a lot and read books. Mama read books, too, but Aunt Eileen would read while she did something else. It was funny. She'd be sewing and have the book propped on a table in front of her.

Aunt Eileen was married to Uncle Ace. Uncle Ace was her sweetheart but she didn't tell anybody because they would kid her. Dr. Clifton found it out though. He came to see Mama and he knew about Uncle Ace, because he'd say, —Saw a piece your beau put in the paper today, and laugh.

Dr. Clifton brought Janice, her baby sister. It was after that that Mama was sick all the time. Janice wasn't much to play with. She was too little, like Aunt Cat's baby.

She thought a lot about Aunt Cat's baby because when it came she and Mama had gotten all dressed up to go see it. She wore her Roman sandals that had to be buttoned with a button hook and pinched awful and a big ribbon on her head. Then when they got there Aunt Cat wouldn't let them come in and see the baby because she said Martha Ann had a cold. Mama got mad and they went away but the next day Aunt Cat came up to the house and cried and told Mama she didn't know what got into her, she worried too much about the baby. So they went to see it after all. It was in a big pink fancy basket and she knelt down and looked, but it was just a baby like Janice and Holder Johnson.

They took the baby one of the quilts Grandmama made. She made quilts for all the babies. They were pink and blue and had blocks and animals on them. This one had a big blue eagle on it too. It was supposed to be funny because everybody laughed about it.

    *   *   *   *   *   *   *

> Mr. Dudley Cartwright, who has been branching out in business the last few years is branching right on out of town. The Cartwright swimming pool will be open for business as usual this June 1st and Dudley tells me he is expanding the Coca-Cola plant in the spring. It is good to see enterprise among our young people. The state of the union can't be as bad as they keep telling us when we have examples like Mr. Cartwright right in our own back yard.
>
> —From the *Maynard County Mast*

    *   *   *   *   *   *   *

This fall she had to go to school. She didn't like it. She poked Veda Johnson with a sharp pencil and the teacher got mad. She threw up one day too. That was because of the kraut. Somebody gave the school 132 cases of kraut and they had it in the lunch room every day. She hated it. She read good, but nobody liked that. That wasn't the important thing. The important thing was to be friends with people. She didn't understand what that meant. People at school were mean to each other. They laughed and ran from each other and whispered and made fun. Sometimes she thought that friends were people who weren't mean to each other. But it didn't seem to work that way either. It always changed around on you. Veda had friends. Veda was cute. That was what all the grown people said: —Isn't Veda cute?

On Saturdays she played with Veda and Van, but they were cousins and didn't count as friends. They played Jimmy Culpepper.

Jimmy Culpepper was an airplane pilot. She thought for a long time that he was like Lindbergh . . . a famous pilot, but once she said so to Mama, and Mama laughed and laughed and said he dusted crops.

That year everything had been wrong. Partly it was Mama being sick, but that wasn't all of it. It started because of something Daddy had to do. It scared Mama. Daddy had to take the car and carry the payroll over to where they were building a school for Mr. Graves. She heard Mama and Daddy talking about it. Mama said, —Please, Morgan. Don't do it. Make him get somebody else to take it. One of those mill hands. They can handle things. And Daddy said, —You know he has to have somebody he can trust. Mama said, —I don't like it. They could hold you up between here and Morgan City in one of those dark places and nobody'd ever know it. And Daddy said, —I'll have the pistol. Mama said, —That scares me worse than anything else.

It happened every Friday night. Daddy would put on his hat and pull the brim down and kiss her and kiss the baby and kiss Mama and go away. Then they didn't sleep that night. Mama thought she did, but she didn't. She didn't because she knew Mama didn't and she couldn't sleep with Mama awake. Everybody would come in and talk to Mama. She'd lie still in her bed and listen and they'd talk about a lot of things, but not about where Daddy was. The next morning everybody would sleep late and wake up feeling better because nothing had happened and after a while Daddy would come home and go to bed and sleep in the daytime.

Sometimes they went out to Pete's. That was when Mama was out of bed and Daddy didn't have to go off at night. They drove out behind Mr. Graves' sawmill and Daddy went in Pete's and came back with a bottle of whiskey. They put it down between the seats in front of the car and she sat on it. Sometimes they went to the picture show to see Mae West. Mae West said, —Come up and see me sometime. She would go to sleep and they would wake her up to hear Mae West say it.

> Mr. Hubert Simmons was the win-
> ner of the Wednesday night Bank
> Night at the Juanita Theater. Mr.
> Bowman, manager of the theater
> tells me the bank night practice
> has done a lot for business at the
> Juanita and that he is considering
> starting a free dish night in the
> near future.
>
> —From the *Maynard County Mast*

*   *   *   *   *   *   *

Most of the time they stayed at home though. She had a playroom and a lot of toys. The best of them was a kaleidoscope. It
wasn't like anything else in the world and it was never like itself
twice. Next best to that was watching the stars at night. In a way
it was the same thing. After she was five they let her sit on the
back steps after dark and watch the stars because Grandfather said
she would probably be an astronomer. Grandfather was always
fixing it so you could do the best things. He would watch the
stars too. He showed her the Big Dipper and the Hunter and
the Little Dipper and the North Star. He told her she would see
Halley's Comet if she was lucky. Once there was an eclipse of the
moon and they sat on blankets on the front walk and watched the
moon go away. She liked the night.

When Daddy went away on Fridays he gave her a nickel to put
in her barrel bank. It held lots and lots of money. Cousin Graham
put money in it when he came and once Aunt Cat put a whole
half a dollar in. When she shook it she could hear the half a
dollar shaking heavier than all the others. It was after she had
to take the Guess Whats back that Mama opened her bank.

In the afternoons Una used to come to play with her. Una was
grown, but she was colored people and talked like you were grown
too. One afternoon Mama sent her and Una to the store to get
some groceries. She gave her a nickel to buy something and said
tell Mr. Hudson to charge it for the groceries.

She and Una walked to the store and told Mr. Hudson about the bologna and bread and things, and he said, —Have you got any money? She said, —I've got a nickel. He said, —Pick out what you want.

She stood at the glass case and looked at all the candy and suckers and Hi-Balls. She wanted Guess Whats. They were wrapped in pink and yellow and blue paper and they had candy and fortunes and surprises inside. Mr. Hudson put five of them in a sack and took her nickel. Then he said, —Have you got the grocery money? She shook her head and Una said, —Mrs. Holder say to charge it. And he said, —No. Can't let you have any more till the bill's paid up.

So they didn't know what to do and they came on home. On the way Una said, —Let's open them Guess Whats. She said, —No. And Una said, —Just one and see what's in it. So they stopped at the bridge over the branch and opened one. It was a ring and a pasteboard Crazy Kat and two candy kisses.

Then they went on home. Mama sat up in bed and said, —Where's the groceries? And Una said, —Mr. Hudson say No'm till the bill be paid up. Then Mama said, —What's in that sack?

She felt awfully strange and bad suddenly because she knew it was wrong to have gotten the Guess Whats and, what was worse, she had known it all the time. That was why she hadn't wanted to open any of them. But she hadn't let herself know it was wrong because she wanted the Guess Whats so very bad. Now she handed the sack to Mama and Mama said, —Did you open any of these? She said it in an awful sort of voice. She shook her head, and Mama said, —Martha Ann! —Just one, she said.

Grandmama came in and said, —What's the matter, Veda? to Mama, just like Mama was a little girl. Mama said, —That old fool wouldn't let them have the groceries. Grandmama said, —God knows what we're all coming to, and R. V. not able to do a lick of work and Bill not making ends meet at that drugstore, and Morgan . . . Well! And Mama said, —Don't you blame Morgan for the damned country's troubles. Grandmama said, —Well, there's plenty in the smokehouse and garden. And Mama said, —There's no orange juice and Pablum. And Grandmama sighed.

Mama turned to her and said, —Take them back. She said it in the funniest way like she was terribly mad and yet wanted to cry. She said, —I can't. Mama just looked at her and said, —Take them back. You've opened one, so keep it, but take back the others and get the four cents.

—Veda, Grandmama said. —Don't make the child . . .

—She might as well start to learn, Mama said.

So she had to. She took the sack, twisted the top real tight in her hand, and said, —Come on, Una. They walked all the way back to Mr. Hudson's. She didn't want to go in the store but she had to, so she hurried right on in and Mr. Hudson came all in a hurry and said, —Well. Come back for your groceries? She handed the sack across the counter and said, —I brought this back. He looked at her and looked at the sack and opened it up and looked in at the Guess Whats and took them out one by one and laid them on the counter. —There's only four here, he said.

She got mad then because all at once Mr. Hudson was acting just like kids at school did and not like a grown person should at all. She said, —I know there's only four. I opened one. You owe me four cents.

He looked at her real mad and rang the bell on the cash register and gave her four cents. When she started out the door she could see him putting the Guess Whats back in the case.

So she wasn't mad or surprised when she came home from school one afternoon and saw Mama sitting on the floor in front of the fireplace with her bank. Mama had opened the bottom with a nail file and she had all the money out stacking it in little piles. There were lots of piles of pennies and a good many of nickels and dimes and a little pile of quarters and the one half a dollar that Aunt Cat had given her.

When she came in Mama got up quick and said, —Go to the kitchen and get yourself some milk and come back. Mama wants to talk to you. Then Mama said that they had to have some orange juice for the baby and you couldn't get oranges in the garden or off the farm and they had to use Daddy's money for medicine and clothes and things for school, and that they'd pay her back, honestly, just as soon as things got better.

—I don't want that old bank anyway, she said. Mama said, —I'm sorry, baby. She said, —I'm not ever going to put anything in a bank again. I don't like it. Mama said, —Don't be that way, baby. And she said, —I don't like orange juice. Do you? And Mama said, —I guess you better go on out and play.

They didn't have Una there to play with her any more so she asked Mama if she could go see Van and Veda and Mama said No, that Aunt Eileen was busy and she asked if she could go talk to Grandfather and Mama said No, that Grandfather was having his nap. So she went out to her playroom and got her kaleidoscope and took it all apart. When she did there wasn't anything in it at all except a bunch of pieces of celluloid and a piece of tin. So she took the pieces out and played buried treasure with them for a while, but it wasn't much fun.

One night Aunt Eileen and Uncle Ace came to play cards with Mama and Daddy. She liked that because Uncle Ace let her sit in his lap and have a sip of what he was drinking. It tasted awful and everybody laughed so she knew it was whiskey. Then Mama made her get down and go play Old Maids with Van and Veda.

Then Aunt Cat came. She had on a black and white dress and earrings and high, high heels. She smelled like flowers. She said, —God, *here* everybody is. I was going nuts down there by myself. Finally got Mother to stay with Gloria and came hunting! Mama said, —Where's Dudley? Aunt Cat said, —Business trip. Where do you think? Where is he always? Ever since he read *The Man Nobody Knows* he thinks he has to gladhand like a politician. Then she said, —Oh! and bit her lip. Aunt Eileen laughed and said, —Is that so bad, Cat? Aunt Cat said, —Oh, don't bring *him* up. And Mama said, —He said he might drop by tonight. —Did he now? Aunt Cat said.

He was Cousin Graham. They always called him He when they

were talking to Aunt Cat. Sometimes when Aunt Cat came he would come too and everybody would talk a lot and Aunt Cat would look especially pretty.

She sat down and Mama said, —You want to play my hand? Aunt Cat said, —You know cards bore me. Uncle Ace said, —Have a pop? Aunt Cat said, —A little one, maybe. So Uncle Ace went to the kitchen and brought Aunt Cat a drink.

Then Mama saw her and made her go back and play with Van and Veda some more. After a while Cousin Graham came. He had already had his pop and he came in smelling good and sat right down on the floor and played Old Maids with them. They kept calling him to come in the other room and play but he said, —I'm happy right here.

After a while he got up and wandered into the other room and Mama said to him, —Where have you been? You're lit up like a Christmas tree.

Cousin Graham said, —By God, I've had a date with the gorgeous Miss Clifton. Nobody said anything at all. Aunt Cat had gone to get another drink. Then Uncle Ace said, —Getting sort of serious, isn't it? and Cousin Graham shrugged and said, —Who knows?

She couldn't see so she got up and went to stand in the door. —Who's Miss Clifton? she said. Then Mama said, —Do you always have to hang around? Cousin Graham laughed and said, —Little pitchers. Miss Clifton is Dr. Clifton's sister, and . . . who knows . . . she may be your Cousin Elizabeth some day. Aunt Cat came back in then looking sort of funny and said, —Well, I guess she's got her eye on the governor's mansion. And Cousin Graham said, —Oh hell, Cat!

Nobody said anything for a while and then Aunt Eileen said, —Do you think Harry Clifton is really going to marry Ruby Marshall? Uncle Ace laughed and said, —Well, her Papa thinks so. I can tell you that. Cousin Graham laughed too and said, —He's probably got the piece all written up ready to sock onto the front page, eh Ace?

Then Aunt Cat got up looking sort of mad and said, —I guess I ought to go home.

Cousin Graham said, —I'll take you. And Aunt Cat said, —Like hell you will. She went out.

Then Cousin Graham put his face in his hands and said, —What the hell does that woman want of me?

Aunt Eileen said, —Life, in that way grown people did that meant it really didn't mean anything at all.

Uncle Ace said, —Have a drink, Graham. Marry your little Clifton girl and forget it all. A politician needs a wife. —Sure. Sure, Cousin Graham said. —And ten kids. You should be one yourself. Uncle Ace laughed and put his arm around Aunt Eileen and kissed her and said, —What time is it getting to be anyway? And everybody laughed some more.

      *   *   *   *   *   *   *

> Mr. and Mrs. Henry Marshall announce the engagement of their daughter, Ruby Clare to Doctor Harry Clifton, son of the late Mr. and Mrs. H. M. Clifton of Morgan City, Alabama. The wedding will take place in December.

> Dr. Harry Clifton announces the engagement of his sister, Elizabeth Ann Clifton, to Graham McCloud, son of Mr. and Mrs. Byron McCloud of this city. The wedding will be an event of December.

> —From the *Maynard County Mast*

      *   *   *   *   *   *   *

That winter Dr. Clifton brought Mama another baby and it died. It was like all other babies, little and red and in a basket. Then one morning Grandmama woke her up and said that the baby was dead. She said, —What is that? And Grandmama said that it had gone to sleep and would never wake up.

They let her go into the living room and look at it. It was in a little box with pink satin pillows and it had flowers on it. She got down on her knees and looked into the box and kissed the baby's head like she always did. It was cold. It wasn't the baby at all. She knew then that Grandmama had it mixed up. The baby hadn't gone to sleep, it had gone away. She went out of the living room and upstairs to Grandfather's room and sat down by his chair.

Grandfather put his hand on her head and said, —What is it, little one? She didn't know. So they sat there together and watched Grandfather's fire burn and after a while she said, —Grandfather. When you're dead you have gone out of this place. When you are dead you have gone away.

Then Grandfather smiled and patted her head and said, —You're mighty wise to be so small.

—It's like when Dr. Clifton brings the baby, she said. —It isn't there and then it is and when it dies it isn't again. It is the same thing.

—Yes, Grandfather said. —All the same. Try not to forget.

—Why will I forget? she said.

—Well, ne'mind that, Grandfather said. —If you do you'll learn it all over again when the time comes.

A lot of people came after that: Aunt Eileen and Aunt Cat and Cousin Graham and Elizabeth. They all went into Mama's room and talked to her. Daddy stayed at home and didn't go to work. Then Brother Jones from the church came and Aunt Eileen took her home with her. She let her cut pictures out of a magazine with the sharp scissors.

When it started to get dark she wanted to go home but Aunt Cat came and brought her pajamas and said she was going to spend the night with her. She had never spent the night at Aunt Cat's house. —I think I'll stay with Aunt Eileen, she said. But Aunt Cat said No, that Aunt Eileen didn't have a place for her to sleep.

Aunt Cat had been crying and that made her feel funny, but she put her coat on and they went out and got into Aunt Cat's

car and went to the Coca-Cola place and got Mr. Cartwright. He
got in the car and said, —Hello, honey, to Aunt Cat, and, —How's
the young lady? to her. She said, —Fine, thank you. He didn't say
anything else to her.

He said to Aunt Cat, —How's Veda holding up? Aunt Cat
shook her head and said, —I don't know. Harry Clifton gave her
a shot and I think she finally went to sleep. Then he said, —Dad
wants to get a new plant manager. Aunt Cat said, —God damn
you! And he said, —Why, honey, what's the matter? Then Aunt
Cat looked at her and frowned at Mr. Cartwright and said, —You'd
talk business with Peter at the gate. He said, —I think you're
crazy. Aunt Cat said, —Oh sure. Start that again. It makes your
part simple as hell, doesn't it?

Then they stopped at Aunt Cat's house and Aunt Cat took her
upstairs and said why didn't she go on and bathe and get in her
pajamas before supper. She went in the bathroom and looked at
the tile and all the pretty towels and weighed on the scales. Aunt
Cat brought a big bottle and said, —Why don't you have a bubble
bath? Come on down when you're through, and went away.

When she came downstairs Aunt Cat was mixing whiskey at
the table. She said to Mr. Cartwright, —Don't you want a sundowner, old boy? Mr. Cartwright put down his newspaper and
said, —Don't you think you've put the sun down enough for one
day? Aunt Cat saw her and said, —How would you like a Coke
in a glass with ice just like a cocktail? and fixed it for her.

While she was drinking it Aunt Cat said, —How do you like
your new cousin? She said, —Who is that? Aunt Cat said, —You
know. Cousin Graham's wife. And she said, —Oh, Elizabeth.
She's all right. Aunt Cat laughed and said, —Elizabeth, Elizabeth.
She's all right!

They had a good supper. They had chicken. They didn't have
chicken so much at home any more. She ate the drumsticks. They
had mashed potatoes, too, and gravy and beans and cranberry
sauce. There was dessert too; it was chocolate pie.

Then Aunt Cat let her go in and see Gloria. Gloria had a room all to herself with lambs on the walls and blue furniture and a little light like Little Boy Blue. But Gloria was just a little girl like Janice and Betty Al. She said, —Where is my sister? Where is Janice? And Aunt Cat said that she was at Cousin Graham's.

Aunt Cat tucked her into a big white bed and brought her a little light too. It was a lady dancing. Then she went out and said, —I'll leave your door open and you call if you want me. You don't have to go to school tomorrow. They hadn't told her that. She was glad.

She went to sleep and after a while she woke up. There was a lot of noise and for a minute she couldn't remember where she was. Then she saw the little lamp made like a lady and knew it was Aunt Cat's house. The hall light was on and she could hear Aunt Cat and Mr. Cartwright talking. Aunt Cat was crying. Mr. Cartwright said, —Don't now. Please don't. Something fell over and made a big noise and he said, —Shhh. You'll wake the kids. Aunt Cat said, —Oh, God. I don't want to do that. Then she blew her nose and said, —It was going to that damned cemetery. It always does this to me. Why can't they put you in the ground at night with nobody around, and forget it? Then he said, —Cat, sort of sad, and she said, —That monument Buz put up there for Marty. It dominates the whole place. It's like a temple in the middle of chaos. Apollo, for God sakes. Apollo . . . in Bellefonte. Do you suppose anybody in this godforsaken place even knows who that is, standing there like that in the middle of all the neat little stones and columns and shafts? Apollo in Cedar Hill. I can't bear it. She cried some more. Mr. Cartwright said, —I'm going to call Dr. Clifton, and she said, —I'm all right. You hear me. I'm all *right*. You know they say she left some stock here in the bank with instructions for them to take the dividends and keep flowers on it and then when there weren't any dividends she came back and sold something of hers and left the money with her lawyer and when the banks closed she wrote Miss Mattie Johnson to get flowers from the place over there and she'd pay her to take them out there. And that bitch takes that money. She actually *takes* it!

Then Mr. Cartwright said, —Why don't you try to get some sleep? Aunt Cat said, —All right. I guess I will. I'll take one of those pills. Then it was quiet for a while and she'd almost gone back to sleep when Aunt Cat said real loud, —Dudley! Mr. Cartwright said real sleepy, —Huh? Aunt Cat said, —Why did your father want to get a new man for the plant? He said, —He doesn't trust the guy we got working. Aunt Cat said, —What does he do? Drink Cokes on the sly? Then Aunt Cat started to laugh, and laughed and laughed, but *she* was sleepy and went back to sleep.

*　　　*　　　*　　　*　　　*　　　*　　　*

SIMMS HOLLY SPRINGS FARM PLACE GOES UP FOR SALE

The R. V. Simms Holly Spring farm place is up for sale. This land has been in one family for about sixty years and it comprises some of the richest bottom land in Maynard County. Mr. Simms tells the editor that he is getting too old to keep up all his properties himself and that rather than turn this farm over to managerial supervision he is putting it on the market . . .

—From the *Maynard County Mast*

*　　　*　　　*　　　*　　　*　　　*　　　*

In the spring the wind blew. One day Van Maynard said, —A carnival is coming. I saw the signs. They were walking home from school and it was so warm they took their shoes off. —I don't guess we'll get to go though, he said.

—We went to the fair last year, Veda said.

—That was different, Van said. —Don't you remember? Nannie Holder took cakes and things to the fair and we went in with her.

—Yeah. It was like that, Veda said.

—Why? she said. —Why can't you go to the carnival?

—Oh, Martha Ann, Van said. —You know how they are about

money. She remembered the bank and the Guess Whats and said, —Is that it? Van said, —It's hard times. She said, —What's that? Van said, —Oh, you and Veda are too young to know. And she said, —I am not.

When she got home she went to Mama's room and asked her. She said, —Mama, are we going to the carnival? Mama sighed and said, —Where'd you hear about that? She said, —Van saw the signs. Mama said, —Well I guess the carnival people are hard up too. So she said, —Is it hard times? Mama said, —Yes. Where did you hear that? She said, —Van, and Mama said, —Eileen's children are so adult. She said, —I'm adult too, and Mama said, —Oh, baby, like she did all the time now. She said, —Well. *Are* we going to the carnival? And Mama said, —I don't know honey. I just don't know.

That night when Daddy came he and Mama talked a long time before supper and after supper they called her into Mama's room and Mama had her sit down on the edge of the bed so she knew it was going to be a talking and it was.

Mama said, —You know you need some new shoes, and she nodded because they had half-soled them Christmas and put new heels and they were all worn out again. —I'm sorry I kick rocks home from school, she said. Mama shook her head and said, —You know they cost money. And even though it's going to be summer you'll need them for parties and to go to town . . . and for the last day of school. She nodded. She knew the very shoes she wanted too . . . not Roman sandals any more, but low shoes with a bow in front.

—Well, Mama said. —There isn't money for the shoes and the carnival both. She felt embarrassed like she always did when they talked about money so she didn't say anything. —It will be up to you, Mama said. —You can either have the shoes or go to the carnival . . . whichever you want. You must decide for yourself. We don't care either way. The money is put up for you. You must decide . . . not now. Take your time, because I don't want you to be sorry whatever you do.

She said, —Can I take my bath now? Mama said, —Run on. And Daddy, who hadn't said anything before, said, —I'll ride you in piggy-back.

She lay in the water for a long time looking at how funny her legs looked with the water up all over them. She thought about the shoes. They would be new and smell good and feel a little too tight. Her feet would look very small and neat . . . like Veda's. The shoes would last for a long time too. She thought about the last day of school and going into the room in her new shoes with the sound the little taps on the heels would make and she thought about the birthday parties next summer.

Then she thought about the carnival. Carnivals and fairs were different from anything else in the world. They always went to fairs and carnivals . . . she and Mama and Daddy, and sometimes Grandfather too. One time Aunt Cat had gone with them in a pair of slacks and a round silk thing on her head.

It smelled different at fairs and carnivals. There was hamburger and onions and sawdust and a sort of paint smell and grease and canvas, and something different about the smell of the ground itself.

At carnivals nothing counted. The people on the little high boxes with their canes and funny hats and checked vests weren't real people. They were just there to stand on the boxes; they never went home and ate and went to bed at all.

There was the noise, too, the whir of things that seemed to be louder than just the whir of the machines that turned the ferris wheels and merry-go-rounds. It was like it came out of the ground and through the sawdust; it sang just below all the men hollering and the hamburgers frying and the bingo man's voice that came louder than anything else, —Twenty-three under N, N-Twenty-three.

They would ride the ferris wheel, high and fast and above everything, and the merry-go-round, even though she was really too big for that. Once Daddy had caught her a brass ring; she never understood why she couldn't take it home. There would be the sound of the merry-go-round music just a little louder than the whir and Mama would be standing waiting with a Kewpie doll or a bird on a stick, because Mama always won things at fairs and carnivals.

They would have a hamburger and Mama would say, —They'll give us ptomaine. But they'd eat them anyway. And after they played bingo a long time and Mama won a blanket they would have to carry her to the car half-asleep and when they were away from it the carnival would still be turning and shining and whirring behind them in the dark.

The water was cold, so she got out and dried herself carefully with a towel. Then she brushed her teeth and put on her pajamas and brushed her hair and went back to Mama's room.

Mama was lying on the bed and Daddy was sitting by the lamp reading the paper. —Did you get your ears clean? Mama said.

She came over to the bed and sat down by Mama. Mama smelled like lavender water and clean sheets. She could see Daddy looking up at her over the paper. —I want the shoes, she said.

Then Mama hugged her and called her a big girl and said they would get them for her the very next day. But she didn't feel very big or very old or very good. She had to wait about fifteen years for that.

3. *Veda 1935*

They said she was pretty. That meant she had curly hair and blue eyes and when Mama starched her dresses they stood out around her nice. But she didn't ever know what to say to grown people. Van did. He talked and talked to everybody but she never knew what to say. She could sing songs, she knew all the songs Shirley Temple sang. They would stand her on the table at the drugstore and she would sing about The Goodship Lollypop. Everybody liked it. But then they wanted to talk to her. And she never knew what to say.

She wasn't very good at school either. Martha Ann, who was in her room, could read all the words and draw all the lines to the right pictures. Martha Ann didn't have to think about it, but she did. Recess was better. Then they played jump rope and house and Bear. Bear was the most fun. Everybody chased everybody else and laughed and felt happy. Even Van would play Bear at recess sometimes.

She had a boyfriend at school. His name was Billy Jo and he gave her part of whatever he brought for recess. When they had chapel he would come sit by her. But after school was out she didn't see Billy Jo any more because he rode the bus.

In the summer she played with Van and Martha Ann. Martha Ann had a playroom and they would play house with all the little stoves and beds and chairs. Martha Ann's Mama was Aunt Veda that she was named after. Aunt Veda was always sick. She would

lie in bed in pretty bed jackets and smell like lavender water. Lots
of times she would have a box of candy and give them all some.
She would save her candy and Martha Ann and Van would eat
theirs all up. Then next day Martha Ann would say, —Give me
some of your candy. She'd say, —No, it's mine, but Martha Ann
would say, —But my Mama gave it to you. Martha Ann was funny
about things like that.

This was the time she got the store dress for her birthday. She
had never had a dress from the store because Aunt Mattie made
all her clothes. But she had always wanted one. Martha Ann had
dresses from the store; Gloria Cartwright didn't have any other
kind of dresses.

She saw the dress in the window at the Kiddie Shoppe. It was
on a little girl with yellow hair standing in front of a white fence
with flowers on it. It was a blue dress with lots and lots of pleats
in the skirt, a bolero jacket that was cut out like flowers, and where
it was cut out pink showed through. The skirt was pink inside,
too, so that if your dress flew up—like it wasn't supposed to—you
could see the pink.

She said, —Mama, that's the prettiest dress in the world. Mama
stopped and looked at it and said, —Five dollars. It ought to be.

But it was there for her birthday in a big pink box with a bow
on it. She saved the big box for last and the first thing she opened
was a new dress from Aunt Mattie. It was blue too, and pretty,
but it looked like all her other dresses. She thanked Aunt Mattie
and then she opened the rubber doll from Van and the real blue-
and-pink washing machine with a crank to turn to wash the clothes
from Martha Ann, and the handkerchiefs from Aunt Trudy. Then
she opened the big box. She was so excited she knocked over the
box with Aunt Mattie's dress in it and got cake on it. Aunt Mattie
got mad and went out to her room and wouldn't even eat any
birthday cake.

Mama said, —Well dammit, I don't care. Daddy said, —Well,
we should have known she'd make her one. Mama said, —She

could have told me. So Daddy shrugged his shoulders and ran his hand through his hair and said, —Oh what the hell, and went out to their little house to get his drink of whiskey.

After that she had the dress for birthday parties and it helped. She didn't like birthday parties but Mama always made her go. Birthday parties were nearly always in the summer and they were supposed to be a lot of fun, but they never had been for her. Mama would comb her hair and put a big bow on it that pulled too tight and she'd have to take the present all wrapped up in tissue paper. It was usually a handkerchief and she knew they wouldn't like getting a handkerchief. She never did.

She would have to walk along the highway that was still sticky with tar and the sun would be hot. She would wish that it was dark and cool and the party over but all the time she walked she could see the white gate or the concrete-post gate or the iron gate she'd have to go through and the walk she'd have to go up and the person whose birthday it was standing on the porch with their hand out waiting for the present that was crumpled up and sweaty now from being held in her hand.

Birthday parties smelled of grass and she'd get green grass stains all over her white shoes. They would play the games like Red Rover where you had to run against people's arms and get hot and tired and messed up, and Marching Round the Levee where you had to choose somebody and everybody was just a face and you couldn't make up your mind to choose.

If you didn't play and sat in a chair the mother would come and say, —Why Veda! Come on and play with the other children. So she always just went on and played to start with so they wouldn't have to come and say it.

Then they had the ice cream and cake and Veda didn't like ice cream and cake at parties. It was so sticky and the cake was always angel food that tasted like a piece of old sponge and sometimes the ice cream would be funny from being made and kept. Everybody thought she was crazy because she didn't like the ice cream and cake. Van always said that to her, —Old Veda's crazy. She don't like ice cream and cake. So she'd say, —You eat mine.

She liked winter parties better. Then they played in the house where it was cozy and they would sit in little chairs and play pass the thimble. They would have cocoa and sandwiches at those and maybe a chocolate cake. Chocolate was what Mama always made for her. But somehow most parties were always in the summer.

Martha Ann had the biggest birthday parties. She had one every August in the big yard at her house. Her Grandmama gave it for her birthday present. Even when they were funny about the hard times Martha Ann had her party. Mama said it was a rite with the Simmses, but she didn't know what that meant.

They would bring Martha Ann's toy box out in the yard and there would be the games and the contests. Martha Ann's Grandmama Mozel always directed the parties because Aunt Veda was sick. At Martha Ann's they had the poppers with the ice cream and cake. They had fortunes and paper hats and little silver charms inside. She had saved all her charms from Martha Ann's parties. She kept them with her silver dollar. Last year she got a bird.

Mama had Aunt Mattie make Martha Ann a dress with pants to match because Martha Ann was her cousin. She walked along the road with Van in his white shirt, and his tie made out of one of Daddy's old ones, and Van let her carry the package. —I don't want to go to this old party, she said. —You just don't like parties 'cause you're not the big attraction, Van said. —That's not so. —Yes, it is, he said. —Nobody asks you to sing and show off so you feel put-upon. That's what I heard Aunt Mattie tell Mama. —Aunt Mattie's mean, Veda said. —Yeah, but she tells the truth, Van said.

They got to Martha Ann's and went in between the concrete posts and up the walk and gave Martha Ann the package. Then they went out in the yard and all the other children began to come. She sat down on the iron bench and Martha Ann said, —Come play with my things, so she went over and looked in the toy box and got a little piano and went back to the bench.

Then they started the games and she saw Grandmama Mozel coming over so she got up real quick and played London Bridge and was on Van's side and they all fell down and she got her blue silk skirt dirty.

Then they brought out the ice cream and cake. It was dixie-cup ice cream, which she liked better than home-made, but it was the same old angel food cake. She sat down on the steps and held her plate with the ice cream and the cake and the popper and the lemonade, and looked at her skirt. She thought about all the trouble the dress had caused and made Aunt Mattie mad and Mama mad and Daddy go get his drink of whiskey, and here it was all dirty and ruined probably because it didn't wash. So she started to cry. Not aloud or anything, but she didn't have her handkerchief. She looked in her belt where she always kept it but it wasn't there and she needed to wipe her nose. She felt so miserable that she tried to eat some of the cake and that was really terrible.

Just then Captain Simms came down the steps. He was old, older than anybody. He just stopped and looked down at her and she could see his black shoes that buttoned up high on his feet and his pants legs and the tip of his cane. —Miss Veda, he said. —Let me loan you my handkerchief. It has been many a year since I could make that offer to a lady in distress.

He handed her a big clean white handkerchief and she took it and blew her nose and wiped her eyes. —Thank you, she said.

—You're quite welcome, he said. —Now. Don't you like that cake? She said, —No sir. Not much. He reached over and took the plate out of her hand and gave her back the popper and said, —How about this ice cream? She shook her head. He took the plate and put it on the banisters and said, —Now. Let's see what's in that popping thing. So she pulled the popper and took out the hat and the fortune and the charm. This year it was a rose. —Well, Captain Simms said. —Look at that. What's your fortune say? She gave it to him and he read, —You will travel on strange ground but always keep your sense of proportion. Hmm! he said. —The things they think of for children. *I'll* tell you a fortune. Your face is your fortune. How's that?

—What's it mean? she said.

—You'll find out, Captain Simms said. —I don't doubt you'll find out. Now let's go pin the tail on the donkey.

He took her hand and they went to the place where the donkey was. When they blindfolded her and turned her round she went right up and pinned on the tail right where it belonged, only just a little high, and won the prize. It was the first prize she had ever won in her life and it was a box of mint candy. She took it over and offered a piece to Captain Simms right then and he took it and laughed and tapped his cane on the walk and she put her arms around him and gave him a big hug.

When she got home Mama was rocking the baby. She said, —How was the party? She said, —I won a prize. And Mama said, —Wonderful.

—I got my dress dirty, she said. Mama said, —It'll clean.

—She went off and wouldn't play again, Van said. —You go on and wash up for supper, Mama said, and Van went across to the big house.

—I'm sorry about the dress, Mama, she said.

—That's all right.

She wanted to say a lot of things, to explain to Mama that it wasn't just getting the dress dirty, that somehow it was even having the dress in the first place; but she couldn't say it. She never knew how to say things. She put her head on Mama's lap and Mama rocked back and forth, and put her hand on her head. It made her feel cozy and good inside. —Mama, she said. —How is your face your fortune? —So soon? Mama said. —That's what Captain Simms said to me. —Oh. Mama laughed low and warm. —Well, that means you'll probably get married and have a dozen babies. —You know, she said, burrowing into Mama's lap. —That's just what I'd like to do. Maybe I'll marry Billy Jo. —Sure, Mama said. —Sure you will.

Little Miss Martha Ann Holder celebrated her seventh birthday with a party for 33 guests at the home of her grandparents, Mr. and Mrs. R. V. Simms on August 23. Games and contests were enjoyed by the guests, and delicious ice cream and cake were served by the hostess.

—From the *Maynard County Mast*

*   *   *   *   *   *   *

4. *Harry Clifton 1931–36*

Harry Clifton had always considered himself a lucky man. He had finished medical school in 1929 and since he had expected his two years of internship to be hard, with money nonexistent, the first years of the depression had no effect on him. Then, just as he was preparing to go into debt to outfit a practice in his home town, had come the summons from Dr. Matthews. Dr. Matthews had practiced medicine in Bellefonte, Alabama, for more years than most of his patients numbered and he had the core of the county's patients. He was getting old and he had no son.

Harry Clifton talked to him in the front room of his rambling two-storied house, drinking the coffee provided by Mrs. Matthews and watching the sunlight through the leaves of the maples in the front yard and along the quiet summer-dusted street. He fell in love with Bellefonte in that moment and he knew afterwards that he would have accepted any offer made to him that afternoon. His parents were dead, he had no girl, no close friends in the town that had birthed him. There was only his sister, a slim silent girl who wanted to get married and who had never been exceptionally popular with the boys she had grown up with. They had no allegiances; no real home.

The proposition Dr. Matthews had made to him was simple and uncomplicated. There was no talk of buying the practice, of contracts and commitments and mutual benefits. Dr. Matthews needed an assistant. Harry would take the patients that Dr. Matthews couldn't find time for any more, he would assist in surgery, he would take on any new practice that came into the office. When Dr. Matthews died the practice would belong to him.

It was an unbelievable stroke of luck, occasioned by one of those tenuous—and to an outsider, incomprehensible—connections of third cousins once removed. They were kin, however casually, in a land where kinship was still supreme and where to have no kin was tantamount to isolation. So he had been sent for, he had come, and he remained.

He rented a house that belonged to Mr. R. V. Simms, a little house by Bellefonte's standards, but a comfortable one, and he brought his sister and what was left of the family furniture and china and his few hard-bought instruments and books to it. In a week he felt that he had never lived anywhere else; in a month he never wanted to.

He was busy, far busier than the size of the town or the poverty of the times had led him to believe he would be, for sickness goes on, babies are born, and people die whether there is money in the banks or under the beds or not; and in Bellefonte, and particularly among Dr. Matthew's patients, a medical debt was a debt of honor. Dr. Matthews—with Harry following his lead—asked little for night and weekend calls, little enough for birthing and healing, less for office calls, nothing for reassurance. But there were enough folded and refolded dollar bills, enough quarters and nickels, enough cartons of eggs and dressed fryers. Because in Bellefonte in the 1930's the doctor was still the medicine man. He was midwife, healer, and analyst and before the first year of his tenure had passed Clifton knew that he was also father confessor, friend, and one of the few remaining threads of hope.

He treated the diseases of malnutrition, impetigo, nose-bleed, the unbelievable respiratory ailments of the young. He brought babies and closed eyes and he found soon enough that the term White Plague as applied to tuberculosis was an accurate and vivid cognomen. In Maynard County it *was* a plague. It crossed all lines and went into all places; there was no stopping it, healing it, or fighting it. He came to know the flushed face and cough in his dreams. He found it in the wide white houses and in the grey sharecropper shacks, in his office and on the streets of the town, in the fields and on the roads—walking consumptives, sitting consumptives, dying consumptives. Because most of them refused to treat it. They couldn't go to bed, they couldn't sit in the sun, they couldn't drink the children's milk or buy a better diet. They lived with it, spread it, and died from it, while he listened to chests and shook his head and prescribed what he knew would not, could not, be heeded. He learned a lot in that first year that they had never taught him in medical school. Most people lived with death and they lived with it much more bravely than he had ever been led to believe. They might deny its very existence, they might wait for it stoically, they might yell like almighty hell against it; but —one way or the other—they lived with it. In 1931 a lot of them had to.

At night he got into the habit of sitting in the kitchen of the little house, drinking coffee with Dr. Matthews, listening to all the things this old man knew about all the people of this town, about their parents and their grandparents and their dim beginnings in the history of Maynard County. He was smart enough to know that he was undertaking another phase of his medical training. The family doctor would be supreme in a town the size of Bellefonte for a long long time and the family doctor had to know not just the age and physical condition of his patients, not just his history of disease and nutrition and general health, but his attitude toward life, his relations with his parents, his way of fitting into the community.

So he listened, he learned, and he worked hard. He loved every minute of it but it wasn't surprising that he fell in love with the most healthy and uninvolved person in town or that he never for a moment gave a damn whether she was a very complicated person or not.

He met Ruby Marshall at a dinner party given for him by Dr. Matthews. She was a small girl, with a pert happy face and a beautiful body. Her father owned the local newspaper and she was pampered and spoiled and irresistible. He sat by her at dinner and took her home afterwards. He made a date with her for the next night and in two weeks time he had possessed the slender body in the back seat of a T-model Ford.

He had never been in love before, he had never had time, and he couldn't get enough of her. He would come in from a day of house calls and deliveries and dusty rides over back-country roads, locking the doctor inside him somewhere while he went for her in a frenzy, leaving only the thread of message in Dr. Matthews' office as to where he might be reached. With Ruby there was no stalker of White Plague, no pill purveyor, no reluctant dispenser of the placebo. There was only a boy who hadn't had time to fall in love at eighteen.

She knew she had him. She had known it before she had ever let him touch her, but he didn't know it. He was even rather surprised to find that they had set a date, timed carefully between the times when he had patients with babies due. She had consulted Dr. Matthews about this; but he didn't know that until long after the wedding.

He had moved through the amenities of family life in such a daze during his courtship that he was shocked and surprised to find that his sister, Elizabeth, had quietly and without saying a word, to him or anybody else, fallen in love with Graham McCloud and was going to marry him.

He didn't like it. He couldn't like it, with his medical knowledge of this town and these people, and when he knew it he had to come back out of that world of passion and frenzy and enthrallment to face it. By then, of course, it was too late.

He had come in from a date with Ruby one night, the smell of her still clinging to him, the feel of her still on him, so that he couldn't concentrate as he should have. Elizabeth was sitting in the kitchen waiting for him, drinking a cup of coffee and tapping her foot in time to a phonograph record of "Shanty Town." "Hi," she said. "What do you think about having a double wedding long about Christmas?"

He stared at her, wondering what the hell she was talking about, then automatically poured himself a cup of coffee and said the words he always said, "Any calls?"

She shook her head. "Did you hear me?" she said.

He sat down. "Who are you going to marry?" he said.

"Oh, Harry." She shook her head. "If there is anybody in Belle-fonte who doesn't know it would be you."

"Not Graham McCloud?" he said, because of course he did know, or would have known if he had ever thought about it. She had several beaus, but it was Graham McCloud who was always there on Saturday night, it was Graham McCloud for whom she wore that look of bright expectancy. He felt cold suddenly, wondering if he could have neglected his patients as he had his own sister. He didn't really think so; he locked Ruby away from his mind in the daytime, he disowned her when he picked up his bag. He had to. But the doubt worried him enough suddenly to make him certain he really wanted the marriage. If he had her at home waiting in his own bed, any night, every night, maybe she'd stop being a fever, a frenzy, a fear.

"Why him?" he said to Elizabeth.

"I'm in love with him, silly," Elizabeth said. "You ought to know *that* diagnosis." She laughed at him.

He smiled back. "He doesn't seem right for you somehow," he said.

"My dear, the McClouds are eminently respectable," she said. "I'm sure even Mama would have approved. He's a gentleman, he's a good lawyer, he's handsome..."

"Yes," Harry said. "He's all that. Do you realize he's going to be shooting for the governorship one of these days? Or is that what you want? Is that part of what you like about him? Somehow I've never pictured you as a politician's wife."

"It doesn't matter one way or the other," she said. "Would it bother you if your Miss Marshall wanted to run for office?"

He poured more coffee. He didn't want to be reminded of himself and Ruby Marshall because he didn't like the comparison. He looked at his sister for a moment and he wondered about the back seat of Graham McCloud's car. Instantly he was sorry. She didn't, she hadn't. He'd have known it. "He drinks some," he said.

"Oh, Harry. How unworthy of you."

It was, and he knew it. Graham McCloud was no drunkard, he never even got more than mildly tight, but he said it because he couldn't say what really worried him. He didn't have to.

"It's because of that Cartwright woman, isn't it?" Elizabeth said.

He shook his head and felt for a cigarette, taking the empty pack from his pocket and remembering with a sensual shock handing Ruby the last one and watching her small red mouth move around it hungrily.

"There's some in the cabinet," Elizabeth said, and brought him a pack. She watched while he lit it, then said it again. "It's because of Cat Cartwright, isn't it?"

He drew on the cigarette and shrugged.

"I know all about that," she said. "It's nothing but a bother to him now. That's all it is now. A bother."

It made him wince.

Catharine Cartwright had come into the office a few weeks after he was settled in, a small thin woman, beautifully dressed, beautifully groomed, something to wonder at in these days of unkemptness. He had seen the twitch, so slight only a doctor would note it, in her left eye and the telltale nicks and burns on her hands. He'd thought, Accident-prone, hyperthyroid.

She'd been coy as hell about what she wanted, wandering around the office and talking sixty-a-minute about Bellefonte and Dr. Matthews and the need for new blood, until he'd been compelled to start glancing at his watch. Then she'd sat down abruptly in a chair and said, "I'm sick at my stomach all the time. That isn't normal, is it? Why the hell should I be sick at my stomach all the time?"

"Have you consulted Dr. Matthews?" he said.

"Consulted him? Consulted him?" She laughed brittlely. "I've got pills to get up on and pills to get down on and pills for in between. We've looked at my liver and listened to my innards and collected nasty little specimens and tried a thousand and one diets. Have I consulted him?" She laughed again. "He suggested I see you as a matter of fact." She got up and started around the office again, picking up ashtrays now and looking at the bottom of them.

"Sit down!" he said loudly. She sat. "Do you have headaches?" he said.

"No."

"Pains anywhere?"

"No."

"Sleep well?"

"Pills. I told you."

"What do you do?"

"Do?"

"With your time? Do you work? Do you have children?"

"Oh. The man means, am I useful," she said. "Hardly. My husband makes money. Isn't that disgraceful? He makes money. Nobody else in town does, but he does. My best friends all have to pretend they don't charge the groceries and that the house doesn't need painting. But my husband makes money. He and his fine ole penny-pinching father are still lousy with it. They didn't lose a damned cent in 1929. They own Coca-Cola, that every fool in the country will go right on throwing their nickels away for, and to make it real nice they figured when folks don't have money they'll spend what little they get to amuse themselves and forget it all so they've opened a swimming pool, and that makes money too. I don't do anything. I try to spend a little of it and get it back into circulation. That's my usefulness." Her voice had risen hysterically. She stubbed out her cigarette and lit another one.

"So?" he said. "Somebody always has money. Somebody always gets out light. Why do you feel guilty about it?"

She shrugged. "Oh don't start that guilt crap," she said. "Freud's not so fashionable this year." She got up. "No ideas about my stomach?"

"Sure," he said. "Plenty. You're bucking for a peptic ulcer, but it may take you a few years to make it."

"Thanks for nothing," she said. "Send my husband the bill."

She slammed the door behind her.

The next time he saw her she was pregnant. She walked in the same way and started her circuit around the office. "Sit down," he said.

"Well, it looks like I'm going to have to be useful," she said.

"Oh?"

"Two months late. I seem to be pregnant."

He examined her. He couldn't be sure, of course, but he was. He always was. He gave his usual talk and told her when to come back. He knew about her by that time. He knew a lot about her.

He knew her mother, who was suffering from angina, and her father, an obstreperous old man with high blood pressure. He knew her husband, calm unruffled Mr. Cartwright of the Coca-Cola plant, and her father-in-law, Virgil Cartwright, chronic indigestion. He also knew that she was in love with Graham McCloud and that only a ridiculous and ill-timed impulse had ever gotten her married to Dudley Cartwright. He knew that she had witnessed what was still talked of as Bellefonte's greatest tragedy, the suicide of Marty Mayhill, which even his limited psychiatric knowledge had neatly pegged the first time he saw that damned statue his mother had put over him on Cedar Hill. People in towns the size of Bellefonte might have skeletons in their closets but they were the damnedest noisiest skeletons this side of perdition.

He delivered her baby, a girl that she named Gloria, and spent more of her husband's money outfitting. She was in labor for twenty-four hours for no reason that he could ascertain except that she resisted having a baby at all. She didn't want to try to nurse it and he—in this case—agreed with her. So they put it on Pet milk and the baby thrived and Cat was up in a week, thinner than ever and more nervous than ever, and she began to be prone to office calls.

She'd come in with a cut finger or an infected bite; she'd come in about her stomach again. He thought that she wanted some-body to talk to. He let her talk. It was the only prescription he had for her. There wasn't anything physically wrong with her. He'd made sure of that.

It took her a long time to get around to sex. It surprised him that she ever did, for in spite of the clothes and the talk she was prim. But she came out with it finally—frigidity. He'd expected it and he didn't have any prescription for that either, unless it was Graham McCloud. She took a lot of his time and he resented it. He had dying patients, patients with no hope, patients with too much hope, but she was entitled to what he could give her. She paid for it. He'd heard about the fees analysts charged and he thought of sending her to one. But he knew she wouldn't go. Bellefonte still connected psychiatry with something "wrong in the head." So she was his cross, the patient he couldn't cure and knew he couldn't. Now his sister wanted to marry the first cause of this.

He tried to see it as a problem in human relations, a chart or a graph: Cat Cartwright deprived of Graham McCloud, Elizabeth Clifton saddled with him. Because he didn't like Graham. He didn't like anything about him. He was arrogant, and too damned handsome, and someday he was probably going to run into Cat Cartwright at the wrong time and precipitate a general breakdown or a murder or a scandal. He didn't want his sister involved in it. Was that asking too much?

He looked at Elizabeth now, her eyes serene, smiling. He shook his head.

"Oh, Harry," she said. "I know all you're thinking. I know what and who Graham is. He's a happy-go-lucky S.O.B. You'd better listen to this now because I'll never say it again. He is that, and he'll probably betray me a hundred times, he'll make me wonder a hundred more. He'll go his happy-go-lucky way and win his elections and glad-hand the populace of his credulous home town. But he'll always come home, my dear. Because that's part of his honorable Southern heritage. And he'll always honor me because I'm the one he had to marry. I'm the one he couldn't get any other way. Yes. That's the way it is."

Harry didn't answer her. She was right as far as she went. It was good to know she knew it, but the thing she didn't know was that Graham had never had Cat Cartwright either. That made the small drop of difference that could precipitate anything. He sighed. "I couldn't stop you anyway, could I?" he said.

Elizabeth shook her head.

"All right. You couldn't me either, I guess. So congratulations."

"I wouldn't try to stop you, darling," she said. "What you don't know about Ruby couldn't really hurt you. She's quite harmless, I suspect. Once you have her safely tucked in."

He asked Ruby the next night. "Did you know Elizabeth was in love with McCloud?"

She laughed and cuddled against him in the darkness of the front porch swing. "Why, honey, everybody in town knows it. Don't tell me you didn't?"

He thought—because he was still, after all, a medical man—I hope the wedding doesn't cause Cat Cartwright to break her neck.

They had a double wedding with Christmas greens for decorations and a reception that featured a groaning board and a yule log and everybody in Bellefonte. And Ruby Marshall Clifton, on her wedding night, spent an hour in the bathroom of the bridal suite in the Park Hotel in Newcastle and when she finally did come out in a white gown with a virginal air Harry knew she was demanding that he take her for the first time. So that's what he did. Because if she wanted to believe doing it in the back seat of a Ford didn't count that was all right with him; and if he wanted to believe, in spite of four years of med school and two of interning and three of being a small town G.P., that he was the first—well, that was all right too.

She gave him a fine Christmas, which was a good thing, because nothing else in Bellefonte that year pointed toward a good Christmas or a happy new year either. Harry lost Veda Holder's baby and it depressed him. For the first time the loss of life seemed personal to him in a way he couldn't figure or fight or understand.

Veda was Harry Clifton's legacy from Dr. Matthews; she was his first patient in Bellefonte. He had still been arranging his meager books and instruments in the office when the call had come in. "You go out, boy," Dr. Matthews had said. "It's little Veda Simms again. It might cheer her up to see a new face. Lord knows she's seen enough of mine." Then he had given Harry the first of many quick off-the-cuff records: twenty-three, married since seventeen, lost one baby, one little girl living, husband working at Graves Lumber Yard, living with her parents, over-protected, delicate, pregnant again.

He had walked up the tree-lined walk to the big house, noticing that it needed a coat of paint, the comfortable look of its porch, the flowers and shrubs that showed signs of needing more tending than they were getting now.

Mozel Simms met him at the door, a big woman, handsome, looking old and worried. "Where's Dr. Matthews?" she said.

He explained to her that he was the new doctor working with Dr. Matthews and that he'd come out because Dr. Matthews thought Veda might like to see someone new. He didn't believe in lying to patients—not even out of necessity—for he had never seen a case of that necessity.

Mozel smiled. "I reckon she would like to get a look at you," she said. "Everybody in town's been discussing the new bachelor."

He went on into the house and down the hall to the bedroom. At the door a little girl stopped him. She was three or four and she held a big doll in front of her. "It's sick in the head," she said.

He leaned over and looked at the doll and diagnosed measles and gave her a tongue depressor. "Where's the chewing gun?" she said. He said, "I beg your pardon?" And she said, "Dr. Matthews has chewing gum in his pocket." So he learned his first lesson in small town patient-doctor relations.

Veda Simms Holder had been sitting up in bed with a blue ribbon around her blond hair. She was very small and pale and the blue veins stood out against her white skin.

"I'm Harry Clifton," he said.

She grinned at him. "I know, all right," she said. "I've been waiting to meet you." He looked her over and prescribed more food. It was the first of an endless number of times he was to prescribe with no hope of the prescription being filled. Veda was very gay and talked to him for a long time. She had her mother bring in some coffee for him. He watched her white face, marveling at the store of vivacity all women of the era of the flapper managed to cling to through marriage, illness, and the dreariness of this new decade.

He liked her. She was young and likable. And sad, because he knew after one look at her that she could fall victim to pernicious anemia without even trying and that she had no business having another baby and that she would go right on having this one, and another one if she could, and another one after that. Because that was life for her.

When he started to leave Mrs. Simms asked him to look in on her husband, R. V., who was in bed with a lingering chest cold. It was seldom, he came to know, that there was only one patient to a call.

After that they called him when they wanted the doctor. He delivered the baby, a girl named Janice, and he came when the old man was down and when Veda was down, and when the little girl had one of her sick headaches. He lanced a carbuncle on Morgan Holder's neck and for the first time saw the sadness and dependence of a man living with his wife's relatives. He would have liked to prescribe a new home for Veda and Morgan Holder but he didn't know any way you could do that.

The next baby came too quick after Janice—he told Veda that, but she grinned at him and said, "Oh, come now, Doctor, you can use the business." It never had a chance because there wasn't enough calcium and iron and plain flesh and blood and bone left in Veda Holder to make another baby. It was premature and weak and listless; the first cold became pneumonia, and pneumonia death, and there wasn't anything at all he could have done. So he didn't know why it disturbed him. The county was full of babies without enough gumption to make it through the first cold spell in the first winter of their lives.

But it did bother him. It was a sign of failure for the Simmses and it pointed toward failure for Dr. Harry Clifton, for Maynard County, and for the United States of America in 1934. It scared him.

The Simmses were the sort of people who couldn't learn to live without money. They had always had it, solidly. It was no great fortune, no ostentatious life of leisure that they had led—the people with that sort of money actually managed better without it than those like the Simmses. People like the Mayhills, who were still talked about in Bellefonte, had simpler solutions when their money went. They jumped out of windows, ending it, or they ceased to live in their big houses and went to live a life of pretence somewhere away from where they had had it all. They had the cavalier attitude that pulled them through. If they didn't go under with a bang in the first shock they adjusted. They had a sense of humor and a belief in their own importance that let them live in a walk-up flat and eat cabbage as though it were a great joke. Like the White Russians, they felt important enough to ignore the obvious.

People like the Simmses couldn't see the obvious. They kept right on living in their too-large houses because they weren't mortgaged and because they *could* be run without a staff of servants, and they kept right on charging their groceries where they'd charged them for years; they went right on drinking Cokes and going to the picture show with what nickels and quarters they had. They couldn't get in the habit of eating the bacon out of the smoke house instead of buying packaged bacon at the store and feeding that in the smoke house to the kitchen help. So they struggled along, living on the capital, not looking beyond the time when the capital went.

Harry Clifton, family doctor, saw too much of it. He had to tell Veda Holder and all the mothers like her that the baby wasn't going to live. He had to tell himself—because it wasn't time to tell anybody else yet—that Veda Holder and the others like her weren't going to live either. Veda was burned out and used up, a pale lovely blond wraith with two big healthy, if nervous, children and a still half-boy husband, and two old parents who probably couldn't survive her for long when she went.

One night at midnight he sat in the kitchen of the Simms' house with Captain Simms. They were drinking coffee while the rest of the family slept, Veda drugged and fitfully—she had a fever and a cold and a cough.

Captain Simms drank from a pint-sized mug, stirring the coffee slowly with a silver spoon. "Don't take it so hard, son," he said. "You're in the business. You got to live with it."

"Captain," Harry said, "when I get to be your age, I hope to God I've learned your serenity."

Captain laughed. "It's not serenity," he said. "It's perspective. I've lived through a lot of depressions and high times and war and low times, and it's the way it is." He refilled his cup. "Don't think it don't pain me. But I've learned that's part of it too. Like that baby girl in there, Veda, that I saw born and learning to walk and talk, and that I've seen the sign on since she was no more than a child. It pains me, but it ain't my fault. It ain't yours. And by and large she got something out of this place. By and large, most folks do."

"She is only twenty-six years old," Harry Clifton said.

"Yes," Captain said. "And that is the part that pains me. But it is the way it is. Ain't you quit asking why yet? And you a doctor?"

When he got home he stood for a long time looking down at Ruby, sleeping peacefully and warmly in the double bed, and when he got in beside her he woke her because he had to feel the

warmth of her against him and around him. For the first time in
his marriage he was annoyed because she insisted on not having
children yet.

Ruby didn't want children—not now. Ruby wanted a hospital
for her husband. Because this was his own dream and his own longing he let her lead him into hope for it, although he knew there
was really no hope; no money, no way to raise money. He didn't
count on the innate practicality and ingenuity of his wife. Bellefonte needed a hospital. Doctors operated, when they had to, in
their offices and when there was time they shipped their patients
across the rough roads to Chattanooga and Hunter City, and
prayed. They delivered babies in homes, they performed what
feats they could where they could with inadequate instruments
and lights and supplies. The hospital was one of the first things
Harry had talked about with Dr. Matthews. He told Harry of
the years he'd wanted one and of what money he had been able
to raise, and how inadequate it was even in a time of a high-
buying dollar. But Dr. Matthews reckoned without Ruby too.

Ruby went to work a month after her marriage. She called her
brother, who was setting up his law practice, and she talked to him
for a long time. She called on Dr. Matthews and found out exactly
how much money he had raised for the hospital. Then she called
on Elizabeth and Graham McCloud. She ascertained that Graham
was running for the state legislature on the next ticket and she
gave him a platform. She drove her Chevrolet coupé out to
Graves' sawmill and talked to W. W. Graves. Then she drove
back to town and talked to a little man in a felt hat with a jackleg
sawmill operation, a man named Whit Wallace. Harry Clifton
knew nothing about any of these calls—not until afterwards.

It began with editorials in the county paper about the need for
a hospital, about the obligation to create a hospital, and about the
young man in their midst with a new idea and the old man with
a long dedication to the same idea. When Graham McCloud
declared for the legislature he promised to try to get state money
to help finance the hospital. And the people of Bellefonte, who

remembered the Lee Highway, decided unanimously that they could raise their own damned hospital money and help out a fine young doctor and a fine old man.

Mr. Graves had been the stumbling block in Ruby's program. He'd told her quite frankly that he was out to make himself a dollar just like everybody else and he wasn't about to help put up a building at what amounted to cost just for the good will of the community. He had all the good will he could stomach as it was, he said, what with Dudley Cartwright for a son-in-law, and he didn't feel obliged to cheat himself to help put up a hospital. "Get some money out of Dudley," he told her as she started out the door. "He could probably put the damned thing up single-handedly if he was a mind. I reckon Catharine patronizes your husband enough she could afford to subsidize him a hospital."

So Ruby had gone to Whit Wallace. Whit Wallace had come down out of one of the innumerable coves in Maynard County to work for some of the easy money W. W. Graves was paying in the early twenties. He and his brother Pete had been the first of the Wallaces to arrive in Bellefonte and they hadn't stayed with W. W. long. Pete had gone into the liquor business. He set up behind Graves' sawmill and by the time W. W. found it out his clientele was so large and so select that there wasn't anything W. W. could do about him. Whit had betrayed him in a worse way. He'd set up a jackleg sawmill on the other side of town. Walter Graves was convinced and almighty sure for the rest of his life that Whit had started that operation on stuff pilfered from his own lumber yard and trucks. But he couldn't prove it and by the time he thought he could Whit Wallace was too important to Bellefonte. Because Whit Wallace contracted to build Clifton's hospital at a cut rate as his contribution to the community.

So the hospital went up in spite of the times—perhaps because of them—and both Ruby Clifton's and Elizabeth McCloud's children were born in it. Harry Clifton saw Dr. Matthews grow older and begin to die, watched Veda Simms Holder begin to lose the small hold on life she had, cut the umbilical cords that brought new life to Maynard County and watched the eyes close out the old life, and tried to tell the poor that 666 chill tonic did not cure T.B.

Of course it was T.B. that finally happened to Veda Simms, because what else was there for her, weak, undernourished, run-down, and living in north Alabama in the 1930's? It was the thing her life had tended toward. Galloping consumption, the old folks called it, the form of this plague that came and went, sweeping before it quickly and thoroughly with no time for sitting in the sun in hope. He brought a nurse in for her; that was all he could do.

His phone rang at midnight on a Saturday night. He answered it, fumbling the cigarette into his mouth with one hand, holding the receiver under his chin while he groped for a match. It was Cat Cartwright. "Can you come over here?" she said.

He sighed. "What's the trouble, Cat?"

"I don't know. Yes I do. I'm scared."

"Where's Dudley, Cat?"

"Out of town."

"I'll call the pharmacist and have him send out some pills," he said.

"I'll come over there," she said.

"They'll put you to sleep," he said. "I'll call him right now."

"Please come." She started to cry.

He drew on the cigarette, feeling the tiredness creeping up behind his eyelids, thinking, Placebo, placebo. What an ugly word. "No," he said into the receiver. "You'll be better off asleep. Drop in the office tomorrow if you're sick."

He hung up then, feeling a small pang of guilt and telling himself it was ridiculous because what the hell could he do anyway and went back to sleep.

She called again the next morning and he went over. She was sitting on a chaise longue in her bedroom, her face pale and drawn, her eyes wide. "Well," she said when he came in the door. "What are you going to do? Are you going to let Veda die?"

"Did you get the pills?" he said.

"Are you?" she said, her voice rising. "Are you? Are you going to let Veda die? You can't, you know. You just can't. She's just a little girl. She's just a baby."

"I'm doing what I can for Veda," he said.

"She's going to die," Cat said flatly. Suddenly she stood up and peered at his face. "How does it feel to be a doctor?" she said. "Not so good, huh?"

"Oh, can it," he said. "There's nothing the matter with you. I've got calls to make."

She started to cry then, her thin body rocking back and forth. "Don't let her die," she said. "I'm scared for Veda to die. Why does everybody have to die, damn it? What the hell makes everybody have to die?"

"I'm a G.P., not a philosopher or a preacher," Harry said curtly. "Try another province."

She stopped crying and stared at him. "Do you think that might be it?" she said. "The church? Somehow I never thought of that. They'd know about hell and all, wouldn't they? They'd know about what it's like to see Marty like that and think about Veda like that . . . shut up, gone, cold . . ."

"I'll give you a shot," Harry said tiredly.

"Uh-uh." She shook her head. "I told you about Marty, didn't I? There wasn't anybody like Marty at all. And then it was over. Just like that. Now it's going to be Veda and she knows it. That's what's so awful, Doctor. She *knows* it. And she's scared. Veda doesn't want to die. She told me that yesterday. She said, 'I'm scared to die, Cat. I'm scared to death to die.'"

He started to curse then, under his breath, unintelligibly, but he could feel the words ripping out of him in neat bright obscenities. He tried to think about Ruby and about his new hospital and about the tree-lined streets of Bellefonte that he loved and lived on. But it didn't work. Because he'd told her the truth; he wasn't a philosopher or a preacher, he wasn't even much of a thinker, and if he was going to let them start to get to him now he wasn't going to be much of a doctor. He tried to think of that.

"There's a man in Chattanooga I'd like you to go see," he said. "I'll write to him today and make you an appointment. I want you to go."

She laughed, the sound sudden and harsh in the sunlit room. "A head doctor, Harry?" she said. "I know. A head doctor. Well O.K. That's fine for me, isn't it? But what are you going to get him to tell Veda Simms? What can a head doctor do for her now? Will he tell *her* not to be afraid of the dark? Because that's it, isn't it? We're all afraid of the dark."

Hell yes, he thought. We're all afraid of the dark. Me too. Sure. Even though I know that it will probably be this muscle in my chest that ceases to function properly and takes me off—because that's what they say takes most medical men off—even if I know exactly how and why the malfunction occurs, it's still going to be the dark for me, too. But damn them all. That's the way it is.

"Shall I write Dr. Threadgill?" he said to Cat.

"Sure," Cat said. She turned away from him and walked across to the window. "Let's try that one now," she said, looking out into the sun. "At least it'll be somebody to talk to."

He went away, fast, out of the clean sunlit expensively furnished house and down the flower-bordered walk and into the Ford and down the street. He drove home. But he didn't go in. He stopped the car and sat for a moment, shocked, realizing that for the first time since he'd first seen her he didn't want Ruby. He didn't want to talk to her or make love to her or even see her.

He shifted gears and drove off. He drove around the square and off the square and down the highway and when he stopped the car he hadn't known he was coming here at all, but here he was, so he got his bag out of the car and, considering why he could conceivably be here, remembered that one of the kids had a cold. "Of course, that's it," he said aloud and went on around to the little house and knocked. When Eileen came to the door he said, "How's the boy?"

She looked puzzled for a moment, blinking at him in the sunlight. Then she said, "Oh, better. Come in and see for yourself," and moved aside.

He went in, looked at the child, drank a cup of coffee and listened to Eileen talking, and after a little he felt like Harry Clifton, M.D., again.

So he had something else to think about now, something he could look at logically and sanely and medically. Why? Why, when he'd felt things beginning to give, when the last blast had been hurled at the breach, had he gone to Eileen Johnson's house? It reminded him of the questions on an exam. Here was a given situation. Here the symptoms, here the age of the patient, the history, the clinical test. Query: Doctor, what do you diagnose? What do you diagnose, and what do you prescribe?

He wondered if he were in love with her. He didn't think so; but he didn't know a lot of things about himself lately. Maybe he was too tired and had gotten too personally involved with his own damned patients to look objectively at himself.

There was one thing you learned early if you were going to be a doctor. You had to learn it or go under. You could not get involved emotionally with your own patients. That was the simple reason doctors didn't treat their own. You could not prejudice your hand or eye at the moment when it had to be objective. Yet there was Dr. Matthews, with his stories and histories and simple gossip, teaching him involvement with every word he spoke. So perhaps the malady was clear after all: he was losing his objectivity, here in this world of everybody-knows-everybody-else he was becoming one of them. Diagnosis: Complete. But why the cure? What had led him into the house of Eileen Johnson?

In the first place he didn't know her that well. He had delivered her last baby, he doctored the children's colds and mumps and cut hands, he'd gone fishing with Ace a couple of Sundays. But he didn't really know Eileen Johnson very well. She was good to look at but that didn't seem to have anything to do with it. He still thought Ruby the best thing to look at in his world or possible worlds. It wasn't sex; he didn't want to touch her. He had that at home, too, just the way he wanted it. He thought for a while that it might be the kids, the household of laughing, running, noisy children, the children he didn't have. But it wasn't that, either, because Martha Ann Holder was his pick of the bunch where kids were concerned and he never wanted to linger in that household.

It became imperative for him to know. Because he couldn't stay away. He started finding excuses to go by. He'd treat a cold for one of the kids until even Eileen laughed at him. When he started to cultivate Ace he knew he had to stop. That was too damned much. You don't make friends with a man so that you can go into his house and be with his wife, no matter how innocent your reasons. And of course there is always that nagging doubt. Can it be innocent? I must be kidding myself.

It was like a puzzle for him, something he needed to work out, the answer to be the answer to Harry Clifton, man in doubt. Involved in his own private and prevailing puzzle, he forgot about Bellefonte, forgot the real structure and smallness of this place of his involvements, so that he was actually surprised when Ruby found it out, and actually indignant, which in itself he knew to be the most perfect of rationalizations against guilt.

He came in one night about eight o'clock and there was no supper waiting. The dining room was empty, dark, and there was no Ruby to touch him and feed him and smile at him. She came in an hour later, dressed neatly and beautifully, smelling of flowers and just a little of good bourbon. "Where the hell have you been?" he said.

She smiled and with the smile he could see the anger in her eyes. "What do you care, darling?" she said sweetly. "You sure the hell weren't here when I left."

"Oh come off it, Ruby," he said sullenly. "You married a doctor, remember?"

"I remember all right," she said, sitting down and drawing off her white gloves. "What I didn't realize was what a splendid alibi being a doctor could make."

"O.K.," he said. "So what's the trouble?"

"I think you know."

"I think I don't."

She threw the gloves onto the table and smiled again. "What's so awful about it all," she said lightly, "is you tramping around fishing with that half-drunken husband of hers. Do you have *any* idea how that *looks?*"

So of course he had to admit that he'd known all along what she'd been talking about. "That's a pretty nasty thing to say," he said.

"It's a pretty nasty thing to do."

"Ruby," he said quietly, "I don't know what people in this dead and dying town say to you about me or about themselves or about anything else. But I'll tell you one thing. I swear to you I have never been unfaithful to you. Not in word, deed, or thought. That's about as simply as I can put it."

"Oh, really, Harry," she said. "Don't tell me you go over there because she makes a good cup of coffee."

He got mad, then, and because he knew the anger was part of the rationalization too it only made him more angry. "Goddam it all," he said, feeling the anger with a sort of love, watching the words forming in his mind and coming out his mouth with a love for them too. "Goddam it all to hell. I will have friends if I want to have friends. I will find a place somewhere among the quick if it kills me and you and the whole damned town. I am sick to death of death and fear and trembling. I am sick to death of weeping and wailing and want. You want to know why I go there? I can tell you. I go because she doesn't whine. Of all the people I know and see day after miserable mocking day she doesn't whine. That's it, pure and simple and whole, Ruby, my love. I bask in it. I delight in it. I love it. Here is someone who doesn't whine."

She was staring at him now, her eyes wide and luminous, and he could see the anger coming into her too, as though she had caught it from him, as though it were communicable. "Do I whine, Harry?" she said. "Damn you. Do I whine? Do I? Do I?"

"No," he said slowly, watching her face. "No, Ruby. You don't whine. But what in God's name do you have to whine about? Just why the hell do you think it's any victory for you not to whine? As far as I can see there's never been one single solitary thing you ever wanted in your whole life that you didn't manage to get, and on your own terms. And that, my dear, includes not only my well-equipped hospital, but me too."

She hit him. She moved fast and gracefully and lovely toward him and hit him in the face with her small white hand and the touch of it drove all the anger in him into a frenzy of wanting. He picked her up and went up the stairs with her and into the bedroom and threw her onto the bed. He didn't even take her clothes off, or let her, and through it all she kept beating on his back with her fists and saying, "Please. I'm not fixed. Let me up . . ." And he didn't give one single solitary damn, because this was the way he'd always wanted her, beautifully, savagely, thoroughly and suddenly, and to hell with how she wanted it or whether she wanted children or not.

Then suddenly she moved under him, around him, and her voice laughed in his ear, low and happy and warm. "Do it again, darling," she said. "Do it all night long. And in the morning I'll make you a good cup of coffee. See if I don't."

Veda Simms died the day that Graham McCloud was elected to the State Senate, the day they were having a celebration in the living room of the McCloud house where Elizabeth and Graham lived when they were in residence in Bellefonte.

It was an old room, high-ceilinged, musty with twenty-year-old drapes and velvet-covered loveseats. There was a coal fire in the converted grate, smouldering blackly and casting light onto the worn, charred floorboards in front of it.

Graham sat on the library table, one leg pulled up under him, a glass in his hand. He was being expansive and charming and—to Harry Clifton—entirely repulsive. Graham pulled Elizabeth to him with his free hand. "Well, baby," he said. "We'll make permanent residence down there yet."

"Harry," Ruby said beside him. "Pour me another drink."

The phone rang and in a moment Aunt Hat put her head around the posts between the front hall and the living room. "Doctor Clifton," she said. "They need you at Simms'. Mr. Graham, from what Mr. R. V. says you might better go with him."

So little Veda has spoiled Graham's celebration, Harry thought, and cursed himself for being more cynical than his new-found objectivity gave him the right to be. He left Ruby with Elizabeth and he and Graham climbed into the Ford.

"Well, what you reckon?" Graham said, and shook his head.

They didn't speak again, driving silently through the bare streets of Bellefonte toward the wide, once-white, house.

He brushed past Aunt Betty and the Captain and Mozel and R. V. and Morgan, standing together in the reception hall, looking at him as though he might have brought the reprieve in his black bag, and he thought, Graham is your boy for reprieves. I'm not a politician either, not a preacher, not a philosopher. And damned little healer, damned little of that.

Martha Ann was sitting on the steps. She was in coveralls and she sat hunched over holding something—a doll?—huddled against her. He turned back into the hall. "Somebody get that kid out of here," he said.

They moved, turning around him in confusion, and he saw the Captain go toward the stairway as he walked on. The nurse was waiting for him at the door. He talked to her and went in to look at Veda, white and only semi-conscious now, her breath loud in the stillness of the room. He found her pulse, feeling like a pretender with the gesture, and turned to the nurse. "Tell them to come on in here," he said. "One at a time. That Holder boy last. He's the last one, and alone. You hear me?"

She nodded and he went into the kitchen and shut the door.

He drank the coffee Aunt Betty brought him and he thought about Veda Holder, who was only twenty-eight years old and

who was finished with what living she was allotted, and he wondered what would happen to Martha Ann and Janice and to Morgan Holder, who had never thought beyond Veda Simms in his
plans for living and who, beginning tonight, was going to have to
think beyond her.

He heard Cat Cartwright come in the front door, because you
couldn't miss hearing her, and he cursed briefly and loudly so that
Aunt Betty jumped and went out onto the back porch where she
put her apron over her head and began to cry.

He reached Cat before she got to Veda's room. "Cat," he said
firmly, "I'm going to shoot enough of something into you to knock
you out right now. Let her die in peace."

She'd been crying and, for the first time since he'd first seen her
making her aimless circuit of his office, her hair wasn't combed.
She looked disheveled and a little hysterical and she had bitten her
lips until they were peeling. She looked at him and began to whis-
per, her voice sounding eerie and shaky. "I'm not going to let her
go," she said.

"Come on in the kitchen, Cat," he said. "Drink some coffee.
Let them say goodbye. People—some people—have a need for
that."

"I'm not going to let her go," she said again. "That's all. That's
it. Period. Definitely."

He took her arm and pushed her into the kitchen and into a
chair. "Where's a cup?" he said, and Aunt Betty came with cup
and spoon. He dumped a folder of white powder into it and
poured coffee. "Drink it," he said to Cat. "Drink it now and drink
it quick. I'm going to be needed in there in a minute."

The nurse put her head in the door and nodded and he went
out, praying she'd drink the coffee and not hoping for it—not for
a minute.

They worked over Veda, doing mechanically all the things that
might give her two minutes more breath, and for the first time in
his years of practice he found himself wondering what that two
minutes was in the scheme of the universe. So I'm getting to be a

philosopher after all, he thought, and held out his hand for the oxygen.

The door banged open behind him and without even turning he said, "Get her out." But she was already past him and leaning over the bed, talking, crooning even, sounding drunk and incoherent and somehow ancient like a witch casting a spell.

"You stay here, baby," she said to Veda. "You stay right here. I am not going to let you go. Do you hear me?"

He pushed her away and looked at Veda. Her eyes were closed and the blue veins showed palely through her skin. She breathed, but slightly, hoarsely, tiredly. "Look at her, Cat," he said quietly. "Hush up and look at her. She's tired, Cat. Don't you understand that? There isn't anything left for her any more. She needs to go."

Cat stared at him, her pupils black and empty. "You're not going to take her," she said and, reaching around him, she picked Veda up, holding her thin body against her and starting in a half-stumble toward the door.

He couldn't move for a moment, the shock wave hitting him, and she got past him and past the nurse who was standing open-mouthed beside the bed. Then he did move but Cat backed against the door, holding Veda's body against her as though she were a child. "You're not going to get her," she said again, still whispering.

"Cat," he said. "Cat, you goddamned idiot." He bent over Veda and Cat pulled her away from him.

"She's gone, Cat," he said.

Still she stood there, backed against the door, her eyes looking past him at nothing except terror and—he knew suddenly—darkness. He was defeated. He was the medicine man all right, the witch doctor whose spell had failed and who was being turned out, sent out, while the women—the unutterable and always present and hovering female—would resort to their own bitter spells. He was a little insane himself in that moment and he knew that she could open that door and walk out into the middle of that family holding the shell of Veda and he couldn't stop her. He was al-

mighty scared himself. He knew that. He knew it objectively because the hairs on the back of his neck prickled and the one clear
thought that came to him then was the names of the bones of
the body, falling neatly into place in their little mnemonic schema.
The bones of the body, named and known, his ticket to medicine
land.

She saved him. She—of course—because only the female can
function when reason fails. Eileen, quiet and sure and beautiful,
opened the door from the back bathroom and walked in. She
didn't even look at him. She went to Cat. "Cat," she said, and
Cat looked at her. Her eyes came back from wherever they were
focused and from whatever they were contemplating and looked
at Eileen. "Cat," Eileen said again. "Lay Veda down."

Cat walked past her to the bed and laid Veda on it and pulled
down the pale lavender gown and smoothed back her hair. Then
she drew the sheet up over the small bare feet and sat down
beside the bed, beginning to cry.

He started to shake, then, but he thought, Hold on, doc. Not
yet. He motioned to the nurse who hadn't moved, standing with
her tray balanced neatly on her square capable hands. She put the
tray down and went to tell the rest of them.

He got to the back porch. He got that far before he sat down
on the steps and let it get to him. After a few moments he heard
the familiar sounds behind him, the sobs and moans and cries and
steps of sorrow. He was all right then, because that was the way
it was and the way it should be. Grief he dealt with daily. He
didn't have to think about grief.

Eileen walked out the door, sat down beside him, and handed
him a lighted cigarette. He took it out of her hand and drew on
it. Then he looked at her and it hit him. It was primitive and
pure animal and enormous. He wanted her so badly that he was
sick. He started to shake again and he thought cleanly and clearly,
I'm going to rape her. He reached out and pushed her back
against the steps.

"Harry," she said quietly, just as she'd said it to Cat. But he was touching her now and he didn't give a damn what she said. He put his mouth over hers and kissed her and he thought very clearly again, I've been waiting for this all my life. And she said, "Harry," again.

He pulled back and looked at her and put his mouth against her throat and said, "Clavicle," and bit her.

He felt her struggle against him then for the first time and he thought, Ah ha, she doesn't trust sweet reasonableness any more, not with the rogue male. This is different from dealing with ordinary female insanity. Then he heard Graham McCloud's voice.

Graham was standing just behind them on the porch and he said very softly, with no expression whatever, "I always wondered what they did at wakes."

So Harry Clifton was dedicated body and soul for the rest of time to getting Graham McCloud into the governor's mansion in Montgomery. Because how the hell could he live with him in Bellefonte? Not that Graham would condemn him; he could live with that. But Graham McCloud forever after would welcome him into the brotherhood of the South, gentlemen all when they came home at night.

He didn't even feel Eileen move and get up and go away from him. He didn't know what he said to the Simmses, remembering only the look of worry and sorrow laid on him by Captain Simms who sat in the front yard with a child on either knee, waiting for Eileen to come and take them home with her.

When he signed the death certificate he was conscious of signing away a sort of freedom, the freedom of uninvolvement, the freedom of detachment, the freedom he knew that every doctor must have. Because Harry Clifton had let death make a man of him. He had let the specter drive him toward life with all the primitive force of a cave man. Science had left him as completely and utterly as though he had never heard of a test tube. And he hadn't learned the courage yet to know that in the long run it would make a real doctor of him. In this day and this time he had only his sense of loss.

5. *Martha Ann 1939*

Grandfather had always sung a song called "Hand Me Down My Walking Cane." It was a gay song—so they said. But it was one of the sad songs for her. They handed down the cane from a closet shelf, from one of the dark and hidden and forgotten places, they handed it down with the old straw hat, and they handed it down so that someone could go away. They went away then on the midnight train and the midnight train was long and black and wet with steam. It went away down a long, lonesome track and it was the train that never came back again.

Grandfather said a train was a knight in armor, and it could be that in the late afternoon. It could wear a plume of smoke and a lance of fire along the side. It could charge away into the cut in the cliffs between the high red walls of clay, toward the dragon, or toward Roncevaux. Roncevaux always got mixed in her mind with dragons anyway. For when you blew the bugle into the void and stood to fight alone there had to be a dragon about somewhere. It was the sort of thing dragons were created for.

Grandfather said Roncevaux happened every day. But then, she thought, so did dragons, and so did the trains that ran at midnight —the ones that never knew when to stop, and that went on forever into the dark.

At school trains were a means of transportation. Just like that. They were always robbing things of their essence at school. They were always making them fit into neat little boxes. Means of transportation took care of trains—and buses and cars and airplanes and horses and ships; took care of whistles and sails and lovely running flesh. Just as means of communication took care of words—and music and poems and plays and signal lights. And arithmetic took care of all the stars. That was the worst of all. She had been so excited the day she found the astronomy book. She had taken it into the back yard to the old arbor and gotten an apple and sat down to read. And it had been arithmetic, it had been figures and lines and graphs, very neat, very nice. The stars were arithmetic and a train a means of transportation. She carried the shock with her for a long time, all the way to psychology class in college where one instructor labeled loving "will," and another labeled joy in little things, "sublimation." After that she learned to go back to the knights at Roncevaux. Because there always comes the time when you have to stand alone in the pass and when it comes the stars are better company than mathematics. Because the only thing that ever measured chaos is the old night longing of the human mind, the human mind that recognizes the sound in the freight whistle without naming it and labeling it and nailing it on the wall.

After her Mama died it was different. Daddy went away. He went to work for the P.W.A. instead of Mr. Graves and he only came at Christmas and on her birthday. Uncle Bill and his wife came to live with them and Granddaddy and Grandmama were always sick. So she talked to Grandfather, Grandfather was the only one who felt like talking any more.

Grandfather was the only one to tell about what happened with Van Maynard. Van was her cousin and he had been there all her life. But one day they went on a picnic in the cove, Van and Veda and Martin and Holder and Aunt Eileen and Uncle Ace. They came and picked her up in their old car and they drove to the cove like they always did in the summer. It was just like all the other picnics had always been. They took sandwiches and potato salad and Cokes, they wore their old clothes, and Uncle

Ace was funny and happy and laughing like he always was on picnics. And she and Veda had a fuss like they always did.

She took her plate and went way up where the pine trees started growing, where she could sit and look down at the old house where Aunt Eileen's renters lived. Then Van came up and sat down by her. He just sat down like he did lots of times, and she turned around to look at him. She liked the way he looked, it was the funniest feeling she'd ever had. It made her feel sick at her stomach and warm inside and unreal like just before she was going to have one of her headaches. She'd never really thought about liking the way anybody looked before.

He said, "What are you doing way up here by yourself?" She looked at him some more then and his face seemed too close and his eyes were gray, and she thought, I didn't know what color his eyes were. Isn't that funny? Then she could see the sweat on his face, just a sprinkling of it, and it made her mad at him. She wanted to hit him. She could feel just how his face would feel if she hit it very hard. She said, "It's none of your business," and he said, "Why do you always have to fuss?" So she did hit him and it wasn't like she had thought it would be at all. Because he just whaled off and hit her back, hard. It made her teeth hit together and her plate fly out of her hand and there wasn't anything for her to say. He got up and turned around and went off down the mountain, and he didn't come near her the rest of the day.

She told Grandfather about it, and he laughed and laughed and said, "It does go on."

She said, "Why did I feel like that?"

And he said, "Hmmm. Well, well. It's because you're getting older, you know. You're starting to see outside of Martha Ann and when you do that the first thing you usually see is some young gentleman."

She said, "Van Maynard's no gentleman."

Grandfather laughed some more and said, "Folks don't ever change."

That winter Dr. Clifton took her tonsils out. Grandmama took her to the hospital and they gave her ether and she had to throw up and throw up, and they wouldn't give her any water. It was terrible and unbelievable, so that after it was over she felt like it hadn't happened. Everything about those days in the hospital was unreal and hazy like something you think of when you're half asleep. She remembered Grandmama and Uncle Bill sitting by her bed, and Uncle Bill making the nurse give her some ice to eat, and she remembered Aunt Eileen holding a little shiny pan for her to be sick in and Dr. Clifton standing behind her getting ready to put the horrible little stick with cotton down her throat. She got all tense waiting but the stick didn't come and she heard Dr. Clifton say, "I'm not ever going to get over it."

Then Aunt Eileen said, "Don't be an idiot, Harry."

He said, "Right here and right now I could."

And Aunt Eileen said, "We're going to move to Florida."

She sat up then and said, "No!" real loud and made her throat bleed again. Because that meant she couldn't watch Van any more, in his knickers and sweat shirt playing baseball on the campus or swimming at the creek with water all over his shoulders.

Then Aunt Eileen rubbed her head and said, "Hush, baby. I have to sell my farm first."

Aunt Cat came to the hospital too and brought her a banana split that she couldn't eat. She lay and watched it melt in a pool of bright colors and after that she cried and felt better. Sometimes it was very hard to cry.

Then Daddy came with a new book about Nancy Drew and a doll too because Daddy couldn't ever make up his mind whether she was a big girl or a little girl any more. She couldn't either so it was all right of Daddy. He looked tired and lonesome and she said, "Why don't you come home?"

Daddy said, "I have to work, baby." Even though she knew that didn't answer her question she pretended it did because that was what he wanted her to do.

After the tonsils were gone life changed and moved, too fast. School went from day to day in a rush of getting up and going off and coming home again. The only thing she ever did any more was read. Because Granddaddy and Grandmama never did anything any more. They went to bed early and they didn't sit on the porch and rock or in front of the dining room fire and rock. They didn't tell the stories any more. All of her life they had told stories at night, about people and places and times before she, or even her mother, was born. They told about ghosts and grave-robbings and idiots, and people who were just a tetch queer. They told about play-parties and weddings and spinning jennies and foot-logs, and buggies and snakes, and singings and storms. Now they didn't tell the stories any more. And because they didn't life changed and faded just a little bit.

Grandfather still told his stories. He still talked about the times before and the times to come. Grandfather couldn't ever change. He wasn't a changing thing like other people. She couldn't imagine looking at him and seeing him different, as she had Van, nor watching him quit and cease and begin to not be any more like Granddaddy and Grandmama. He was like the things in books ... there forever.

In some ways Grandfather was like the president, bigger than other people. Martha Ann had seen the president once. Like this: he was coming through Bellefonte on the afternoon train. Veda and Van told her. They ran all the way from town to her house to tell her when their daddy heard it at the newspaper office. She begged to go up to the crossing with them to watch him go by on the train. They didn't want her to go. Grandmama and Grandfather were Republicans and Grandmama didn't think much of her "high-tailing up to a railroad crossing just to look at that man." But in the end they said she could go because Grandfather said, "Let her have her look at history. That man is history, think what you like about his brand of it."

Granddaddy was a Democrat, like her Daddy, and he said, "Go on and look. I'll come with you." But Grandmama sniffed and talked about a foolish old man, so he didn't go after all.

But they went, she and Veda and Van. It was coming on toward dark, and cool in the air from the night and the damp, the way it got when the wind came off the river in the late afternoon. They went up the road toward the crossing, kicking a rock all the way, cut through the field across the highway, and came to the grading.

She sat down on a rock by the road and looked up the track but the light was green. "She ain't in the block yet," Van said.

"I know it, smarty," she said.

"Don't kick at the gravel," Veda said. "You'll get us all dirty."

Across the track and on down the dirt road they could see the place where the Negro houses began, all the rows of slanting, yard-swept houses with the ragged plants on the banisters and the chickens in the yards and the children with their rubber tires and tin-can tommy-walkers. After a while all the colored people started coming out on their porches and Martha Ann thought, I reckon that's why Grandmama didn't want me coming up to look at him. It's a thing that the colored people do.

Van was looking at her. "You'll remember this all your life," he said suddenly. "That's what my Mama said. You don't ever forget things like seeing the president like this."

"I reckon I know it," she said.

Veda began to whine. "I'm tired," she said. "I wish that ole train would come on."

"Oh, stop it," Van said. "You should have stayed home anyway. You always try to spoil things."

I am happy, Martha Ann thought. I am happy right now this minute. It was funny how seldom you ever thought that. Often you looked back and said, I was happy then, and sometimes you looked ahead and thought, I'm going to be happy when tomorrow comes, but it wasn't often you just thought, I am happy. Mostly it happened when you had just waked up in the morning, feeling happy for no reason you could name, like it had been told you in your sleep last night and you still remembered it a little bit after you woke up. But that went away by breakfast; this was different. This was because the air smelled cool and clean and the light was happy. Sometimes the light could be terribly sad, especially in the autumn or in February. Sometimes the light in February made her cry.

And, of course, there was Van, standing in the slanting light, his hands in his pocket, looking up the track, waiting to see the president go by.

He looked at her. "What's eating you?" he said. "You look sick."

She didn't answer him. Because you couldn't ever answer boys when they said those things. She thought it was because they meant something else besides what they said. And how on earth could you answer something you never heard at all?

"It's in the block," Van said, and she could hear the whistle.

She got up then and they stood in a row on the edge of the track, looking up the road toward the red light that burned in the distance. We'll wait forever, she thought, just like this now, and the train will never come if we don't let it. Then it was there. It came slow and dark through the afternoon, and in her mind she could see all the crossings and all the gradings down the track where the people were standing waiting just like they were.

First there was the engine, then the line of cars, and finally the end came into sight. He was standing on the observation platform, leaning on a cane, and there were two men beside him. But you didn't look at them at all. You just saw the president. He said hello to them and she could see the gleam of his glasses where the sun was going down, shining on them, and the way his hands held the cane, and that he smiled. Then the train went on past the crossing and into the trees that lined the track toward the station. Finally there was the whistle again, coming back to them this time, and he was gone. After a while she looked across the track and there were all the little colored children, standing quiet, their eyes big like they got about candy, standing quiet, like the way the night was coming, on the other side of the track.

When Grandfather was ninety-six years old they gave a birthday party for him. Grandmama was busy for days seeing that the cake got made just right, and the supper planned, and all the silver and good china gotten out and shined and washed. Grandmama even got out the lace cloth and mended the torn places.

Everybody came. There were old people like Mr. Cartwright and Mr. and Mrs. Graves, young people like Aunt Cat and her husband and Aunt Eileen and Uncle Ace. Dr. Clifton came, but his wife didn't come with him.

Van came, too, but he wouldn't talk to her and after he ate his cake he went home. He was like that sometimes.

The cake really had ninety-six candles on it. It was made in layers and layers, all different sizes. Grandmama and Aunt Betty had spent a whole day making it in the kitchen and Grandmama decorated it with the silver decorators that she kept in the back of the sideboard with the timbale irons.

They had nectar too, from the fruit jars on the top shelf of the pantry. It was sweet and sad somehow like the fall days. She told Aunt Eileen that and Aunt Eileen smiled at Dr. Clifton over her head and said, "This one!"

Dr. Clifton smiled, too, and said, "Yes. How sweet and sad, the days that are no more."

Grandfather sat in the chair with the arms at the head of the table and smiled and smiled. He ate the cake and drank his coffee out of the big cup. Everybody stayed late and all the lights were on. It was like a long time ago before Mama died. She went out on the side porch once and there were all the lights, lying across the yard in patterns the shape and size of all the windows, and when people moved inside the house they crossed the light and went away again.

When she came back in Grandfather was motioning to her. She saw him from the door and went over. He looked tired and happy and he had cake crumbs in his beard. "I reckon it's about time for me to go on up, Martha Ann," he said. "How about handing me my walking cane?"

She brought it from where it leaned against the sideboard and he took it and went on upstairs to bed. After he was gone most of the people left but Aunt Eileen and Uncle Ace and Dr. Clifton, and a few other close friends, stayed. They stayed to talk to Grandmama and Granddaddy and they forgot about her, she guessed, because nobody told her to go to bed.

After a while she went out and sat down on the steps in the hall. She could still hear them talking around the dining room fire and it made her feel safe. After a while she leaned her head against the wall and went to sleep.

She could tell it was late when Dr. Clifton started up the steps, the night had that dead feeling, and she could tell that Dr. Clifton was in a hurry too, because he didn't even see her. Aunt Eileen did when she started up, though, and she made her go to bed. She lay there, listening to the steps and sounds, the slamming doors, and she knew that Grandfather was going to die. She knew because that was the way it had been with Mama. Later they had come and told her and she'd pretended she hadn't known, but she had known; and she knew now. She felt lonesome and sad and afraid and she tried to think of some of the stories Grandfather had told her, but that made her cry; then she tried to think of the president on the train, but that made her think of trains and it frightened her. She got up finally and went to the dining room.

The party litter was still there because Aunt Betty had gone back to bed and was going to clean in the morning. She sat down by the half-dead fire in the middle of the dirty plates and napkins. She tried to think about God, but that didn't help either.

When Mama died they all told her that she had gone to heaven and that God took care of her. But that didn't seem a very good thing because when she thought of God and heaven she thought of Sunday school, and Sunday school was the smell of oil heaters and having your feet cold under the table. It was Miss Mayfield reading about Paul on the road to Damascus and John, the best-beloved. It was all those men who were far away in a dead time, who wore bright flowing clothes and beards, and who knew Jesus who was the son of God. It didn't seem to her that her mother would be happy in a place with those people, nor with a God who liked to be talked about where it smelled like oil heaters. She knew Grandfather wouldn't like it. Grandfather always liked something new. He wouldn't like something that happened hundreds of years ago, or something that Miss Mayfield read out of the cards that smelled of paste.

Grandmama had told her once that eternity meant with no end. That meant Grandfather and Mama would be in heaven forever, with no end, up there somewhere with all those stern people in robes. It wasn't likely. Maybe, she thought, it was more the stars. Maybe it was the eternity of the stars that they went to, the spaces between the stars where it took the millions of years for light to travel. That made her feel better because there was bound to be something new and wonderful out there somewhere in the quiet places between stars.

She was cold and she was afraid to put anything on the fire because she wasn't supposed to. Then she remembered all the coats and got one from the pile on the couch. It smelled of men and the newspaper office and she knew it was Uncle Ace's. She snuggled into it and felt better still. They were moving around upstairs, but quieter now. There was something she kept trying to remember, something about Grandfather, and just as she felt herself going off into sleep she knew it. She could see them sitting in his room together and she could hear herself telling him, "When you die you've gone somewhere. . ."

So it was all right. Because it was like getting on the train, the midnight train that never came back again. Any train had to be going somewhere, that's what trains were for. They took you away, but away to somewhere else, and there weren't any trains in Galilee so it wasn't there. They went on, like everything else, on— and out. That was what Grandfather had always wanted. When they read about Flash Gordon in the funny papers he'd say, "You'll live to see it," and she figured maybe he'd get to see it too, the places between the stars where the wind stopped, and where whatever happened happened after the sun went down.

Of course they all thought it was scandalous and Grandmama

couldn't see where she got such ideas. They told her she didn't understand. But she knew they were wrong, so it didn't really matter. That afternoon she sat in the kitchen with Aunt Betty and sang it for him anyway, just like she'd wanted them to do at the funeral, the sad song that they said was a gay song, "Hand Me Down My Walking Cane."

Beachhead

Through the long days of summer Eileen watched her daughter, Veda. The doctor had put her on tranquilizers, but she was still too tense, too quiet. The tranquilizers made Eileen think of Harry Clifton. The last time she had been in Bellefonte they'd had a Coke together in Simms' Sundries and he'd said everybody in Bellefonte was on them, how about her? She'd said she'd be damned if she wanted to go round half alive. He'd laughed and said that was typical. And she'd said, of course, that he still didn't know enough about her to know what was typical of her and what was not. She and Harry were good friends now, she usually had a talk with him when she was in Bellefonte, always in the drugstore. She hadn't seen him alone since the day Veda Simms had died.

She'd think about Harry sometimes, about the way she could have wanted him if she'd let herself, about how all her life there were the places where she might have let herself do this or do that, but where there always seemed to be the little sign post, like the pictures of the prayer stations in the Swiss alps, a little peaked-roofed house pointing the other way. She'd figure she was pretty lucky because most people didn't seem to have the sign posts at all, or if they did they didn't have the ability to follow them. Her own daughter, for instance, writhing against her era like a snake in a cage, like the new snakes Vance used to bring in from the woods, spitting and hissing and coiling inside the wire. And none of it any good, because everybody is born into a time of trouble, there isn't any other time. It's the human condition, like two arms and two legs. It's always there, the challenge to be met. After all, it was what kept it all going in the right direction. When the

challenges stopped it would all stop, like if suddenly all the elec-
trons became protons or vice-versa. Nothing. Stasis. Poof!

It tickled Cliff to hear her talk like that. He'd say her knowledge
of science was about as advanced as Newton's had been. But she'd
say, All right. I get along right well, even today. And I reckon if
they came tomorrow and said, We've scanned them all and you're
it, told me I'd have to climb into that first cylinder and be shot off
into the dark, out of earth and home and air and light, why, I
reckon I could do it. I wouldn't like it, mind you, but I'd go. I'd
go sweating and praying and sick at my stomach, but I think I'd go.
And Cliff said, I know damned well you would, and God help us
if the Russians get the idea that women are the stronger sex before we admit it.

Eileen tried that summer to think of ways to help Veda but
none of them seemed to amount to much or come to anything.
What her daughter really needed, Eileen thought, was a way of
seeing history, the way Captain Simms used to make them all see
it and feel it. She thought of it as riding on a train, going by the
stations, looking out the windows, watching the wayside stops
come into view. There were the Egyptians under a hot red sun,
the stone station with its strange carved beaks and square-cut
figures flanking the mud of the river bottom; the Greeks, white
marble and behind a wall the sound of the breaking sea; the Ro-
mans, heavy wheels and the sound of brass. Here the roads ran
straight and the train went faster—into Galilee—a barren stony
place where birds circled and a cross stood naked and ugly under
a gray-black sky. Through the tunnel then and past the monks,
chanting into morning through the night, past the knights and
castles and the dying fall, through the dust of pilgrims and the grit
of empire, through the rabble to the ocean fronts. All of it bright
and beautiful, naked and dangerous, and no place anywhere to
pause or hide under the blue unseeing sky. Because it was wound
up and going, from east to west and on, out of the garden into the
wilderness, out of the wilderness into the sky. All of it in every one
of us somewhere, if we could only learn how to look at it. That
was the trick man couldn't master, the looking in and seeing the

wholeness of it. Maybe we weren't supposed to, not yet anyway. Maybe the brightness and nakedness and danger were too close yet, maybe they'd kill the beauty and wholeness if we saw it plain. But you had to have a feel for it, or not do much living. Eileen had been seeing that all her life.

Her own life, on its own segment along the line, seen closer but all a part of it somehow. Boarding the train in the rural fastness of morning, the cove and Vance, and having to stay right on the train and watch him fade out the window and be gone behind her, gone with the trenches and Tipperary and a world made safe for democracy. While they blew the whistle and she stayed right on, on into the station where they played jazz and drank bootleg gin, where Floyd Collins died and Rudolph Valentino ceased to be, where Lindbergh flew across the ocean and Al Capone laughed in Chicago; past that and through it while they sang Bye Bye Blackbird and Buz Mayhill erected a statue to Apollo in the middle of Cedar Hill.

Faster now, through the bread lines, the hunger, through fear; past the gray sad faces that listen for the dead music, and into the station where the booming voice begins . . . Nothing to fear but fear itself. And the train moves faster. On the way to a rendezvous, on the way, on the way, on the way. Leaving Veda behind now, and Captain, and the future waiting to claim someone else at the next stop.

She had an old photograph album filled with yellowing pictures, and with glossy bright new ones, the old ones written across with the autographic pencil, the new ones dated in bright black printer's ink. She didn't look at them often, she was too busy. But sometimes, on a rainy afternoon, she and Bambi would get the book out and she'd tell over again who they were: Vance, in puttees and overseas cap, squinting into the camera with a barracks wall behind him, her mother and father, sitting stiff and overdressed on a horsehair settee, Morgan and Veda like paper dolls, Veda's long loops of beads swinging forward, her hat in her hand, her mouth fixed as though to say, "Wait a minute," Morgan sheepish beside her in a buttoned vest. Ace in his Sunday suit, Cat in a sweater and a straw hat, and nothing else, posing her knees prettily above the satin high-heeled shoes, Graham McCloud sitting in Marty's Playboy, and one of Marty in his French beret.

The children: Van naked on a bearskin rug, Van sitting on the chicken coop, Van in his graduation suit, Van on the flight deck of a carrier; one of Veda in her first bought dress, and one of Martha Ann standing beside Van, both of them embarrassed and grimacing in the sunlight of 1941.

She'd look at those pictures and long to say to Veda, "You can't get off here, my girl. This just isn't your stop."

On a Sunday night Martha Ann called from Montgomery. She came to Eileen's for most of her vacations, which occurred any time she could talk Graham into giving her a few days off. Martha Ann didn't like her job, she didn't like office work at all, but she did like the South. "I don't know why I stay here," she'd tell Eileen. "I can't make any money at all unless I work for my relatives, I can't walk down the street to a movie alone without being frowned at, and I can't even serve on a jury. But I love it. There just isn't any other place I like to live. They're all in too damned much of a hurry everywhere else. This is the only place in this country where people still amble to lunch."

Eileen picked her up in Orlando. Veda hadn't wanted to come with her, Veda and Martha Ann had never gotten along.

They drove through the sunshine, being themselves behind their dark glasses and kerchiefs, together in the way they always were, companionably, comfortably, not aunt and niece, but friends.

"Veda's got the heebie-jeebies," Eileen said.

"Veda? Why? I wish to God I had as much as she's got."

"Are you being bitter?"

"No. Just that it always seems to me it's the people with the most that get the heebie-jeebies. That's all."

"Sometimes it does seem like that," Eileen said. "I guess other people don't have the time to spare."

Martha Ann laughed. "I'm sorry," she said. "I'm tired. It's a mad house in that damned capitol."

"How's your Daddy?" Eileen said.

Martha Ann shrugged. "I don't know, Aunt Eileen. How would I know? He seems all right. I never see him much. It's way too late now for me and Daddy, you know."

"I know."

"He goes over and plays poker with Graham one night a week and they manage to get maudlin about the good old days, he works, buys a new car every year. I guess he's happy. Though he's not exactly the government type, is he?"

Eileen grinned. "Nope. He wasn't the farm type either. I think what Morgan would really have liked would have been a garage— or his own lumber company."

"Fat chance!" Martha Ann said.

"Yeah."

They could smell the ocean now. Martha Ann sniffed. "One of these days I'll get up the nerve to take myself away from Alabama and live on a beach."

"What's stopping you?"

"I'm afraid I'd go native."

"I doubt that."

Martha Ann lit a cigarette. "I get influenced," she said. "Remember Walt."

"I remember him quite well, thank you," Eileen said. "Light me a cigarette, will you?"

Walt had been Martha Ann's husband, a charming intelligent drunk. They'd been married three years before Martha Ann had given up on him. Luckily, Eileen always thought, there had been no children. Walt hadn't wanted them.

"I was thinking about Walt the other day," Martha Ann said. "I hardly ever think about him any more. But one afternoon, just sitting in the park waiting for one of those damned messengers to bring me a court order, I thought about the first time I met him. And I wondered just then, for the first time, if I didn't marry him because he smelled of bourbon and had hands like Uncle Ace."

"Martha Ann, for God's sake!"

Martha Ann laughed and lit another cigarette. "We're nearly there, aren't we?" she said, looking out the window and smiling contentedly. "I'm going to stay a whole damned week this time. The office can go to holy hell."

"Were you serious?" Eileen said.

"About Walt? Halfway. You know Uncle Ace was the real love of my life—before Van." She threw her cigarette out the window. "I always seem to be loving someone of yours, don't I? It's rather silly, come to think of it."

"That's probably what all the smug Yankees mean about our ingrown culture," Eileen said, grinning.

"Um-hmm. Decadence, incest, and violence," Martha Ann said. "Only from where I sit it's more likely to be inertia, flirtation, and damn foolishness."

"We're home," Eileen said.

They had a drink before Martha Ann got into her bathing suit. Then she was gone toward the ocean and Eileen walked down to Veda's.

Veda was in the bedroom again. She stayed there more and more. The kids were patching sail on the back porch. "Well, I reckon she got here," Veda said, propping her chin on her fist.

"Um-hmm. You all want to come down to my house for supper tonight?"

"I don't know. I don't feel like cooking. Don't spccially feel like seeing Martha Ann either."

"Oh, hush," Eileen said crossly. "Get up off that bed and comb your hair before Cliff gets here. You look like hell."

"Well, thank you, Mother," Veda said. But she got out of bed and went into the bathroom.

She came back with her hair combed and a pair of shorts on. "Hand me those white pills in the kitchen, will you?" she said.

"No. I think you can get along without them this week."

"The doctor said . . ."

"He said for a week or so."

Veda pouted. "You sound like Cliff."

"We'll expect you all for supper," Eileen said. "I'm going to take the kids down for a swim. You dress up a little."

"No."

"All right." Eileen went on out the door, collecting the kids as she went. She tried not to let herself push Veda. It was a hard thing to decide when these aberrant moods needed firmness, when sympathy. The thing was, she always remembered Cat, she couldn't keep the thought of Cat away from her when she looked at Veda. Damn it, she'd think, I will not let my child turn into a psychotic mess. But then, what the hell can I do about it? What could any of us ever do for Cat? That's what it always came back to, the sense of failure with Cat. Harry Clifton had tried to talk her out of that. He said they'd all done everything they could. But you couldn't ever feel sure about human relationships, they were too damned tenuous. She thought of Martha Ann and smiled. Now why wouldn't she, daughter of Veda and Morgan, be the one to get snowed by atomic weapons? But she wouldn't. Martha Ann was like Betty Al. You could lay it on 'em with a shovel and they'd manage to crawl out and take a bath.

When she got back from the beach Martha Ann and Cliff were sitting on the porch drinking vodka. "Where's Veda?" she said.

Cliff shrugged. "Said she wanted to wait till later," he said. "I had an idea the liquor cabinet would be open for the company so I came on."

"Well, you can get up and mix me one too," Eileen said.

He went to the kitchen. Eileen looked at Martha Ann. She was wearing black pedal pushers and a black Chinese jacket, sandals. She looked cool and relaxed and almost pretty. "What were you two talking about?" Eileen said.

Martha Ann sipped her drink. "Graham McCloud. Cliff says he's the only politician he's ever heard of that's been around the length of time he has and held as many offices as he has and never been governor."

"Shouldn't matter," Eileen said. "He's always been on the gravy train, one way or the other."

"Um-hmm." Martha Ann crossed her legs and stretched. "They do say the Wallaces didn't want him governor."

"Probably not," Eileen said. "He's too old south for them."

"Are they all that important in Maynard County and all the north of the state now?"

"I imagine so."

"Poor old Harry Clifton should never have let that Whit help him build the hospital," Martha Ann said.

"Who's Harry Clifton?" Cliff said, handing Eileen her glass.

"A nice guy from Bellefonte," Eileen said.

"Ah. From the light of the world. Did you like Bellefonte, Martha Ann?"

"Like everybody, yes and no."

"To go back to?"

"No."

Cliff picked up her empty glass and went back to the kitchen.

"Feeling better?" Eileen said.

"You know it. This place is the relaxation spot of the universe for me," Martha Ann said.

"That's good," Cliff said, handing her her glass. "Veda thinks it's pretty grim."

"I don't know, Cliff," Eileen said. "Maybe she needs a good spanking."

Cliff sighed. "Maybe. Or for me to get another job."

Eileen shook her head. "She needs a sense of history," she said, and went on to tell them about her idea. She hadn't voiced it before, but she knew Martha Ann would understand it. Martha Ann always liked her notions.

She was nodding now, sipping her drink and smiling. "But it's more too, Eileen. Life, I mean. It's a kaleidoscope too, you know, not just a train ride."

"How's that?" Cliff said. "You sound like my esteemed mother-in-law yourself."

Martha Ann laughed. "Well," she said slowly, "you know. A kaleidoscope is different every time you turn it, at least the pattern is, but the pieces are all the same. The same pieces in a different pattern. That's life . . . yours, or the world's."

"I'll have to think about that one," Eileen said.

"Well you ladies will have to excuse me," Cliff said. "I'm just an ordinary scientist. I don't know a damned thing about metaphysics."

"But that's what I'm trying to say!" Martha Ann said. "That's what I keep trying to tell everybody. Metaphysics and science are really the same thing, just a twist of the kaleidoscope apart. See?"

"Yeah," Cliff said, stretching his long legs across the porch. "I see I need another drink. I can't keep up with the esoterics here without it."

"No. Listen," Martha Ann said. Her eyes were shining now and she reached up to push her hair out of her face. "Listen, Cliff. Have you ever tried to lose anybody?"

"Huh?"

"You know, really lose somebody you've known. Lose them never to see or hear of or find out something about by coincidence. It can't be done, my friend. They keep coming back like the well-known song. If they were anybody significant, that is, and most people you know are significant to you, one way or the other."

Cliff stared at her. He was a little high now, Eileen noticed, thinking, This is the first time I've seen him relax since Veda started this business. "Wait a minute," he said. "Wait a minute. You may be right. It's like matter and energy, that right? Destroy one you've got the other—stuck with the other, in fact. Right! So why couldn't it work with people, or . . . Oh hell!" He threw back his head and laughed loudly. "You two have got me doing it."

"I've got to get supper on," Eileen said.

"It's on," Martha Ann said. "You said gumbo. And gumbo is cooking."

"Well, thank you," Eileen said.

"You're quite welcome," Martha Ann said. "Where's Veda and the kids?" She got up and went to the door, looking down the beach toward the other house.

Cliff looked annoyed for a moment, then he smiled. "Want me to go get them?"

"Why don't you?" Martha Ann said. Her voice suddenly had a sharpness in it. Eileen looked at her and back at Cliff.

Cliff shrugged and got up from the lounge chair. "I'll go get 'em," he said.

Martha Ann stood at the screen, watching him walk off down the beach. Then she turned and went into the kitchen. Eileen followed her. "What's the matter?" she said quietly.

"Nothing." Martha Ann stirred the gumbo. "No." She turned around. "I'm a liar. It's . . . it's that, sitting out there on the porch with Cliff, talking to him like I haven't talked to anybody in a long time, I suddenly, well, just liked the whole idea of a man again. The idea of Cliff. That's all. I'm sorry. When I realized it I made him go get Veda. Because, after all, I've never cared much for Veda and that makes it pretty bad, doesn't it?"

"Well, my God, I hope we're not all responsible for our thoughts the same as if they were actions," Eileen said.

"Why not? One becomes the other."

"Not necessarily," Eileen said. "That's where free will comes in."

"Keep talking," Martha Ann said. "We can talk it all away."

Eileen looked at her. "Oh," she said. "You mean you don't want to talk it away."

Martha Ann turned back to the gumbo. "I remember when we were kids," she said softly. "We used to get those Easter eggs that came one inside the other. Remember? Each egg is smaller than the last and you keep opening one and finding another one." She turned the stove down and turned back to Eileen. "We used to call them infinite Easter eggs because, even though you knew that eventually there would come the time to open the last one and find either the toy inside or only emptiness, it never seemed that way. It always seemed as though there would· go on being another one to open forever. Today has been like finding another egg to open."

"You ought to get married again," Eileen said. "Or something."

Martha Ann laughed. "I thought that's what we were trying to talk away," she said. "The 'or something.'"

"No," Eileen said. "I'm not worried about Cliff. He's in love with Veda."

"I know it," Martha Ann said.

"All right," Eileen said. "I'm not preaching. Honest."

"I never knew you to," Martha Ann said. "Want another drink?"

"All right. Mix another for Veda and Cliff too while you're at it."

"You want me to go back to Montgomery?" Martha Ann said.

Eileen looked at her for a moment, watching her hands mixing the drinks neatly and efficiently. "No," she said. "Let the damned kaleidoscope have this round."

PART III

September in the Rain

1. *1941*

The summer of 1941 was the last summer for a lot of people. For some of them it was the last summer before the war, for others it was the last summer of childhood, for Van Maynard it was the last summer of Bellefonte.

It was a long summer, filled with sunshine, and looked back on, it seemed incredibly beautiful, as though sun and air and trees had lain in a haze, green, fragrant, still.

They belonged to a gang that summer, Van and Veda and Martha Ann. They called themselves the Bicycle Club. Van was president, but the membership varied. Sometimes only the boys got together, sometimes they let the girls go with them. They weren't sure they wanted the girls, but they weren't sure they didn't, so they vacillated. But on the night they wrangled a car from reluctant parents the girls always went. They didn't talk about this; it was understood.

They usually got the car on Sunday night after B.Y.P.U. and church. Their parents felt that if they went to B.Y.P.U. and church first they could be allowed the privilege of the family automobile for a few hours afterwards. They furnished their own gas, chipping in a nickel or dime apiece.

For Van it was best on the nights he got his Dad's car. He could always tell on Sunday morning if he was going to get the car on Sunday night. If his Daddy got up cross it was no go, no matter what happened during the day, but if he got up loving

Mama, even with his splitting headache, it was all right and he'd get the car. There wasn't any telling on Saturday, because his Dad drank every Saturday. He didn't drink because he was unhappy like Aunt Cat did, ending up crying and having to drink coffee, or to impress people like Graham McCloud did, bringing scotch with him. He drank mostly because he liked the taste of bourbon. Mama'd drink with him, even though she didn't keep up with him.

They'd sit in the kitchen over in the big house and drink and talk, and somebody always dropped in, Aunt Cat or Graham, or Uncle Morgan when he was in town. Every once in a while Dr. Clifton came, but Mama wasn't ever very nice to him, so he never stayed long.

Van slept in the big house now that he was too old for three in a bed. He had a bed to himself in a room to himself back in the house away from Aunt Trudy and Aunt Mattie. He could come in the back door and go to bed, but he knew Mama always heard him when he came in, no matter what time it was, so it wasn't ever too late.

If Dad got up feeling good on Sunday morning Van would go on to church with Aunt Trudy and Aunt Mattie, and during the afternoon he'd get together with the gang and tell them he thought he'd get the car. They always got together on Sunday afternoons. They'd cut a watermelon, or sit in the yard furniture at Martha Ann's, or make ice cream at Sue Kirk's house where they had a big electric refrigerator. They kidded him about Sue Kirk, but he really didn't like her. She was little and blond and cute but she reminded him of Veda and somehow you couldn't get much interested in a girl that reminded you of your little sister.

Late in the afternoon when the shadows began and the grass turned greener they'd start getting ready for B.Y.P.U. One by one they'd drift off home and he'd go to collect the car keys from his Dad.

It was a good feeling, driving through the late afternoon, smelling grass and dust through the open car windows, parking in front of the church and going in the basement door with the keys in his pocket.

After church it would be dark getting into the car and they'd drive away feeling peaceful and happy. Van didn't like church but he had to admit that, like Martha Ann said, it made Sunday night a lot more fun if you went on to church first. He thought about that and it bothered him, because it was like paying off beforehand, but Martha Ann said there wasn't any point arguing about your conscience. If you had it, you had it, and best placate it. Then he'd said, "But what's wrong with Sunday driving?" She'd said, "Oh, Van. That hasn't got anything to do with it. It's doing what our parents want us to do first so we can be free to do what we want to do the rest of the night." But he wasn't sure that was it.

Because they did smooch on Sunday nights. It wasn't a very private or a very comfortable sort of smooching, because there were always at least eight and sometimes more than a dozen people in the car, especially when they had his Dad's Buick. But they did smooch, which was why they kidded him about Sue Kirk. She always jumped up in front by him and if they parked there she was.

The Buick was a good car but there had been something funny about his Dad's getting it. When Mama sold the farm she wanted to move to Florida and Daddy hadn't wanted to. They'd bought this car instead, and a lot of new clothes. Now they were talking about adding to the house. Only Mama hadn't quit talking about Florida and he knew she had the rest of the money in the bank. He didn't like to think about it because he didn't want to move to Florida. He had lived here all his life and he liked it. He had his gang, his favorite places, and his life was pretty well planned up to graduation from high school, anyway. His Dad, he figured, sort of felt the same way.

Van's favorite place on Sunday nights was the ridge road. It was still woody there, quiet and undeveloped. You could park and look down on more woods and empty fields toward the highway. It was one of the few places left like that.

One night they all got out of the car and walked to the foot of the ridge, all of them except him and Martha Ann. It was a slow night with the stars low, not hot, but drowsy. Martha Ann was sitting in the back seat and after a while he said, "Why don't you come on up here?" He didn't know why he said it because they'd probably have a fuss if she did. They always fussed, nearly as much as he and Veda did. But she came up anyway and turned on the radio.

"This won't run down the battery or anything, will it?" she said.

He shook his head. They were playing "Green Eyes" by Tommy Dorsey, his favorite record right then. Martha Ann smelled good. She always did. It was one of the things about her. It wasn't perfume or any of those things, just good clean skin, like she'd just scrubbed her face. "Why didn't you go with them?" he said.

She shrugged. He could just make out the gesture in the moonlight. "I don't care about walking," she said. "Not tonight." The radio was playing "This Love of Mine" by Frank Sinatra now. "I like that," she said.

It was terribly quiet. They couldn't even hear the sound of the others on the gravel road. "I reckon they're nearly to the bottom now," Van said, and reached over and took her hand.

"I reckon," she said.

He sat very still, playing with her fingers one by one. "Would you like to go swimming tomorrow?" he said.

"All right."

They went swimming together a lot, sometimes with Veda, sometimes alone. They'd go up to the pool, or out to the creek. It wasn't anything unusual, but suddenly he felt as though it were. Hell, he thought, this is my cousin, Martha Ann. What am I getting uncomfortable about? He turned his head and kissed her. Her lips tasted like she smelled, good clean flesh, and all of a sudden it excited him. He wanted to do all sorts of wild crazy things to her, just because she tasted good. It felt wonderful and at the same time it made him mad. Her lips were cool and neatly closed.

He kissed her again, working her mouth open. She pulled away from him and turned the radio dial.

". . . Music from the Trianon," the announcer's voice boomed.

She turned the volume down. "What'd you do that for?" she said.

She was sitting bent over with her hair falling around her face and he couldn't see her. "What?" he said.

"Kiss me like that."

"Don't you like it?"

She swung around, her hair brushing across his arm. "It's nasty," she said.

"Oh hell," he said, hating her. "It is not. You don't know anything."

"And don't want to," she said.

"Well, that's all right by me," he said. He turned the key and started the car, moving out of the trees and going slowly down the hill to overtake the walkers.

"Do you still want to go swimming?" she said very low.

"Why not?" he said. "What's it got to do with swimming anyway?"

They went swimming at the pool next day but it wasn't much fun. They didn't enjoy being together for a week or two. Then one morning, early, she stopped outside his house on her bicycle. "Come on, let's go to the creek," she said when he came out onto the porch.

He got his bike and went with her. It was hot and still already, even though it was only nine in the morning, and they were tired and sweaty when they got to the creek. They took off their shorts, put on on top of their bathing suits, and went right in. Then they lay in the sun, still wet and almost cool.

"This has been a damned good summer," Van said.

"I know it. It's like we'd just been waiting for it."

"What's that mean?" He felt easy with her again, and grateful. He almost put a hand over hers, but stopped before he began the gesture.

"I don't know," she said, "but it's what it's like."

"I guess so." He sat up and looked out at the creek. "Let's go back to town and get a watermelon off the square," he said.

"All right."

He thought she sounded disappointed but he couldn't see why. He felt good. It was a fine day and school starting still weeks away. They were friendly again for the first time since the night in the car and he wanted it to stay that way. "You want to go back in?" he said.

She shook her head and stood up, pulling her shorts on quickly over her damp bathing suit. "I wish we didn't have to pedal all the way home," she said.

"Plenty hills."

"Yeah, but going up them."

They rode back slowly, feeling their bathing suits steam dry under their clothes, pedaling quickly up the hills to coast down the other side, the rush of wind on their hot faces sudden and sharp.

On the square the watermelons were piled in neat pyramids at the corners of the courthouse. Van got off his bike and expertly thumped two before choosing one. He gave the overalled farmer the nickel and put the melon in his basket.

"Who you want to get?" Martha Ann said. "Sue Kirk?"

"No," he said. "I don't want to get anybody. Let's take it over to your house and eat it all ourselves."

"No, your house," Martha Ann said. "It's always more fun there."

"Yeah, but it'll hardly go around to all the others."

"I wish Sue Mayhill hadn't come back here," she said. "That old house would have been just the place."

He nodded. He didn't want to talk about it. It had never seemed right for the house that had been his playground for so many years to be usurped by the tall woman with her crew of painters and carpenters who turned it into an apartment house and robbed it of all enchantment. It was like his mother selling the cove. Things changed too fast; he didn't like to think about it.

"Let's go over to your house anyway," Martha Ann said. She pedaled off and he followed her.

Martha Ann Holder was in love. What she didn't realize was that she was in love with a family. Being a girl, she thought that her being in love involved males, so for a long time she'd thought she loved Uncle Ace; now she thought she loved Van. What she really loved was the feeling the Johnsons gave her. She liked to be with them, any one of them—except Veda. She liked the little house with its crowded room, she liked sitting around the kitchen table in the big house, she liked rocking on the porch with Aunt Eileen. She wished Van wasn't her cousin so that she could marry him and belong with him. What she really wanted was just to belong.

It was lonesome at her house now. Since the Captain had died nothing felt right any more. Nobody was particularly interested in where she went or what she felt. They nagged her about it, sometimes, but they didn't really care. Her Uncle Bill and his wife wanted to move out to themselves again but they didn't feel they could leave her Granddaddy and Grandmama; nobody seemed to think much one way or the other about her and Janice.

Her sister, Janice, didn't feel about it as she did. She didn't remember when the house had been full of people and there had been Mama and Daddy and Captain. She liked everything the way it was now. She read. That was the way Janice filled her days. It wasn't enough for Martha Ann.

Being with Aunt Eileen's family was. Then being with Van was. He made her feel safe. Even after he kissed her that way it was all right, because he didn't do it again. In a way she wished he would, but the part of her that wanted things to stay the same was glad he didn't.

There were summer storms in the late afternoons, coming up suddenly with a lot of wind and thunder and then a hard driving rain leaving the ground smelling of dampened dust. Martha Ann and Van sat on the front porch of Eileen's house and watched the water drip off the bushes onto the packed dirt around the house. "Here comes Aunt Cat," Van said.

She came around the big house, stepping neatly over the puddles in the yard, leading Gloria by the hand, making her step daintily around them too. Aunt Cat still dressed better than anyone in Bellefonte, even though she was thinner than ever and her mouth always looked drawn. She had on a purple and white suit now, with padded shoulders and gold braid on the collar. Gloria was dressed in a full white dress with butterflies embroidered on it. "What a little snob that one is going to be," Van said.

"Hi," Cat said, coming onto the porch. "Where's your mother?"

"Out at Nannie Holder's," Van said. "She's sick again."

"Your grandmother is?"

"Yes."

"When's your mother coming back?" Cat said, beginning to frown.

"Tomorrow, or maybe tonight."

"I have to see her."

"Well come back tonight, Aunt Cat," Van said.

Cat looked agitated, biting on her lower lip and holding Gloria's hand tighter until Gloria pulled away from her and went to sit on the porch railing.

"I'm sorry," Van said. "Sit down with us a while."

Cat shook her head. Suddenly she went quickly through the door into the house. Van and Martha Ann looked at each other. Gloria swung one white-slippered foot against the banisters. "She's gone to be sick at her stomach," she said.

"I better go help," Martha Ann said. She started toward the door, but Cat came out, looking pale and smiling a little.

"I can't stand it when I come by and Eileen's not here," she said. "It's really awful somehow. Like the end of the world."

Martha Ann stared at her. "You ought to go home and lie down, Aunt Cat," she said. "I'll go with you."

Cat shook her head. "No. I'm all right now. I'm going down

and buy a new dress. That always helps, doesn't it?" She patted Martha Ann's cheek. "You don't look at all like your mother," she said. "Janice does, but not you." She straightened and looked across the field toward the Mayhill Apartments. "I despise to look at that house," she said. "They've ruined it."

Van spoke suddenly. He'd been sitting silently in the rocker watching them. "I always sort of thought *she'd* come back and open it up," he said.

Cat looked at him. "Me, too, Van," she said. "I waited a long long time for her to do that. But when they turn the lights off you might as well quit waiting for them to go back on. Come on, Gloria. Don't get your feet muddy."

They stepped off the porch and went around the house.

They were silent for a long moment after she left. Finally Martha Ann looked at Van. "What's the matter with her?" she said.

Van shook his head. "I don't know. Mama says she ought not have ever married Mr. Cartwright. And that she needs something to do."

"She gives me the creeps sometimes," Martha Ann said. "Sometimes she's so bright and gay and lovely. It's the most fun in the world to have her around. Like she always used to be when we were kids. Now she's just as likely to be this way though."

Van tilted back against the wall in his chair. "Let's go walk in the puddles," he said.

Mrs. Holder was sick most of the time now but she insisted on staying on the farm alone with only Ida and the hired family to look after her and to farm the few acres they still had in cultivation. Eileen had been trying since her father's death a year ago to get her mother to move into town, but she refused. Today she had sent the hired man into town for Eileen. She looked small and frail, Eileen thought, coming into the room where she lay propped on pillows in the iron bed, her little battery radio beside her.

"Whit Wallace wants to buy this place," she said as soon as Eileen was inside the room.

Eileen smiled. "What's he want this for?" she said.

"I don't know," Mrs. Holder said. "I wanted you to ask around. It's for some reason, that's sure, and I want my full money's worth if it's something important. I'm not going to stand on principle like you did and refuse to sell to him. I just want to be sure I get what it's worth."

Eileen laughed. She had refused to sell the cove to Whit Wallace and she wasn't really sure why. He'd made the first offer back when there began to be a little money lying around again. But she'd refused, she'd waited, and sold finally to Mr. Wright, the mail carrier. She'd sold it to him to give his daughter for a wedding present, sold it to be farmed and loved, which was worth as much to her as the money. The money was worth plenty. For a good many years it had been her goal, her planned escape route, the way to pry Ace away from Bellefonte and his aunts, to give him self-respect, a new business, a better life. But it hadn't worked. Not yet.

Her mother was watching her. "You still think you can get Ace Johnson away from that damned newspaper and those two old bloodsuckers?" she said.

"Mama," Eileen said.

"Do you?"

Eileen straightened. "I do, and I will, one way or the other. Now why do you *think* Whit Wallace wants this place?"

"I don't know. But I know Whit. It's for something. He wanted that cove because it's the best land this side of town. This farm isn't, it's always been mediocre. He don't want it to farm."

"I'll find out," Eileen said. "You planning on coming into town now?"

"Maybe." Mrs. Holder smiled. "I might like town living in my old age. Can't you see me and Ida in a steam-heated apartment with a bathroom? Maybe we could get one in the Mayhill house."

"Maybe you could at that," Eileen said.

Eileen drove back to town, thinking about Whit Wallace and why he would want the farm. She knew Ace hadn't heard anything about it; he'd have told her. Driving past her own house, she made her decision and drove on to town. She would ask Harry, because Harry would know, and Harry would tell her. Since the day Veda died she had avoided Harry. He still came by to go fishing with Ace sometimes, or to have a drink on Saturday nights, but she did her best to discourage him. Eileen was still in love with her husband and wanting Harry Clifton didn't change that any. So she didn't let herself be around Harry Clifton.

She looked at her watch. It was the time he went to the drugstore for a Coke, so she knew she had known all along that she'd ask him and that she'd planned her trip to town to coincide with that time. She went into the drugstore, smiling wryly.

He was standing against the counter drinking a Coke. "Hi, Doc," she said. "Have a Coke with me."

He followed her back to a booth and sat down across from her. "What's on your mind?" he said.

She laughed. "Why should anything be?"

"Why else would you take the trouble to speak to me?" he said.

"Oh, Harry. But of course you're right. Whit Wallace wants to buy Mama's place."

He grinned. "Airport," he said shortly.

"Airport?"

"That's right. Best place for it in the county."

"What are we going to do with an airport in Bellefonte?" she said.

"We'll need one. If not this year, the next or the next. You asked me. That's it."

She sipped her Coke. "What's it worth to him?" she said.

"Enough. Best place in the county."

"Thanks, Doc."

"You're welcome." He took out a crumpled pack of cigarettes and offered one to her. "You still planning on moving to Florida?" he said.

"I am."

"Why Florida?"

"I like the ocean."

"I didn't know you'd ever seen it."

"I haven't."

He laughed. "O.K.," he said, "I give up. It's none of my damned business. I saw Van and Martha Ann Holder this afternoon, walking down the road carefully stepping in every puddle they came to. They're sort of old for that, aren't they?"

"I wouldn't think you'd ever get too old for that," she said.

"That kid looks lonesome as hell to me," he said.

"Martha Ann?"

"Yeah."

"She'll be all right. One of these days she'll go off to school and she'll be all right. She's really fine."

"I guess. Hangs around with Van a lot, doesn't she?"

"Harry, for heaven's sake. She's his cousin."

"That's what I mean."

"Forget it. They're fine. If you just have to worry about somebody this afternoon, try Cat. She's the one I worry about."

"With reason. But I've done all I can. She's got that ulcer now, you know."

"I know."

Harry sighed. "I even tried talking to Cartwright," he said. "That was a bust. He informed me that his wife wasn't crazy."

"You hadn't said she was, had you?"

"Hardly. I suggested she go back to the psychiatrist."

"Do you really think that would be worth anything?"

"I doubt it."

"So?" Eileen spread her hands.

"So. Oh Eileen, it's so good to talk to you. Why won't you ever just let me talk to you?"

"You know why." She picked up her purse. "I've got to get home," she said. "If Van and Martha Ann have gone off somewhere Veda won't half look after the kids."

"Where are the esteemed aunts?"

"They're there. They don't think the kids need much looking after. Just Ace."

Harry snorted. "Maybe you should move," he said. "Only I don't want you to."

"Way inside you do, Harry. Way inside you know it'd be best for you too."

In August she moved her mother into a first-floor apartment at the Mayhill house. Sue rented it to her. She looked old already, gaunt and with black circles under her eyes. "I'm glad to let you have it," she said. "You know you're one of the few Mama still asks about when she writes. How is Eileen Johnson? she'll say, and Cat Cartwright? She asks about Cat too."

"How is Buz?" Eileen said.

"All right. In fact, better than Daddy, I guess. They stay in Los Angeles all the time now. That's why they said go on and do over the house. Mama suddenly admitted to herself, I guess, that she'll never come back here."

Eileen looked around the room. It was hard to realize that this tight snug little apartment, in which Sue Mayhill lived, had all been created out of the old living room. She thought of the parties they'd come to and the lights shining through all the long windows, and smiled. "It's certainly changed, isn't it?" she said.

"I like it," Sue said. "I like it fine like this. It was too big. Nobody needs all that much room just to loaf in."

"I reckon not," Eileen said. "But it was pretty."

"Was it?" Sue said. "Now it's comfortable and profitable. That's more than can be said of most of the Mayhill enterprises."

"Does your father still own part of the gin?"

"On paper."

"Who does own it?"

"Who owns everything? I don't know which one. L. D., I think. Not Whit himself. Not in name."

"I hear Whit's planning on putting up a couple of brick apartment buildings himself," Eileen said.

"Maybe so," Sue said. She poured coffee into Eileen's empty cup. "But he can't buy the name Mayhill, can he?" she said.

It turned cool early in September and it was over. Martha Ann sat on a pile of lumber behind the high school with Van, watching the light fall cold on the campus. "It's over," she said.

"What?"

"The summer."

"You sound funny about it. I thought you liked the fall."

"Not this year."

"Why?"

"Because this is the best damned summer we're ever going to have," she said. "I know."

Van got up and went to watch the sun shining on the windows of the school. It was a new school, put up only a few years before with government aid. It was a pretty school, a modern school, with shiny new lockers and desks and lab equipment, with rows of shiny new typewriters, and completely equipped home-ec kitchens. "I'm sort of glad for school to start," he said. "I always am. I think I won't be, but I am."

"Me too, usually. I like the new books and the football and the way the air changes and the smoke smells. But not this year."

"It'll be all right," Van said.

"I know it. Let me be sad about it now though. I like to."

Van laughed. "You're funny."

"I know that too. In one way I'm all excited about school and my new corduroy coat, and going to Montgomery for the Auburn game."

"What's that?"

"Oh, Cousin Graham's got tickets for me and Janice, for the first game played there."

"Oh . . ."

"And in another way I feel like everything's over. Riding Sunday nights won't be the same."

"Sure it will. In fact I bet I get the car this week."

She laughed. "I know it. I think I just don't want to grow up."

"I don't guess anybody does."

"Van." She got up and went to stand beside him. "Maybe Cousin Graham'll get you a ticket too. You want to come to Montgomery with us?"

"Sure."

"It'd be fun, wouldn't it? Being out of Bellefonte together? It wouldn't be like anything else we've ever done."

He wanted to go with her but he knew he wouldn't when the time came. It wasn't anything he understood, only that he wouldn't. Because he didn't want to risk being outside Bellefonte with Martha Ann. He couldn't say why, even to himself. "Yeah, I guess you're right," he said, turning to look at her. "The summer's gone."

Behind the Cartwright house the maples were red and yellow now. Cat sat on her iron bench and watched them, waiting for the single one to let go and fall onto the pile beneath the tree. Gloria sat beside her, neat and clean as always, not running to play in the leaves like the other children, not interested in them.

"Aren't they pretty, baby?" Cat said.

"Yes, Mama."

Cat sighed. "Go on and play," she said. "You aren't interested in pretty leaves."

"All right." Gloria got down obediently and went into the house. Cat lit a cigarette, leaning back on the bench, stretching her legs out in front of her. Dudley was in Newcastle on business again and she was free for the whole weekend. She wondered what to do. I could go down to Hudson's and buy grapes and make pies, she thought. Or drive out to the mountain and look at all the trees turning, or go to Eileen's for the whole afternoon. She got up and went into the house. She walked from room to room looking at

268 IT'S ALWAYS THREE O'CLOCK

the expensive and perfect furnishings. Then she went to the kitchen.

"I'm going out for the afternoon," she said to Mable. "Where's Gloria?"

"Playing with that dollhouse," Mable said.

"All right. Feed her the chicken for supper. If Mr. Cartwright calls tell him I'm at Mother's."

"Which Mr. Cartwright?"

"Either one."

She got her jacket from the closet and went to the car. She didn't know where she wanted to go yet so she drove aimlessly around the town, looking at the falling leaves and the bright splashes of autumn flowers. After a while she felt hungry but she remembered she couldn't have a hamburger and it was the only thing she really wanted. She drove down to the new drive-in and got a pint of milk and drank it, watching the new cement-block front of the drive-in and the cars passing on the highway in the slanting afternoon sun.

After a while she stopped fooling herself and drove out behind her father's lumber company and bought a pint of Seagrams.

Ace kept his whiskey at the newspaper office until time to go home on Saturday afternoon. He didn't want Mattie and Trudy finding it and besides sometimes he got the chance to get a little start after Mr. Hudson was gone in the afternoon. He came home feeling pretty good.

Eileen was sitting in the kitchen waiting for him. "Want some supper?" she said. "We've got liver and onions."

"And kill this glow?"

"O.K. I'll go on and feed the kids then."

He sat down and poured a drink into a coffee cup. "Where's the aunts?" he said.

She grinned at him. "Gone to a shower for somebody," she said. "Won't be back till all hours—ten, at least."

He stretched his legs out and winked at her. "Time enough."

She went out and he could hear her calling the kids in. While they ate he sat watching them, sipping from the cup. Van was dressed in a white shirt and a sweater and his good pants. "I bet Van's got a date," Veda said, cutting her liver daintily.

"Shut up," Van said.

"Why's he got a date?" Holder said. Holder was only ten and his conversation still consisted primarily of questions.

"Why do you think, silly?" Martin said. Martin, twelve and completely uninterested in girls, was scornful.

"He's hoping he'll get the car," Veda said.

"Well now," Ace said. "I haven't heard anything about it. I thought Sunday night was car night around here."

Van continued to eat without saying anything. He had a date with Sue Kirk. He'd started dating her suddenly after the day he and Martha Ann had talked behind the high school. But he didn't really care whether he got the car or not. He didn't care that much about Sue Kirk.

"Who've you got a date with?" Ace said.

Eileen looked up from cutting Betty Al's meat. "You really got a date?" she said. "Not just the gang?"

Van nodded. "And it's about time to go," he said.

"Who is the young lady?" Ace repeated.

"It's Sue Kirk," Veda said.

"Who asked you?" Van said.

"Nobody. But that's who it is. Martha Ann told me."

"How the hell did she know?" Van said. He could feel himself turning red.

"Sue Kirk told her, naturally," Veda said. She laughed nastily. "Martha Ann didn't seem real happy about it."

"I'm going," Van said.

Ace reached in his pocket and took out the car keys. He held them out toward Van on the end of his finger. "Take the car, son," he said.

"Well, thanks Dad." Van took the keys and stood holding them for a moment.

"I don't see why Van has to get the car just because he's sixteen," Veda said. "Maybe if I could have it I could get somebody sixteen to drive it for me."

"Well, young lady," Eileen said, "produce him and maybe you will get it." She kept watching Van. "Go on, honey," she said finally.

"Sure. Night Mama. Thanks Dad." He went to the door and stood there a moment looking at them. "I guess I better go on," he said.

"I don't think having the car tonight will keep you from getting it tomorrow night," Eileen said suddenly. "Is that what's bothering you?"

He looked at her gratefully.

"Huh?" Ace said. "Why, no. I reckon not. I just thought maybe if he was dating now he would rather have it for Saturday night than to haul around a whole bunch of kids on Sunday. But no, I don't reckon this would stop that." He poured more whiskey into the cup. "No. Go on, Van."

Van shut the back door and went out to the car.

"What's eating him?" Veda said.

"Growing pains," Eileen said. "Eat your liver."

"I don't like it."

"That doesn't matter. Eat it."

Later, after Veda and Martin and Holder had gone off to the Saturday movie and Betty Al had been sent across the yard to the little house to bed, Eileen poured herself a drink and put the dishes in the sink.

"I didn't know Van was courting," Ace said. "When'd that start?"

"Just has as far as I know," Eileen said. "I don't think he's courting though. I think he's running from Martha Ann."

"Martha Ann?" Ace said. "Now why in hell would he do that? Martha Ann's got more to her than any little girl around here. I thought they were great friends." He was feeling pretty good now and he found Eileen's statements a little hard to follow.

"I know," she said, pouring soap powder into the sink. "But they're cousins."

"Huh?" Ace said. "Sure they're cousins. What the hell are you talking about?"

"Well Martha Ann isn't unattractive, Ace."

"That's what I just said, baby. You're losing me again. What's wrong with a little flirtation between cousins? Lots of people do that."

"I know it." Eileen sipped her own drink. "But Van and Martha Ann both take things so seriously."

Ace frowned. "You aren't worried about it, are you?"

"No."

"O.K. then." He smiled at her. "Come on over here."

"The dishes aren't washed."

"I said come on over here."

She went over and let him pull her into his lap. "Honey," she said a few minutes later, "it's early. Somebody's liable to come in."

"Oh hell," he said. "Come on. Let's do it on Mattie's bed, just for the hell of it."

"Ace!"

"O.K., Trudy's then. I'm not particular."

Eileen giggled. "Better be Van's."

"O.K."

She got up and went in front of him into the back bedroom where Van slept. She stepped out of her clothes and lay waiting for him, feeling the warmth of waiting spread through her. "It's ridiculous how much I still want you," she said when he lay down beside her. "Just plain silly."

"Yeah." He ran his hands over her expertly. "But nice, wouldn't you say?"

"Nice," she murmured. "Wasn't exactly the word I had in mind."

Spreading up the bed while Ace put the coffee pot on, she thought about bringing up the subject of moving again, but she didn't. She had never yet taken advantage of Ace and she wouldn't do it now.

They drank the coffee and she warmed up some supper for Ace. Then he settled back in his chair and put the bottle on the table. "Well, I'm ready to do some serious drinking now," he said. "Ain't it about time those kids got in from the show?"

"Just about," Eileen said from the sink. "It seems to take them longer to walk it the older they get. They have to loiter around the drugstore a little, I guess."

"Should Veda be doing that?"

"It never hurt us, did it?"

He laughed. "I don't know. That's probably why we're here right now."

"So?"

He shrugged. "She's just thirteen."

"So's Martha Ann. And you were going all to bat about her and Van awhile ago."

"O.K., O.K., Mother," he said. "Drink up. I won't worry."

"You don't have to. Veda'll take care of Veda. She's that way."

"You don't sound especially pleased."

"I guess I'm not. It shows a lack of warmth, you know."

"Well, it's better than illegitimate grandchildren."

"I know it."

"Ah, how'd we get onto this on Saturday night anyway?" Ace said. "We sound like Trudy and Mattie bewailing the younger generation."

"I know it," Eileen said. "It's the penalty of being a parent." She took her hands out of the dishwater. "I hear them now," she said. She went out on the porch and peered into the darkness. "Who's that with you?" she said.

"Martha Ann," Veda said. They came into the light from the back door.

"Oh. Hi," she said. "All of you come on in here and I'll fix some hot chocolate. Or have you already been to the drugstore?"

The boys bolted past her into the kitchen. Veda and Martha

Ann stood at the edge of the porch looking at the sky. "Isn't it gorgeous tonight?" Martha Ann said.

"It is," Eileen said. She looked up, seeing the stars high and brilliant with the fall chill, smelling the acrid odor of burned-out leaves. "Want me to bring your hot chocolate out here?"

"No. It's chilly," Veda said. "We'll come in."

"I can't stay," Martha Ann said. "I've got to get on home."

"He's not here yet anyway," Veda said snippily. "The car's not back."

Martha Ann didn't say anything. Eileen tried to see her face but it was turned away from her. "I've got to get on home," she said again.

"You're not going to walk by yourself," Eileen said. "I'll get one of the boys to go with you."

"No. I've got my bike. I'll be all right." She ran around the house and Eileen could hear her pedaling off down the road. Looking up, she saw there were clouds forming between them and the stars.

"Why were you so mean to Martha Ann, Veda?" she said, watching her daughter's face in the light from the kitchen door.

"Oh Mama. She and Van always think they're so damned much smarter than anybody else," Veda said. "You know they treat me like I was two years old. They always have done me like that. And they're not so smart. Neither one of them. Martha Ann's got a crush on Van and she thinks nobody knows it. Anybody can see what a fool she is."

"Veda," Eileen said, "love never makes anybody a fool. You remember that."

"Oh, love," Veda said.

"Yes. Love," Eileen said. "There's nothing wrong about it, ever. You remember that."

"I'm going to bed, Mama," Veda said.

"All right." Eileen watched her go across the yard, then she went back inside to make hot chocolate for the boys.

When they heard the extra pair of footsteps coming up the walk

with Miss Mattie and Miss Trudy, Eileen thought for a minute
it must be Van. Then she remembered that he had the car. It was
Dudley Cartwright. Miss Mattie left him in the parlor and came
on back to the kitchen. Her back stiffened and her nose twitched
when she saw Ace at the table. "Dudley Cartwright's out there
in the parlor," she said. "You all seen Catharine?"

Eileen shook her head. "I'll go talk to him," she said. "Why
didn't you bring him on back?"

Mattie grunted. "Didn't reckon he'd want to come into a drinking party, poor man. He has enough of that to put up with."

"Oh, hell, Mattie," Eileen said cheerfully. She smiled at Ace
and went out of the room.

"Goodnight Alvin," Miss Mattie said.

"Night, Mattie. Don't forget to wind the clock and all that."

"I don't know what's going to ever become of you," Mattie
said. "Drinking every Saturday night like a . . ."

"Bum?" Ace said. "That the word you're hunting?"

"Lord knows we did the best we could with somebody else's
child," Mattie said. "It was marrying that girl . . ."

"All right." Ace stood up. He was tight, but he wasn't drunk.
He swayed a little, then straightened and looked coldly at Mattie.
"You ever say another word about my wife to me or to anybody
else and I hear of it, we go," he said. "We go like Eileen wants
us to. And that means my salary goes. How'd you like that?"

"Go on," Mattie said. "Go on with your bottles and your lally-
gagging around with your wife in front of your own children. You
won't be missed around here."

"I bet," Ace said. He sat down and poured another inch of
bourbon into his cup. "Go to bed, Mattie," he said slowly. "I
don't want to see you any more tonight."

She went out of the room and he sat staring morosely into the
cup. He knew that Eileen was right and they ought to leave. He
didn't know why he couldn't do it. It was funny, him a grown
man with a houseful of half-grown kids and he didn't want to
pull up roots and try something new. He knew that it wasn't sen-

sible of him, but there it was. He didn't want to leave Bellefonte. He was afraid to leave. It had to be fear, there wasn't anything else to hold him here. He wasn't going to get the chance to buy into the paper, he knew that now. Mr. Marshall was already talking about bringing in somebody from Morgan City. There wasn't anything holding him to his aunts any more either. They'd killed that with their bickering and pettiness, their refusal to be half decent to Eileen. So it was fear—fear of failure, fear it was too late, that he was too old, that he wasn't strong enough. Of course he had Eileen; but that, he thought, was just it. If they went, if, this late in life, he tried something new, he had to be able to do it without Eileen's help. He had to do it *for* her.

He heard her coming back into the kitchen with Dudley and he looked up at her, loving her as he had every moment since he was sixteen years old. She smiled at him. "I'm a lucky son-of-a-bitch," he said.

"Ace," Eileen said, "Dudley's hunting Cat. I told him we haven't seen her all night. You didn't see her around the square when you came home, did you?"

He shook his head. "Sit down and have a drink, Dudley."

"I guess not," Dudley said, but he took his hat off and sat down anyway. "I got a chance to finish up and get on home tonight," he said. "Couldn't wait to get in, but Gloria was already in bed and Cat gone. Reckon I might as well of stayed." He looked bewildered for a moment. "She told Mable she'd be at her mother's, but I went by there and Mrs. Graves said she hadn't been there all day. Made the square too, and the drive-in, but I didn't see the car anywhere. I figured sure she'd be over here."

Eileen shook her head. "I haven't seen her all day," she said. "Maybe she drove down to Hunter City shopping."

"I don't think so. Mable said she had her slacks on."

"Dudley, you're really worried, aren't you?" Eileen said.

"Yes," he said slowly. "Yes, I guess I am."

"We'll find her then. Won't we Ace? Come on. Let's go help Dudley find her."

"Find her?" Ace said. "Where?"

"I don't know," Eileen said. "Maybe I'll get a hunch. You go on out to the car, Dudley, and we'll be out soon as I look in on the kids."

Dudley went out and Ace squinted up at her. "Now what's this all about?" he said. "Dudley can't keep up with his wife, that's his business, not ours!"

"Oh, Ace, you know she's not well. He's worried. For the first time I think he's really concerned about her. And, frankly, I am too. She's usually been by here by this time on the weekends he's gone."

"O.K., O.K. We'll go hunt her up. Fresh air would do me good anyway. Where you gonna look?"

"Over at the cemetery," Eileen said.

"Huh?"

"That's right. That's why I want to go with him. He won't go over there by himself. He won't even believe it."

"All right. You seen my sweater?"

"You're sitting on it."

"What would I do without you?"

"It doesn't matter, does it? You don't have to . . . ever."

Catharine parked the car by the stone wall on the side of the road. The gates were closed and she didn't want to see if they were locked. She felt that if she tried them and they were locked it would frighten her, and she didn't want to be frightened. She was frightened enough on the nights when she stayed at home and lay in bed and heard the courthouse clock strike at her. Now, free out under the night, she wasn't going to be frightened, not by the little minds of Bellefonte that would lock in the dead. Lock in the dead, lock out the living; that pretty well took care of the caretaker function. If you could manage to do those two things you wouldn't have many problems left.

She felt along the front seat for the bottle, held it up, looking at it in the dim light from the street lamp a block away. There was a half-inch in the bottom. She nodded and got out of the car. Holding the bottle carefully in one hand, she climbed onto the low stone wall and stood still, looking in.

The hill lay quiet in the starlight, the cedars dark and soft and sweet-smelling in the September air. She slid down, standing ankle deep in the needles that had drifted against the side of the wall. They felt soft and sharp at once, like memory. She walked on up the hill, passing the flat broad tombstones of the older part of the cemetery without pausing to glance at them, seeing in her mind the moss across the letters and the mud rain-splashed almost to the lettering. There was wind now, coming up in the cedars, blowing their pointed branches against the high sharp stars.

At the crest of the hill where the three cedars stood together she could see the gleam of the gray block of granite that belonged to the Simms family. It bulked huge and strange in the starlight, not akin to the slender white pillars and slabs around it. "Hey look at you," Cat said softly. "What lies under you may be gone. But you're going to by-damn last a long time, aren't you, old fellow? Aren't you now, ole whale of the sea?"

She walked carefully now, anxious not to step on a grave. "I'd like to step over you, Veda-love," she crooned softly. "You're around here somewhere." She stood still suddenly. "Where's the lamb one?" she said. She looked around slowly, getting her bearings between the likenesses of stone, hunting the different one, the one with the lamb with the curly marble hair. "There you are," she said. She crossed over to it and knelt down, putting her arms around its neck. The bottle clinked against the base of the monument and she groped for it in sudden panic, her hands shaking until she picked it up and clutched it to her again.

"Now ten paces past you, lamb, and six to the left and past the ironing board one to the iron fence." She threaded her way slowly, like a mouse in a maze, keeping the picture of the baby in the shell in front of her eyes as the reward. Her hands reached out, felt the iron railing, and she stopped to peer in, waiting until her eyes adjusted to the starlight. "Sleep well, love," she said.

Far back behind the fence the iron baby lay asleep in the iron shell, curled warmly against the cold. She had seen him first when she was ten years old, when they came to bury Uncle Dan. She said, "Why is a baby here?" and her father said, "The Lord giveth and the Lord taketh away. Blessed be the name of the Lord." It was the baby sleeping in its shell that first brought her here. She had remembered it one night when she couldn't sleep, remembered how quiet it was, how still. At first she hadn't been able to find it. She'd hunted and looked all one afternoon after putting out the flowers for Veda brought for an excuse. She'd gotten panicky almost, rushing between the upright marble slabs, the rusting lavender baskets with their dead weedy smells, the freshness of turned earth, the mold of old.

I dreamed it, she kept saying to herself. It wasn't ever there. It's just one of those things I dream, like the wheel and the place with the funny sun. They seem like something I've seen too. Only I dream them. And I must have dreamed that baby in its shell. Then she had stumbled over the lamb and, looking up, she'd seen the iron fence. "Why is it hidden?" she'd said. "It's right here in the middle of the cemetery and yet it's hidden. It doesn't want to be come on suddenly."

Now she sat down by the fence and looked up at the sky. The wind was blowing wisps of cloud across the stars, but it was still a warm wind. It won't be cold until November this year, she thought. I don't believe it will be cold. On the road below her she heard a car pass and she started, wondering who would be using this road on Saturday night and if they'd see her car and think some of their crazy evil little thoughts. She looked back at the baby. "We don't care, love. Do we?" she said.

She walked around the fence to the back of the shell and patted it once gently, then she turned and struck out across the cemetery to the newer part. The tall white temple stood alone on the flat level across the gravel road. It was very high and white in the moonlight; around it the ornamental shrubs moved gently in the wind. She walked through them and up the little steps into the room, pausing for a moment to look up at the tall white statue with its perfect lips and limbs and carved dead eyes. Then she sat down on the top of the steps. "Hello, Marty," she said. "I brought you a little drinky."

Eileen stood in front of the moving shrubbery and called to her, not lowering her voice for the place or the hour or the mind, just calling. "Cat. Let's go home now."

Cat peeped out at her from behind one of the slender columns. "Eileen!" she said. "Come on in. It's the cat's pajamas, it's the cat's meow."

"Sure," Eileen said. "But it's time for coffee."

"Is it?"

"Yep. Time to go to the drive-in."

"What about Marty?" Cat said.

"He wants to go to sleep."

"All right." Cat came down the steps, moving slowly in the darkness. The wind was stronger now and clouds covered most of the sky.

"It's fixing to rain in half a minute," Ace said from behind Eileen. "Hurry up."

Dudley stood on the edge of the gravel road, staring unbelievingly at Cat coming down the marble steps, her empty bottle still in her hand. She came up to Eileen and Ace. Then she stopped and put her hand over her mouth, giggling. "Who is yon spirit?" she said, shaking with laughter and pointing at Dudley. "Is it my husband? The late, right honorable Dudley D. Cartwright of Coca-Cola? Or is it his shade doomed to walk the night?"

"Come on, Cat," Eileen said briskly. "It's starting to sprinkle." She took Cat's elbow and steered her toward the car.

"Where we going?" Cat said. "Your house? To visit the two weird sisters?"

"Home to put you to bed," Eileen said.

"I'm not going home," Cat said. "See, there's my car. I'm going for a drive."

"O.K.," Eileen said. "We'll both go." She motioned Ace. "You and Dudley go on over to Cartwrights'. I'll get her home." She shoved Cat into the front seat of her car and went around and got in under the wheel. "You left the damned keys in the car," she said. "You're lucky somebody didn't take it. You know what a hellacious part of town this is."

"Sure," Cat said. "They even have to lock the dead in."

Eileen started the motor and drove toward town. Cat watched her for a moment, then she collapsed against the back of the seat, crying loudly. "Oh now why the hell did Dudley have to come home tonight?" she said. "Why couldn't he stay in his damned hotel suite in Newcastle? Now he'll take my car away from me. I know it. I know it. And I can't live without this car. I cannot."

"Hush, Cat," Eileen said. "We're going down to the drive-in and get coffee and something to eat."

"Let's just drive."

"Nope. Something to eat." She swung the car onto the gravel apron and stopped the car. "Sit up and fix your face, dear," she said. "People, people, everywhere. Saturday night."

Cat sat up and opened her lipstick. "It's raining," she said. Outside, the rain came down on the gravel, all but hiding the front of the drive-in. The carhop ran for the awning over the front of the building and around them automobile windows were rolled up quickly.

Rain beat against the windshield, the windows; and dead leaves and crumpled napkins rolled helplessly in the wind before being beaten soddenly into the gravel. Eileen leaned back and lit a cigarette. "Switch on the radio," she said. "Let's have music while we wait."

Cat obediently turned the dial. "Listen to that," she said. " 'Everything Happens to Me.' Ain't it the truth?"

Eileen looked at her out of the corner of her eye. She seemed herself again, composed, a little tense still, but all right.

"Cat, why don't you try to calm it down a little?" Eileen said.

"Oh hell, Eileen. I try. I do try. But then something always happens. Like yesterday. Here comes Ruby Clifton into the drug-store. 'Well, guess what we hear from Graham and Elizabeth,' she says. 'Graham has a new office. With a rug on the floor.' Rug on the floor my you know what!"

"Oh, Cat. Let it go."

Cat shook her head. "I hate her," she said. "I hate her. Her prim little nothingness. Those beautiful children she thinks are her right. I hate her."

"But it's you you're hurting."

Cat shook her head. "Eileen, you're just strong. You don't un-derstand."

Eileen winced. "I wish I were," she said. "But nobody is. No-body is, Cat. Don't you understand that? It's hard for all of us, all of it, all the time."

"It's not raining so hard now," Cat said. "I guess we can get a carhop."

It rained the night of December 7, a fine misting rain that turned harder as the night grew later. Ace let Van have the car anyway. He usually wouldn't when it rained. "Be careful," he said, but he handed him the keys. Then he and Eileen sat by the fire in the little house and talked about everything except what was on their minds.

Van drove slowly, watching for other cars, easing carefully when he had to apply the brakes. Sue Kirk sat beside him, her blonde head on his shoulder, and on the other side of her Veda sat in Billy Jo Winston's lap. Martha Ann was in the back seat with a half-dozen other kids. He didn't turn his head to look but he was conscious of her, sitting next to the window on his side of the car, looking out into the rain. They had the radio on, picking up the newscasts as they broke into the regular programs. They were all a little excited and they talked wildly, referring to last times as though they were all older and the war had come closer than it actually had. But in a way, he knew, they were right. Because everything had changed suddenly when it happened today. It was like the day behind the high school with Martha Ann. You knew summer was over and whatever happened with fall would be, at least, different.

"We'll all be in before it's over," Billy Jo was saying to Veda. "Wait and see. Every boy in this car'll be in before it's through."

"You're just fifteen," Veda said.

"Wait and see."

Beside Van, Sue Kirk moved softly. "Why don't you park?" she said.

He didn't want to, but he couldn't just tell her so. "All right," he said. He drove to the ridge and parked there, wanting to be there again just for a few minutes anyway, just to look down into trees where there were no houses. Sue Kirk snuggled against him. "Oh don't, Billy," Veda said.

He could see Martha Ann reflected in the windshield from the radio light. She was still looking out into the rain. He put his arm around Sue and kissed her. She opened her mouth and he pulled back. "What's the matter?" she said.

"Nothing."

Martha Ann turned from the window and looked at him. He could feel her looking at him and he half turned around.

"I don't think we ought to be smooching on a night like this," she said suddenly, loudly, viciously almost.

There was silence in the car, you could hear the sound of the rain outside in the sudden quiet. Then Sue Kirk turned on her. Sue was usually mild, coy but mild. She wasn't mild now. She turned and glared at Martha Ann and for a moment Van could have sworn she was going to hit her. "Oh, why don't you leave us alone!" she said.

Van could feel himself growing red, a cold place in his stomach, and in his head the words forming, Oh, no. Don't. Please don't. No.

Nobody said anything at all. Then Veda giggled, a tiny sound. Then there was only the rain again, falling on the soaked earth outside the car.

Van turned the key in the ignition and shifted gears. "We'd better get in," he said. "It's getting late."

He drove them home, one at a time, not saying anything to any of them, the boys first, then Martha Ann, then Veda, then Sue, the way he always did. He couldn't do anything about it. He couldn't say anything. Because this was a situation he had created and he hadn't time to think his way out of it now. Martha Ann got out of the car and ran up the walk to her house. He didn't even stay until she got to the front door as he usually did, he shifted gears and got Veda home quick because he was directing most of his rage and frustration toward Veda. He had to put it on somebody and Veda had giggled.

He walked Sue to her door, still not saying anything. "What's the matter?" she said, putting her hand on his arm. "Aren't you going to kiss me goodnight?" So he kissed her, quickly and absently, and got back in the car.

He drove then, by himself, through the wet deserted streets, out the highway, past the darkened farmhouses. He drove to Lansford, the little community five miles from Bellefonte, and turned and drove back home again.

When he came into the drive and switched the lights off he saw Martha Ann sitting on the back porch waiting for him. She was cold and wet and miserable. She'd not even gone into her house, getting her bike off the porch and coming back and waiting. She'd seen Veda come in and had hidden behind the old fireless cooker until she was inside the little house. Then she'd cried, thinking about how long he was staying out all alone with Sue and that they were laughing at her and that she had no pride and ought to go on home. But she didn't. Because seeing him meant more than being hurt or laughed at or made a fool.

Then he came. He sat down by her on the steps and neither of them said anything at all. The rain was coming down hard now, leaving mud in the yard and filling the air with the smell of wet bark and molding leaves. After a while he spoke. "It goes too fast," he said.

"I know it. You'll go to the war."

"Not yet a while."

"But you'll go."

"You gonna write and send me cakes and cookies?"

"Every day."

He smelled her skin and wet hair and the smell of leaves. "You've been crying," he said.

"Yes."

"Well don't any more."

"All right."

It was late now. They could feel the night pass midpoint and go on into morning. It was cold and they didn't have anything to say to each other but they sat there, watching the sky become blacker and the rain slow and turn to mist again.

"Do you love her?" she said finally.

"I don't know," he said.

"All right." She pushed her hair back with her hands and rested her forehead on her knees.

After a while the rain stopped and he walked home with her.

They were waiting in the living room. There was her grandmama and her granddaddy and her Uncle Bill and Aunt Carrie, all of them in robes and slippers, sitting stiffly on the chairs in the reception hall.

Her grandmother got up when she came in the door. "Where have you been?" she said in a terrible voice that Martha Ann had never heard her use before.

Martha Ann just stared at her. For a long time now her Grandmama Mozel hadn't paid much attention to her. The days of stories and planting flowers and picking nuts for the fruit cakes were gone. Grandmama Mozel sat and knitted by the dining room fire and Granddaddy stayed in bed most of the time. They weren't in bed now. They loomed over her, large and remembered from a long time ago as the arbiters of fate.

Her grandmother shook her. "I said where have you been?" she said.

"Who's that with you?" her Granddaddy said.

Uncle Bill and Aunt Carrie didn't say anything. They looked at her and at each other and didn't say anything at all.

Van came on into the room. "It's me, Van Maynard, sir," he said. "I'm sorry it's so late."

"Sorry it's so late? Sorry? Sorry?" Mozel turned on him and Martha Ann backed into the corner by the door. "Do you know what time it is? Do you know we've been half out of our minds? We thought you were at church or over at Eileen's. Then Bill and Carrie came in here and I got up to get your granddaddy some hot milk and saw that you weren't in. How many times have you been out at three o'clock in the morning? What have you been doing?"

Martha Ann stared at her. Mozel's hair was standing out wildly from her hair pins and her glasses were on crooked. She looked as though rage had twisted her face permanently. Martha Ann could never remember seeing her look like that before in all her life. Mozel took her by the shoulders again.

Martha Ann shook her head and began to cry.

"Mozel," her granddaddy said. "Mozel. Calm down a little. You're scaring the child to death. Give her a chance to explain."

"Explain?" Mozel said. "Explain? At three o'clock in the morning? You know what I thought. You *know* what I thought," she said, turning on R. V.

"Mozel," R. V. said gently. "She's only thirteen years old."

"Veda was only seventeen," Mozel said.

"Van," Bill said suddenly. "Where have you and Martha Ann been?"

"I'm trying to tell you," Van said stubbornly. "None of you'll let me or Martha Ann say anything. We've been sitting on our back porch. That's all. Sitting on our back porch."

"Till this hour?" Mozel said.

"We ... we were talking about the war."

"The war? What in God's name do you two have to say about the war?" R. V. said.

"I guess they have got something to say about it," Bill said. "I imagine before it's over it'll have effect enough on them."

"Oh pshaw," Mozel said. "They're children."

Bill laughed. "Which way do you want it, Mama?" he said. "Children, or old enough to be into trouble?"

"Bill Simms I'll tell you to keep your mouth shut," Mozel said, but she was calmer now. "You go to bed, Martha Ann. And you go home, Van. I'll take this up with your mother in the morning."

"Yes ma'am," Van said. He tried to get Martha Ann to look at him but she went on through the doorway into the hall without looking back. "It was my fault," he said slowly. "I should have brought her home. But she felt bad. We just wanted to sit together a little bit. That's all."

"I said I'll talk to your mother in the morning," Mozel said. "Go on home now, Van."

He went down the steps and down the walk and across the highway home. He knew he should have done something, but he didn't know what. The whole night had been that way, feeling the wrongness of it and not knowing what to do. He went home and sat on the porch until it was light enough and late enough to wake his mother.

It was snowing when Eileen closed the last of the suitcases. Not a real snow, white and heavy the way she always thought snow should be, but the thin gray half-rain kind of snow they always had in Alabama in January, the icy rainy snow that gave you pneumonia and sore throat and sinus trouble, and that made you wonder why this was called the South.

She went to the window, looking toward the Mayhill house, thinking she'd barely have time to see her mother for a minute and that it was a terrible time to leave even if she had wanted to do it for ten years. She smiled. I'm homesick, she thought. Already I'm homesick and we haven't even started yet.

In her mind she went over her list again, checking off what was done and what was still to do. The children's school records were all sent in and they were registered in the new schools, the house was rented and Graham and Elizabeth had promised to have it aired and cleaned and the beds up by the time they got there. She wasn't taking any furniture from here. She wasn't taking anything except clothes and the crocheted bedspreads and afghans from the cove.

Ace was cleaning up at the newspaper, which meant they'd have a party for him and she'd have to drive the first hundred miles at least while he slept it off. The other kids were at the big house, being stuffed and pampered and wept over by the aunts, and Van was somewhere—off by himself or with Sue Kirk. He wasn't with Martha Ann because Martha Ann was sitting in the kitchen over there with the other kids waiting for him, with or without familial permission, Eileen wasn't sure and didn't care. She was going to give them a chance to say goodbye and Mozel Simms could drop dead for all of her.

It had been a hell of a time, last December. Mozel weeping and wailing at her about Van leading Martha Ann astray and Trudy and Mattie siding with Mozel. All of them telling Eileen she was too lax and that all the kids would come to no good end. They'd even gone so far as to talk about poor dead Veda's child, and that had done it. She'd made Ace send in the advertisements to all the southern newspapers the next day. And she'd written Graham and Morgan and everybody else she knew herself.

But Harry Clifton got Ace the job. She hadn't seen him or talked to him, or even known he knew she had to get out. He'd just walked in one afternoon a few days before Christmas. She had the tree up in the little house. She always had one in spite of Mattie and Trudy's protests that it was silly when they had Christmas in the big house. He'd gone over to it, looking at the little ornaments and lights, smiling and rubbing his hands together.

"Take your overcoat off," she said. "You'll freeze when you go out."

"Can't stay. Just got a little good news for you," he said.

"That'd be good," she said. "There's been little enough of it lately."

"There's a guy in Montgomery," he said, "looking for a good linotyper."

"Montgomery?"

"I know. It's not on the ocean, but it's in the right direction." He smiled at her. "Good set-up too, little shop, chance of going partners before long."

"Oh Harry." She went toward him, stopping just out of touch and smiling. "How'd you know?"

He shrugged. "Grapevine. Nothing a doctor doesn't hear, you know. I think this might be just right. Talk it over with Ace and then we'll contact Graham. He knows the guy."

"It's not political?"

He shook his head. "I wouldn't do *that* to you. It's just what it looks like. A good clear chance at something better. It probably won't pay much to start, but . . ."

"It'll be awful strange living in a city."

"Montgomery's not much of a city. I figure you'll find it's not much different from Bellefonte after you've been there a while."

"I'll talk to Ace tonight," she said.

"All right." He went to the door. "Merry Christmas."

"Merry Christmas, Harry. I guess this is the best Christmas present I ever got."

On the ridge the snow fell onto the wet ground with no noise, but where the banks of dead leaves lay against the tree trunks there was a soft faint patter in the silence and soon there was a silver mist on each pile of leaves. From where he sat on a rotting log Van could see the start of patterns of white lacings on the fence posts and down below the clearing the snow seemed to fall faster and thicker, going toward the ground with abandon. Here it felt like cold rain.

He would have to get up and go in a few minutes now. It would take him an hour to get back to town walking, maybe longer if the ground began to freeze. He hoped it didn't freeze. He didn't want his mother to drive in that. And he didn't think she'd let him.

He hadn't driven the car since the night with Martha Ann. He hadn't wanted to drive it. He sat with Sue Kirk in her living room on the maroon divan and listened to Tommy Dorsey on the radio. Christmas Eve and Christmas day he had stayed at home. Sue had cried even though he'd bought her a set of Evening in Paris with most of his Christmas money. He stayed home anyway.

He got up and stood in the clearing for a moment, looking out toward the last stand of trees before the highway turned the woods to town. Then he struck off down the hill toward home.

They didn't want Eileen to go with it snowing, but they couldn't stop her. "I'm going to sleep in Newcastle tonight," she said. "We'll get that far anyway."

Veda and Martin and Holder and Betty Al were already in the back seat, fighting for the windows without looking back at anybody or anything. Mattie and Trudy hovered over Ace, still talking and talking in the lightly falling snow. Eileen slid under the wheel. "If you people are going with me you better come on," she said.

Van and Martha Ann stood behind the car. She had on her corduroy coat and her head was bare. Her nose was turning red with cold and the snow fell onto her hair, turning to water before it had time to cling. They didn't say anything, just looked at each other. Van thought for a minute that he would kiss her, but there really didn't seem any point in it now. He shook her hand and got into the car beside his mother. Then Ace slammed the door and they were gone.

The long sleek convertible that belonged to Cat Cartwright came around the corner before they were out of sight. She saw Martha Ann standing in the gutter, shivering, and pulled over and jumped out of the car. "They're not gone," she said wildly, looking toward the house and back at Martha Ann.

Martha Ann nodded numbly. She was cold now, shaking, but she didn't want to go home. They'd want to know where she'd been, and why. She didn't think the rule forbidding her to see

Van would hold for goodbyes, but she wasn't sure. Besides, she didn't want them to know. She wished they didn't even have to know that he was gone.

"They can't be gone," Cat said.

"Aunt Eileen said she told you goodbye last night," Martha Ann said, trying to talk out of her misery, feeling her feet cold in the wet gutter.

"But I wanted to see her again for just a minute," Cat said. "Now they're all gone. Everybody. Every single one." She looked at Martha Ann closely. "Honey, you're freezing. Get in this car."

Martha Ann got in beside her, feeling the warmth of the heater start to thaw her aching feet, watching the little swish the windshield wipers made across the glass. She could feel her head beginning to tighten at the temples and knew that she was going to have a sick headache. But it didn't seem to make much difference.

Beside her Cat sat still, watching her own windshield wiper clear the triangle of glass before her. "Where will we go, huh?" she said.

Martha Ann smiled wanly at her. "Home, I guess," she said. "There isn't anywhere else."

"Yeah," Cat said. "Nowhere else at all."

2. *1943*

They lived in a big house on an old street, a street where there were still white columns and oak trees, and iron deer grazing behind iron fences. They had an apartment, but it was an apartment every single room of which was bigger than all of the house in Bellefonte had been. They were rooms with high ceilings and tall windows and ridiculous marble fireplaces; and beech floors and high and heavy transomed doors.

The postman left the mail on a big oak table in the downstairs hall. He came at eleven o'clock every morning and Eileen tried not to be waiting for him. She would stand in the kitchen that had once been a sun parlor and stir diligently at something on the stove, or hang clothes in the too-shady enclosed back yard, which was the only place she could hang clothes because the landlady thought doing your own wash was common. She would read a book, or sweep the floor or take a bath. Anything except wait for the postman.

She heard from Van regularly. At first, when he was in preflight in North Carolina, twice a week, during the rough period of flight training at Norman, Oklahoma and Corpus Christi, once a week, and even now from the expanse of water in the west at least once a month. More often than not the letters were frustrating because they were nothing but cut-up scraps of paper, tidy paper jig-saws with only the salutation and signature holding them together. "Do you have to write so many things they'll cut out?" she'd write him, or "Just write on one side of the paper. Then, at least, they won't get the innocuous on the other side with their nasty scissors." But he always forgot or couldn't find but one sheet of blue-lined paper, and she'd get another jig-saw puzzle. V-mail was worse. There wasn't room for anything at all and it never felt right to her. It wasn't a letter. It seemed to her that it had been written, somehow, by a machine.

Ace liked the V-mails, he was fascinated by the process. He liked keeping the big map on his office wall, too, and moving the bright headed tacks around in simulated employment as the news reports came in.

She didn't like it. Because little red tacks today didn't represent Van on the edge of peril yesterday for her. It was a game and she didn't have the West Point mentality, she'd tell Ace.

Ace drank from fifths now, tall round bottles of blended whiskey because there wasn't any bourbon, and Eileen couldn't stand the taste of it so she didn't drink with him much any more. He did a lot of his drinking at the shop before coming home. She didn't mind, because Saturday nights she always had trouble with Veda anyway. Saturday nights there were dances, for officers, for enlisted men, at the USO, even at the church.

Veda had to have this dress ironed or that dress sewed, she had to have a new pair of shoes even if it took one of the boy's ration stamps for them, she had to dress for two hours while Frank Sinatra sang over and over and over from the phonograph, "Sunday, Monday, or Always." Once Eileen counted and she played it twenty-five times.

On Sundays they had some boy to dinner. He'd be tall or short or blond or brunet, wearing wings or ground crew stripes. He'd drink blended whiskey with Ace, and eat Eileen's dinner, and end up sitting on the floor with Holder's electric train while Veda fussed and fumed and went out to powder her nose and finally talked him out and downtown to the picture show.

They hadn't been back to Bellefonte much this year. Last year it had seemed as though they were on the road all the time: when her mother died, when Trudy died, when Van volunteered—when, as Mattie said, *she'd* sent him off to be killed. Because she'd signed the papers. She could have stopped him, and she let him go. She let him go because he was gone anyway, already enlisted and off and away and gone in his room on Saturday nights with his own maps and books, on the edge of the airfield on Sundays, watching the planes take off. She'd thought he'd want to join the army air corps here at Maxwell Field, but it was the naval air corps he wanted. And that was all right with her, even if she hadn't gotten a look at the ocean yet.

She thought about the ocean a lot now that Van was on it somewhere. She'd never seen an aircraft carrier and the pictures Ace brought home to her didn't tell her much. Boats were a surprise —she still thought of them as boats no matter how often Martin and Holder informed her that they were ships—they were always smaller than they ought to be for what they carried. She knew that if she saw an aircraft carrier she'd never for one moment believe they could fly airplanes off them, much less get them back on. So she didn't visualize the carrier at all, just the ocean, which in her mind looked always as she'd imagined it when she read *Moby Dick*. And Van was Ishmael and would manage somehow to find a coffin to cling to.

There was always somebody in the apartment, spending the night, staying the weekend. When they couldn't get in a hotel they called her or Ace, and they put them in Van's old room or on the living-room studio couch. Morgan came, going through on his way to another construction job, always traveling, always in a hurry, his zippered satchel proclaiming him one of the transients as much as if he wore a uniform. There was always somebody from Bellefonte coming down to see a son or brother or lover, there were friends of Graham's he and Elizabeth couldn't find room or influence for.

Once Cat came, on a Saturday night. Eileen saw her coming up the walk, her high heels clacking along the cracked concrete, her alligator bag in her hand. She stayed the rest of the weekend watching the telephone.

"Go on and call him," Eileen finally said. "It's war. Nobody gives a damn."

"But I do give a damn," Cat had said sadly. "I can't do it. This isn't what I want at all. That's what I came for, of course, but I can't do it. Because what I want isn't in any hotel room."

"It isn't anywhere," Eileen said. "You've passed that stop."

"Bye-Bye-Blackbird," Cat said. "Does Ace keep any whiskey here?"

"I can get hold of a fifth without any trouble if you want it," Eileen said. "This isn't Bellefonte."

So Ace and Cat drank whiskey, and moved pins around the map, and Veda played the phonograph. It was a dismal weekend between news broadcasts and the smell of whiskey and the rain that finally started late on Sunday afternoon.

"Isn't it funny about Frank Sinatra?" Cat said, holding her glass to the light. "He's so different from Rudolph Valentino or Rudy Vallee. He seems so negative to me."

"I sort of like him," Eileen said. "Or I did before Veda played the grooves off that damned record."

"Veda's so pretty," Cat said. "She's the prettiest little thing I ever saw. She sort of glows here in the middle of all the uniforms, if you know what I mean?"

"I know," Eileen said. "It's a hell of a time to be fifteen in."

Cat shrugged. "What isn't? She makes me think of Daisy in *The Great Gatsby*. Have you ever thought of that?"

"I admit it's crossed my mind," Eileen said, "but I haven't seen anything resembling Jay Gatsby around, so I don't worry about it." She watched Cat's face. "Did I tell you about Van seeing Buz while he was in California?" she said.

"Oh, hell, no!" Cat said. "This damned war makes the strangest bedfellows."

Eileen laughed. "Well I hope not," she said.

Cat laughed too. "You know what I mean," she said. "How come him to see her?"

"Coincidence. She runs parties for service men. Turns her place over to them on weekends. Van said he'd have known her anywhere. Still the long earrings and cigarette holder, still very swish. And very drunk too, I take it."

Cat looked at her. "Why not?" she said.

"Why not, indeed?" Eileen said. "It seems to be the great national pastime these days."

"That and the other one," Cat said. "Which maybe is what the drinking's for."

"Not for Buz—or for you."

"No. I reckon our motives are more complicated. Don't you drink at all now, Eileen?"

"Not that stuff."

"Same results," Cat said.

She went back home on Monday without ever picking up the telephone.

So, of course, after all the watching and waiting and busying herself against the postman Eileen forgot that it would be Western Union and when she came in from her Red Cross afternoon and saw the yellow envelope on the table she didn't believe it was for her at all. She picked up her mail and went right on up the stairs without looking at it. She put the coffee on and was reading a letter from Martha Ann when the landlady came up the stairs and knocked on the door.

"All right," she said, not even looking up, and then Mrs. Harris was standing there, her face contorted behind the round shining glasses, her neat blue-white hairdo looking, for the first time that Eileen could remember, a little rumpled. "Is there anything I can do?" Mrs. Harris said.

"Do?" Eileen said, thinking with another part of her mind, No. It was not for me. It certainly was not for me. They wouldn't have left it without me to sign.

And then like the governor saying, No reprieve, Mrs. Harris said,

"I signed for it. The little messenger boy looked so . . . I don't know . . . afraid. I thought it might be better for you to find it by yourself . . ."

"Find what?" Eileen said, hearing her own words loud in the room. "Was there something you left for me?" Her mind went on quietly, Of course not. They wouldn't send it in a simple telegram. Maybe it's from Cat. She sends the things.

"The telegram," Mrs. Harris said, her face breaking into pieces and seeming to cascade around the room, "The telegram . . . from the War Department."

"Please," Eileen said, getting up and carefully holding Martha Ann's letter in front of her, her eyes going on to register the last sentences—*I had a letter last week. It didn't say much. He never says much of anything*—"Please," she said again to the old lady with the cast-iron back who had suddenly deserted her. "You mustn't take on so."

Mrs. Harris gasped. "Mrs. Johnson," she said, "I'm going to call your husband." She was gone, leaving the doorway blank behind her.

Eileen walked down the stairs, putting one foot carefully in front of her, then the other even more carefully, her mind busy telling her not to fall, the panic held tightly in the back of her head somewhere, screaming at her, It isn't. It isn't. It isn't.

After a long long afternoon in and out of the patches of sun on the polished stairs she reached the hall table and put out her hand and picked it up and read it, the one word, MISSING, jumping off the page intact into her mind with sudden reprieve until she thought, OCEAN, and knew she hadn't really been reprieved at all.

It was the pictures her mind threw up that were very bad, worse than it had been when Vance died, because Vance was a man at least and not the one she'd had to lean over a crib and say, Watch, Watch, Please, about for so many years. Because certainty and peace don't exist after a baby comes. Unless you're some sort of imbecile or iceberg you learn about life. You know you're just a little tiny step away from the safety of the trees and that anything at all is out there in the dark. So when it happens one part of you keeps saying, See, I told you. I told you. And it's very hard not to agree with the ones who gave up and never tried at all.

The pictures that came and went when she closed her eyes varied with the night but they were never good to look at, never bearable. She didn't know anything about ships and airplanes, but she knew about pain and fear and it was these that haunted her and made her get up nights and sit in the kitchen hugging the coffee cup. Don't let him have been afraid, she'd say to whatever existed or didn't exist outside her kitchen. Don't let him have hurt too much too far from home.

It was three years before she got the letter that told her about it. After it was all over and they were coming home with their ruptured ducks and hot pants, and Veda was her prime worry. After the confirmation telegram had come and gone with no ripple, because she had always known, after the things arrived in the neat foot-locker, the clothes and books and letters from her and Martha Ann.

Dear Mrs. Johnson,

I have wanted to write you this letter since Van went off the carrier, but they wouldn't let us write nothing like this until after the war. I got out yesterday and I'm writing to you and Mrs. Koski (that's our belly-gunner's mother) first thing after I called my family.

It happened laying off the Marianas. It wasn't even a combat strike, we were doing target runs with dummy torpedos. There was a lot of sun that day. It was still and hot and quiet like Sunday. Van was laughing and talking like he always did just before we had to go out. He was a good pilot to have to fly with ... I mean, if you got to go off one of those flight decks with anybody it sure was good for it to be somebody cheerful. I never had another one like him.

We just climbed in like always. I was the radioman and Koski in the belly, and Van up front, like always, and the guys ran up and cleared us. I remember it was shiny out on the water, with the top of all that ocean smooth and dead in the sun and the convoy spread out across that water like a bunch of toys in a tub of water like we

used to play when we were kids, and I was singing "Beer Barrel
Polka," because I always sang up there. It kept the sky from coming
in and the water from coming up.

Then they yelled and pulled the chocks and we went down the
deck and off of her. We just ditched. We never had before, though
lots of the fellows did, some of 'em almost regular. Those TBM's
are heavy things to take off a flight deck. There I was on top of the
sky, singing, and then we were in the water. I didn't think at all. I
just pushed like hell and opened that turret and got out. Then I
looked. I looked a long time, Mrs. Johnson, but she went down like
lead, with Van and Koski in her. I kept trying to dive and hunt and
the rest of those sob's (excuse me) taking off over me, but it wasn't
any use, and after a while I grabbed the mae west floating by me
and they got me back on board.

He was a good pilot, Mrs. Johnson, and a good friend, and I
think he liked the Navy even though he crabbed about it as much
as the rest of us. I won a silver dollar off him once in a poker game
and I have felt bad about that a lot since, because maybe it was
his good-luck piece. But I try to feel like if it was that I won it
because his number was up anyhow. You have to think like that,
Mrs. Johnson, if you are going to come home and get married and
go to work and start doing all those things again.

I am enclosing the silver dollar.

Yours sincerely,
DWIGHT ELSWORTH JONES

She sent the silver dollar, that Captain Simms had given Van
when he was born, to Martha Ann, just as she had given away the
books and clothes, sent Martha Ann her letters, and burned her
own. She had learned a long time ago not to hoard what should
have been thrown off the train at the last stop. Hurt or loss might
never vanish, but it eased and there was no reason to rub salt in
it for the rest of time.

It could have been worse, she always tried to tell herself. There
are worse ways for the last Maynard to stop belonging to the air
of the planet than by going off a flight deck on a sunny day while
toy ships floated on the surface of the western eye of the world.

3. *1946*

From where she lay in the high white bed the ceiling looked
like a honeycomb. It was a good idea; she liked it. Besides it gave
her something to think about since Gloria and Dudley hadn't been
to see her all week and the vases of tall red roses and the stacks
of new magazines and the private nurse with the pretty face didn't
make up for that.

Last time they'd come twice a week. This time not since last
weekend. She counted the days, hearing them unwind on a creaky
spindle in her mind. My mind is a long black corridor with a million doors that open onto bright neat little scenes in which the
people grimace and dance and prance and say their piece, she
thought, and down the corridor go the days, unwinding on that
creaky spindle toward the eye of the world.

She sat up in bed suddenly. "Why did Dudley send me roses?"
she said out loud. "He knows I can't stand roses. He knows it."
Her fingers fumbled, found the buzzer, pushed.

The pretty nurse who always smiled came in. "What is it, Mrs.
Cartwright?" she said.

"The roses," Cat said.

"Roses?" The bland face smiled for commercial consumption.
"There aren't any roses, Mrs. Cartwright? Or do you mean you'd
like some?"

Cat whimpered. They'd fooled her again, switched the vases
probably. She looked around at the table—jonquils, cool yellow

and green, smelling of summer and sunshine. Jonquils. "They *were* here," she said.

"Not now." The face smiled.

Cat smiled sweetly back. "You bitch," she said behind her clenched teeth.

When the nurse closed the door she got up and got her clothes out of the closet. They were there, hanging neatly on wire hangers. This was not the kind of place where they took your clothes. It was a high-priced rest home, the people here had everything from diabetes to upset stomachs. She dressed and slipped into the corridor. Then she remembered her purse and had to go back and start all over again. This time it was harrowing, this time she had to tiptoe and open the door slowly and quietly, and look stealthily up and down the hall. Because this time she'd thought about it and knew it to be dangerous. She even went down the stairs, instead of using the elevator, and stopped at the foot of them and watched the nurses talking in the brightly lit cubicle until they turned away to pour coffee and she could dart past and out the door. Outside it was cool and dark with the stars like summer overhead, close and blurred as though it were already hot, not cool with spring.

The hospital was on a hill and she had to walk down it, but the gate was open and she just walked through and under a street light and down another hill to the bus stop. In a few minutes a bus came, yellow and green and lighted inside like a stage, the people hanging from straps and sitting looking out the windows. There was the hiss of airbrakes and she got on, got her purse open and put the dime in the box, and a man stood up and she sat down.

Then she remembered that she hadn't looked to see if the bus was going uptown or downtown and she began to shake. It has to be going downtown, that's all, she told herself. If it isn't I'll die. I'll have to get off somewhere out in the suburbs in the dark and try to get back, and I can't. It's simple. I can't.

She looked out the window, trying to gauge whether the lights were coming closer together or further apart, and finally deciding she couldn't tell yet. At each corner the bus hissed and slowed and stopped and people got down clutching packages and holding their coats over their arms. It's uptown, she thought. It is. I should get off right now so I can start back. But she sat on, looking at the thinning crowd of passengers, watching the lonely pools of light at the street corners where they got down and went off into the dark. Once they stopped in front of a drugstore and she tried to stand up and get off but her legs wouldn't hold her and after that she didn't try again. She sat still, feeling her palms sweat and trying to pray. Last year when she'd had all the talks with Reverend Duskey he had said prayer would always help. But it didn't now. She could feel the words come into her brain like the steady little taps a woodpecker makes but they didn't mean anything. Father. Jesus. Help me. Save me now. Let it be going downtown, please. Grant me this one thing. Let it not be going out of town, in Jesus' name.

After a while there was only a fat woman with a shopping bag and two giggling twelve-year-old girls with a movie magazine. Then they all got off at a deserted corner and the bus went on for two more blocks and stopped.

The bus driver turned around. She could see his eyes behind the rimless glasses, blue and blurred, and she was afraid of him. "End of the line, lady," he said.

"I'm all right," she said.

"End of the line. You'll have to get off, lady. I got to take her back to the barn."

She swallowed. "Which way is the barn?"

"It don't signify," he said.

"Couldn't you take me back with you?" she said. "I . . ."

But he kept staring at her and she knew she couldn't stay on the bus with him. She kept trying to remember something her father used to say when she was a little girl. White Slavery. That was it. He wanted to sell her. "I'll get off here," she said.

The bus went away, not back but on down the road, and she

thought, I was right. He wanted to sell me. She looked behind her. There was nothing, nothing but the darkness. There was a green bench in front of some bushes and on down the road a pale street lamp lighting up a crossroad with a white house back in some trees but, behind her, nothing. She backed into the bench and sat on it. After a while her eyes pierced the darkness and she saw another house opposite, with no lights in it. Somewhere a dog barked twice and stopped. She tried to see her wrist watch but there wasn't enough light. She felt in her purse but there weren't any matches, or cigarettes either. I have to have a cigarette, she thought, and she could see them, lying in the pack on the sterile little bedside table, one of them just outside the edge of the pack, waiting. "I have to have a goddam cigarette," she said.

She got up and walked down the road to the street light, feeling the dark closing in behind her as she walked. Wait a minute, she kept saying to whatever was behind her. Wait a minute till I can get to the light. Then there was the street light, casting its lonely pool, and she stepped into the pool and saw that it was ten o'clock.

Then the bus came, the bus going in the right direction, downtown, coming fast. She held up her arm, trying to stop it, then she tried to run back to the bus stop, her feet refusing to obey her command fast enough so that it was past her and past the bus stop and gone. "It was the last one," she said wildly. "It was the last one and I can't get to town till morning." Panic started to close in and she stood still, staring toward the disappearing tail lights while the night closed in on both sides now.

Then she heard the roar of the second bus. She couldn't believe it for a moment because nothing good had happened to her for a long time and there was no reason why it should now; so she almost missed that one too, standing staring toward the approaching headlights until she thought, My God, the stop, and ran toward the bench by the bushes and raised her hand just as the bus roared up.

She climbed on, fumbling for the money, and there was only a fifty-cent piece so that she had to hand it to the driver, and look at him, and it wasn't the same one after all. This one had brown eyes and no glasses. She took the change and heard the little ring as the coin slipped in, and sat down on the front seat. There was a little sign that said, "Your Driver, safe, courteous, dependable, Harry Griffin," and a bigger sign that said, "No Smoking." She stared at them while the bus went back past all the lonely little pools of light and past the drugstore and finally past the bench at the foot of the hill by the hospital and then past more and more lights and across a set of tracks and into town.

She looked out at the neon and the wide-fronted windows with the clothed dummies and the draped material and the shining ornaments, and she said to the bus driver, "Have you got a cigarette?"

"No smoking on the bus, lady," he said.

"All right. I'll get off," she said. "Have you got a cigarette?"

"No'm," he said. "I don't smoke."

"How far is it to the Greyhound station?" she said.

"Couple blocks."

She stood up. "I'll get off here."

The bus pulled to the curb by a triangular sign and she climbed down, not looking back, and went into the drugstore on the corner. There were little signs hanging on strings of wire all across the store and piles of junk on tables all down the center aisle, and a fan that blew the little signs back and forth, back and forth, in the heavy air. There was a boy behind the soda fountain in a dirty apron and an old man on a stool eating a sandwich. Neither of them were real.

"A package of Herbert Tareytons," she said to the dirty apron.

"Ain't got none," he said. "Lady bought the last carton this afternoon. Man'll be around tomorrow."

"Anything then. Pall Malls."

He pushed the bright red pack across the counter and took her bill. She watched his hands ringing up the sale. They were long muscular hands. "What time do you get off from work?" she said.

"Ma'am?"

She looked at him. He was about fifteen years old, with a thin discontented face. "Nothing," she said. "I made a mistake."

"Cup of coffee?" he said.

She sat down on one of the red stools, smelling the sour smell of old ice cream and spilled coffee and wet counter rags. He set the cup in front of her. If he doesn't slosh coffee into the saucer I'll drink it, she thought. She looked carefully at the saucer, moving the cup. It was clean. "All right," she said.

"Do you feel all right, lady?" the boy said.

"What?" For a minute she couldn't remember who he was. Then she saw the dirty apron. "Oh, I'm fine. Sure. All right." She looked at him. "My head hurts, though. Have you got anything for a headache?"

"Sure. Fix you a bromo," he said.

"Oh I don't think that would do."

"No'm?" He'd begun to look worried now, the discontent had given way to bewilderment and somewhere behind the eyes a touch of fright.

"No. Have you got any whiskey?"

"Ma'am, that's not good for headaches."

"It's *my* head," she said. "Or at least it was." She peered into the mirror behind the fountain, seeing her pale face gazing back at her. "It was. Wasn't it?"

The boy had moved away now, looking toward the back of the store where there was either someone else or a telephone. Cat laughed. She laid a dollar on the counter and slid off the stool. "It's all right," she said. "I'm just leaving. Do you have a girl?"

"Nope. Not me."

"All right," she said. "I'm going."

The old man looked up from his sandwich and she went to the door quickly. Outside, the streets were empty except for a few late cars, a few late buses. She walked along looking into windows, wondering where the bus station was. There was a crowd of boys on the corner, clustered around a lamp post, and they called to her.

She began to run then, against the light, across the street, and down another block until the back of her mind registered the running dog in blue neon and she could push open the doors and cross to the little window and say, "When is the next bus to Bellefonte?"

"It's loading at Gate 2 now," the voice in the little cage said.

"Isn't that funny?" she said. "The back of my mind had this all planned out. I even got on the wrong bus at first so I'd get here just in time."

"Ticket?" the voice in the cage said.

"All right." She shoved a bill at him and waited while he made the little stamping motions and clicking noises and handed back the yellow square with the change.

"Punch, brother, punch," she said laughing.

"Pardon?"

"Oh quit pacing your cage, tiger," she said. "Where's Gate 2?"

"Through the glass doors and to your right."

"Yes sir." She saluted him and went out the door. There were a lot of animals on this side of the cage, too, but she didn't look at them. They were carrying things and holding their young and they all looked pretty nasty. She skipped down the concrete ramp and climbed on the bus.

Most of the people on the bus were asleep. She went to the back and found a seat by a boy in a tweed suit with a duck in his buttonhole, and sat down. He nodded, and shut his eyes again.

She shut her eyes too, shutting out the hospital and the nurse who would be coming around now with the red pill or the gray pill or the yellow pill, and the dark corner of nowhere under the street-light and the soda jerk's dirty apron. But she couldn't seem to shut out the smell of the soda fountain. It hung inside her nasal passages, lingering in her head like a dirty song.

The bus swung sideways and she felt her stomach turn over. Then they were out of the station and back on the streets and she put her hand over her mouth.

"Can I help you?" the boy said beside her.

"All right now, I think," she said.

"Get by the window." He got up and changed places with her and she held her face to the half-open window, feeling the wind on her cheeks with the city smell still in it, rubber and tar and concrete, and somehow, popcorn.

"Thanks," she said.

He was fumbling in his pocket. "Gun?" her mind said. "Gum?" He drew out a bottle.

"Would you like a shot of this?" he said.

"Well now, thanks." She felt her hands, reaching like claws. "But not a tiger," she said. "That's for people in cages."

"Ma'am?"

"Don't say that," she said. She screwed off the top of the bottle and put it to her mouth. Then she took it away, teasing herself for a minute. "Cheers, ducky," she said. Then she turned it up and drank. It was like Mizz Mozel Simms' nectar used to be, cool and fresh. "Why's it cool?" she said.

"Cool?"

She handed the bottle back. "Uh-huh. Just like the musicians say. Only in my day the word was hot."

"Yes, ma'am," the boy said.

"Did I drink all your whiskey?" she said.

"No'm. There's some more. Have it." He gave the bottle back to her. There were two good inches in it. She drank them.

Outside, the city had disappeared. They were going up the mountain now, the bus pulling heavily in low gear. There was nothing but darkness on the side of the road. Then they reached the top, leveled out, and started down. The whiskey had warmed away some of the unreality of the night and she could let her mind open some of the doors now. Here was one with Eileen and Ace in the old T-model Ace used to have. Coming home from shopping down this very mountain and the brakes going out. And here she was, and Veda, laughing, sitting on the front porch of Eileen's little house, saying, "What did you do, Eileen? What did you *do?*" Eileen tossing her head and laughing and saying, "Hung on and prayed and let 'er go."

But that opened another door and here was Eileen leaving, driving another car out of Bellefonte. Now she only saw her once a year. She cried.

"Jesus, what is it, lady?" the boy said.

"I'm all right. I've been sick. I'm still weak."

"Oh." He dropped the empty bottle onto the floor.

But it was too late now. When you stopped letting the spool unwind by itself and started letting the doors open they kept opening, on people and places and bright little technicolor scenes, and after a while she'd come to the one where Marty was and the one where Graham came into the empty apartment, and the one where Veda was so cold and still and . . . "Don't you have any more?" she said.

"No'm."

The bus roared on. It is only sixty miles, she thought. We've come at least ten, at the least that. Only about fifty miles to go and I'll be home and everything will be all right. It's being in that terrible hospital and nobody even coming to see me. That's all. When I get home it will be all right.

Around them people slept slumped in the awkward seats; outside, cars came along the highway, spaced and swift in the night.

"Where are you going?" the boy said.

"Home. To Bellefonte, that is. Home."

"Me too," he said. "I live in Montgomery."

"Oh," she said. "Oh. Do you? Do you? Do you know a Graham McCloud?"

"The Fixer? Oh, I know *of* him. But I don't know him personally. No'm."

"The Fixer," Cat said, and laughed so that a man in front of them raised up and glared at her. "That's the name for old Graham all right. He's been at it for years. Who does he fix things for this year?"

"The governor, of course."

"Of *course*." She put a cigarette in her mouth and waited until the boy fumbled a match out for her. Then she leaned back, pulling smoke gratefully into her lungs and trying to get the spool unwinding smoothly past the doors again.

"You talk," she said. "You talk about something. I'll be all right."

He did. But she never knew what, something about being discharged and the Pacific. The words soothed her though, issuing into the silence of the dark bus, the sound of youngness in them, the pauses when he lit a cigarette.

I'm going to make it all right, she thought. It can't be much further, and then Home. They passed through Sinclair. Halfway.

The boy went to sleep. Or pretended to. She didn't know which. She looked at him, blond, stolid, healthy. "I bet you won't ever put a bullet through your head, my boy," she said.

He stirred in his sleep. She patted his head and shut her eyes, dozing. She jerked awake suddenly, unable for a moment to tell where she was. Then she remembered, I was in the hospital again, but I got out. Why was I there this time? Then she remembered that too.

A bad week, got off her diet and her stomach giving her hell, and Harry Clifton saying, "Got to get you off the sleeping pills. I know you're taking dexedrine in the mornings whether you'll admit it or not." Dudley with his new presidency in the J. C.'s and Gloria pitching a fit in the dress shop because she bought herself a new dress and didn't get one for Gloria. Couldn't sleep, no pill. Got up and took the car. Another bright little picture now: sitting in front of the drive-in waiting for the milk and there was Martha Ann Holder and some boy in a car, and she went over and said, "Honey, could you go out and buy something for me? They won't let me have it."

Martha Ann said, "Aunt Cat, I can't do that."

And the boy said, "Well, what a little prude you are."

And Martha Ann said, "Go to hell," to the boy.

Then she had said, "Please. Please. Please. If you don't I'll get somebody else. Maybe that boy that drives a taxi." So Martha Ann said, "All right," and got out of the boy's car and got into hers and they went out behind the sawmill and she gave Martha Ann the five dollars and she went in and came back with the bottle and she took her back to the boy in the car.

After that it was pretty blurred. Except that somewhere Dudley and Gloria came into it and took her away from Marty's party and sent her up here. No. Up there. She was going home now, though, and it would be all right.

The bus was on the causeway now so she knew they were nearly home. She tried to see out the window to tell when they got to Larkin's Barbecue place, but she missed it because there was the old convict camp and the little grocery store and then Five Points and the bus was pulling into the main street. It stopped at the corner across from the dark bus station and she stepped across the sleeping boy's legs and got off.

There was a taxi sitting under the oak tree across the street and she went over and looked in. The driver was half-asleep over the wheel. She didn't know him but she shook his shoulder and he blinked and said, "Oh. Hi, Mrs. Cartwright. Want a taxi?" And she got in and he took her home.

The lights were out but she found her key in the bottom of her bag and let herself in, her mind racing ahead, thinking, It's all right now. It's all right now. I'm off that impossible bus stop. I'm home and safe.

Then a light went on upstairs and she felt the hair rise on the back of her neck. There were footsteps coming down the stairs and she tried to hide behind the big chair by the door but she knocked over the magazine rack and knew it was too late. Her mouth was dry now and she could hear her heart, beating and beating inside her, trapped. Then he shone the flashlight right in her face and said, "What are you doing here?", and she began to scream, loudly and unreasonably and forever. Because it was Dudley Cartwright's house she was in and he was the one who wanted to sell her. He was the one she had been trying to run from all the time.

Harry Clifton crumpled the empty cigarette pack in his hand and threw it onto his desk and sighed. "I don't know, Dudley," he said to the man across the desk. "I don't know. She's all right now, this week. I cannot tell you about next. If you could keep her off whiskey or pills or . . ."

"Should I send her back up there?" Dudley said. "She hates it so."

"No. Not now. Try it at home a while. Try getting out a little. Go to Newcastle and see a play, do something . . . Oh hell, Dudley, I'm lying. I don't know."

"Well, I don't," Dudley said.

"Do you think you could talk her into going back to the psychiatrist?" Harry said.

"You know that never did much good."

"I know."

"The preacher?" Dudley said.

Harry shrugged. "Use your own judgment about that," he said. "I don't know."

Dudley stood up. "It's that I don't ever know what's going to set it off," he said. "Sometimes I can understand it. Like when Daddy died and we had to go over to that cemetery in the miserable cold and rain and she got hysterical that night because I wasn't going off *my* rocker. But this last time I couldn't find any reason at all."

Harry looked at him, handsome, conservative, unimaginative. He stood up. "Let's go get a cup of coffee, Dudley," he said. "Sometimes these things work themselves out." He knew he was lying.

From her room she could see the maple trees, green now and silver, waiting for summer, waiting for fall. Last winter they had talked to her. It was grim hearing those bare black branches saying,

Look out, there it is, let me tell you about it. They sang sometimes too—"Bye Bye Blackbird." Why do you like those old songs? Gloria said. Gloria liked Eddy Howard and "To Each His Own." Gloria liked "Doin' What Comes Naturally." Gloria wore bobbysox and dirty saddle oxfords and big sweaters over plaid skirts. But she was pretty. As pretty as I was, Cat thought, or prettier, pretty as Veda.

Since she had come home this time she hadn't been able to get through the glass at all. At first it was only sometimes that the glass seemed to be there, a clear pane between herself and other people, people who moved and talked and must surely feel, somewhere in another world out there. Now the glass had shut down for good. It wasn't the glass itself that worried her, though. You could cope with that because sight and sound and even smell were perfectly plain from the other side. What worried her was that she didn't want to get through any more. Whether she liked to remember it or not she could hear that nasty little doctor with his manicured nails saying from behind his bare shiny desk, "Don't worry about a sense of unreality, everybody has it sometimes. Start worrying when you begin to like it."

She went to the mirror and put on some more pancake make-up. She was never satisfied with the result and she would put on more, watching her face anxiously until only the pale even mask stood out around her eyes. Then she felt better. Everything was hidden then. No blemishes. It said so right on the box.

She wanted to go down to the bus station and buy some magazines. It was cozy there, warm and steamy with the coffee waiting in the big silver urns, and the kids sitting on stools reading comic books. But she couldn't go there any more because the Winston girl who worked there had called Dudley one day and he'd come and gotten her. She had been reading a magazine and drinking coffee, not doing anything at all really, but Dudley had come and told her to go home.

Later she tried to reconstruct the morning and understand what she had done wrong in the bus station, but she couldn't think of anything. She had sat in a booth, very proper, and sipped politely, and turned the pages of the book. Finally she'd had to brace herself and ask Dudley, and he said that she was tight and her skirt was unbuttoned, but she didn't think so. She hadn't had anything to drink. Two dexedrines, but that wasn't dope. The kids took it to diet. After that day she started wearing the pancake make-up. It made her feel very bland.

She told Reverend Duskey this and he frowned. She didn't like him to frown because he was very handsome and frowning made him look like Dudley or her father, which was not good for a preacher. She told him this, too, and he told her that perhaps she was working too hard helping with the mission work and to take a rest. So she'd given him up too.

She looked around the room at the things she'd gotten from her mother's house. There was her old screen with the paint peeling off. She was going to paint it. There were her old pillows with the fringe coming off too. She couldn't fix that. And her scrap book. Harry Clifton said not to look at the scrap book so it was hidden, because Dudley would just as soon as not burn it up—or bury it.

After a while she looked at the door. She had a game with the door this week. She tried as long as possible not to look at it so that she wouldn't start thinking she couldn't go through it. The only way to get out was to walk toward it and through it without looking or thinking. She still needed to go through it. There were a lot of places she still had to go.

She put on her earrings and her fur jacket. Then she remembered it was spring and took the jacket off and put on a print dress. It felt big at the neck so she pinned it with the diamond pin Dudley had given her to stab herself with. It was a pretty pin, but dangerous. Then she was outside on the landing and had gotten through the door again. It was easy going downstairs and out the front door and down the walk. She could smell the flowers bloom-

ing but she didn't see them. She walked down to the taxi stand
and got a taxi and had them take her to the Coca-Cola plant.
Dudley had taken her car keys when she ran into Sue Mayhill's
garage one night.

She went in and back to the office. He was sitting at his desk,
checking papers, of course. "Hello honey," he said.

"I don't have any money," she said.

"Your credit's good all over town."

"But I want some money."

He frowned and reached in his pocket and handed her two one-
dollar bills. "That do you?"

She took the two dollars because it was two dollars. "Dudley,"
she said, "you are the stuffiest man in Maynard County."

He went on checking his papers. Just as she got to the door he
said, "Don't you think you'd better leave that pin here with me?"

She didn't even bother to look at him, just went on out and
looked at the sunshine falling crazily into the branch across the
street. Somebody's washing was swinging on the line behind an
apartment house and there was a dog lying happily in the middle
of the road. She turned left and started out of town.

It was warm in the sun on Marty's little porch. She sat there
for a while before she reached down behind the statue and took
out the bottle. The bottle was warm too where the sun had gotten
to it even here in the shelter of Apollo himself. She had a drink
and poured a little onto the stone as libation.

The grass was sweet here and the breeze soft; she could look
across the gravel road at a lot of Bellefonte under tree and stone.
Behind her was the brown and gray and dirt of the Negro district,
hovered over by the blue of mountain, separated from the hill by
a field of shining grass. If she was very quiet she could hear the
wind blow through it, like wheat. Scene in some book, wheat rip-
pling. She'd never seen wheat, but it was like that grass. Keep off
the grass Walt Whitman. Nearly as bad as roses or Millay. They
said that when they had to move the old Martin Town Cemetery

away from the river when they took up Ole Mrs. Clopton Wright her hair had grown and grown, all over the inside of the casket. Used to tell that at Veda's on the porch on summer nights. Scare each other. All fake. Graham had a blazer jacket, new that year, navy and white. And Ace played on the uke, "Doo Wacka Doo." Then there was poor ole Floyd Collins. Had it happen to him alive. Why didn't he gnaw his foot off, like foxes in traps with their teeth on edge? I could go make grape pies again.

She squinted at the sun. It was almost overhead. I believe there's something wrong with it today, she thought. This was the really bad one, waiting for the sun to novate. She had days when she waited all day long, only to jump out of bed at night remembering suddenly that it could happen then, too, that it was still up there balanced in its share of space even when you couldn't see it shine, and she'd lie tense waiting for it to go on and blow. In a way she wanted it to happen because it would be a real finality. You couldn't ask for a bigger, more final, thing than that. Melting into space like hot wax, dripping down the candlestick of matter into the void of night.

But it wouldn't happen. Not this life, not this side of time. They'd go on one by one into the ground where Rudolph lay on pink and white and Marty's hands were folded across his new plaid vest.

And leave Cat, Sittin' on Top of the World through a megaphone. C? C for see like they used to write it on notes in study hall with Miss Jones in her collars and pins with a ruler tapping along the window ledge. Had a picture of her from the autographic camera, written across the bottom, Our English Teacher. Out here now too, like Elaine the fair. High in her tower to the east, guarding the sacred shield of Lancelot. Old Edison record of William Jennings Bryan on Immortality. They got him too, of course. How was it? Crucified him on a cross of gold. Over there next to King Tut waiting for the archaeologists. Yes, We Have No Bananas. We have no bananas today.

She threw the bottle toward the whispering grass, cause the

trees didn't need to know—and went into the old part of Babylon and looked at the baby in its shell. It slept quiet, waiting for the sun.

Jack Burke had one of the only specialty stores in Bellefonte— he owned a sporting goods shop. The shop had been an inspiration on the part of Jack's father, who had given up attempting to educate him after he was thrown out of two military academies, St. Andrew's School for Boys, Vanderbilt, the University of Alabama, and Auburn.

He bought Jack the shop and it kept Jack happy. He could sit in the sun on a splint-bottomed chair and watch the world go down the street. He could talk to the passersby and whittle toy guns. On weekends he could raid his own stock and go hunting or fishing in his second-hand Ford. His wife, a former waitress at the Majestic Café, liked it too. She came down after wiping a cloth over the furniture and stacking the dishes in the sink and sat with him. She went along on the hunting trips in pants and a pair of hip boots. When the baby came they took him along too.

The store made a living—barely. Jack eked it out by selling some of his hunting and fishing trophies to less lucky sportsmen, an arrangement that paid well after the lakes opened to tourists. There was money for hamburgers and milkshakes for the kid and whiskey for Mama and Daddy and gas for the second-hand car. It was a good life.

When Jack looked up and saw Mrs. Cartwright standing in front of him in the noonday sunlight he wasn't surprised, because she came in fairly often and bought things for her husband. She was one for spending big and giving big. He'd even ordered things for her out of Memphis and Chattanooga and Newcastle, things the store didn't carry regular, like a fancy duckblind with sleeping bag and decoys all together in a passle. So he felt right glad to see her because he was sure it meant money.

Like everybody else in town he'd heard she was hitting the bottle but half the town was doing the same, as far as he could see. They said when Pete Wallace sold out his bootlegging business, because the Wallaces were getting too big in the county for him to go on with it, that the price he got was sending all his younguns through college besides building him that house out on the river and paying for the fancy cars he and his wife drove. So he figured Mrs. Cartwright's drinking was her business. She'd been sick a lot and that was enough to drive anybody to the bottle. He'd had a touch of malaria once and it'd about driven him to a permanent place behind the bottle himself. He shoved his chair upright and stood up. "What can I do for you?" he said.

Cat went on into the store in front of him, blinking at the dimness of the interior after the hard glare of sun on the sidewalk. "I'd like to see your guns," she said.

"Shotguns?"

"Oh no. Pistols, I think. Of course, I don't know anything about pistols . . ."

He was behind the counter now and he grinned at her. "Well, I do," he said. "You tell me what you want it for and I can sure tell you what kind will do the job."

She smiled at him and opened her eyes very wide. "Why, it's for Dudley, of course," she said. "A surprise. He wants it to practice on a range with, or whatever you call those things. He and some of his business friends from Newcastle are all excited about some sort of contest or something . . ." She let her voice trail off and smiled again.

"You want a .22 Target," he said. "I can show you the best thing in stock and, if I do say so, the best in the country. Here."

He put the gun on the counter and looked down at it admiringly. "How does it work?" she said.

He showed her, loading the rounds, pushing the safety off and on.

"It looks heavy," she said.

"No'm. Not for what you want. Just try it."

She took the gun up in both hands, looking at it closely, then hefting it on her palm. Then she pointed it at him and laughed. "Boom," she said.

He laughed too, uneasily. "It's loaded," he said.

"But the safety's on," she said brightly. "See, right here where you showed me."

"Yeah," he said.

"I'll take it. You just put it in a box so I can wrap it up fancy, huh?"

"Wrap it myself," he said. "I got some old Christmas paper here somewhere, some blue and white that'll do for anything."

"Fine." She waited, tapping her foot on the floor and humming until he came back with the wrapped package. Then she rummaged in her purse and frowned. "Well," she said. "You'll just have to trust me till Saturday."

"Yes, ma'am. Perfectly all right," he said. "Shall I send a bill?"

"No. I don't want Dudley to see it yet. I'll just come in Saturday and pay you."

"Yes, ma'am."

She put the package in her purse and went out of the store, still humming. After Jack was sitting back in the sun he found himself humming the song too. He couldn't place it for a while, but he finally got hold of it—Three O'Clock in the Morning, a mighty gay tune, back a long way. He remembered his older sister had a record of it that she used to play on the victrola. That was when they cranked 'em up by hand.

On Saturday she came in and paid him for the gun in cash. She got the money from her mother, telling her it was for a debt at the dress shop.

"How'd Mr. Cartwright like it?" Jack said.

"Oh, I haven't given it to him yet. It's for his birthday." She smiled and went out of the store.

The gun lay in the locked drawer of her dressing table. She didn't intend to use it. She wanted it to make her feel safe. And it did. She felt so much better that even Dudley commented on it.

She even began making the dessert for dinner again and spending the mornings working her flower beds.

The gun pushed the panic away. Knowing that it lay there safely in the tiny drawer pushed the pulsing sun back, rid the morning hours of the waiting in terror. If it were to get too bad, if she ever got too afraid, the gun was there to take her out of dark and fear and waiting, to put her safely on the hill to wait in peace.

She let Mable start the spring cleaning and put the lawn furniture out, she bought a new slack suit for gardening, and she told Gloria that she could have a wiener roast. Then on Friday Buz Mayhill came home. Sue called Cat early in the morning when the sun was coming into the breakfast room in a normal happy slant. "Cat?" she said, "Mother's here. She's going to stay a whole week with me, she says. You're the first one she asked about. Can you come over this afternoon for coffee?" In the kitchen Mable slammed the refrigerator door and the sun changed, coloring with the tinge of uncertainty. "All right," Cat said.

"Well, here I am again," Buz said, fitting a cigarette into a long holder. "I never thought I'd come back to this place. Even after Martin died I just couldn't make myself come—even to see my baby girl." She patted Sue on the knee and Sue pulled back from her slightly.

"The war, darlings," she went on, "the dreadful war. I entertained those boys and, I must say, it took a hell of a lot out of me." She reached into a voluminous tapestry bag and took out a silver pill box. "Time for the mid-afternoon sedative," she said. "If I don't start now I won't get to bed before two A.M."

Cat set her cup into her saucer with a clink. She didn't want to look at Buz but it was impossible not to. Buz's face was painted white and her mouth was purple. Her eyebrows, plucked to pencil lines, had been dyed to match her hair, dyed sable. When she talked, gesturing, her hands shook. She had put on weight from the waist down but her arms and legs were bird thin. There was a tick in her left eye.

"More coffee, Cat?" Sue said.

Cat nodded, trying to put Buz behind the glass where she belonged, but she kept breaking through, shrill-voiced, sick, sad.

"Tell us about California," Cat said.

"Oh, it's fabulous," Buz said. "Always something new. Lately I've gotten interested in one of those mad groups out there. They run around in bed sheets and plant gardens. I don't know. Maybe I'll join them. All they want is your money. But what the hell . . ." She smiled sweetly at Sue.

Sue smiled back, just as sweetly.

Buz took out the bag again and pulled out a silver whiskey flask. "Want your coffee sweetened?" she said.

"All right," Cat said, watching the claws pour whiskey into the china cups. She drank the coffee in one gulp and Buz poured straight whiskey into the cups, winking at her as she did so.

"If you'll excuse me," Sue said, "I've got some things to attend to in the kitchen. Some other people are coming in later," she said ominously.

"All right, darling," Buz said. "Do your little duties in your closet-kitchen." She turned to Cat. "Isn't it ridiculous what the child has done to this house?" she said. "But I can't let myself care any more. I just overlook it. One can always have another drink, can't one?" She poured from the flask.

Cat drank with her, watching the level of whiskey against the edge of the thin cups, thinking, What the hell, love, what the hell, as ole Dorothy used to say.

The room was pleasantly blurred around her when the bell rang and Sue came in from the kitchen, opened the door, and let Graham and Elizabeth in. Buz got up and went to kiss Graham, to look Elizabeth over, to lead them back to where Cat sat, holding her cup carefully between both hands.

"Hi, Cat," Graham said. Elizabeth nodded and they sat together on a Mayhill loveseat.

"Have a drink, loves," Buz said.

"Don't care if I do," Graham said cheerfully.

Elizabeth shook her head and Sue poured coffee for her.

"Someone told me they called you The Fixer," Cat said loudly.

There was silence and she could see Buz's painted face turned toward her in amusement, Sue's raised brows, and between Elizabeth and Graham a look, the quick glance of marriage that welded them in the alien room, a look that shut Cat behind her glass forever. She set down her china cup. Her words still hung in the quiet room until Buz spoke, dropping them into their rightful place as conversation.

"How charming," she said. "It sounds like somebody working for Al Capone."

Graham smiled feebly. "It's a term my political opponents use," he said.

"Of course," Cat said. She did not want to say anything more, to witness the round impenetrability of her own words in the room, but she said it anyway because the glass was up permanently now and it didn't really make one continental damn what she on this side said to those on that side. She knew now that she was never going to get through into their world again. "It must be a term of your nasty opponents," she went on. "Everyone knows what a southern gentleman you've always been."

"Cut it out, Cat," Graham said.

"More coffee?" Sue said.

"Just like old times," Buz said comfortably. "You two always scrapped."

"Really," Elizabeth McCloud said, "I think we'd better be getting on."

"You smug bitch," Cat said.

Graham stood up. "Cat," he said, "don't. You're going to be sorry . . ."

"In the morning? No. I don't think so. If you feel your wife's reputation has been impaired you can probably collect damages from my husband. He's filthy rich." She stood up, swaying a little. "Buz," she said, "Buz, don't look worried. It's still afternoon. The bad time only comes early in the morning, early in the morning between the night and day. Along about three o'clock when you wait for the explosion, or the silence, or the sound of the front doorbell." She peered at the tiny watch on her wrist. "Right now it is only four P.M. Four P.M. plus six and one-half minutes." She picked up her purse. "Goodbye, Graham," she said. "I would rather have waited for autumn." She went out the door before any of them could say or do anything.

Outside, the sun shone through green leaves and somewhere around the house was the scent of roses. She knew there could only be a few, the first ones, blooming budlike through the trellises, but the smell went with her, strong and nauseating in the late afternoon. She got in her car, watching her fingers fumble uselessly through somebody's pocketbook, finally feeling the touch of metal and fitting the key to the lock. She drove straight home, went to the kitchen, and told Mable to take the night off. "Where's Gloria?" she said to her.

"Band practice, I reckon," Mable said. "It's Friday."

She watched Mable leave by the back door, seeing through the kitchen window her heavy body going down the lane, her paper sack hugged to her, knowing without being able to hear her that she was humming.

She went back to the living room and picked up the telephone book. She couldn't read the numbers very well but she remembered the one she wanted and gave it to the operator.

"Hello?" Reverend Duskey's voice said.

She wanted to cry for the first time then because he had been kind to her. He had helped her through bad places more than once and he had ignored a lot of things other people would think unforgivable. "Look," she said. "This is Catharine Graves."

"Who?" he said.

"I'm sorry. Cartwright. Look. Would you pray for me?"

"I always do, my dear," he said.

"Well, today special," she said, crying hard now. "Just in case."

"In case?" His voice began to sound alarmed.

She tried to brighten her own. "That's right, darling," she said. "Just in case."

She put the phone down and looked through the open window. The trees were silver and green, the sky pale blue. She shut her eyes and thought of red and yellow leaves, the sound they made on the sidewalks when you walked, and the sky a blue so deep that it had to contain something, that inverted bowl of Omar's, cupped around her world.

She called again and got Mozel Simms. "Is Martha Ann there?" she said.

"Catharine," Mozel said, "what's wrong with you?"

"I'm all right."

"No you're not. You sound sick. Are you there by yourself?"

"Just let me speak to Martha Ann please. She's home, isn't she? She's out of school for the summer, isn't she?"

"All right," Mozel said.

Then Martha Ann's voice, reminding her of Veda. "Aunt Cat?"

"Honey." She tried very hard to sound like the people on the outside of the glass. "Do something for me, will you?"

"Sure."

"Go over to the high school and pick Gloria up after band practice. Will you?"

"Yes'm."

"Take her somewhere with you for tonight. Let her spend the night with you too."

"Why?"

"Please. I just want to be by myself a while. Will you?"

"All right. Maybe I can get up a double date. That all right with you? Somebody nice."

"That's fine, honey. Thanks."

She put the phone down, quickly, and went on upstairs.

Inside her room the blinds were drawn. She opened them, letting the sun with its pregnant pulsing shine onto the carpet. "Was there anything else?" she said aloud. And thought of Eileen. She took a page of her note paper and sat down and wrote her a letter.

Dear Eileen,

It is a lovely day here, green and silver. Buz Mayhill's back in town—looks much the same. Martha Ann's home for the summer. I think she's getting along fine now. Saw Graham and Elizabeth today. They seem prosperous. Harry Clifton asked for you last time I saw him. I think of you often and wish you were still here, but know it's better for you in a bigger place. I have some beautiful big yellow chrysanthemums planted out behind our back hedge. If you'll take a little trouble you can transplant them in time for them to bloom this fall.

Love always,
Cat

She signed the letter, took it downstairs and put it in the mailbox to be picked up in the morning. Then she went back upstairs and took the blue and white box out of the drawer and undid the clumsy ribbons Jack Burke had tied. She loaded the gun, went into the bathroom, and locked both doors. Then she opened the blinds and looked out at the slanting sun. "I beat you to it, you son-of-a-bitch," she said, and put the gun to her head and pulled the trigger just the way Jack Burke had told her to do.

They didn't find her until the next morning because Dudley went out of town and when he couldn't get anybody on the telephone he just went by the house and left a note on the hall table. Gloria and Martha Ann went to the picture show with a couple of naval veterans to see "Rhapsody in Blue," and Mable was spending a long-delayed evening at Pink's Café listening to the juke box.

She was late getting to work because she'd been up late the night before and she was surprised to find the door unlocked. She went through the house calling, Miss Cat?, stopping to read Dudley's note and deciding that Miss Cat must have spent the night at her mother's. She put coffee on in case somebody came in and called Mrs. Graves. Mrs. Graves said she hadn't seen Catharine since the day before yesterday.

Mable had worked for Miss Cat for sixteen years and she had

nursed her through a good many bad spells. She set out with effi-
ciency and a little judicious worry to locate her. She went upstairs
and saw that the beds hadn't been slept in and that Cat's clothes
were all in the closet, but she didn't think to try the bathroom
door. She went back down to the telephone to try the most likely
places.

She called Harry Clifton first and after talking to him she began to be really scared, because he was. "She was in a pretty bad
state yesterday afternoon," he said. "You better try to find her.
I'll be out there."

She called the Simms' house next. Mozel answered the phone
and when Mable told her that Cat couldn't be located Mozel
didn't even answer her. She just slammed down the receiver and
started.

Mable was standing on the porch when Dr. Clifton drove up
and Mozel came up the walk. "Have you heard anything?" Harry
said.

Mable shook her head.

"Harry," Mozel said. "Gloria's at my house with Martha Ann.
Catharine called yesterday and had Martha Ann pick her up at
school."

Harry seemed to relax then. Resignation replaced worry on his
face. He looked at Mable. "Have you looked everywhere in the
house?" he said.

Mable started to nod, then her eyes went blank and she put
her hand over her mouth, moaning suddenly. "The upstairs bathroom," she said. "Oh Lord, Mr. Harry. The upstairs . . ."

Harry went past her and up the stairs, leaving Mozel to cope
with Mable who was swaying back and forth now, her eyes rolling.
"All the time," she chanted softly. "In there all the time."

Dudley Cartwright drove up from Newcastle with a feeling of
relief somewhere under his grief that he had to spend the rest of
his life trying to deny. At eleven o'clock Graham McCloud went
into Burke's sporting goods shop and beat Jack Burke within an

inch of his life before Harry Clifton and the deputy sheriff pulled him off. Everybody knew why, but nobody ever told Dudley Cartwright about it.

"It isn't right, Eileen," Mrs. Graves said, helping her wrap the dirt-clogged roots of chrysanthemums in damp cloths. "It isn't right for old folks to have to outlive their children."

Eileen shook her head.

"I'm sorry, child," Mrs. Graves said. "I forgot. But war's different. It's just as bad, but not so abnormal somehow."

"You're right," Eileen said. "At least as human beings talk of normal. In this world I reckon war is the normal thing."

"I'm sorry."

"No. I know what you mean. You and Mr. Graves and the Simms and the Mayhills. I know what you mean."

"I mean take me and Mozel Simms. Here we are, should be old and ready to go ourselves, and we've had another generation of our children's children left to us to raise. It's like the generation in between just wasn't there. It's like they just skipped them somewhere in the scheme of things."

Eileen wiped her hands on her skirt. "As adults, yes," she said. "You think of Cat and Veda and Marty, even Morgan and Graham, like they used to be, always wearing their twenties plumes and laughing. Like snapshots. Or . . . I don't know. But somehow they never got through the next decade."

"Maybe they all had too much all at once," Mrs. Graves said. "Like one big Christmas morning, and they never could take January."

Eileen put her hand on her shoulder. "Let's go now," she said. "I'm going to plant these in my new back yard. We're moving this fall, you know."

Flora Graves nodded. "You don't ever think of moving back home?" she said.

Eileen shook her head. She looked across the back yard toward the neat brick house, silent and deserted in the morning sun. "Just visiting sometimes is all," she said.

In the high old smoky kitchen of the McCloud house they—Graham and Harry and Ace and Morgan—sat around the oak table, the whiskey bottle in the center, a pool of light cast by the glare of the overhanging bulb. They didn't say much, drinking the whiskey while the afternoon went.

Graham rested his bruised knuckles on the table and squinted down at them. "Y'all remember that play we had back when we were sophomores in high school?" he said.

"God yes," Ace said.

"Today at the funeral I saw Sara Downs," Graham said. "It was the funniest damned thing. She came up to me and I didn't know her—wouldn't have recognized her at all. She said 'We never meant to leave you kids in the lurch like we did, Kenneth and I.' Just like that, and went on away. Wasn't that a hell of a thing to say?"

Harry poured drinks around again. Through the shades a late afternoon sun shone steadily but it didn't reach into the dark kitchen. "When you moving to Florida, Ace?" Harry said.

"Fall. Soon's we get the printing deal all set up. I'm buying out a guy in Orlando. Lock, stock, and you know."

"Orlando's not on the ocean, is it?" Harry said.

"No. But it's pretty near. I figure a year or two we can get a beach place."

Harry smiled. "I figure you will," he said.

Morgan was silent, moving his glass in circles around the old oilcloth. He looked older than any of them, graying now, but his face still the same handsome wholeness under the wrinkles, still waiting, still pointed toward something that hadn't materialized.

"Morgan," Graham said, "why don't you come work for me? After all, you ain't so all-fired attached to what you're doing you couldn't quit it. Come work for me. I could use somebody to help out with state construction. I could use a good blue-print man."

Morgan shrugged and sipped the drink. "Maybe," he said. "It'd put me closer to Eileen and the kids, see 'em sometimes. I never get to see nothing of Martha Ann and Janice here anyway."

"Do it, by damn," Graham said. He shook his head and grinned. "I reckon I'd just like to have you around," he said. "Sometimes it's lonesome . . ." His voice trailed off and he looked apologetically at Harry.

Harry shrugged. "Anybody want another drink?" he said.

"Sure," Ace said. "Sure. Fill 'er up. It's one damned thing that never changes anyway."

Outside, the sun set on schedule.

Beachhead

From where they sat on the edge of the tide-line Martha Ann could see the two houses set apart from each other with the path worn between them so that the sand lay more solid there. She could see the cars parked and the kids on Eileen's sleeping porch steps and although she couldn't see her she knew that Veda was just inside her porch. Cliff sat beside her on the sand. If she moved her hand she could touch him, but she didn't. She hadn't, and now she knew she wasn't going to. It was enough that she had loved him with her mind and showed it in her eyes, let it show, given it to him. Too much, already. She was going to leave. She'd meant to come out here and tell him so today but she hadn't done that yet either. She couldn't. She wanted one more afternoon to talk, to possess mentally what she couldn't have physically. Then she was going to let herself know that the only thing he was really interested in was the physical, and the only reason for that was Veda's illness. She'd already bought her plane ticket, but she hadn't told even Eileen that.

"What's the matter with you?" he said.

"Nothing."

"All right, if you don't want to talk about it."

"I don't."

"Look at the sun go down," he said.

"I'm looking. Looking like crazy."

He touched her hand, just a brushing movement on the sand between them.

One night, maybe, she thought. And then, No. I've decided. She stood up and looked down at him. He stood too.

"You go swimming every night?" he said.

She nodded, not wanting to say it, yet knowing he'd say What time? He said it, and she heard herself say, "Around midnight." Then she walked away toward the house. He followed her.

Inside the porch the shadows were already dark. Eileen was sitting on a cot watching them. "We're going to Veda's to supper tonight," she said.

"Well, good," Martha Ann said. "She decided to come out of the old shell after all, huh?"

Eileen grinned. "She had to," she said.

Martha Ann stood still, looking at her. "You mean she's really out?" she said.

"I think so."

"Because of me and . . ." She nodded toward the door where Cliff was standing on the steps with the children.

"She's not blind," Eileen said.

"You devil," Martha Ann said. "You're glad of it. You wanted it to happen."

Eileen stopped smiling. "I didn't want you to get hurt," she said. "You know I'd never want that. But Veda's my child, Martha Ann. I want her alive, to everything. I can't help it if this is what worked it for me. I can't help that."

Martha Ann lit a cigarette. The sun was gone now and the wind off the water felt cold. "You're not even giving me the chance to give him up," she said.

"Were you going to?"

"Hell yes, I was going to. I've got my ticket. I'm leaving in the morning." She laughed a little. "Nothing could have happened in one night, could it? I was going to tell him tonight."

"Tell him then. Tell him now."

Martha Ann shook her head. "No. Give her her chance. Let him see her fixing the gala meal, let him sleep with her again tonight, and go back to his goddamned rockets in peace. He can feel very superior about the girl he couldn't even lend a night."

They were throwing a beach ball now between the houses. She could hear Cliff's voice rising above the kids' shouts.

"You didn't really want it to happen, did you?" Eileen said.

"I wanted to get the credit for preventing it myself."

"You still can."

"No. I'll just leave in the morning. You can take me to the plane. You know all my life I've felt that trains take you away from something and buses toward. That's why I want to leave on an airplane. It isn't certain either way."

"Back to Montgomery?" Eileen said.

"For now. Not for long, though. I've decided something else while I've been here. I'm going to sell the old house in Bellefonte and go to Denmark."

"Denmark?" Eileen said. "Why Denmark?"

"I don't know. I want to get over and get a look at things before something else happens to the world. And Denmark . . . well. The place that produced Hans Christian Andersen must have something pretty special about it. Don't you feel that? I've always had a hankering to see that little mermaid sitting in the harbor. I think I'll do something about it."

"Don't guess I'll ever get to Europe now," Eileen said, lighting a cigarette. "I used to want to, but I don't much any more. I sort of got comfortable here, seems like."

Martha Ann smiled at her. "You like being where they're making these launchings, too, don't you? It's just like you, Aunt Eileen, wanting to be in on something new."

"I like it. Sure. There's a lot of your great-grandfather in me somehow. Even if we weren't kin."

Martha Ann got up and looked out onto the darkening beach. "You don't think it's coming then?" she said.

"What? The end of the world? Not a chance. Oh, the atomic war, maybe. The end of the world, no. God, Martha Ann, can't you feel it? The going out? The rightness of it? I used to be pretty bitter about war, after Van. But I don't know. Maybe it takes the war and the hate and the fear to produce the initiative. Maybe we just aren't ready to go it without the spurs yet. Sure, a lot of the energy and money and time go into rockets for weapons but, on the other hand, they've got 'em going out. It's like they can't stop themselves. It's the time for it. Just like the crossbow killed feudalism. Wait and see."

"You're an incorrigible optimist."

"Guilty."

They smiled at each other in the dark of the porch.

"You know," Eileen said. "I always did my best to make Ace see things that way, but I don't think I succeeded very well. Sometimes I've wondered if I did the right thing, taking him away from home."

"You did."

"I don't know. After Van was killed he never cared a lot about anything again. It was like he wouldn't let himself. He just drank and ran his press, and talked a lot. Talked a lot about Bellefonte. Kept looking the wrong way."

"Hell, Aunt Eileen, that's the curse of your whole damned bunch," Martha Ann said. She couldn't hear Cliff's voice any more. It had retreated down the beach. She stopped straining for it. "You know, when I think of my mother now," she went on, "I think of the fact that she was a little girl. That's an odd thing to think about your mother. But it's true. My mother was a little girl till the day she died." She paused. "Aunt Cat too, I guess," she added.

Eileen shivered. "Let's get dressed," she said. "I don't reckon you want to grace Veda's table in a bathing suit."

They went into the house. Martha Ann went to the shower and turned the knobs, letting the water warm up while she stood talking to Eileen through the door. "I still feel bad none of us got here when Uncle Ace died," she said. "I always loved him so. I felt like I'd deserted him."

"My fault," Eileen said. "I didn't really want any of you here. It happened quick. He just came home from work one day feeling bad and went to bed. It was over by morning." She was silent for a moment. "The doctor said he'd been drinking too much for years," she added.

"We could have got here," Martha Ann said.

"I told you. I had to do it by myself. If any of you'd come, I'd have gone back to Bellefonte. Take your shower."

Martha Ann stood under the soothing water, letting it take away the salt and the sand and the one stinging touch on her left hand. She felt tired and empty and sleepy. She guessed she'd skip the swim tonight and go to bed.

"Martha Ann," Eileen said as they walked down the beach to Veda's. "It's that I know you can take it, don't you see?"

"Yeah. Good old Martha Ann. It's easier for her."

"No! That is not what I said. I'd say it's harder. It's just that you won't let it stop you. You're one of the lucky ones."

"I must say I don't feel like it."

"You probably never will."

They could hear the sound of laughter from the cottage. "So maybe your Veda is going to quit being a little girl now, huh?" Martha Ann said.

"I can hope now anyway."

"Maybe I should have slept with him. That would really have given her a chance."

"Yes, I think so. A better one. But it would have been harder on you."

Martha Ann shrugged. "Well, past another little crossroad anyway," she said.

"You find your life full of crossroads too?"

"Infinitely, infinitely. Oh well. Let's go enjoy supper, Auntie dear. Life is an infinite Easter egg."

The house was empty after Eileen put Martha Ann on her plane. She couldn't seem to settle down to reading. After a while she put her sweater on against the wind and went to sit on the steps in the soughing dark. Down at the water line she heard Cliff shout something to Veda, and her answer coming back through the darkness, cheerful, whole, sane, with just a trace of snappishness.

She lit a cigarette. Behind her the phone rang, shrilling suddenly into the evening. She went inside. It was Betty Al, crying a little, saying she just had to get home for a day or two. Would it be all right if she came right on tonight? Could Eileen meet her in Orlando? She asked what time. "Midnight?" she said. "Don't you kids think I ever need to sleep?"

"You never have," Betty Al said. She sounded happier.

"I'll meet you," Eileen said.

She went back outside and sat down on the steps, wondering what Betty Al's trouble was. Some boy? Probably. It had taken her long enough to get around to it. The beach was purple now with night and the tide was going out, retreating, with the going of daylight, toward the other shore.

She looked up, watching the stars come into being suddenly like a light turned on in a many-windowed cave. Down the beach behind their wire and striped boards they were putting together the parts of another try, stringing together with steel and plastic, with flesh and blood and bone, another light to go up over Cape Canaveral, another tiny searching candle in the dark.